Dair
Devil

LUCINDA BRANT BOOKS

'Quizzing glass and quill, into my sedan chair and away —— the 1700s rock!'

Lucinda Brant is a *New York Times*, *USA Today*, and *Audible* bestselling author of award-winning Georgian historical romances and mysteries. Her books are renowned for wit, drama and a happily ever-after. She has a degree in history and political science from the Australian National University and a post-graduate degree in education from Bond University, where she was awarded the Frank Surman Medal.

Noble Satyr, Lucinda's first novel, was awarded the $10,000 Random House/Woman's Day Romantic Fiction Prize, and she has twice been a finalist for the Romance Writers' of Australia Romantic Book of the Year. All her novels have garnered multiple awards and become worldwide bestsellers.

Lucinda lives in the middle of a koala reserve, in a writing cave that is wall-to-wall books on all aspects of the Eighteenth Century, collected over 40 years—Heaven. She loves to hear from her readers (and she'll write back!).

lucindabrant@gmail.com | lucindabrant.com

pinterest.com/lucindabrant | twitter.com/lucindabrant

facebook.com/lucindabrantbooks | youtube.com/lucindabrantauthor

A GEORGIAN HISTORICAL ROMANCE
ROXTON FAMILY SAGA BOOK THREE

Lucinda Brant

A Sprigleaf Book
Published by Sprigleaf Pty Ltd

Dair Devil: A Georgian Historical Romance
Copyright © 2014, 2020 Lucinda Brant, all rights reserved.
Editing: Martha Stites, Cathie Maud Cabot & Rob Van De Laak.
Art & design: Sprigleaf. Model photography: GM Studio.
Cover models: Jam Murphy & Guy Macchia.
Custom jewelry: Kimberly Walters, Sign of the Gray Horse
Reproduction and historically inspired jewelry.
Rory's Pineapple fleuron design by Sprigleaf.

Garden and foliage images of Chelsea Physic Garden, Chiswick Gardens,
& Syon House by Lucinda Brant (author's own photographs).

Georgian couple silhouette is a trademark belonging to Lucinda Brant.
Sprigleaf triple-leaf design is a trademark belonging to Sprigleaf Pty Ltd.

Typeset in Adobe Garamond Pro.

Also in ebook, audiobook, and other languages.

ISBN 978-1-925614-71-8

10 9 8 7 6 5 4 3 2 Studio Art Perfect Bound Paperback Edition (s.i) I

for my daughter

Cinda Ann

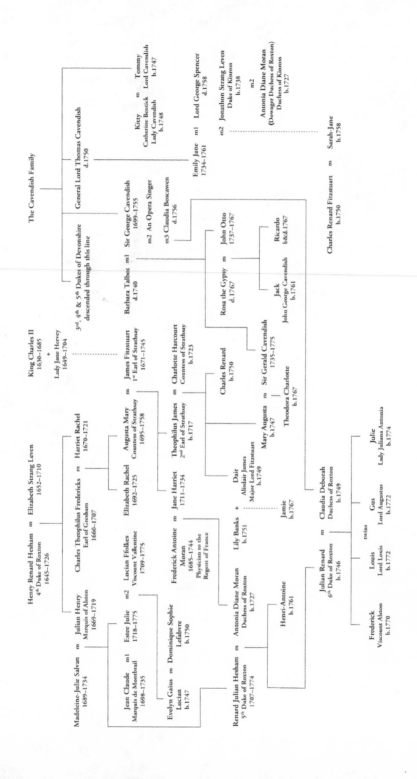

The Cavendish Family

Henry Renard Hesham m Elizabeth Strang Leven
4th Duke of Roxton   1652–1710
1645–1726

King Charles II
1630–1685
+
Lady Jane Hervey
1649–1704

General Lord Thomas Cavendish
d.1750

3rd, 4th & 5th Dukes of Devonshire
descended through this line

Madeleine-Julie Salvan m1 Julian Henry
1689–1734   Marquis of Alston
1669–1719

Charles Theophilus Fredericks m Harriet Rachel
Earl of Gresham   1670–1721
1660–1707

Sir George Cavendish m1 Barbara Talbot
1699–1755   d.1740
m2 An Opera Singer
m3 Claudia Boscawen
d.1756

Kitty   m   Tommy
Catherine Bentick   Lord Cavendish
Lady Cavendish   b.1747
b.1748

Jean Claude m1 Estée Julie m2 Lucian Ffolkes
Marquis de Montbrail 1718–1775 Viscount Vallentine
1698–1735   1709–1775

Elizabeth Rachel
1692–1725

Augusta Mary
Countess of Strathsay
1695–1758

James Fitzstuart m Augusta Mary
1st Earl of Strathsay
1671–1745

Emily Jane m1 Lord George Spencer
1734–1761   d.1758

m2 Jonathon Strang Leven
Duke of Kinross
b.1738

m2
Antonia Diane Moran
(Dowager Duchess of Roxton)
Duchess of Kinross
b.1727

Evelyn Gaius m Dominique Sophie
Lucian   Lefabvre
b.1747   b.1750

Frederick Antoine m Jane Harriet
Moran   1711–1734
1685–1744
Physician to the
Regent of France

Theophilus James
2nd Earl of Strathsay
b.1717

Charlotte Harcourt
Countess of Strathsay
b.1723

Rosa the Gypsy m John Otto
d.1767   1737–1767

Charles Renard Fitzstuart m Sarah-Jane
b.1750   b.1758

Renard Julian Hesham m Antonia Diane Moran
5th Duke of Roxton   Duchess of Roxton
1707–1774   b.1727

Lily Banks
b.1751

Dair
Alisdair James
Major Lord Fitzstuart
b.1749

Charles Renard
b.1750

Sir Gerald Cavendish m Mary Augusta
1735–1775   1747

Theodora Charlotte
b.1767

Jack   Ricardo
John George Cavendish   b&d.1767
b.1761

Henri-Antoine
b.1761

Jamie
b.1767

Julian Renard m Claudia Deborah
6th Duke of Roxton   Duchess of Roxton
b.1746   b.1749

Frederick
Viscount Alston
b.1770

Louis
Lord Louis
b.1772

twins

Gus
Lord Augustus
b.1772

Julie
Lady Juliana Antonia
b.1774

ONE

CAVENDISH SQUARE, LONDON. THE FIRST WEEK OF MAY 1777

ALISDAIR 'DAIR' FITZSTUART PULLED THE WHITE LINEN SHIRT UP over his square shoulders, scrunched it into a ball and tossed it to his batman. Bill Farrier caught this crumpled article with his one hand and shoved it inside a large canvas haversack, atop his lordship's midnight blue silk waistcoat and matching frock coat. His master's black leather jockey boots he had set beside a high stone wall, out of the way of passers-by. Pedestrians, however, were unlikely given the location and the hour.

Red Lyon Lane was at the rear of a row of elegant townhouses that fronted Cavendish Square. Tradesmen and their ilk used it. It was not an address frequented by gentlemen, unless engaged in mischief. The three inebriated gentlemen taking hearty swigs from a wine bottle being passed amongst them were definitely up to no good. Bill Farrier knew this for fact. The phlegmatic ex-soldier also knew no good would come of their antics.

It was dusk and there was a new moon. It meant the night would be as black as soot. This was just as well, thought the batman. His master and two friends might have a chance of escaping into the night without being caught or recognized. He had every confidence in Major Lord Fitzstuart. Five years as his lordship's batman had given Farrier a measure of the man. He would follow him to the ends of the earth, and fall off the edge if required.

He did not have the same confidence in his master's two civilian companions. They looked to have as much courage under fire between them as his lordship had in his pinky. But as they had been the Major's boon companions since his days at Harrow, it was not his place to pass comment unless asked. Farrier had not been asked. He remained silent and patiently waited for his lordship to divest himself of the remainder of his clothing: Stockings, buckskin breeches, and drawers. He then flicked a finger at a linkboy to step forward, as if illumination by a flaming taper would shed light on the discussion taking place, or, at the very least, provide a spark of warmth for the bare-chested Major.

Dair was oblivious to the cool spring air, toes curling in the cold earth beneath his stockinged feet as he unbuttoned the three covered buttons at his knees, and then proceeded to undo the fall of his breeches. He looked up when directly addressed.

"Hold on!" demanded a tall white-blond gentleman, stripped to his breeches. He pointed the neck of the wine bottle in his friend's direction. "There was no mention of getting naked as a newborn babe."

"To raid Romney's studio as an American Indian, you can't be dressed as an Englishman," Cedric Pleasant enunciated as if talking to a small child.

Dair let his breeches drop to his feet, stepped out of them, removed his stockings, wrapped these in his breeches and tossed the lot to Farrier.

"Breechcloth, Mr. Farrier, if you please."

"So you *do* wear drawers," Lord Grasby stated with satisfaction; he of the white-blond good looks. "That's one wager I will win. A guinea is now owed to Yours Truly!"

Cedric Pleasant slipped his silver pocket watch into a deep frock coat pocket.

"Wager? About Dair's *drawers?*"

"Whether he wears 'em, or not," Lord Grasby said. "*I said*, contrary to what *others* might think, *I know* Alisdair Fitzstuart for a gentleman."

"Thank you, Grasby."

Lord Grasby saluted Dair with the neck of the wine bottle to his temple.

"Who the devil would wager otherwise?" Cedric Pleasant wondered aloud.

"Or care," Dair added with a huff.

Lord Grasby drank heartily of the wine then said, "Brother Weasel. That's who! Weasel said a soldier—a *dragoon* no less—would have no use for such a useless article of clothing as drawers, because a soldier is required to have his weapon at the ready *at all times*." He snorted. "Did you hear that, Cedric? Weasel—weapon at the ready—at all times."

Cedric grunted in acknowledgment and made a grab for the bottle Lord Grasby was swinging about, and missed.

Dair rolled his eyes to the blackening night sky and motioned Farrier to his side.

"Carriage up the laneway?"

"Yes, m'lord."

"And the beadles paid off?"

"To be deaf as a plank of wood? Yes, m'lord. We won't hear a cry for assistance from that lot."

"Good. Once Lord Grasby and I slip through the garden door, you hare off with the kit and we'll see you at the carriage in the Square. Not outside Romney's house. Position it across the street. We'll make a dash for it." He caught Farrier's glance of skepticism at his drunken blond school friend. "Don't worry. I'll sling him over a shoulder if necessary."

"Very good, m'lord." Farrier said no more about it. "Breechcloth?"

"Breechcloth."

Lord Grasby propped a bony elbow on Cedric Pleasant's shoulder, so he could lift a foot to remove his stocking without falling flat on his face. "Oi! Dair! Tell me again—Why are we undressing in a laneway?"

Cedric Pleasant sighed his annoyance and was about to answer when Dair said patiently,

"Two reasons: We are breaking in to a painter's studio in an attempt to spark Cedric's non-existent love life. Secondly: You want to embarrass your no-good-weasel-of-a-brother-in-law; your words, not mine. Thus, your best friends are obliging you with this piece of theater."

Lord Grasby took a moment for this to penetrate his inebriated brain.

"Good. Glad to help, Cedric. Hope Weasel chokes on a lamb chop! Ugh," he added, pulling a face as if he had tasted something unexpectedly bitter. "Why did I have to be shackled with Weasel Watkins for a brother-in-law? The man is a-a..." He searched his limited-by-alcohol vocabulary. "*Weasel.*"

Dair grinned. "That's the spirit! Now get undressed."

Lord Grasby obediently pulled off his other stocking. "You know what I detest about him more than anything else, more than his sanctimonious whining, more than his small-minded self-importance, more than the way he hovers about m'sister—"

"Surely that's enough of a list—"

"—It's that he had the vileness to put forward the opinion Charlie Fitzstuart would make a more fitting Earl of Strathsay than Dair. He even said that's what Dair's relatives think, too! Damned cheek!"

"My brother *would* make a more fitting earl," Dair agreed, pulling on the drawstring bow of his drawers. "And, yes, my esteemed relatives think likewise." He shrugged. "Nothing new there. The Weasel is a boot-licking understrapper, but I'll grant he uses to advantage what brain matter he does have between his shop sign ears."

"Cowpats to that!" Lord Grasby declared, and took another swig from the wine bottle. He wiped his mouth on the back of the hand that held fast to the discarded stocking. "I like your brother well enough, Dair, but Charlie ain't you. Is he, Cedric?"

"Certainly not!" Cedric Pleasant agreed. "Charles is a bookworm; you're not. What does a bookworm know except what's on paper? Written by dead people, books. Ghastly lot, authors."

"Can't have a bookworm inheriting an earldom," Lord Grasby stuck in. "Would make the rest of us look less than the full deck of cards. There's nothing wrong with being all brawn and no brain, and so I told the Weasel. If it weren't for you brave chaps in uniform, sniveling fellows like the Weasel would spend their days shivering with fright under their bedcovers! And so I told him."

Dair gave a huff of laughter. "I'm not in uniform now, Grasby. But thank you for your spirited defense; well, at least I think that's what your speech was about."

"I'd take what Grasby says with a pinch of salt," Cedric Pleasant said as a confidential aside. "The claret is doing most of the talking."

Dair's dark eyes held Cedric Pleasant's gaze.

"But Weasel Watkins does not drink... Of course I won't take it to heart, Cedric," he said, forcing a grin when his friend looked uncomfortable. He clapped him on the shoulder. "As well as not having a brain, apparently I don't possess a heart either. Ha! I wonder what internal organs Weasel Watkins will allow me to own?"

"No heart? That's a new one on me," Cedric Pleasant replied with a smile, following Dair's nonchalant lead. "Perhaps he secretly thinks you're an automaton? You come to life with the turn of a key. What do you think of that, Grasby? Mystery solved! The Major survived nine years in the army because he's not flesh and blood, but made from cogs and coils!"

"Automaton? No brain and no heart? Well that might explain why he'd accept a God-awful wager to tup a cripple for a shilling," Grasby declared, rounding on Dair with an instant of lucidity. "Did you? Did you accept such a contemptible dare, *Dair*?"

Cedric Pleasant was astounded. "The devil he would! Who says so?"

"The Weasel, that's who!"

Cedric looked at Dair, astonished. "You never did! You couldn't!"

Dair was momentarily uncomfortable but quickly masked this, saying with a forced nonchalant laugh, "If she's halfway to being pretty and willing, why not?" He looked from one grim face to another, not comprehending the sudden tension between his two best friends. "What of it? I was drunk. It was years ago." And to make them laugh, added with a sheepish grin, "Lame doesn't mean *lame-brained*. As I don't have a brain, she'd find me out for an automaton and remove my key before I could no more than kiss her luscious lips!"

"You'd not get close enough to do even that! *My* shilling on *that*," Lord Grasby proclaimed.

They laughed and amity was restored.

"Isn't it about time you removed your breeches, Grasby?" Cedric demanded, steering the conversation back to the matter at hand.

Lord Grasby's shoulders slumped.

"Is it absolutely vital I remove m'breeches *and* drawers?"

"It is," Dair replied with a hint of apology. "It's crucial to the success of our mission."

"And the pocket watch is ticking towards the half hour…" Cedric Pleasant added with a lift of his eyebrows.

"All right. All right," Lord Grasby grumbled as he reluctantly pulled at the large horn buttons of his linen breeches. Unable to stifle the bubble of air in his throat, he let out a loud belch and felt better for it. He chuckled. "Methinks I've drunk rather too much claret. Drusilla— Silla—my dear lady wife, will scold me severely when I return home. *Harvel Grasby, you are drunk and will spend tonight in your own bed.*" He looked up from tugging on the fourth and final button. "You know the wife, don't you, Dair? Cedric?"

"Yes," Dair replied, rolling his eyes at Cedric, who grinned. "We were both at your nuptials."

"Ah! That's *right!*" said Grasby. "It was m'sister who was missing from my big day. Bedridden. Fever."

"Dair wore his regimentals," Cedric Pleasant added. "It was just before you were shipped over to deal with that *ghastly* business in the Colonies…"

Dair grimaced at the word *ghastly*, as if the war in America was akin to suffering toothache. As had always been his practice, he made no comment about his time in the army, particularly his involvement in the bloody struggle across the Atlantic, between those loyal to the crown and the troublemakers who had taken up arms against their king. He had made choices in life to which he now wished he had given more thought, but he had no regrets, and he was philosophical enough to hope he had learned something along the way.

He stripped out of his drawers, and when Bill Farrier handed him a thin braided leather belt, he slung it low on his bare narrow hips, fastening the ties into a knot. He gave it a tug to ensure it was secure.

He then slid the knot to sit just below his right hip so that the two rectangular flaps of soft calfskin sewn to the belt were positioned front and back, providing a covering between his legs. Looking up, he saw Lord Grasby frowning in puzzlement.

"It's called a breechcloth. Farrier has one for you, too."

Lord Grasby stared at his best friend, naked but for the strip of cloth between his muscular thighs, and his self-confidence plummeted into his stomach.

"Is that *all* an American Indian wears?"

"In summer—Yes."

Lord Grasby gave a snort of panic. "You're hoodwinking me!"

"No. It's this or nothing at all," Dair responded, comfortable in his own skin. "Make your choice." When Lord Grasby made an agitated motion with his hand, as if shooing away a bee, Dair did his best to reassure him, adding, "You'll feel more the warrior once the war paint is applied. Every man can hide behind war paint. Now, do get a move on, Grasby, before the ladybirds flit away into the night."

Lord Grasby liked the idea of hiding behind war paint. He whipped off his drawers, snatched the belt with breechcloths attached from the ever-patient Farrier, who had been standing at his side for some little while, and threw it around his waist. Being acutely self-conscious, he secured the belt ends in a rush, and breathed a sigh of relief to have completed the task in record time. Unbeknownst to him, the two breechcloths were not front and back as he thought, but left and right, against his bare flanks.

When Cedric Pleasant burst into laughter, Grasby glared at him, hands on hips, wondering what was amiss. Unable to speak because he was laughing so hard, Cedric waggled a finger in the direction of Grasby's groin. His lordship glanced down, gave a start, and was swift to try and set matters to rights, face ablaze.

"Blast it! It's all caught up now!"

"May I be of assistance, my lord?" Farrier asked at his most bland.

"Yes. Yes. All right! And be quick about it!"

Grasby suffered the ministrations of the batman to adjust the breechcloths, chin in the air, and with all the dignity of a man in his dressing room and not naked in a laneway.

"If you would just check to see that the knot you tied is still secure, m'lord, then all will be well."

"Can't you do that for me, too, damn you?" Lord Grasby demanded through clenched teeth.

When the batman remained silent and held up his left arm, Grasby finally looked at him. Where the man's hand should be, there was only air. Curiosity got the better of him, and he peered into the void of Farrier's coat sleeve. In response, Farrier thrust his arm up through his sleeve and out popped a stump. It was capped with a small polished silver hook, the fitted silver cap secured by a leather strap buckled about his forearm.

Grasby leapt into the air.

"For king and country, m'lord," was Farrier's bland response to Lord Grasby's reaction to his amputated hand.

"You scared me half to death! Damn you!"

The batman bowed, and with a flourish wriggled his arm so that the stump was again hidden, with only the tip of his hook visible within his coat sleeve.

"Thank you, Mr. Farrier," Dair said, taking his bare shoulders off the stone wall. "You've had your amusement for the evening; ours is yet to begin. Time to fetch paint pot and ash."

The batman bowed and retreated, leaving behind him a heavy silence.

"Nine years in the army and you come out of it with a few knocks and dents, but poor Farrier has the rotten luck to lose a hand," Cedric Pleasant said into that silence. "Still, you both managed to keep a head on your shoulders, and that's the main thing, isn't it?"

"You could have damn well told me!" Grasby threw at Dair. "I'll have nightmares for weeks." He gave a shudder of revulsion. "Damned unpleasant…"

Dair's face tightened. He was on the verge of reminding his friend that there were thousands of Farriers out there who had lost limbs, not to mention those who had made the ultimate sacrifice, all in the service of their king and country. All so gentlemen such as Grasby were at liberty to go about their daily lives undisturbed and unfettered. Instead, he pushed the unspoken diatribe back down his throat and turned away to take the paint pot from his batman.

"Watch and learn, Grasby," he said, beckoning his best friend closer.

Dipping his index finger into the small ceramic pot of white paint, then peering into a hand mirror his batman held up in the soft orange glow of the linkboy's lantern, Dair painted a continuous stripe from cheekbone to cheekbone across the beak of his nose. Two stripes were added to each cheek and a single stripe from bottom lip down the center of his square heavy chin. Satisfied with his war paint, he exchanged the paint pot for a cloth dusted in charcoal. This he rubbed into his closed eyelids, then blackened under his eyes, extending the blackness out across his temples into his hairline. He then applied soot to the beefy rounded tops of his shoulders. Peering back into the mirror, he grinned. The whites of his eyes were now stark and menacing, and the paint and soot somehow also made his large white teeth brighter and sharper.

Dair turned this macabre grin on his friends, who opened wide their eyes and smiled their appreciation of his transformation. And when he threw back his head of black hair and howled at the moon, Grasby joined in, infected with his friend's enthusiasm.

With both gentlemen sufficiently decorated in war paint, soot not only applied to Lord Grasby's face but dusted through his hair to turn it gray to disguise its blondness, Cedric Pleasant took one last look at his friends and declared they were ready to carry out their mission. And while Farrier and the linkboy gathered up the gentlemen's belongings, Dair went over the particulars one last time.

"And when Cedric threatens to stick me with his sword," Dair concluded, "that's our signal to get the hell out of there—"

"—looking suitably terrified," Cedric Pleasant added.

"We'll be scared stiff, dear chap," Grasby confirmed. "Petrified, I stop chasing dancing girls and dash out of the house after Dair. And we make for the carriage across the square."

Dair smiled. "Cedric saves the day, and the divine Consulata Baccelli has eyes only for her newfound champion. Couldn't be easier." He stuck out his hand. "Gentlemen, let the adventure begin!"

All three men shook hands, a gleam of mischief in their eyes, and wished each other luck before going their separate ways. Mr. Cedric Pleasant proceeded back down the laneway, a gloved hand to the hilt of his sword and a spring in his step. Major Lord Fitzstuart and Lord Grasby entered the garden of George Romney's townhouse by stealth and the back gate.

At the very same moment, Lady Grasby, Mr. William Watkins, and Lord Grasby's sister Miss Talbot, were being welcomed inside the townhouse by Mr. Romney's butler.

TWO

MR. WILLIAM WATKINS NOTED THE LATE HOUR UNDER THE LIGHT cast by a flambeau, then slipped his engraved timepiece on its silver chain back into his waistcoat pocket. He paused at the base of three shallow stone steps to allow his sister Lady Grasby and Miss Talbot to enter Mr. George Romney's residence before him.

"Tell me again why you insist we view your unfinished picture now?" he asked Lady Grasby in a voice of resignation, waving away a footman who had stepped forward to take his cloak, a sure sign the visit was to be of short duration. "We do not have an appointment and Mr. Romney is possibly away from the house, or perhaps he is with a client…?"

"It will take but a moment, William," Lady Grasby replied flatly, removing her gloved hands from an oversized mink muff. She shoved this at the butler. "As we had dinner two houses from this door, it would be foolish of me to be in such close proximity and not call. Mr. Romney is unlikely to refuse me. I have had nine sittings to date. Yet, there is something not quite right that has been keeping me up at night. I am so distracted by it I cannot remember any of the dishes at Her Highness's table. Only that there was a centerpiece, an elaborate sugar confection of sheep grazing—"

"Cows."

"Cows? Were they?" Lady Grasby frowned, momentarily diverted. "Are you certain those sugar lumps were cows, Aurora?"

Rory (no one but her sister-in-law called her by her birth name) nodded, and pretended to cough, a gloved hand to her mouth to hide a smile at the pained look of tolerance on Mr. Watkins' long face as he listened to his sister's prattle.

"A delightful pastoral scene of bovines," Mr. Watkins confirmed. "And there was a dairy maid—or were there two, Miss Talbot?"

"I cannot recall, sir. But it was delightful," agreed Rory, allowing a footman to take her red wool cloak. "Lady Cavendish says Her Highness has the most talented confectioner in all England, and I believe her."

Lady Grasby shrugged. "I am sure it was delightful, and I would have found it so, were I not worried over my portrait. I heard only one word in five of the conversation, though that prattlepate Lady Cavendish had a great deal to say."

"As did her corpulent husband." Mr. Watkins gave a loud sniff of derision. "Which was surprising, given he rarely pauses between mouthfuls to breathe, least of all speak. One day I fear Lord Cavendish will—*pop*."

"Oh dear, I hope I am not the unfortunate sitting beside him when he does," Rory quipped, amusement in her clear blue eyes. "One trusts Lord Cavendish will have the good manners to *pop* in privacy…"

"It is of no interest to me if Lord Cavendish bursts all over the dining room!" Lady Grasby announced, exasperated. "You both have the most extraordinarily tasteless conversations sometimes that I wonder at *your* good manners." She glared at her brother. "You do want me to sleep at night, William, do you not?"

"Nothing is dearer to my heart, nothing more important to me, than your well-being, Silla, but—"

"Did you catch Lady Cavendish's prattle over the trifle, Aurora?" Lady Grasby asked as she moved further into the hall, the butler following in her wake, her question to her brother, he realized too late, rhetorical. "Can it be true? Did a merchant's daughter, a Miss Strang, *reject* an offer of marriage from Lord Fitzstuart?"

"That is what Lady Cavendish reported," Rory replied. She paused in thought. "Though… I am more surprised that an offer was *made*, rather than one was rejected."

"Far be it from me to continue such a conversation in a painter's hallway, but Miss Strang's rejection of Lord Fitzstuart's offer shows a good deal of sense on her part," Mr. Watkins replied. "His lordship is a womanizing scoundrel. No female in her right mind would accept such a man for a husband."

Rory managed to suppress a smile. Leaning lightly on her walking stick, she said steadily, "I have not heard it said Miss Strang is anything but in her right mind. But perhaps that is debatable. She rejected the elder brother and ran off with the younger, if Lady Cavendish is to be believed."

"She has *eloped* with Fitzstuart's *brother?*" Lady Grasby was so astounded she shooed quiet the butler who was giving her the good news Mr. Romney was free to receive her. "Say it is not so! A girl who has the odor of the Covent Garden market about her person has the barefaced cheek to reject the heir to an earldom, in preference for a younger son who has no prospects and even less fortune? The girl must indeed be mad!"

"Or in love...?"

"Rot, Aurora!" Lady Grasby stated dismissively. "The children of merchants are raised to believe first and foremost in the value of a *thing*. Love is an ideal, an emotion of the highest order. As such it cannot be measured, so can hold little or no value for such practical people."

Rory wondered if her sister-in-law was speaking from the experience of having a grandfather whose vast wealth had been accumulated over a lifetime as a Billingsgate fishmonger. But as she had used the third person, Rory could only hope, for her brother's sake, that her sister-in-law had quite forgotten her own family's fishy beginnings.

"Now let us say no more about this Miss Strang and her mental deficiencies. Nor do I want to hear another word about Lord Fitzstuart," Lady Grasby continued. She covered her sister-in-law's gloved hand with her own and said quietly, "Truth be told, it is your brother's slavish friendship with Fitzstuart that keeps me awake at night. Sometimes I think...sometimes I think Grasby cares more for that man than he does me! I wish—"

"Grasby is devoted to you," Rory interrupted.

"—Fitzstuart had died in the Colonies!"

Rory gasped. "You do not mean it, Silla!"

"Unfortunately, he is possessed of the devil's own luck," Mr. Watkins said on a sigh, offering his tearful sister his perfectly pressed and folded white linen handkerchief. "The more dangerous the mission, the more daring the cause, the more willing Fitzstuart is to play the hero. And he came out of the army with all four limbs and his head intact!"

Rory looked from sister to brother, stunned.

"I cannot believe my ears. Mr. Watkins, you may decry the man for being a womanizer, and you, Silla, may dislike him heartily and be jealous of the time Grasby spends in his company... Indeed, there is not much Lord Fitzstuart can say in his own defense for his want of conduct, but neither of you have the-the *right* to wish him *dead*. How-how uncharitable, and his lordship a war hero!"

"No. No, Miss Talbot. You misconstrue me," William Watkins apologized. He smiled thinly and looked secretive. "As secretary to the Committee for Colonial Correspondence of Interest, I am privy to certain—*communications* and-and *particulars* about the war in America… There have been occasions—dangerous occasions, Miss Talbot—when his lordship was required to involve himself, and did so willingly, at considerable risk, not only to the men under his command but to his person. He is considered *reckless* in the extreme, so much so that I am not the only one who has wondered aloud if he has made a pact with —" He paused, looked over his shoulder at the butler, who quickly looked away, and pointed a gloved finger to the floor, and whispered, "*You-know-who.*"

Rory blinked at the man's outrageous suggestion that Lord Fitzstuart had managed to undertake and survive perilous and often life-threatening missions only because he had sold his soul to the Devil. But before she could make comment, Lady Grasby confronted Rory, saying with a pout,

"If you are not careful such a spirited defense of a gentleman you do not know in the least, and who would not know you from Eve, but whom you readily admit to observing, will be misconstrued as the unhealthy interest of a delusional and plain spinster for a handsome rake."

Rory's face ripened. Spinster she may be. Delusional she was not. Nor was she plain. Her hair might best be described as damp strawblonde. Her eyes were blue, but so pale as to be thought cold. But her face was heart-shaped, and her skin unblemished, so on balance, she was considered sweet and pretty, if not beautiful. If she was plain, it was only when in the orbit of the dark-haired beauties with cheeks flushed from flitting about the dance floor. But at two-and-twenty she had no expectations of marrying for love or anything else. With no fortune and not enough beauty to overcome a meager dowry, Rory was resigned to living her days as she had begun them, as her grandfather's dependent.

Thus, for her beautiful sister-in-law, who was a remarkably pretty brunette with damp brown eyes, to underscore the reality of her situation, in such a blunt manner, *and* in public, was a piece of spite that bruised Rory to the core. She was only surprised Drusilla had not gone one step further and stated the glaringly obvious; that was left to William Watkins, who shared his sister's unwitting lack of tact.

He made Rory mentally wince and wish she were a mouse to scurry through a hole in the kicking boards when he said with a sickly-sweet smile of understanding,

"I am certain Miss Talbot's interest in Lord Fitzstuart goes no deeper than an appreciation of his exceptional athleticism. As is often the way, what is lacking in ourselves we greatly admire in others. You, my dear Miss Talbot, cannot help being lame, just as I cannot be blamed for my poor eyesight. It is God's will, and thus we abide it with good grace and forbearance."

"If you will follow me to the upstairs drawing room, Mr. Romney will be with you presently," the butler intoned in the silence which followed Mr. Watkins' homily, a toe on the first step.

"You do have your eyeglasses, William?" Lady Grasby asked, bunching up her apricot silk petticoats to ascend the staircase as rapidly as possible in high-heeled mules. "I so want you to examine the portrait, to tell me what it is about it that is vexing me." She paused on a sudden thought and looked over her shoulder, a gloved hand to the polished balustrade. "Don't trouble yourself to come up, Aurora. We will not be above half an hour."

"That would be for the best," Rory responded cheerfully, standing at the base of a staircase that would take her twice the time to ascend than anyone else but a child taking its first steps. "I know so little about art that I would be of no help to you whatsoever." Her gaze swept the hall for a settee or a wingchair. "Mr. Romney must have a suitable vestibule for visitors on this level…"

She was talking to herself. The butler and Lady Grasby, with her brother a step behind, had disappeared up the staircase.

One of the painter's assistants rescued her. He stepped into the hall from the studio at the back of the house, dressed in a smock covered in all manner of colored daubs, and in time to be privy to the conversation. He offered Rory to follow him to a small viewing room off Mr. Romney's painting studio. There was a fire in the grate and a comfortable chair to sit upon and wait.

The fire was welcoming, but her interest was not in the many painted canvases stacked against two walls, or in those propped on easels ready for inspection, but in the sounds of commotion coming from the other side of a door left ajar by the assistant. Interest piqued, Rory entered the large well-lit room uninvited, and found it brimming with activity and laughter.

She was halfway across the room and beside a canvas propped on an easel before her trespass was finally noticed by those on the stage in front of her. She took only a cursory glance at the canvas of a half-finished painting, more interested in the group of scantily-dressed females whose modesty was saved by strategically draped diaphanous silks. While these draperies covered their torsos and flowed to their stockinged feet, the sheerness of the fabric did little to hide their limbs and female attributes. All possessed the long shapely legs of the opera dancer. This was confirmed when three of their number broke from the group and danced out across the stage, holding hands and twirling this way and that on the balls of their stockinged feet, slim graceful arms offering an elegant counterpoint to their footwork.

They appeared as Greek statues of glistening white marble come to life with their sculptured white limbs and powdered faces; their graceful movements, as they danced about the stage, mesmerizing. Rory delighted in their exuberance and agility, so much so that it was several moments before she realized she was being addressed, and by the principal ballerina fanning herself by the chaise longue.

"I beg your pardon. I was so taken with your companions I did not hear your question."

CONSULATA BACCELLI DID NOT IMMEDIATELY RESPOND, TAKING HER time to appraise Rory's gown of striped mint green taffeta with underskirts of embroidered lilac silk, the outer petticoat ruched and bunched behind to affect the fashionable polonaise. Here was a lady of style, if not of the first society, and she wondered where the young woman's male chaperone could be—a personal maid at the very least—particularly at this late hour. She did not have to wonder why the young woman used a walking stick.

Watching Rory cross the room, it was evident from her awkward gait that she needed it to move about. The short hem of her polonaise, which was some three inches off the ground, exposed her trim ankles in their white clocked stockings and matching heeled silk shoes; an inwardly twisted right foot answered to the uneven gait.

Rory was all wide-eyed interest, and Consulata thought it a great shame the young woman would never dance or be graceful in her movements, which surely meant she could never show herself to advantage. But her spontaneous delight at watching the ballerinas playfully spin out across the stage decided Consulata here was a young woman without malice, and she immediately decided to befriend her.

"Signora—"

"Signorina. Signorina Talbot," Rory corrected with a smile, gaze turning to Consulata Baccelli as the dancers were ushered back into formation by a weary assistant; another hurriedly coming to his colleague's aid to help adjust drapery and flowered headpieces. "They dance delightfully. I'm sure you all do."

"*Sì*. We do. But me, Consulata Baccelli, I am the most delightful

dancer of them all." The principal ballerina laughed behind her fluttering fan at her conceit. "I would show you but for these outrageous
robes Signore Romney he has made us wear." She indicated the blue
damask chaise. "Come, sit here with me."

When Rory looked about her, as if a chair closer at hand would be
more suitable than sitting upon the stage with the dancers, Consulata
smiled and patted the damask cushion.

"Come. Amuse me until the excitement, it begins."

Rory reluctantly climbed the three wooden steps and sat where
requested, careful not to disturb the bunched petticoats at her back.
Her walking stick she kept close to her side, a gloved hand about its
ivory handle.

"You must be thrilled to have a painter of Mr. Romney's skill and
reputation to immortalize you and your beautiful dancers."

"Signore Romney he paints us not as dancers but as part of a Greek
allegory. Me? I prefer to be painted as I am, a ballerina most famous.
But this—" She waved a plump wrist covered in pearls at the large
canvas propped on the easel. "—this painting that has us all dressed in
these ridiculous sheets of annoyance, it is painted for the Duke of
Dorset. He will hang it in the gallery at Knole." Consulata leaned in
with a sly smile. "And then, because Dorset he is my lover, he will have
me painted, dancing. And *that* painting he will hang in his private
apartments, for his eyes only." Her large brown eyes danced merrily,
adding so only Rory could hear, "Dorset, he wants Signore Romney to
paint me nude. Perhaps I will allow it, eh?"

Without wishing it, Rory blushed. Consulata Baccelli's suggestion
was an outrageous one, and most inappropriate to a spinster who lived
a sheltered existence in the household of her aging grandfather. He
would be horrified to learn his only granddaughter was in the company
of a troupe of dancers whose morals were questionable at best. That
Rory was conversing with the notorious mistress of the Duke of Dorset
was an encounter she decided to keep to herself. And lest she be considered prudish, she summoned her courage and looked into Consulata's
large lovely eyes, and said with a smile she hoped oozed a worldliness
she did not in the least possess,

"The Duke is sure to treasure such a painting. Your graceful figure is
to be admired, and deserves to be immortalized."

Consulata was pleased with this response and beamed.

"I think we will be good friends. Very good friends indeed, Signorina Talbot. I will have Dorset invite you to dinner. Then you and me,
we can laugh and reminisce together about the little escapade Major
Fitzstuart he arranges for his pleasant friend."

Rory tried to keep the interest from her voice and the surprise from her features. "Major? Major Fitzstuart?"

The dancer's dark eyes crinkled with amused mischief. Before she could enlighten Rory, she turned on the group of females giggling and jostling each other behind the chaise and slapped her fan down hard across the back of the chaise's gilt frame. The dancers instantly swallowed their mirth and were silent and still long enough to be chastised.

"Stop this instant or not one of you will dance at the Haymarket again." She jerked her dark head at the windows. "Keep your eyes on the windows, and when the handsome Major and his friend they appear, you will all do as instructed. *Sì? Bene,*" she added, when the dancers nodded obediently. "Now please to contain your impatience. When you see Major Fitzstuart in all his glory, then you have my permission to screech the excitement so loud his pleasant friend will run into this room and save my life."

She turned back to Rory and said merrily, "Soon it will begin, and so you are not alarmed, me I will tell you what is to happen. But first promise me not to tell Signore Romney's servants. It is most important to keep the surprise so the Major's pleasant friend, who is naturally infatuated with me, believes I am terrified and he has saved me from a fate worse than death."

Rory was so intrigued she could only nod. She shuffled down the chaise longue in anticipation of receiving Consulata's confidence regarding Major Fitzstuart. But no sooner had she done so than the dancers at her back began jumping up and down and squealing their delight. This had Consulata Baccelli on her feet. At the same time, one of Romney's assistants threw paints and brushes into the air as if in panic and fled the room, while two of the dancers swept up the trailing folds of their drapery, skipped lightly down the three steps of the stage and ran across the studio towards the windows.

Such was the instantaneous outburst of excitement that Rory instinctively swiveled to look over her shoulder—at the dancers, not out across the studio to see what had caused their agitation. By the time she reoriented herself to the windows, an intruder, who had dropped into the studio via an open window, was chasing two dancers across the room.

Rory was shocked into speechlessness by such outlandish behavior, and while she blinked several times in response, as if convincing herself the scene presented before her was indeed unfolding, she did not sense any immediate danger to her person, or to any of the dancers. This surprised her, because the intruder was male, and naked but for a belt around his waist that positioned a modesty cloth between his legs.

Watching him chase after the giggling dancers, who were showing no resistance to being caught, the cloth proved no covering at all, and Rory's face flooded with the heat of outrageous embarrassment.

And then, within the blink of an eye, her acute embarrassment turned to profound shock, and from shock, panic sprang, not for herself but for the intruder. When he came running up the room towards the stage and caught the squealing dancers about the waist and held fast, Rory saw that his hair was powdered gray, his eyes blackened, and his laughing face disguised with thick stripes of white paint. But it was a thin disguise and would fool no one who knew him. Rory knew him better than anyone else. The naked intruder was Harvel; Harvel Edward Talbot, Lord Grasby; her only brother.

THREE

Earlier, Lord Grasby had tiptoed behind Dair, staying
close in the darkness as his friend navigated the pathways of the small
garden at the back of George Romney's townhouse.

"Dair! *Psst*! Dair?" Grasby hissed. "Is this it? Is this the window?"

Dair nodded. He had crouched under one of three sash windows,
this one with the lower sash pushed up off the sill and the velvet
curtains pulled back on the night. He took a peek through the
window. Grasby joined him, nose just above the sill, blue eyes very
wide.

Candlelight blazed everywhere. At the far end of the room on a
raised platform, with a backdrop of white linen drapery, half a dozen
scantily-clad beauties giggled and flirted with two soberly-dressed
gentlemen attempting to position them in some sort of order around
the back of a damask-covered chaise. Here on a chaise reclined the well-
known Italian ballet dancer Consulata Baccelli, fluttering a fan and in
conversation with a female who was obscured from their line of sight by
a third Romney assistant, who was ordering his two fellow assistants
about.

Neither Dair nor Grasby was interested in this unknown female. If
anything, her presence was a complication Dair could do without.
Consulata had made no mention of a companion, and the fact she was
not dressed like the dancers meant she was possibly an annoying
patron, come to see the painter about a portrait. Dair dismissed her as
unimportant, and soon forgot all about her as he joined Grasby in
admiration of the mesmerizing sight of a troupe of beautiful ballerinas

in thin silks, their milky white breasts freed of the restrictive confines of stays.

Had Grasby been less inebriated and less mesmerized, he might have noticed the partially obscured female's walking stick, an anomaly amongst a group of dancers. And having noticed the walking stick, he would have wanted to see the face of the owner of what was quintessentially a male accoutrement, only used by females who were elderly or infirm, and by his sister Rory since he could remember.

It was fortuitous for Dair that his friend remained oblivious to the walking stick, and that the assistant continued to obstruct their view of its owner's face. Recognizing his sister, Grasby would not have jumped through the window and run towards the stage with arms raised, howling like an escaped Bedlam inmate. He would have turned his skinny behind away from the window and fled back down the garden path and into the blackness of night, leaving his friend stranded and bemused by such a cowardly act.

"That's a stroke of luck. Romney's not in the room. The canvas is unattended. It's now or never, Grasby!"

"What? Me? *First?*"

"Yes. I'll be one foot behind you. You head left towards the stage, hollering as loud as you can to get attention. I'll take the right flank, and creep up on those fellows and take them on, should they prove to have a brave bone in their body."

Grasby liked the idea of Dair dealing with any ensuing violence, but he remained reluctant.

"We could seriously upset such delicious creatures with our carryings-on, and I don't think I can—upset them. One must remain a gentleman. It doesn't feel right to frighten them."

Dair understood. He had no wish to terrorize females, defenseless or otherwise.

"I'll let you in on a secret, something Cedric doesn't know because he is determined to be the hero of the hour. Consulata is well aware of what's about to happen; I had her tell the girls. They are expecting us. I presume that's why there's so much giggling and jiggling going on. Have another look and you'll see they can't keep still." When Grasby popped his eyes above the sill, he grinned. "Lovely, aren't they?"

"Heavenly…" Grasby dropped back down again. "I like this plan much better." He pretended to button his lips. "Not a word to Cedric."

Dair stuck out his hand. "Good luck."

Their handshake was firm. Both grinned with the anticipation of running after semi-clothed dancers squealing with delight.

Dair slowly pushed up the sill, and when it was high enough to allow human trespass, he nodded. When Grasby straightened from a crouch, Dair briefly gripped his shoulder to give him courage. Grasby scrabbled over the sill and dropped into the room.

Thirty seconds was all it took.

The studio walls reverberated with the piercing squeals of half a dozen dancing girls jumping for joy. Two of their number ran with open arms across the studio to greet the intruder playing at being an American Indian.

Lord Grasby was in seventh heaven.

RECOGNIZING HER BROTHER, RORY WAS UP OFF THE CHAISE longue and leaning on her stick. When a hand caught at her gloved wrist, she tore her gaze from Lord Grasby cavorting with two giggling dancers and stared unseeing at Consulata Baccelli.

"Do not be alarmed," the ballerina reassured her. "There is no danger. The Major and his friend, they are merely playing a game—"

"I must get down from here at once!"

Consulata's grip tightened but her smile remained.

"That is not possible, not until the performance is over. Sit and be calm."

"You do not understand. I cannot be seen here. I must go, without delay!"

"It is natural we females become anxious by the games men play, because always they are unpredictable," Consulata replied, misunderstanding Rory's determination for feminine anxiety. She tried to make her see reason. "But their games they are harmless. And these two, they are like little boys who pretend to be savages. And my dancers, they are greatly amused to be so entertained. So, signorina, you will sit and not spoil our enjoyment of their performance, *sì*?"

"I assure you, if I do not leave here at once, the consequences for those men will be far worse than spoiling your enjoyment. Now, please, let go of my hand."

"Why are you such a wet goose about a trifle of a thing?" Consulata demanded indignantly, voice rising as she tried to be heard over all the excitement.

A quick glance across Rory's shoulder and she saw the reason for the increase in the dancers' vocal admiration. A second male intruder had now dropped into the studio via the sash window. It was Major Lord Fitzstuart. Her gaze reluctantly returned to Rory. She was now furious with this young woman to whom she had given a front row seat to the handsome Major's outrageous display.

"You are tiresome in the extreme!" she declared, up off the chaise. "And me, I do not apologize to one who goes frigid with fright at the sight of a man uncovered! Eh? The male body 'tis beautiful, powerful, *stupendo*. If one is to faint, it is in appreciation! You want to run away over a thing that is most natural, but Consulata, she will not allow you to do this! The perfect opportunity it has arrived for your eyes to be opened and for you to *see*."

The principal ballerina grabbed Rory's shoulders, swiveled her to face into the studio, and gave a snort of satisfaction.

"Now take a good look at what is before your eyes, because me, I have a vast experience of men, and none is more impressive in its handsome masculinity than the figure possessed by Major Fitzstuart. *Ecco!*"

Rory did not struggle to be free of Consulata's hold, neither did she do as requested and search out the Major. She kept her gaze on the middle distance, where strewn across the floor were the paints, artist's brushes and paraphernalia that had been tossed into the air and left scattered and spilled by a retreating assistant. In so doing, Rory hoped to avoid catching sight of her brother, so that if he chanced to take his focus from the dancers in his arms and recognized her, he would not be instantly acutely embarrassed. For surely finding her amongst a troupe of scantily-clad dancers of questionable morality, while shocking in itself, was as nothing when compared to the fact his little sister had discovered him cavorting with these very same females.

Her second thought, and the one that consumed her the most, was how could she possibly forestall her sister-in-law and Mr. Watkins from entering the studio? They were just one floor above, and the disturbance was so deafening and constant that had they been three floors higher, they could not fail to hear the high-pitched squeals and laughing protests of the dancers as they were being chased. It was only a matter of time before every person within the Romney household came rushing to find out what all the commotion was about. And if Lady Grasby discovered one of the intruders was in fact her husband of three years, Rory was certain her brother's married life would not be worth living thereafter.

To save her brother's marriage from ruin, the family from scandal, and for the sake of domestic harmony, Rory knew it was her duty to make every effort to cross the studio and lock the door on the outside world. Her sister-in-law and Mr. Watkins must be prevented from entering at all costs. If she were able to lock the door, then she was confident Grasby and the Major had every chance of escaping from the house the way they had entered it, without further detection and with no one of their acquaintance the wiser as to their outrageous behavior.

And then the little voice within her, the voice that came to her when she was alone with her thoughts in her bedchamber, or out in her hothouse nurturing her precious pineapples, uttered the two tiny words she knew so well.

What if?

When she was much younger, and thus more impetuous and less level-headed, these two words had caused her heartache and strife more times than she cared to count. They had allowed her to entertain alternatives and possibilities for a future that had been ordained the day of her birth.

Her mother had died in childbed, and she was born lame. The man midwife who delivered her postulated that there was a likelihood she was also brain-damaged. He deemed she would never walk, never develop in body, and would have impaired brain function. It was best if she were left to go hungry and let nature take its course. Her grandfather saved her. No one, however, could save her father. The death of his beloved wife sent him into a deep depression, and two months after her birth he did the unthinkable. He was found drowned in the Thames. A boating accident, so the world was told.

What if she had been born without a deformity? *What if* she had been able to walk without the aid of a stick, upright and confident, and with the grace shown by all young ladies wishing to present themselves to best advantage? She would have found a suitor. She would have married. She would have born babies by now.

What if her grandfather had not saved her? And that was the most profound *what if* of all.

And as she stood on the stage in indecision, held against her will by Consulata Baccelli, those two little words came to her, and she dared to consider the consequences of *what if?*

What if she remained on the stage and did as Consulata Baccelli demanded and looked upon Major Fitzstuart dressed as a savage? The ballerina insisted and would be offended if she did not. And after all, as the main actor, surely he wished every member of his audience to be attentive to his performance. It would be the height of bad manners not to show him some consideration...

Rory smiled to herself, smoothed out her petticoats and resumed her seat on the chaise longue. With back straight, one gloved hand resting lightly in the lavender silk folds of her lap and the other about the carved ivory handle of her walking stick, she slowly lifted her gaze and allowed her light blue eyes to calmly survey its principal performer, one Major Lord Fitzstuart.

Oh my...In all her daydreams, he had never looked like *that*.

Stripped to his breeches and white shirt was as undressed as her imagination could take her. And at the recent Roxton Easter Regatta, Major Lord Fitzstuart had unwittingly obliged her by fulfilling this daydream when he strode into her marquee in search of refreshment after his exertions in winning the boat race. He had walked straight past her without a second look, which was to be expected. He did not know her. She was six years younger than her brother, and the Major was in the army, abroad before she even put in an appearance downstairs. And as always at such functions, she was seated with the elderly, the infirm, and those guests unwilling to make the trek to cheer on the rowers from the lakeshore. Ignored, Rory was at her leisure to admire his lordship in damp breeches and even damper white shirt clinging to his manly physique.

But never, in all her conjured fantasies, was the Major wearing nothing but a cloth between his taut thighs. When he stopped and threw back his head with laughter to find her brother gleefully writhing about the floorboards with two dancers collapsed on top of him, she was given further opportunity to appraise him. And just as the dancers appeared to her fashioned from an ethereal marble, so, too, did the Major. His broad back and shoulders were smoothly polished, the muscle contours to his arms and legs as chiseled as a classical statue of Apollo. But when he turned and ran across the room towards the stage, she was so taken aback she gasped, breath short and quick, as if needing air to stave off lightheadedness. It was not his darkened eyes or war paint, or the two braids either side of his handsome face, that caught her completely off guard. It was the shock of the unexpected.

Gentlemen of her social circle were always close shaven; some wore a blue cast to their cheeks and chins between shaves. She knew that if left unshaven, men grew facial hair, and if left to grow, this hair turned into a beard. Major Lord Fitzstuart had this blue cast to his strong jaw and heavy chin, and while his throat was smooth-skinned and hairless, the rest of him was not. The covering of dark hair to his expansive chest was a complete surprise. This dark hair not only covered his chest, but continued south, over the hard contour of his torso in a neat dark line, to disappear under the modesty cloth hanging between his legs. A quick glance to the floor and she saw that his bare feet were large and hairless, but his solid calves and muscled thighs were not. It was a revelation. Rory's throat burned dry. The Major's masculinity far exceeded the girlish expectations of her daydreams. Small wonder then that the dancers were applauding and jumping up and down in admiration! Mentally, she was engaged in doing the same.

Recovered from the shock of revelation, she allowed herself to be caught up in his display of male bravado and athletic prowess.

One of Romney's assistants, who was brave enough—or was he stupid?—to stand his ground, put up his fists. The Major laughed and welcomed the challenge. Yet he kept his hands on his hips, goading the assistant to make the first strike. When the man did just that, the Major nonchalantly ducked this way and that, avoiding contact with the run of jabs punched into the air in front of him. Seemingly tired of the game, he finally went in for the attack. His fist caught the assistant's jaw first punch and the man reeled back, shocked.

Rory half rose from the chaise.

The dancers at her back cheered.

The Major followed up with a series of strategically placed short sharp blows to the man's body. The assistant collapsed, crumpled onto the floor, winded.

Rory applauded.

The dancers cheered louder than ever.

The Major turned to the stage in recognition of the acclaim, but the dancers, Rory included, gasped, smiles replaced by agitation as they pointed at something or someone over his shoulder.

A second assistant was foolish enough to make a run at the Major from behind with chair raised. Instantly, the Major swiveled on the balls of his feet, saw the chair in the air, dropped to a crouch and put his shoulder forward. The assistant ran straight into the Major's shoulder whereupon he was lifted off his feet, lost his balance and hold on the chair, and was flipped into the air. As the Major straightened, the chair and the assistant crashed to the ground. The chair bounced and splintered. The assistant landed on his back, winded, self-esteem shattered. When he could breathe, the man scurried from the room on all fours to the accompaniment of the Major's hearty laugh and the taunts of the dancers.

All resistance at an end, Major Lord Fitzstuart turned to the stage and bowed with a flourish, quick to revert to character as an American Indian. He skillfully traversed the battlefield of strewn artifacts to be found in a painter's studio, scattered in panic by one of Mr. Romney's assistants: Paint brushes strewn like broken sticks, a palette dropped like a soldier's shield, and paints of all colors spilled out of their mixing pots and splashed across the floorboards like the blood of the wounded vanquished.

Cheers and squeals of delight from the stage accompanied this successful crossing of such a perilous battlefield, and in celebration, the Major howled at the moon, fists raised in victory. The dancers continued to applaud, and all hoped they would be the one the Major captured when he invaded the stage.

Consulata Baccelli leaned forward on the chaise longue, the diaphanous silk slipping off her shoulder invitingly as she called for him to join her. And when the Major looked her way, she beckoned him with a sultry smile and one crooked finger. It was all the encouragement he needed to take a flying leap for the chaise longue.

What Major Lord Fitzstuart could not see and thus did not know, and what the dancers saw but promptly ignored, was the sudden activity at his back. A raiding party had invaded the studio, the door was flung wide and banged against the wood paneling. The smack of wood hitting hard up against wood was lost in the din of the dancers screaming for the Major's attention.

Rory not only saw the door burst open but also was witness to Mr. Cedric Pleasant striding purposefully into the center of the floor before dramatically drawing his sword and holding it aloft, like a valiant knight of old on a quest to smite the enemy. He followed his theatrical entrance with the bellowed pronouncement that he, Cedric Pleasant esquire, had come to save the day. Disappointingly for Mr. Pleasant, no one but those at his back heard this brave declaration.

Mr. George Romney, Mr. William Watkins, and Lady Grasby, with a gentleman unknown to Rory following on their heels, all pushed through the doorway, almost at one and the same time.

Rory instantly shot to her feet.

Someone—*she*—had to warn Grasby.

At the edge of the stage, her gaze shifted from the intruders to her brother, who was sprawled on the floor and content to stay there. His sooty head rested in the lap of a dancer while another straddled his lap. Both women were running their fingers over their captured savage in search of the most sensitive spots along his body that were ticklish. And by her brother's giggling fit, with his long thin legs kicking out wildly, he was enduring their chosen method of torture as best he could.

It said much for her sisterly devotion that despite the shocking nature of her brother's circumstance, watching him enjoying himself had her smiling with loving indulgence. It had been years since he had been so at ease. She had almost forgotten he could laugh so heartily.

Rory's indulgent smile sealed her fate. Had she not paused in contemplation to watch her brother with loving affection, she might have had sufficient time to avoid disaster by flinging herself out of harm's way. Returning her gaze to the doorway, where the raiding party was as stone, mute with stupefaction, she was met with a terrifying sight. It was so startling that every fiber of her being conspired against her, and she could not move a muscle. Major Lord Fitzstuart had taken a mighty leap and was in full flight of reaching the chaise longue. He was hurtling straight towards her and there was nothing she could do to save herself. She closed her eyes tight and took a deep breath. Braced for disaster, she hoped for the best.

FOUR

While Dair was dealing with Romney's assistants, he wondered at the whereabouts of Cedric Pleasant. His short wide friend had yet to make his grand entrance. And where was Grasby while the affray was taking place? Not that Dair needed his help to get rid of the two men. He had toyed with them, and then become bored with their antics, dispatching both in quick succession. Discovering his blond friend flat on his back and being tickled into submission by two dancers was a delightful surprise, and Dair couldn't have been happier for him. Not since before his marriage to that cold beauty Drusilla Watkins had he seen Grasby so carefree. So he decided to leave Grasby undisturbed, and made a move on the stage, alone. And when Consulata beckoned him to her, he needed no further encouragement.

Dair made a flying leap for the stage.

The cheering, squeals and clapping was deafening.

And then the unexpected happened.

It was so unexpected that time slowed to allow the moment to be etched in the collective memory of those present. There was such disbelief that no one spoke and no one moved for a matter of seconds, wondering if it was all part of the Major's display of outrageous bravado. He had not received the moniker Dair Devil for sitting about White's playing at cards.

Dair was in full flight of his leap when into his path stepped the female in the mint green and lavender silk petticoats. Where in the name of Jupiter had she sprung from? Her timing was disastrous. Did she have a brain the size of a pea not to comprehend what would happen to her by such an idiotic move? It was impossible for him to stop mid leap. His soldier's instinct told him that if he did not take immediate evasive action, his large beefy carcass would slam full force into this simpleton. Bones would be broken. Hers. There was no time and no possibility of being heard, even if he did shout out a warning.

The bevy of beauties, who only moments before had been jiggling and giggling and calling out encouragingly, now saw the disaster about to befall him, and they scattered, screaming, to get out of the way.

Dair took the only action left to him to avoid catastrophic consequences. He tucked in his arms, twisted his body and braced, hoping this would be enough to alter his trajectory and throw him wide of the idiotic creature. His quick thinking would have worked had the female remained where she was and not turned. It was as if she sensed an ominous presence, and in trying to escape it she again stepped into his path. There was no option left to him.

He landed heavily on the stage, momentum carrying him forward, and scooped up the female, pulling her hard against his torso as he kept running. His feet scrambled to resist inertia. His thigh slammed into the corner of the chaise, startling its occupant, who flopped forward before sprawling backwards across the cushions with an involuntary screech when the tipped chaise fell back on all four of its spindle legs with a thud.

Dair judged the edge of the platform to be a few feet in front of him, that there was then a drop and a gap of some five feet before the plastered wall at the back of the studio. The last thing he wanted was to fall into the gap with his captive; she might land under him and be crushed. And even if he did leap the gap, there was nowhere to go. They would slam into the wall. While he might suffer a few bruises and abrasions, there was no guarantee he could prevent his captive from breaking bones, possibly ribs.

He needed to do something, fast. Out of the corner of his eye, he caught sight of the linen drapery, used as the painter's backdrop. It was billowing in the breeze from the open sash window. He calculated it was within reach. With his captive in one arm, he stuck out the other, grabbed a handful of this material and prayed the curtain rod did not snap in two. The material needed to remain stitched to its rings long enough for them to become entangled, which should stop them from falling off the edge of the stage.

His strategy worked. Speed coupled with motion spun them into the folds of linen. The curtain swung wide. Dair's shoulder hit the wall with a thump, and then the curtain and its two occupants swung back to the stage and came to a halt. The couple were rolled up in the material, but remained upright and unharmed.

Pleased with his efforts at averting a disaster, he let out an involuntary chuckle. For several seconds, all he could hear was his own heavy breathing, and all he could feel was his heart thudding against his ribs. Far off, at the other end of the studio, there was a great deal of commotion, but here, wrapped in this linen cocoon, there was only silence... and breathing. His captive was breathing heavily, too. He felt her breath on his bare chest, where her forehead was pressed, and she was trembling, no doubt from fright. But she was not screaming or moaning, which told him she was unhurt. No broken bones then. Good. He possibly had a nasty bruise to his thigh and to his shoulder, but that was as nothing compared to the bruise to his ego, courtesy of this idiotically unaware female wrapped safely in his arms.

Who the devil was she, anyway? Where had she come from? Why was she on the stage surrounded by dancers dressed as Grecian nymphs when she herself was dressed from head to foot? His wine-befuddled brain searched for answers. She must be a friend of Consulata. Perhaps a singer, or an actress, or a high-class whore who catered to the needs of men of his social class. Mistress of one of Dorset's cronies, perhaps? That made sense.

She was certainly not one of those delicately nurtured females, like his sister and cousins, and his mother, who wouldn't dare dip an expensively shod toe into a painter's studio without a male chaperone, and for fear of encountering the very women for whom he and Grasby had been performing. A drawing room miss would have fainted or be screaming her lungs out by now. The severe shock of being swept off her feet by a naked man playing at savage would surely bring on a fit of hysterics. Yet she was not hysterical. Perhaps his captive was too frigid with fright to put up a struggle? Which would explain why she was adhered to him as tightly as an eager bride clinging to an enthusiastic groom on their wedding night.

He determined that she might not be idiotic after all, but rather a cunning little minx. Idiotic in the execution of her gambit—no one in her right mind threw herself in front of a dragoon whose chest was the width of a sedan chair—but cunning in that if she had been wanting to get his attention, she now had it, undividedly. And she was not backward in coming forward in letting him know what she wanted from him, either. Vixen.

What was that saying Cedric repeated *ad nauseam* after one too many bottles of claret? *Carpe* something? *Carpe... Carpe diem...* Seize the day! That was it. He certainly had something in his hands right now, warm and soft and no doubt, delicious… He grinned. And he wasn't above seizing the moment. Be damned what was going on beyond their cocoon.

How convenient her petticoats were in disarray, bunched up to one side, the panniers concertinaed up off her hips, pinioning his left arm to her waist and his hand to her firm round derrière. Her light linen chemise was no barrier to the pleasurable tactile sensation of warm, rounded female flesh, and he wondered if she smelled as good as she felt.

He dipped his head, expecting one of the more sweet headier scents concocted by Floris and splashed about by his lovers, as if it were water and he with coins to pitch into the sea. But what price the bedding of a beautiful woman?

He was pleasantly surprised. This scent was much more subtle, and alluring…

He closed his eyes, and snuffled her, wondering at the component parts of such a beguiling fragrance. It was an indefinable, barely-there mingling of scents, of vanilla, and lavender, and mostly of her feminine allure. It triggered within him a deep longing that he could neither describe nor wished to acknowledge. All he knew was that he wanted more of her, then and there. His hand convulsed in her thin chemise, scrunching up the linen between his long fingers as he drank her in.

She lifted her head off his chest and he tilted away from her, but just enough to see her face, to see if she was as caught up in the moment as he. Her big blue eyes, limpid under heavy lids, blinked up at him, and when her lips parted, slowly and ever so invitingly, he needed no further invitation. He pressed his mouth to hers and gave himself up to the moment…

It was the wooden pegs in the plasterwork that gave way first. They held the metal brackets to the wall. One metal bracket came away and fell with a clang to the stage, just as the wooden curtain rod, bowing under the weight of its two entangled occupants, snapped in two. There was a great whoosh and clatter of wooden curtain rings as they slid off the splintered ends of the broken rod. Dair and his female captive found themselves drowning in drapery.

It was over within seconds. Caught unawares, the cocooned couple struggled to stay upright, now they were no longer supported by the curtain pulled taut by their weight. With lightning reflexes, Dair's arms enveloped and tightened about his captive. And as they were knocked to the ground, he stuck out his elbows and took the brunt of the fall. Trapped in the drapery, they rolled over and over, fell off the stage and into the narrow gap between it and the plastered wall.

Dair landed on his back, his captive on top of him, clinging to him as if he were the only piece of flotsam in a raging sea. Both were shaken but unhurt. Both lay still, taking deep breaths, to recover their equilibrium, if not their dignity. Then suddenly both realized their latest predicament. As they had rolled off the stage, the linen unraveled, setting them free as they dropped into the gap. They were now a tangle of naked arms and legs, with breechcloths askew, panniers twisted and broken, layers of carefully-constructed silk petticoats crushed and disheveled, and all of it on display.

Dair thought it a great lark.

Grinning, he put an arm behind his head and settled in, not at all perturbed. His grin turned to genuine good humor watching his captive struggle to disentangle her limbs and her garments from his brawny form. And without his help, with not much success. He could see by her mulish expression his lack of assistance annoyed her, but when she managed to sit upright and rake her mussed blonde hair from her face, he caught at her wrist. He had every intention of pulling her back down on top of him to continue where they had left off wrapped in the curtain, everyone else be damned.

Then a voice boomed out across the studio, above the commotion. Dair stayed his hand around his captive's wrist, a finger to his lips lest she speak, and rose up on an elbow to listen. It was not Cedric Pleasant declaring he had come to save the day. He did not recognize the voice, but he recognized the bark of command. It was accompanied by footfall. And that, too, was familiar. It was men in boots marching in synchrony. At best guess, he would say a dozen men, maybe more.

Soldiers.

FIVE

RORY HAD NOT MEANT FOR HIM TO KISS HER. ON THE CONTRARY, she was one breath away from vocalizing her affront that it was the height of rudeness to sniff at her neck, at anyone's neck! She should have been terrified, distressed, even hysterical, to be pressed up against a naked man with nothing between them but a flap of doeskin. And that was proving not much of a shield. A particular part of his anatomy was not behaving as it ought, or perhaps that was the dilemma, it was behaving precisely as it should, but without permission to do so. Not that she knew anything about *that*, except what she had gleaned from studying the tapestries in a folly temple on her godparents' Hampshire estate.

Twenty-two years old and a complete ignoramus about matters of the heart, more precisely, matters of lust. Twenty—*two*. She could hardly believe her own ignorance!

As a spinster she had a duty to faint. If not, she should do everything in her power to fight him off and thrash her way out of the cocoon. Scream. Anything to get her virginal body as far away as possible from such potent masculinity. Her unsullied reputation demanded it. Her family would expect it. Polite Society would condemn her for not doing so.

But Major Lord Fitzstuart had shaken her well-ordered world as if it were a mesmerizing show globe. Afloat in a sea of colored liquid possibilities, she came to the realization that this impromptu visit to George Romney's studio was turning out to be the most exciting night of her staid life. Nothing ever happened in her day-to-day existence that was not sanctioned by convention, considered acceptable, peaceable and *safe* for the unmarried granddaughter of a peer.

And now here she was in the arms of the handsomest, most wicked war hero of the age. What should she do? She knew what she wanted to do, but it was contrary to everything she had ever been told or taught. What was that saying Cedric Pleasant used at every opportunity... *Carpe... Carpe—Diem.* That was it! Well, she would seize it and the consequences could go hang!

What was the harm in a single simple kiss? One kiss and she would know one way or the other if kissing was overrated. She had never been kissed, and certainly never in the way females wished to be kissed by handsome men, ardently and without restraint. While alone in her Pinery one day, she had allowed herself to daydream about kissing, the mechanics of a kiss, and how it must make a person feel. She concluded that if two people thought about it before committing to the act, they would not do it. Her daydreaming had led her to completely cover a maturing pineapple plant with tanner's bark, until the gardener alerted her to her abstraction. Two people with their lips pressed together? What was so special about that...?

He was so warm and so—so *male*. He smelled of pepper and musk, and—freshly squeezed limes... Fascinating how the skin on his face appeared smooth and yet, when she rubbed against it in an upwards motion, his chin was rough, like the sharp punched points of her grandfather's silver nutmeg grater... His nose really was large and beak-like. She'd noticed that about him before... And his eyelashes... They were quite long and dark... She was sure her lips were swollen... He tasted salty and delicious... Had the windows been closed on the night air and a fire started in a grate...? She was suddenly hot and heady, and there was a tingling sensation, more a pulse, somewhere...

Oh my!

It had never occurred to her that to truly enjoy a passionate kiss, their mouths must open. It was so—*decadent*. And he was so —*delicious*. She pressed herself against him, wanting more and not wanting him to stop. She wanted everything about the moment to be burned into her consciousness: His warm hand cupping her bottom; the feel of him large and bare, pressed up against her; his fingers entwined in the hair at her nape, tied with a lavender satin bow; and the wondrous way he kissed, as if he truly, fervently desired nothing and no one more than he did her.

Oh how easy it was to spiral into erroneous belief. And all it took was one kiss...

IF RORY WAS DISCONSOLATE TO HAVE THEIR DELIGHTFUL KISSING interlude brought to an abrupt end by the snapping of the curtain rod, she was shocked into speechlessness when she landed, straddling him, a disheveled wreck. Never mind she might have broken ribs. She knew she was bruised from head to foot from being tumbled and crushed under him as they rolled across the stage and then landed on the floor. And when they came to a crashing stop he just lay there on his back laughing, and so heartily that she bounced on his abdomen.

But the tumble jolted her awake to her behavior, and all she could think about was setting her clothes to rights and getting away from him as quickly as possible. She had to distance herself before Drusilla and Mr. Watkins discovered her whereabouts, and before Grasby realized his little sister had seen him drunk and disorderly, cavorting with females of low repute. But what could she tell them had happened to her? Her panniers were twisted and broken, the buttons and strings that gathered her petticoats into a polonaise had snapped, and the material was now hanging loose and haphazard. And where was her walking stick? The last she remembered seeing it was when she was hit by a wall of male muscle and it flew out of her gloved hand. She hoped it had not caused any of the dancers serious injury...

She was brought back to the immediate present when Dair gently squeezed her upper arm and, with a wink and a finger to his lips, signaled for her to remain silent. No explanation was necessary. The loud regular clatter of boots on floorboards, accompanied by the squeals of alarm from the dancers, had her scrambling off him and kneeling at the edge of the raised platform to see what was happening.

Just inside the doorway was Mr. George Romney, arms folded, shoulders hunched, and looking troubled. Beside him was his brother Peter, grinning from ear to ear. They shuffled out of the way of a contingent of uniformed militia who were marched in by a ruddy-faced captain of the guard. The soldiers came to an abrupt halt halfway up the length of the studio, where stood a stout gentleman in an eggshell blue frock coat with metallic thread and spangles, legs splayed and thus displaying his strong calf muscles to great effect. What lessened the impact of his stance was that he had stridden into the middle of the spilled paint, and now had splatters all over his buckled shoes. He was holding aloft a sword before an audience of crying and panicked dancers and declaiming. He quickly terminated his rehearsed speech when he was interrupted by the captain of the guard barking out orders, but his arm holding the sword remained in midair. Rory suspected he had frozen in tongue and body upon hearing, and then seeing, the soldiers. She recognized the frozen swordsman. It was her brother's best friend Mr. Cedric Pleasant. She surmised that he was the "pleasant friend" to whom Consulata Baccelli had referred.

She wondered at the whereabouts of her brother. She prayed he had managed to go into hiding somewhere in the room. Perhaps he was crouched behind the stack of canvases up against one wall, or under the table draped in cloth that had upon it all the paraphernalia needed by a painter of portraits? Better still if he had managed to dive back out the open window he had climbed in through. He was not amongst those now gathered in the studio, so when Dair tugged on the lace at her elbow to get her attention, she readily turned away from the melodrama. She was surprised he remained nonchalantly propped on an elbow out of sight.

"Report, fair scout! What's happening out there?"

"You don't want to see for yourself?"

"Let me guess," he said. "Twelve—maybe fifteen—militia, not including their captain...?"

Rory looked out into the studio, counted, then nodded, impressed.

"Couldn't ask for better odds! I would be insulted if there were fewer than a dozen. Six, and the wagtails would mistake them for customers. Eight, and our canary birds think they're for the round house for soliciting. Now with a *dozen* of our city's finest invading the premises, they suspect something far more serious is on the boil."

Rory frowned.

"Wagtails and canary birds? On the boil? I have no idea what you're talking about but it's nothing to do with aviaries. And, I would hazard a guess, contrived for your own amusement?"

Surprised, Dair stared hard at Rory for the first time since crashing into her. While he liked what he saw, she was a shapely little thing with big blue eyes and glowing hair, her self-possession and the intelligence in her expression unsettled him. He wasn't sure if she was laughing *at* him or *with* him. Instinct said the latter, so he took a leap of faith and confided in her, saying at his most nonchalant,

"You aren't particularly perturbed that Mr. Romney's studio is overrun with uniformed ruffians?"

"Why should I be?" she said with a shrug, adding with a cheeky smile, "I have a war hero to protect me."

"Ha! That's true!" he replied, and felt his face grow hot. God! Was he blushing? He felt sick to his stomach at such weakness. Plenty of women had used that one-line gambit on him, fluttering their eyelids and pouting their reddened lips, and to bed the most beautiful of them he let them think it had worked. But he had never blushed at the remark.

"A war hero masquerading as a savage," Rory teased.

"For a wager—all of it," he blurted out, as if a confession were required of him.

"Yes, I thought that might be why. But those poor—wagtails and canaries—they don't know that, do they? And the militia... I hope you aren't out of pocket for their invasion? Or will your winnings cover expenses, too?"

"Clever." His mouth twitched. "I'll wager my breechcloth you know what *perturbed* means, too."

Rory turned away to look out over the stage again; anything to stop him staring at her so fixedly. She was feeling quite faint. She told him what was happening, adding, "The captain has two of his men guarding the door, which is now closed. You won't escape that way, if that was your intent?"

He tugged again on her lace and gestured with his thumb over his bare shoulder. "Door behind us. And it's unlocked. What's the gentleman with the sword doing now?"

"He's put away his sword and is conversing with the captain."

"Mr. Pleasant will be as grumpy as a kicked toadstool to have his performance upstaged. Wise of him to sheath his sword and not play the hero. He's no coward but it would be idiotic to challenge men in uniform, particularly with such odds stacked against him."

"A war hero would. You would. Nothing frightens you."

For the second time in as many minutes, Dair was startled by such ready conviction. But he quickly recovered his sangfroid and inclined his head in acknowledgement, saying with a grin, "I will frighten them into submission. I doubt any of those boys have seen a Colonial least of all a native of that continent."

Rory's gaze flickered over his painted face, with its two braids dangling either side of his ears, and then across his wide shoulders, but dared not let her eyes drop any further, and quickly brought her gaze back to his face with its blackened eye sockets. That he was watching her intently was evident in his fixed stare.

"Yes, you will," she said calmly. "And it wouldn't require you to wear such an absurd disguise. You don't look like an American Indian in the least."

"Absurd? And how many American Indians have you—"

"I've seen etchings!"

An involuntary burst of laughter was quickly muffled when he clapped a hand over his mouth. He leaned in to her with a raise of his eyebrows. "I'll show you mine if you show me yours…?" But when she frowned, not understanding the inference, he sat back, suddenly uncomfortable and said with unusual brusqueness, "Next time I need to appear ridiculous I'll seek your advice!"

"You don't need my advice. You do quite splendidly on your own! Oh! Oh! Now that was rude of me! Forgive me!"

He grinned, watching her fluster and flounder her apology, cheeks apple red with embarrassment. He chucked her under the chin, then pinched it affectionately.

"You, my sweet-mouthed delight, are nothing like Consulata's usual coterie of female friends… I'm glad you threw yourself in my way."

"Threw myself?" Rory gasped loudly. "*Threw myself?*" She did not know what else to say to such a startling accusation. She was saved further embarrassment and explanation when Dair put a finger to her lips to quiet her and jerked his head at the stage.

"Listen! Sounds like an argument. Female tearing strips off some poor fellow. It's not Consulata. When she fires up it's all Genovese and gestures! Who did you say was out there?"

"I didn't."

Rory peeked over the ledge, but she knew who owned the agitated voice without needing to do so. Into the startling diorama of soldiers standing to attention, dancers huddled together, and a painter's studio in disarray, swept the Lady Grasby, followed by William Watkins a stride behind. Both rushed up to Mr. Romney demanding answers. Rory had no idea what was being said, there was too much competing noise. She could well imagine the painter was being accused of the world's ills by her sister-in-law, who was gesticulating widely with her folded fan.

Dissatisfied with the laconic painter's responses, when he pointed out the captain, she readily turned on this uniformed officer and proceeded to flay him with no regard for his rank, his mission or their audience. Drusilla's weapons of choice never wavered: The Talbot family pedigree that stretched back to Edward the Third; her grandfather-in-law's earldom, which her husband would one day inherit; and the Earl's noble connections to every Privy Councilor, which would see the captain shipped off to St. George's Island in the southern ocean, if he did not do as she commanded.

Rory sighed and said somewhat apologetically, "Lady Grasby is threatening the captain and he is looking most decidedly intimidated."

"Grasby? *Lady* Grasby?" Dair's ears burned and he sat up. "Tell me, Delight, do you see a wide-eyed ginger-haired fellow, thin as a whipping post—a scribbler with a blotter and pencil? Is he making copious notes?"

She nodded. "He is. And he cannot write quickly enough for the conversation. He's just broken the tip from his pencil and it's jumped out of his hand. Oh no! The poor fellow went to ground trying to recapture it and has had his hand trodden on by Mr. Watkins—"

"Mr. *William* Watkins? *Weasel* Watkins is there too? Hallelujah! It is a happy day indeed!"

Rory looked over her shoulder in time to witness Dair punch the air with joy.

"Weasel? *Weasel* Watkins? Is that what you call him?"

She tried to stifle a smile but Dair saw it and pointed a finger at her.

"Admit it, Delight! The moniker fits him like a glove. Those squinty eyes! Those bushy brows! Those thin, disapproving nostrils!"

"I will admit to nothing. And shame on you. Not everyone can be an Adonis. Certainly not Mr. Watkins. But he does dress his faults well."

"But he does dress his faults well," Dair mimicked, pulling a face of disgust.

Rory couldn't help herself—she giggled.

"Never in my wildest imaginings would I have believed Major Lord Fitzstuart capable of envying another. You could wear a sack and females would swoon at your feet. Poor Mr. Watkins must use all his sartorial skill to fashion himself into something worthy of a female's attention. You enter a room in a sack and poor Mr. Watkins' efforts would be for naught."

"Come here, Delight," he commanded gently, and pulled her down beside him, a firm grip on her gloved hand. There was no roguish smile when he looked into her eyes and said quietly, "It's time for me to end this charade. I must, before my friend the scribbler uses up all his parchment. But before I make my grand exit, I want your name. You're not a dancer, and you are not an actress. Your conversation—everything about you—tells me you've been well cared for, or were, in the past. No. Don't struggle. I don't want to cause you distress. I want to offer you—" When Rory continued to look at him blankly, he huffed, glanced away, then looked back at her in exasperation. "The Devil! What am I offering you…?"

Rory swallowed hard, throat dried with expectation, gaze riveted to his handsome face. By the deep lines between his black brows, she knew his mind was in a turmoil of indecision.

"How am I to know if you don't?" she asked in a small voice.

His gaze dropped at that, but not away—down, down to her mouth. Then down further still, to the swell of her small firm breasts contained in a tight striped silk bodice, the square décolletage low-cut, and just peeping out around its silken edge, the pretty lace border of her chemise. He caressed a fold of the delicate lace between the tips of thumb and forefinger, itching to fondle much more... Finally, he lifted her chin with his forefinger, and brought his gaze back up to her face.

"You know what I want, Delight. You don't kiss a man the way you kissed me without expectation of a result. Well, this is your lucky day. I'm going to give you what you want."

Rory blinked. It was her turn to experience turmoil. Her mind throbbed with the competing emotions of joy and dread. Joy because she saw that he desired her. She might be ignorant but she was no simpleton. The handsomest man in London found *her* desirable. No one had looked at her like that, ever. He certainly had never known of her existence before today, despite her attendance at the Roxton Easter Ball less than a month ago. But joy was quickly swallowed by dread, the dread of what he was about to propose. One kiss and he presumed to know what she wanted? Men were such immediate creatures!

She did not want to hear what he had to offer and shifted away, to brush down her petticoats, to get her gown and herself in some sort of order before she was discovered, as was inevitable. Her sister-in-law had stopped verbally abusing the captain, and he was now addressing his men. The dancers had quieted, too. A thump close by made her jump. There was footfall on the stage. The chaise longue was set upright. For the first time since they had landed in the ditch, Consulata Baccelli was heard complaining in her own tongue.

Yet, before Rory could take a peek to see what was going on, Dair pulled her into his arms and kissed her swiftly on the mouth.

"What is it about you that compels me? I must be mad! No matter. It is done. Whatever you want. House. Carriage. Clothes. Give me a week to arrange it. 'Till then go to Banks house in Chelsea. It shares a wall with the Physic Garden. Lil—Lily Banks. She'll take you in until I come for you, no questions asked. Just mention my name. Repeat the directions so I know you won't forget. Say them!"

"Banks House in Chelsea. The house shares a wall with the Physic Garden. Lily Banks will look after me, no questions asked. Who's Lily?"

"A friend—a very good friend." He grinned. "Mother of my son."

All the blood drained from Rory's face. She was in shock. Though why this was so, she had no idea. It was not as if she were unaware the Major kept a mistress and had spawned illegitimate offspring. The habits of noblemen and their mistresses were readily talked about in

every drawing room. She had even been present at a discussion between
two long-suffering wives of peers conferring on the care and nurturing
of their husbands' children by various mistresses, one of the ladies
lamenting her husband's ability to impregnate every woman he set eyes
on. Her sister-in-law had whisked her away before she could hear more.
Yet, to her, such conversations were just that, conversations like any
other. So she had never really given much consideration to what was,
for many wives of peers, a fact of life. But to have it baldly stated to her
face, and by the man himself! She was not sure what was the greater
upset, his lordship in nothing but a breechcloth or having him tell her
he had an illegitimate son by a woman named Lily Banks.

For several seconds she could neither feel nor hear. She watched
without seeing as Dair peered over the stage, then ducked down again
and said something to her. But she did not hear him. All she could
think about was a house in Chelsea, his mistress and their son. What
had he offered her? A house? Clothes? A carriage? But what about Lily
Banks and the boy? Was Lily Banks being cast aside for her, or was she
an addition to his harem? How many other women were there? And
children? What would her brother think? *Her brother?* Why had Grasby
intruded into her troubled thoughts about the Major and his nefarious
lifestyle?

Grasby! She could hear him. She mentally shook her mind clear
and discovered Dair had disappeared.

"DAIR! DAIR. FOR PITY'S SAKE! DON'T LEAVE ME HERE TO ROT!"

It was Grasby, pleading. But from where? His voice was muffled, as
if he was down a deep well. Soldiers were now scrambling over the
studio. Soon she would be discovered! Oh where was the Major? No
sooner had Rory wondered this than he appeared, out from under the
platform. He slithered on his stomach far enough out so he could raise
his shoulders then twisted his body around onto his bare buttocks,
Rory turning her head so she did not see him sit up. When he huffed
she looked back at him. He was covered in cobwebs and dust.

"Coy little thing aren't you?" he stated without criticism. He jerked
his head at the stage. "Friend in dire straits. He's stuck under a beam.
Must get him free. So you'll have to excuse me. And a warning, I would
stay low until the fighting—"

"*Fighting—?*"

"—is over." He leaned down and called out under the platform,
"Never would abandon you, Grasby! Just do as I say! You can't come

forward. The gap is too narrow, even for your skinny carcass! You have to back out, rump first!"

"Oh God! No! Not that way! Dair! Dair! You've got to *save* me!"

"Will do, dear fellow! Got to create a diversion first. When you hear a roar of noise and the girls screaming, that's when you scuttle backwards the way you came in, and as fast as you can. Got it?"

"Got it! A great noise and screaming and I back out."

"As fast as you can!"

"As fast as I can!"

"That's the spirit!"

"Dair! Dair? What the bloody hell do I do then? Where do I go? Make for the window?"

"No! Not the window! Across the platform. On the other side there's a door—"

"A door? On the other side of the platform? Oi!? What's that racket? Sounds like a damned rhino stomping above me!"

"Soldiers looking for—"

"She's sent *soldiers* to look for me? Bloody hell! I'm done for!"

"Not you! Nothing for you to worry about!"

"Worry about? I don't care about the bloody militia! It's the bloody wife—dearest Silla—she's out there, Dair! She's going to *kill* me! Dair! Dair... I've lost my bloody breechcloth... Dair?"

Dair swiveled on his toes, hunched over, shoulders shaking and a hand clapped to his mouth to stifle an outburst of laughter. Tears of glee filled his eyes. He turned back to face the black void under the platform when Grasby called to him in a thin high-pitched whisper.

"Dair? Dair, did you hear me...? You're laughing! I know it! This isn't amusing! This is *my* head on the block!"

Despite controlling his laughter, Dair could not hide his grin and it sounded in his voice. He wiped tears from his eyes, smudging the soot.

"No. Not amusing at all! But it's not your head that's the concern."

"Damn you to hell for getting me in this fix!"

"Yes. Yes. I'll be there soon enough. Just put your hands over your gadso and get across the stage and through that door as fast as you can! Make for the carriage. Grasby? Grasby!"

"Yes! Yes! Door! Carriage! Have a care with Silla. Be gentle. Her nerves. The shock... Are you listening to me, Dair? Dair? Dair! Devil take you! Bloody stupid prank! Bloody..."

The rest of Lord Grasby's tirade of abuse was swallowed by the noise of the dancers being herded under protest back onto the platform.

Dair took a look across the stage to ascertain the position of the soldiers. Most were still in formation awaiting orders. The civilians were still by the door, as was Lady Grasby and the Weasel, and two soldiers guarded the exit. Strange they were positioned there; that was not part of the agreement with the captain. The dancers were all huddled on the stage, and blocked his view of the right side of the studio. He presumed it was Consulata prone on the chaise longue; all he could see of her was a fan fluttering to and fro in agitation above the back of the chaise. And there, standing in the center of the room beside Mr. Cedric Pleasant, was the newssheet reporter, pencil and blotter in hand, looking wide-eyed and interested, as if he had hit on the story of the Season! Dair smiled. He would give him his story all right, and more.

Finally, he decided it was time to make his move. In farewell, he tugged on a long lock of Rory's hair, come loose from her mussed coiffure, then stood up and stretched his legs. When she went to do likewise, he signaled for her to remain seated, out of sight.

"Stay here. There's bound to be blood spilled. Nothing serious, but I don't want you getting mixed up in the fracas—"

"*Blood?* You will be careful, won't you?"

He instantly thought of his nine years in the army and the bloody carnage he and his comrades had survived. No one had ever asked him to be careful then, or cared. He laughed harshly, a look over his shoulder to see if he had yet been noticed, and brushed away her apprehension.

"Not mine! That lot out there. Well, maybe a little drop of mine," he conceded at her frown of concern. In an impulsive move, he leaned down to her, whispering near her ear, "I'll be careful, just for you..."

With his teeth, he tugged free the lavender satin ribbon tied in her disordered hair, chuckling at her sudden intake of breath.

"Did you think I meant to bite you?" he asked as he hastily tied the satin ribbon to the end of the braid hanging in front of his right ear.

No. Rory thought he meant to kiss her, and when he did not, was annoyed with herself for such an expectation. It must have shown on her features, because he said with a smile of apology,

"Every warrior gets his share of the spoils of war. This is mine. Now wish me luck, Delight!"

She was not given the opportunity to wish him anything at all. He was up out of the gap and onto the stage, standing tall with arms akimbo, before she could utter a syllable. Then he bellowed into the room with all the enthusiasm of a man relishing the result of his invitation,

"Well, lads! Who wants to come at me first?"

All hell broke loose.

SIX

Lord Shrewsbury was in his seventieth year, but today he felt a hundred and seventy. It was on days such as this that he contemplated resigning his post as England's Spymaster General. He would retire and live out the rest of his days here, at his Dutch house at Chiswick, with his beloved granddaughter for company. Together they would watch watercraft sailing up and down the Thames—all the ills of the world, all the vileness and intrigue consigned to the pages of his secret history.

But he had made a promise to his sovereign to remain Spymaster General until the "trifling upset" in the American colonies was resolved. Those members of the Privy Council who referred to the ongoing war across the Atlantic in such terms were either hopeful idiots or just plain ignorant fools. His Majesty was unshakeable in his belief that the "trifling incident" would soon be over, and his American "children" would return to him, their English parent.

Privately, Shrewsbury believed the American colonies were already lost. He believed this because he, more than any other man in the kingdom, had access to secret correspondence and intelligence from a network of spies that stretched across the kingdom, across Europe, out across the vast Atlantic Ocean and into every colony in the Americas. And he knew the American child had reached out to another parent, a rival, the great enemy of Britain—France. The French Ambassador to the Court of St. James's was at pains to reassure King George that France would not go to war to assist the American rebels: It would remain neutral.

Bollocks to that! thought Shrewsbury. He knew the French for liars. Louis' government was secretly providing aid in its various forms so the rebels could wage a full scale war on British troops defending His Majesty's colonial subjects. He was breeches-deep in secret intelligence that told him so. He had recently received intelligence that an agent of France based in Lisbon was, for the right price, willing to not only betray his countrymen, but divulge the name of the traitor within the bureaucratic ranks of Lord Shrewsbury's own spy network. Shrewsbury knew this traitor existed because he had been about to pounce on the traitor's intermediary, Charles Fitzstuart, a young idealist who had managed to evade capture with the help of his noble family.

It brought the bile up into his throat to think Charles Fitzstuart had escaped to France. He could not now be brought to justice for his treasonous activities, and he had taken with him the identity of the traitor within England's spy network. It was now vital that contact be made with the French double agent in Lisbon. Shrewsbury would send his best man, who possessed the skills to disappear into the local setting, could speak whatever language was required of him, was expert in handling all types of weaponry and, if caught, would be able to withstand the torture meted out to foreign spies. It was a dangerous and challenging assignment requiring great courage and cunning, but he was confident Major Lord Fitzstuart was up to the task.

The Major was presently licking his wounds after a particularly riotous evening the night before at a painter's studio. Shrewsbury had not read the finer particulars of a report into what had occurred, but he knew whores, drink and fists were involved, as it always was with the Major. Half a dozen souls and an aggrieved painter were seeking reparation and revenge. None of this bothered Shrewsbury in the least. He had been the same at the Major's age. Young men, particularly young men who risked their lives, needed distraction. And such men would be naughty boys given enticement and opportunity.

How ironic that the Major, his best agent, just happened to be the elder brother of the escaped traitor Charles Fitzstuart. But he trusted the Major implicitly. The same could not be said for the other members of Charles Fitzstuart's family. Two of their number sat across from him in his study. Both were noblemen of the highest rank and both were likely suspects in aiding and abetting Charles Fitzstuart's escape.

The Duke of Roxton was the most powerful duke in the kingdom, son of his best friend and Charles Fitzstuart's cousin; the other, Jonathon Strang, newly elevated Duke of Kinross, was the wealthiest peer in Scotland, and certainly the most outspoken. An intimidating duo. Both men were arrogant, opinionated, and fearless. But both had a weakness, the same weakness: Antonia, Dowager Duchess of Roxton.

The Duke of Roxton demanded to know why they had been summoned before him.

The Spymaster General was remarkably composed and smug.

"Do you not know, your Grace?" Lord Shrewsbury was unconvinced. He looked at Kinross. "Perhaps your Scottish Grace would care to enlighten his English Grace?"

"There's no need to be convivial on our account," Kinross stated dryly. "If Roxton says he don't know, believe him."

Shrewsbury looked Kinross between the eyes.

"Very well. Then I need only arrest you for treason, your Grace."

"*Treason?*" both dukes said in unison, but it was Kinross who gave a bark of laughter, as if Shrewsbury was in jest, which he knew he was not. He blew cheroot smoke into the air.

"For helping a couple elope? Don't be a fool, man! There ain't anything treasonous in that!"

"For knowingly aiding a traitor to evade capture, the penalty is—I see that you do not know what transpired earlier today, Roxton?" Lord Shrewsbury continued, and was interrupted by Kinross.

"I'll tell you what happened this morning. Shrewsbury here gave permission for the militia to storm your mother's house at dawn. Imagine! The house was overrun with troops. It was a damned frightening experience for Mme la Duchesse—"

Roxton half rose out of the armchair.

"*What? Soldiers* stormed *my mother's* house?" He looked from Kinross to Shrewsbury. "What game are you playing at? It's intolerable you have me summoned here not five minutes after I reach town, leaving my wife, *my pregnant wife*, troubled as to the nature of your business. And now I find you have distressed my mother even more so? I will not allow—"

"What you will and will not allow is irrelevant, your Grace," Shrewsbury cut in politely. He looked over the rims of his spectacles, blue eyes cold. "You need to ask yourself how Kinross knew your mother's house was searched by militia on my orders. And at such an early hour of the morning, when most of Westminster is still sleeping…" He looked directly at the Duke of Kinross and said without blinking, "My guess is the Duchess was still in bed… None would know that better than you, your Grace."

"Ha! You short change yourself, Shrewsbury. Given your sinister line of work, I'll wager my silver cheroot case you not only know the answer to that, but which side of the bed she prefers!"

Shrewsbury inclined his white head at the backhanded compliment.

"And when not in bed, the preference is for a chaise in the book room, or the public space of Her Grace's pretty summer pavilion, is it not? The infinite variety of settings you choose for your torrid couplings is limited only by your imaginations."

Kinross bared his white teeth. But there was no laughter in his eyes. He drew back deeply on his cheroot and deliberately blew smoke at the Spymaster.

"What a sad little man you are, Shrewsbury. The salacious reports about a beautiful woman being pleasured by her lover get it up for you, does it? Keep those under your pillow? Take them out to salivate over when you need some relief? Ha! My bet is you've been spying on Mme la Duchesse well before I—"

"For God's sake, Kinross! You're talking about my mother."

It was Roxton. He was hard gripping his chair, face the color of puce. He looked about angrily at Shrewsbury's secretary, Mr. William Watkins, who instantly dropped his gaze to the quill in his hand. "*My mother*, Kinross," he said in a fierce, whispered aside. "Not a common harlot. A duchess. I thought you—God! I don't know what to think now!"

Kinross patted the younger man's velvet sleeve affectionately, and leaned in to speak to him quietly. "My apologies. He got under my skin. Made me as mad as hell. He has no right, no right at all, to spy on her. I didn't mean to upset you. Julian…" He waited for Roxton's green eyes to meet his gaze. "I love and adore Antonia, most sincerely and devotedly. There isn't anything I wouldn't do to make her happy. I mean to marry her, and without delay. Your blessing, or not." He gave a lopsided grin. "I would prefer to have your blessing."

"Good. Roxton can present you with the Special License he recently procured from Cornwallis, once you've taken your leave of me. Perhaps he has it now, in his frock coat pocket…?"

"How did—?"

Shrewsbury smiled thinly, unconcerned and pleased with himself for managing to rile both noblemen within minutes of their discourse. Matters were progressing more quickly than even he anticipated. Both dukes stared at one another and then at Shrewsbury.

"Don't expect him to tell you!" Kinross said with a dismissive wave of his hand. He grinned sheepishly. "But I'll gladly accept the license, if indeed you have one."

"Of course I have one! Damn you!" Roxton blustered. "I cannot say I'm overjoyed to gain a father who is a mere eight years my senior. That you sincerely love my mother, and come with a dukedom, sweetens that bitter pill. Besides, it's what she wants. You make her happy. And that's all I've ever wanted for her—to be happy. So for God's sake, marry her without delay. This afternoon wouldn't be soon enough!"

Kinross shook his head with apology. "Not today. Promised to accompany her to the theater. Opening night of Sheridan's new play. She's been lookin' forward to it for weeks. Can't disappoint her."

"Tomorrow morning then. No later." When Kinross nodded, Roxton audibly sighed his relief. He took from a deep frock coat pocket a packet with the Archbishop of Canterbury's seal upon it and handed it over. "The rest of the details I leave to you... You, sir," he said, addressing Shrewsbury, "I shall have your apology for casting aspersions on the character of the Dowager Duchess of Roxton, and I will have it now or I leave your house, and never will I or my friends speak to you again."

Shrewsbury was not the least intimidated, and he leaned forward in his chair and crossed his arms on the blotter on his desk.

"What is it with you, Roxton, that you have this inherent belief that your dukedom puts you and your family above the law and its statutes?"

"My father certainly believed so," Roxton quipped, then added seriously, "You know me for a stickler in doing what is right. That a member of my family could well be a traitor to his king saddens and appalls me." He glanced at Kinross. "I confess I only became aware of Cousin Charles's treasonous activities recently. That family members felt obliged to assist him evade capture is not something I applaud. But I believe such actions were taken with the best of intentions, even if they were *misguided*."

"Best of intentions? Misguided? Balderdash!" Shrewsbury stated dismissively. "For their *assistance*, your mother and Kinross may as well be in league with the French!"

"Charles Fitzstuart eloped with my daughter to France, and I gave my consent, so it's not a crime," the Duke of Kinross stated. "That's all anyone outside these four walls needs to know. And there's an end to the matter!"

Shrewsbury stared at Kinross with half-closed lids.

"Do not insult my intelligence, or the intelligence of Roxton and my secretary. You and the Dowager Duchess were instrumental in Charles Fitzstuart evading capture and fleeing to France. Punishing Fitzstuart has now become academic. But just because that bird has flown does not mean others cannot be punished and made an example in his stead. Those contemplating treason must be shown that even if they manage to avoid capture, it does not mean they are free, particularly when they leave behind friends and family. There are a myriad of possibilities of inflicting punishment without putting a finger on the traitor."

Shrewsbury's mouth twitched with self-satisfaction. He put up his arm and beckoned someone out from the shadows of the long room.

"Your family will be held accountable, and I will make certain Charles Fitzstuart is punished. In fact, I mean to kill three crows with the one stone. And I have just the instrument to do that."

"Instrument?" Roxton asked, exchanging a look with Kinross.

When that nobleman shrugged and pulled a face of incomprehension, Roxton looked behind him. Kinross did likewise. Both Dukes were taken aback when out of the shadows Major Lord Fitzstuart appeared. But their surprise was not that he had been there the whole time and overheard the entire conversation, but at the state of his appearance.

Kinross could not help exclaiming, "Good God! What happened to you?"

DAIR SMILED, BUT EVEN THIS SMALL ACTION MADE HIM GRIMACE. He instinctively touched the corner of his mouth where his lip was split and where an ugly blue-black bruise was getting uglier by the hour. Above his left eye his brow was also black and swollen, and there were abrasions and bruises to his knuckles. Every part of him felt raw. But for all that, he could still stand upright. A good hot soak in his bath had gone a long way to easing his aches. A shave, a clean white shirt and stock, and a suit of coal black linen with silver lacings and matching buttons, and he had regained the appearance of a gentleman, even if the state of his face and hands made him look the street ruffian.

"Come and take a seat, Major," Shrewsbury said with genuine warmth. "Do the honors with the teapot, Watkins."

When the secretary half rose out of his chair, pulling a face in the process, Dair waved a hand at him to resume his seat.

"I'd prefer an ale, but tea will do. Don't put yourself to the bother, Watkins. I'll fend for myself. You might need to consult your notes on the off chance I don't get my facts straight. Was I pummeled by ten, or was it twelve, soldiers?"

"I—I can't—I don't—" William Watkins blustered and pretended to look through his notes by shuffling paper.

He wondered how the Major knew, not only that he had written up an extensive report of the drama played out at Romney's painting studio the night before, but that he had been there to witness the entire inexcusable episode. The man was an animal. He couldn't wait for Lord Shrewsbury to read his report, and for that, he waited with gleeful expectation of this arrogant luggard getting his comeuppance.

"It was ten," Dair stated, dropping a sugar lump into his tea cup and stirring. He sipped gingerly at the black brew. "Not the best odds, but I came out of the lacing better than some of those leather-heads."

It was the Duke of Roxton's turn to furrow his brow.

"*Ten* soldiers set upon you?"

Dair sprawled out in a chair beside William Watkins, making that gentleman feel instantly so inadequate beside such a colossus of brawn that he instinctively shrank away from him. If he noticed the secretary cowering beside him, Dair ignored him and stretched out his long legs, one polished black jockey boot heel upon an upholstered foot stool.

"I'm surprised I wasn't poked with a cheese toaster into the bargain," he replied nonchalantly. "Still. Can't complain. Bruises heal quicker than a sword slice."

"Why would you be stuck with a sword?" Kinross asked.

Dair lifted his black brows with mock surprise; and even this made him twinge. He had no idea eyebrows had so much feeling in them. Still, he managed to appear unconcerned and unhurt.

"Isn't that what happens to traitors?" He looked to Shrewsbury. "Or do the traitorous sons of noblemen get the block and axe?"

Shrewsbury inclined his head and said, "I cannot prosecute your brother for his treason, but I can throw *you* in the Tower—"

"*What?* Commit *Dair* to the Tower? For-for *treason*? Are you mad?" the Duke of Roxton demanded. "Don't be absurd! No one will believe that for an instant! Why would a war hero, who spent nine years in the army, three of those years fighting the rebels, suddenly decide to betray everything he holds dear? Not possible! Not plausible!"

"So you think? Yesterday no one would have conceived that a mild-mannered idealist, who spent his days with his head in a book, capable of treason, but Charles Fitzstuart has committed just that by passing on state secrets." Shrewsbury glanced at Dair, who continued to sip at his tea, unconcerned, and addressed Roxton and Kinross. "You are both going to help make the muck stick. It's the least you can do for the part you played in allowing Charles Fitzstuart to escape. As for why the Major failed his countrymen? Take your pick: Conscience, war-weariness—debt?"

Roxton brushed this off. "Nonsense! Never. None of those will wash."

"No matter. One will have to do," Shrewsbury replied, saying with a lift of his brows at Roxton's continued frown, "Please don't concern yourself unnecessarily, your Grace. I don't intend for the revelation to reach the newssheets—nothing so sordid. It only needs to reach the ears of society that the Major has been committed to the Tower under suspicion of committing treason. If you both refuse to confirm or deny the allegation, then society will believe it true. No doubt you'll hear whispers at your back, but no one will be brave enough to voice the accusation to your face. But I'm afraid such a revelation will cause heads to turn in your direction and for all the wrong reasons." Lord Shrewsbury shook his head in disapproval and addressed the Duke of Kinross. "What a shame it is the war hero and not his brother who must be branded a traitor. I hope you can sleep at night knowing you assisted—"

"You're an utter whoreson, Shrewsbury."

The Spymaster spread wide his hands and smiled in response to the Duke of Kinross's name-calling disgust.

"For the greater good, I assure you, your Grace. And I am doing you the courtesy of informing you before news the Major has been arrested and thrown in the Tower reaches Westminster breakfast rooms."

"And you...? What do you think of this?" Roxton asked Dair.

"He don't seem too concerned about it, that's for certain," Kinross muttered.

Dair gingerly sat up and took his boot heel off the footstool. Every square inch of him throbbed with pain. It made him irritable and insolent.

"It doesn't matter what I think. All that does is making reparation for my brother's unconscionable actions. If that means shackling me in the Tower, then so be it."

"You are not required by law to take your brother's place," Roxton stated. "He would not want you to. If he thought you—"

"That's just it. He didn't *think*, did he?" Dair threw up a hand. "And I'm considered the dullard of the family!"

"No one said you—"

"I don't want your pity or your help, Roxton. Traitors get what's coming to them!"

"But Charles is your *brother*."

"And did my brother once think of me, his brother, when he was acting as go-between for the French and the Colonial rebels, while I was fighting for king and country? Did he ever stop to think that the numbers on the scraps of paper he passed to the French were in actuality flesh and blood? Each number a man with a family, a man fighting thousands of miles from his home, in foreign fields, being cut down where he stood, a limb hacked off here, a leg blown off there? That man left his wife a widow and his children orphans, all to fend for themselves. Did he give me or any of those men a thought? His treachery added to our dead and wounded; possibly lost us a battle or two. He deserves the same consideration he gave me; none. But as he is a coward and did not stand his ground, then it is left to me to stand mine, and take what is his due. And I am no coward."

"That answers that," Kinross murmured into the deafening silence, color to his cheeks. He squared his shoulders and took out his silver cheroot case for something to do. When he saw Dair glance at it, he offered him a cheroot, then handed over his smoldering cheroot so the Major could light his, saying conversationally, his cheroot back between his teeth, "If you like the blend, I'll send you a box. I'm supposed to be giving the bloody things away." He grinned guiltily, a glance at Roxton. "She says it's not a good example to the boys…"

Dair lifted an eyebrow at this, not entirely sure who Kinross was referring to, but sensed it had everything to do with the Dowager Duchess of Roxton. Smoking the cheroot put him in a more convivial mood, and he nodded to Kinross, saying,

"Thank you. A box would be welcome…" He glanced at his cousin, and in an about-face said, "Charles is a traitor and a coward, but you are right. For all that, he is still my brother. I don't wish him dead, for my mother's sake as much as mine own. I hope he and Miss Strang have a long and happy life together. Sorry, sir, but it's the truth," he apologized to Shrewsbury. "In the Colonies I saw brother fighting brother, and that should never be. It's just not right. Besides, if the earldom is to go beyond my generation, it will be Charles who will produce the earl to follow me. It wouldn't do to the memory of our grandfather, the General Earl, for the line to die out with me, now would it?"

"Balderdash!" Roxton stated. "You'll marry and have a son—I mean a—"

"—legitimate son?" Dair smiled crookedly. "I don't think that likely, do you? The odds of Charles and his wife having a legitimate heir to the Strathsay earldom are better than my making it through the next winter, given my chosen employment. So I want him kept alive," he said to Shrewsbury. "I'll do whatever it takes. I'll rot in the Tower on whatever charge you care to invent, but Charles and his family are to be left alone. Your word on it, sir."

Shrewsbury held the younger man's gaze, as if mulling over the consequences of agreeing to such a promise and allowing Charles Fitzstuart his liberty. He had thought of quietly sending in an assassin to have the man disposed of; it would have given him a certain sort of satisfaction for the French and American rebels to know he could deal out his particular form of justice from the comfort of his book room in London. Yet, he was a traditionalist. As well as not wanting to cause the Countess of Strathsay undue distress at losing one of her only two sons, he did not want to be the one to cause the extinction of the earldom of Strathsay, particularly as the line was begun by Charles the Second's coupling with Lady Jane Hervey, the younger daughter of a duke, who just happened to be his ancestor on his mother's side. The English aristocracy were such an incestuous lot.

His gaze flickered over the bruising to the Major's handsome face and to his long fingers that held the cheroot, the grazing to his knuckles still raw, and he had to agree with him. The man had a reckless disregard for his own safety. It had always been thus, since he was a boy. He was not the least surprised dispatches and letters from the colonial war front praised the Major's heroism. Foolhardiness was mentioned more than once. That he had survived into his twenty-ninth year was close to a miracle. So it was not the following winter that he worried the young man would survive, it was the next couple of weeks in Portugal. England and Portugal might be allies, but with a new Queen just three months on the throne, there was unrest around every corner. Lisbon was crawling with cutthroats and spies, both Spanish and French, and he prayed that Alisdair Fitzstuart would return to England alive, and not in a lead casket. Finally, to the relief of everyone in the room, he nodded.

"Yes. All right. You have my word, and those in this room as witnesses to it."

"Thank you, sir," Dair said solemnly, then grinned, which hurt his lip. "So it's through Traitor's gate and a spell in the Tower for me, is it?"

"Don't be idiotic, Fitzstuart!" Shrewsbury said dismissively. "A fearless, trained killer like you, willing to risk life and limb for king and country, clapped up in prison? A complete waste of talent and energy. No. I have use of your particular—*skills*—on the Continent."

He looked past Dair to Roxton, and then at Kinross and said, "As for anyone believing you could be a traitor… Those who entertain the idea must have a pebble for a brain. But there are just enough pebbles out there of our acquaintance to form a seashore, more's the pity! Still. The conjecture will serve its purpose and bide us time; time enough for you to set sail, and hopefully reach your destination and your contact before the calls are loud enough to demand your release. Now, if your Graces will excuse us, I need to speak to Fitzstuart alone."

"And why did I turn traitor?" Dair asked. "Conscience? War-weariness? Or debt?"

"Debt. Roxton. Kinross. Tell the Dowager Duchess her cousin got into a lot of debt, and stands accused of passing on sensitive documents to his brother to sell to the French on his behalf. As far as she and the rest of society are concerned, Fitzstuart is spending a sojourn in the Tower, while the matter is further investigated."

"She won't believe it," Kinross said flatly, standing and stretching his legs, the rest of the gentlemen in the room doing likewise.

Dair agreed. "She won't. She knows me better than my own mother."

"Well, Kinross is going to make her believe it!" Shrewsbury grunted. "If Antonia Roxton believes it, then others will, too. And it is vital to our war efforts in the Colonies that our friends and relations believe Fitzstuart is locked up in the Tower. So I don't care how you do it, Kinross, but make the Duchess believe it."

The Duke of Roxton tugged at the lace ruffles at his wrists. "If anyone can convince her, it's you, Kinross." He regarded the Major a moment and said, sticking out his hand for him to take, "I don't know what Shrewsbury has in store for you, but I have the greatest dread it is something as life-threatening as charging into battle. Good luck."

"All so we can sleep safely in our beds, aye, Dair," Kinross said, gripping the Major's forearm.

Dair pulled him closer, so only he could hear. "I need to see Cousin Duchess before I head off on my Continental jaunt. Tomorrow morning."

Kinross nodded. "I'll let her know you're coming. Time?"

"Before noon."

Kinross put up his brows at the early hour but nodded his agreement. And without another word, he followed Shrewsbury and Roxton out of the book room to the anteroom, where farewells were made.

"I presume I will see you both at the theater tonight?" Shrewsbury asked cordially, as if the conversation in his book room had never taken place.

"It will be *me* for the Tower if we miss Sheridan's new play!" Kinross exclaimed. "Come to our box. Antonia will be expecting you."

Shrewsbury was not the least surprised by the invitation, or the fact that in sharing a box at the theater, Kinross and the Dowager Duchess of Roxton were making a public declaration of their relationship. Still, he could not help glancing over at the Duke of Roxton to gauge his reaction to this interesting piece of news. Roxton merely rolled his eyes in response but remained tight-lipped, which had Shrewsbury suppressing a grin that the principled Duke had silently capitulated to his mother's *force majeure*.

"I would be delighted," Shrewsbury replied, "and so will my granddaughter. Rory has been looking forward to this new play almost as much as Her Grace. In point of fact, I believe it was the Duchess who wrote and told her…"

And so in discussing the upcoming evening at the theater, Lord Shrewsbury farewelled the two noblemen in a much better mood than he had received them. When he returned to his book room, Dair and William Watkins were still on their feet.

"For God's sake, my boy, sit down! Sit down! Standing about with you and your relatives, makes me feel as if I'm at the bottom of a bloody well! You, too, Mr. Watkins. Now, before we discuss what it is I want you to achieve in Lisbon, there is something I need you to do… For me—" He looked at his secretary, "—and Mr. Watkins."

Dair settled his shoulders into the upholstery of the wingchair directly opposite Shrewsbury's desk, smoldering cheroot between his fingers, and crossed his booted ankles. Not a glance at William Watkins, he met the old man's bespectacled blue eyes.

"Whatever it is, if it's for you, sir, consider it done."

"Good. I want you to forget the incident at George Romney's studio ever happened."

SEVEN

"PARDON, SIR? INCIDENT?" ASKED DAIR.

"Yes. Very good," replied Shrewsbury. "That's precisely how you will react and respond if anyone asks you."

Dair glanced suspiciously at William Watkins. "At Romney's studio?"

The old man nodded.

"It was just a piece of tomfoolery with some pretty dancers, and a bit of a beat-up with the militia." Dair shrugged a shoulder and drew back on the cheroot. "Nothing to write home about, sir, and tame into the bargain."

"*Tomfoolery*? A bit of a—of a—*beat-up* with the-the militia? *Tame*?" William Watkins' voice was reed thin. "The damage alone to Mr. Romney's studio, I calculate to be in the hundreds of guineas! As for the great distress to—"

"Thank you, Mr. Watkins," Shrewsbury interrupted. "I understand your concerns, and I have your report—all twenty-five pages of it."

Dair pulled a face. "Only twenty-five pages. No embellishment then?"

"When his lordship has had time to digest my report, he will see that your preposterous posturing—"

"Say that five times, Watkins. I'll wager you can't."

"—has caused immeasurable damage to the—"

"Yes. Yes. Hundreds of guineas damage," Dair stated flatly, with an exaggerated sigh. "Send me the account. Romney should be thanking me. The write-up in the newssheets alone will increase his trade in portraits tenfold. Not to mention those just calling on him for a gawp at where the action took place; he might persuade them to buy something in oils, too."

"There will be no write-up in the newssheets," Shrewsbury said smoothly. "The reporter's notes were—confiscated."

"Burned, my lord," Watkins primly assured him. "I saw to it personally. And the editor was informed spirits were detected on the reporter's breath, so his verbal account cannot be relied upon either."

"Well, aren't you a treasure," Dair drawled sarcastically. "What did you do for an encore? Offer the girls the contents of your breeches to keep them quiet too?"

While Watkins was genuinely shocked, Shrewsbury chuckled.

"A secretary's loyalty only stretches so far—"

"—and his gadso not far enough."

Mr. Watkins had no idea what a gadso was, but when the old man laughed with genuine good humor he was convinced he was being slandered; with Shrewsbury's next comment he knew it was so, and his face flushed purple with embarrassment.

"That's not fair on Watkins, is it? Few men are blessed with good looks and equipage worthy of a prizewinning bull. So the rest of us don't experience a stab of inadequacy, let's keep the conversation above our breeches buttons, shall we? If you must know," the old man continued more seriously, "your cadre of female admirers have been threatened with Newgate if they so much as squeak a word about last night. And Signora Baccelli will keep her pretty mouth shut, if she wishes Dorset's continued devotion. Romney will be compensated, several lucrative commissions sent his way to sweeten his silence; his wastrel brother's debts paid into the bargain. Mr. Cedric Pleasant has given his word never to speak of the incident, as has my grandson. There only remains for you to give me your word of honor to do the same. In fact, I want you to do more. I want you to claim to have been so drunk that you have no recollection of the evening whatsoever."

Dair was annoyed by Shrewsbury's high-handedness for what he considered nothing more than three friends having an evening of fun and games. That it ended in a riot was not strictly his fault. That was the fault of the militia, and the Spymaster's orchestrated means of having him arrested. He had willingly fallen in with Shrewsbury's plans, was prepared to be thrown in the Tower, if necessary, or sent off on some God-forsaken mission abroad, all for the cause of furthering British war efforts against the colonial rebels.

But what he was not prepared to do was be reprimanded for a harmless prank that had seen his friend Grasby the happiest he had

DAIR DEVIL

57

been in years, and all because Weasel Watkins and his stiff-necked sister had taken offence. For Weasel to go squealing to Shrewsbury about an incident which was none of his business stuck in his throat as cowardly; a twenty-five page report indeed!

Anger with Weasel Watkins' interference in his affairs did not stop him feeling the sort of discomfort he had experienced on the numerous occasions he was brought before the headmaster at Harrow to be thrashed for some minor infraction. One glance at the secretary, and he knew that was precisely how he wanted him to feel.

He was sorely tempted to put a fist into Watkins' self-righteous smile. Instead, he lifted his heavy chin and said belligerently,

"That could be difficult. I mightn't be too bright, but I do have an exceptional memory... And I haven't yet been drunk enough not to remember the night before. Now Grasby, he was drunk, and shouldn't be held accountable, because I was the one who got him drunk. I'll take the blame for his actions, readily. But I'll not cower in a corner all because your lily-livered secretary and his nose-in-the-air sister took offence about something they should not have witnessed in the first place!"

Shrewsbury removed his eyeglasses, closed his eyes and pressed the bridge of his nose between thumb and forefinger. When he sighed, as if even *he* had been pushed beyond the limits of his patience, William Watkins was convinced the old man was about to give the Major a dressing down, and about time too! So he was astounded then when the Earl said,

"As you can both appreciate, the past twelve hours have been exhausting, twelve hours I could have better spent—but it is done... Watkins... Be so good as to take yourself off."

"Off? But... My lord! I understand that as your secretary I should do as you request... But as Lady Grasby's *brother*, it is my duty to be present as her representative if you intend to discuss the inexcusable infractions that occurred at Mr. Romney's house."

Shrewsbury opened his eyes and focused on his secretary, who stubbornly remained seated behind his desk, and behind a cloud of smoke. He did not have to wonder where that had drifted in from, with the Major deliberately exhaling smoke from his cheroot over his right shoulder in Watkins' direction. The lad was irredeemably mischievous, and Shrewsbury had to force himself not to smile.

"You may have such feelings, Mr. Watkins, but they are irrelevant. The day your sister married my grandson she became a Talbot and part of my family, and thus no longer your responsibility, whatever your strong brotherly feelings. But I have no objection to you seeking out

Lady Grasby at this hour of the day. She may well be up and in need of
your brotherly shoulder to cry on. No doubt there are plenty more tears
to come," he murmured to himself as Watkins quietly closed the door
to the book room.

"Aside from almost ruining my grandson's marriage," Shrewsbury
said, as he leant back in his chair and crossed his hands over his round
belly in its silken waistcoat, "and that it could take an immaculate
conception for my granddaughter-in-law to conceive, as she won't have
her husband within twenty feet of her person, what happened last night
I couldn't care less about, but for one important fact. It is this fact that
compels me to seek your word of honor as a gentleman that you will,
from this day forward, not reveal to anyone, in word or gesture, that
you remember a single detail of what occurred within the walls of
George Romney's studio."

Dair sat up, all attention.

"Sir, if it means that much to you, then yes, I readily give you my
word as an officer and a gentleman. If you wish me to say I was drunk
beyond cognition, then so be it. But may I know why? Why the secrecy
and the need for me to forget? If Lady Grasby wishes to blame someone, then that someone should be me—"

"Oh, she blames you, all right! And I do not blame *her* for that! You
made a mockery of her husband, and in turn her marriage, and before
witnesses. She is a prideful, vain creature and may never recover from
the humiliation. She certainly will never forgive you. That does not
bother me in the slightest. That you have forgotten the details of the
entire evening will go a long way in appeasing her self-esteem. She may
yet be able to look you in the eye with her head held high upon your
return from Lisbon. An absence of some four or five weeks should also
soothe Grasby's anger with you."

"For getting him drunk? I admit I cut his breechcloth a tad too
short—"

Shrewsbury waved a dismissive hand.

"I wish I'd been there to see your play-acting for myself. I have no
doubts Grasby enjoyed himself immensely, until he realized his wife
and her brother had become part of the audience. A most unfortunate
happenstance. But that's not what angered Grasby, or why I extracted
your promise. Lady Grasby and Mr. Watkins were accompanied to the
studio by my granddaughter, Grasby's younger sister. As to what she
saw, and how much, I have yet to find out…"

Dair's expression of polite interest to this piece of news told
Shrewsbury everything he needed to know. Somewhere in the deep
recesses of the Major's mind there was possibly a dim awareness that his

best friend had a sister. Given time, he might even be able to recall in his mind's eye a picture of her as a child, when he had occasionally come to stay between school terms. That he had no idea as to her age, and would not be able to point her out if ten young ladies of good family were lined up for his inspection, did not surprise Shrewsbury. In the Major's world, Aurora Christina Talbot did not exist. And why should she?

They would have been introduced at some stage when Rory left the schoolroom. They came from the same wider social circle, and their more intimate circle of friends and relations would have intersected from time to time when attending polite society engagements. This social interaction would have increased over the past six months since the Major resigned his commission from the army.

The most recent of these was the Roxton Easter weekend at the Duke's Hampshire estate. He was so grateful to Deborah Roxton for including Rory in the small parties made up of people her own age when they played at charades, picnicked by the lake, attended evening music recitals, and danced at the gala ball. The dance floor was where most social interaction between eligible young men and women occurred; a chance to look each other over without a chaperone breathing down the back of a girl's neck.

Rory could not dance. But Deborah Roxton sat Rory close by her, so she had an excellent vantage point to watch the dancing, and by association, guests saw that his granddaughter was a favored guest. And to those doyens of Polite Society who put great value on such things, those who wondered at Rory's place within it were politely reminded that as well as being the granddaughter of the Earl of Shrewsbury, Miss Talbot was the goddaughter of the old Duke of Roxton and his widowed duchess, Antonia Roxton.

There were occasions when unsuspecting guests wondered aloud why such a pretty little thing was not married, and needed no answer when Rory rose to her feet with the aid of her stick. The look of abject embarrassment, often pity, that crossed these same puzzled powdered faces when his granddaughter limped off—she transformed in their eyes into a wholly different and undesirable being because of her uneven gait —made him want to pummel to dust each and every one of them.

But what broke his heart, what never failed to bring tears to his eyes, was the never-ending sparkle in her blue eyes, blue eyes just like his, of wonder and excitement for the world around her. This was never more evident than when she watched the country dancing, cheeks flushed with the joy of living. It was as if she were out there upon the dance floor, taking every step with the dancing couples. He would have given anything and everything to be able to make that happen for her…

"Sir…? My lord? Lord Shrewsbury?"

It was Dair, on his feet, at Shrewsbury's desk. The old man looked to have taken ill suddenly, such was the paleness to his cheeks and the glassiness to his eyes. But just as quickly, he snapped to his old self and waved Dair away. The Major retreated to his armchair, carefully stubbing the cheroot on a small silver tray at his elbow, giving the old man time to completely recover his equilibrium.

"I want my granddaughter to forget last night ever happened," Shrewsbury snapped without preamble. His inability to offer Rory a cure for her physical infirmity made him feel frustratingly inadequate. "I pray that in time it will become nothing more than a distant nightmare. And it must have been a nightmare—a bloody nightmare—for a carefully nurtured female who has never stepped outside this house without a chaperone, and has never been left alone in the company of a man who is not her brother or her grandfather, *ever*. She is unmarried and likely to stay that way after witnessing your disgusting and unsavory behavior!"

"I beg your pardon, sir?" Dair asked with civility, racking his brain to make sense of the old man's emotionally charged rant, when not ten minutes earlier he had been having a chuckle about the whole episode. Nor did he know of any female present at Romney's studio, other than the uninvited Lady Grasby, who fit the description of carefully nurtured, and she was married to his best friend. "Aside from Lady Grasby, who was an unintended witness to our—um—shenanigans, there was no other female that—"

"Goddammit Fitzstuart! My granddaughter was witness to the whole sordid episode! And from what Lady Grasby has been weeping into her pillow, it sounds as if she and my granddaughter were subjected to a scene ripped straight from the pages of a bacchanalian orgy!"

He shoved at the papers in front of him, as if wanting to distance himself from the event and the Major, and did his best to bring his temper and his tone under control.

"Getting your tackle out for the admiration of sylph-like whores and their ilk, I couldn't care less about. How many you rut and how often is your business, and I say good luck to you! You play a dangerous game for your country, and the stakes are impossibly high, so you deserve to play equally as hard. But… There are times—*this time*—when such behavior goes beyond the pale. My granddaughter, Grasby's little sister, is an innocent. She was there, damn you!"

"I understand, sir. You don't have to tell me twice," Dair said in a rush, feeling uncomfortably warm under his stock. He sat forward in the armchair. "You can't think I would have carried on the way I did, would have allowed Grasby to compromise himself, if I'd had an inkling that she—that the sister of my best friend—would be a witness? My word on it, sir!"

Shrewsbury nodded, calmer, hearing the sincerity in the man's voice. "I suppose not... You were not to know... It's just that her presence, it alters the entire episode, doesn't it?" He cocked an eyebrow. "I wonder if you would have acted any differently knowing Lady Grasby and Mr. Watkins were part of your audience?"

Dair could not hide his grin.

"I did know, sir."

This elicited a reluctant laugh from the old man.

"Almost makes me wish I'd been a flea in Watkins' wig, just to see her ladyship's face. Now *that* is between you and me and no other." He pushed back his chair and Dair got to his feet. "So when next you see my granddaughter, you will act as if last night never occurred; feign complete ignorance. She will be comfortable then—we all will." He came around the desk. "And that goes for Grasby and anyone else who mentions Romney's studio, or asks a question. You were too drunk and have no recollection of events. You're a good actor. If anyone can convince my grandchildren, you can."

"And Watkins? What about him?"

"Mr. Watkins will do as he is told. And he knows what's at stake. He wants his sister to give the earldom of Shrewsbury an heir as much as I do. It will cement his place in the family. Better to be thought of as uncle to an earl than remembered as the grandson of a Billingsgate fishmonger." When Dair snorted his skepticism, Shrewsbury smiled. "All very well for you not to care, you've got royal Stuart blood in your veins, not estuary water like the Watkins. Now put on a good show and you'll be believed. My granddaughter, for all her youth and inexperience, has a keen mind and an even keener eye; comes from all that sitting about observing people. She'll see through the façade if you don't make yourself believe it, too." He put out his hand to Dair. "I'm relying on you, my boy."

"You can, sir," Dair replied, taking the old man's hand in a firm grip. He was still trying to put a face and a name together for Grasby's sister and coming up blank. Ultimately, that was unimportant. He had given his word, and to Shrewsbury, the last man in this world he would ever want to disappoint. "I won't let you down. My word on it."

Shrewsbury smiled, mind at ease. "I know you won't. You haven't yet. Thank you. Now let me have a pitcher of ale fetched, and we'll drink it on the terrace and take a walk in the garden. Fresh air helps clear the mind, and to focus it. There's still much I need to tell you before you set sail for Lisbon—"

"Grand! Grand? The most wonderful thing has happened! Crawford was the first to make the discovery! It's just like the one in the book. Oh, you must come to the Pinery and see it for yourself! Oh! Do-do forgive me. I thought you were alone. Crawford said your guests had gone…"

"Rory. Come in! Come in, my dear!" Shrewsbury coaxed as his granddaughter took a step backward, to retreat from the room. "I know you've been introduced before today, but I shall do the honors again, because introductions at a function, where there is always a crush of persons filling up a drawing room, is no introduction at all, really, is it? This is Major Lord Fitzstuart, your godmother's cousin; Grasby's friend Dair from his Harrow days. Major, this is my granddaughter, Aurora Talbot."

The only sound in the room was the thud of Rory's book hitting the floor.

EIGHT

Speechless, Rory watched Dair slowly retrieve her book. Her eyes did not leave him for a moment. He went to his haunches to collect *A General Treatise of Husbandry and Gardening* by Richard Bradley, then straightened to his full height, leaving her eyes level with the engraved silver buttons on his black linen frock coat. For some inexplicable reason, fully clothed he looked taller and much wider. He completely blocked her view of her grandfather's desk.

He made her a slight bow of acquaintance, murmured a platitude that the pleasure was all his, and held out the book; and all this without making eye contact. She was so happy to see him again that the coldness in his manner and tone did not immediately register. She was also too preoccupied with wondering if he would notice she was not wearing panniers with her petticoats, something she avoided when at home, and if there was dirt smudged on her cheek. She had remembered to remove her gardening gloves, so her hands were clean, but her flimsy white apron over her white muslin gown (not the most practical of colors to go trowelling in amongst the compost) was also smudged with dirt. She had not meant to go to the Pinery after nuncheon, because she had to ready herself for the excursion to the theater. But the gardener had sent word of the most marvelous news, of an emerging pineapple flower, and so she just had to see it for herself there and then.

When her grandfather gently reminded her to take her book, that the Major was still holding it, she was suddenly shy at forgetting her manners. She realized, too, that she was rudely staring fixedly at the front of his broad chest and had not looked up at his face. Yet, when she went to take her book she noticed the state of his thumb. The skin was ragged and bloody at the knuckle. Her concern for his well-being far outweighed her embarrassment and uncertainty. Without permission, she gently turned over his right hand and saw that the rest of his knuckles were similarly raw, and there was bruising, too. She was sure his fingers were swollen. What she failed to notice was that the moment she touched his bruised flesh, he reacted, his grip on Bradley's treatise tightening, so much so that she could not have pried the book out from between his fingers had she used both hands and all her force to do so.

"You took a dreadful beating... I'm afraid I wasn't brave at all. I fainted with your first blow..."

With her fingers still resting on the back of his hand, she lifted her gaze from his injuries to his chin and then to his mouth. Here she paused, blue eyes widening with concern at the split to his lip. She then looked up into his eyes. The bruising to his face caused an involuntary intake of breath.

"I hope—I hope you took something to ease the pain. You really ought to apply a raw steak to that eye, to bring out the bruising, and so your lip doesn't scar there is a remedy—"

"Thank you, my dear," Lord Shrewsbury interrupted gently and removed the book from between Dair's fingers. "I'm sure the Major has done all he can for the time being."

"Of course. Of course," Rory murmured with a nod, again embarrassed to have forgotten her manners, and for speaking so frankly.

Coming to a sense of her surroundings, she discovered the Major no longer had her book and that she was holding his hand. She instantly let go of his fingers and whipped her fist to the middle of her back to clutch at the bow that tied on her gossamer apron. Her right hand tightened about the carved ivory handle of her walking stick because she had the sensation of swaying, as if aboard a ship in rough seas.

"Please excuse me, Miss Talbot," Dair said dully. "I know the way to the terrace, sir. I'll see you there at your convenience."

He gave a small nod, stepped past Rory, and left the room.

She watched him go, a strange lump forming in her throat; all at sea. She had no idea what had just happened but it left her desolate. Why did he not know her? Neither of them needed to speak of the particulars of the previous evening, but there was no need for him to pretend nothing at all had occurred between them. He had given her an address in Chelsea. They had kissed! She had seen him, and he had embraced her, for all intents and purposes, naked. Perhaps he was embarrassed? Perhaps it was the presence of her grandfather that made him stilted and cold? But he could have winked down at her, to let her know he was well aware of her existence. She would never have betrayed him.

And then she had a sudden awful thought that could account for his behavior. It was not coldness, it was embarrassment, and an awkward embarrassment she had encountered many times before but which she ignored because she could not alter herself.

Last night he had not seen her walking stick. He had not seen her walk. Now he had. And now he knew her for a cripple. She could not blame him for being surprised by such a discovery. But did he now disdain her because she had such an imperfection? His features had not changed. He had not shown a disgust of her, or worn an expression of pity. In fact, he could have been a brick wall, such was his lack of emotion. Something, call it intuition, but something deep within her told her his coldness in manner, more correctly lack of any reaction whatsoever, was not because he was being judgmental. Whatever his foibles, she did not think intolerance one of them. Then why was he like stone?

Her grandfather gave her the answer, and his explanation left her more forlorn than she thought possible. Had the Major looked upon her with disgust, that was at least a show of some emotion, and she could then have dismissed him as unworthy of her.

With her book pressed to his chest, Lord Shrewsbury put an arm about Rory's shoulders and kissed her temple.

"There. That was not so difficult, now was it, my darling? Did I not tell you and Drusilla the Major was so drunk last night he was unlikely to remember a single detail of what happened? And I was right. He doesn't. No recollection of events past the point of trespassing into Romney's studio. It seems he and your brother and Mr. Pleasant polished off a goodly number of bottles of claret before the start of their mischief-making. Blind drunk, the three of them. We ought to forgive them their disgrace, don't you think? Particularly the Major. Any man who fights as bravely for his country as he has deserves to play just as hard. The horrors of combat can greatly affect a man. Even a strong-minded man like the Major must have his dark moments. A bit of drunken tomfoolery allows such men to forget those moments, however briefly."

He kissed her again and hugged her to his side, adding with real regret,

"What a piece of rotten luck for the three of them that your small party happened to pay a visit on Romney at the same time. All three are, when not drunk to dissipation, true gentlemen and are abjectly apologetic to have caused you and Drusilla the slightest distress. If it is acceptable to you, I will not have them apologize in person, it will only further distress your sister-in-law. The sooner the entire episode is behind us, the better. Don't you agree, my dear?"

Rory nodded, not entirely convinced that her brother and his friends were so drunk as to have lost all memory of their behavior, particularly Mr. Cedric Pleasant, who was perfectly lucid and clothed the entire time. Her brother was drunk, that was true, but the Major? If she detected spirits on his breath it was not so marked as for her to think him drunk, and she had not tasted alcohol on his tongue... Instantly, heat flooded her face at the remembrance of his deep kiss. If he went about kissing females unknown to him in a way that made them melt against him, what must his kisses be like for females he truly cared about?

"Are you perfectly well, Rory?" Lord Shrewsbury asked, arm still about her shoulders. He had felt her sway and shiver. "You told me at breakfast you did not suffer any nightmares, and you would tell me if there is anything else troubling you...?"

She forced a smile and took back her book. "Yes. Of course, Grand. I slept well indeed."

"Shall I come to the Pinery to see your great surprise?"

"No. No, Grand. The Major—Lord Fitzstuart is waiting for you on the terrace. The surprise can wait. Besides, I must change into my outfit for the theater..."

Shrewsbury flicked her under the chin. "We have been looking forward to this afternoon for some time, have we not? And I have an added surprise for you. Your godmother has invited us to visit her box."

"Oh? How-how lovely. I shall enjoy discussing the play with Mme la Duchesse."

Shrewsbury walked Rory from the book room and through the anteroom to the long gallery, his conversation all about the upcoming visit to Drury Lane to see Sheridan's *School for Scandal*. They stopped before a small closet with a half door, inside which was a bench with a velvet cushion upon it. Running vertically through the closet was a silken rope that threaded through a system of pulleys attached top and bottom. This allowed the closet, which was in fact a lifting chair, to be raised and lowered with ease by its occupant.

Shrewsbury had the lifting chair installed fifteen years ago, patterned on the one in the French king's private apartments at Fontainebleau, allowing Louis' mistress, Mme de Pompadour, to visit him in secret. For Rory, it gave her independence of movement. As a child she had been required to call on a footman to carry her up and down the broad staircase, with its many steps twisting up through the center of the Dutch house. Seated on the velvet cushion, she could pull herself up and down with ease to the first floor where her rooms were located. Shrewsbury could still recall the look of absolute delight on her little face when she took her first ride in the lifting chair, her brother racing up the staircase to try and beat her to the first floor. It was a game they never tired of, even now.

Two footmen stood sentry either side of the lifting chair, and one opened the half door for Rory, but before she could step inside, Shrewsbury put his hand over hers.

"Rory. My dear. I do not want you to recall particulars of last night that might distress you, but Mr. Watkins told me he found you crumpled in a gap at the back of the stage—that you had fainted…"

"Yes. Yes, he did. I did."

"Do you remember how you got there, or why you fainted?"

"I cannot—I cannot recall the precise moment, no…"

"Mr. Watkins has written up a report of the evening—"

"A-a report? Why?"

"Please. Do not alarm yourself. None shall read it but me. And if in the meantime if you do recall any particulars… I hope you will confide in me…"

Rory hesitated, then slowly met her grandfather's blue eyes. She smiled weakly.

"Of course, Grand."

LORD SHREWSBURY NODDED, AND WITH A KISS TO HER FOREHEAD let Rory step into the lifting chair. He watched the chair ascend, Rory waving to him when he just stood there looking up into the void. He smiled and waved back. His granddaughter's hesitation to respond to his questions, the way she avoided his gaze, her smile that was not a genuine smile, were all signs of concealment. He had not been a spy for His Majesty for as long as he had and not know she was hiding something from him. Knowing Rory as he did, she would only withhold the truth to protect another. He suspected that other was her brother, Harvel, Lord Grasby.

He was fond of Grasby, who was his heir, but it was Rory he loved. From him she had inherited the Talbot blue eyes and quiet determination, and from her mother a sweet nature and delicate Nordic features. Shrewsbury had despised the children's mother, his daughter-in-law

Christina, with every fiber of his noble being. She had brought out the worst in him in every conceivable way.

Ironically, for all his experience as a spy, and his ability to see through the subterfuge of a person's public face to their hidden desires and machinations, he had failed to see that Christina wore no mask. She was what she appeared: A beautiful woman with a heart of gold. Shrewsbury knew only one woman who fit such a description, Antonia, Dowager Duchess of Roxton, and he was not prepared to believe two such women could exist in his lifetime. What's more, he was too bitter, too eaten up with shame that his son and heir had married so far beneath him, to entertain the idea of accepting such a female for a daughter-in-law. She was not only a foreigner—a Norwegian!—but the illegitimate daughter of a minor court official and a seamstress.

When his son and new family returned to England he was so eaten up with resentment, he refused to have anything to do with them, until one day his daughter-in-law paid him a visit. It was the first time he had set eyes on her, and he was instantly smitten. She brought with her his little grandson, who was not quite five years old, and father and son were soon reconciled.

He had no clear recollection of how he spiraled into such depths of depravity, and at the time he had blamed her completely. She had bewitched him body and soul. Only hours after his daughter-in-law gave birth to Rory, she was told her baby was not normal and would, in all probability, not live beyond a few months. She blamed herself, for what she had allowed him to do to her, and threw herself off a balcony. The world was told she had died in childbed. Her husband was inconsolable. He would not have suspected the truth in a thousand years or more, but his wife left him a note. He drowned himself, leaving Shrewsbury bereft and with the care of a little boy of six and a newborn.

It was these two orphans who finally set him free from his bitter loneliness. Grasby was not much older than seven when he had made an impromptu visit to the nursery, impelled by an enquiry from Antonia Roxton as to how her goddaughter was progressing. The wonder for Shrewsbury was that the Roxtons had willingly sponsored his granddaughter, particularly when no physician could assure him she would walk, or if indeed she had impaired brain function, as was often predicted with malformed children.

The Duchess's enquiry had shamed him into visiting the nursery he had never entered. He had needed a footman to show him the way. He, England's Spymaster General, was ignorant of the layout of his own house! What confronted him not only piled shame upon shame but shocked him into action.

His seven-year-old grandson was huddled in a dusty corner, being beaten with rushes. With his thin little body he was trying his best to shield his year-old baby sister, who was screaming uncontrollably. But it was not fear which had her screaming, it was the iron shoe clamped about her twisted little foot and secured with iron rods and bolts just below her chubby knee, forcing it into the correct alignment. Her brother had been attempting to remove the iron shoe, and for his compassion got a beating that broke the skin on his back.

That very day, Shrewsbury took control of every aspect of the children's lives. New servants, new tutors, new, bright surroundings. No more beatings, no more iron shoes or clamps, and talk of "curing the cripple" was forbidden. He had agents scour the Continent for a physician able to treat his baby granddaughter's deformity, and found one in Professor Petrus Camper in Amsterdam. An expert in many fields, Camper was also an expert on feet. And while unable to cure Rory's club foot, he gave Shrewsbury, and in turn her little brother, the necessary assurances Rory was normal in every other way. From that day forward, brother and sister grew up inseparable. Grasby was his sister's champion, and Rory her brother's greatest supporter and confidant.

So it was easy for Shrewsbury to believe the siblings would protect each other, even lie for one another; that Rory would keep from him certain particulars of events at Romney's studio all to shield Grasby. He would not press her for information. He would find out in other ways. Watkins' report would be a start. Having those who were present questioned would provide a more complete picture. Writing out his instructions to trusted agents could be postponed until tomorrow morning. The Major was waiting for him. Tonight he meant to set aside the troubles of the kingdom, and more importantly, within his own family, and spend a leisurely evening in the company of his granddaughter. Yet, he could not shake the belief that Rory had not been honest with him— that she felt the need to lie, and that troubled him more than he cared to admit.

NINE

RORY HAD LIED. SHE HAD NEVER LIED TO HER GRANDFATHER AND it made her heavy of heart. She had lied, not to protect her brother, but to protect Major Lord Fitzstuart. If the Major had no recollection of the night before, more precisely his encounter with her, then what was the sense in her recalling the incident, and to her shame? What purpose would it serve for her grandfather to know the truth? It would only cause him great distress. And for the Major to be prompted to remember an episode he clearly couldn't care less about and, had he been sober, would not have engaged with her, was a humiliation she could not endure.

She did not blame the Major for his lack of memory. For him the encounter was just one of many; *she* just a number in a long line of countless females whom he had trifled with over the years. *Trifled with...* What an inane expression! In her case, it was apt. But she was certain the Major had done a great deal more than *trifle with* other females. She had engaged in nothing more than a brief kiss. A brief kiss that was not worth his remembrance. But to her, not only was that kiss a moment to treasure, the entire evening had been so exciting she had committed it to memory. Such an encounter was never likely to happen again. Which just underscored her sheltered existence. She looked down at the book in her hand. In her day-to-day life she was a spinster whose prime interest was the nurturing and cultivation of the pineapple.

Distracted with her thoughts, she handed her walking stick to her maid without seeing her, and climbed up on the window seat with its view of the formal gardens. Bradley's treatise on gardening she dropped on the rug, all the joy of her discovery overridden by her malaise. Her head ached and she felt hot, and yet strangely cold. Perhaps she was coming down with a fever? The studio had been without heat and she without her cloak... But in his arms she had not felt cold at all; quite the opposite...

She found her woolen shawl at her feet and went to put it about her shoulders, when her maid, Edith, did this for her.

"You look worn to threads! Too much time spent in the heat of that Pinery," the older woman castigated her lovingly, fussing with the sit of the shawl. "And after the upset last night, I dare say it's all added to the extra color in your cheeks. Now you sit there nice and quiet and I'll have a cup of tea fetched. You have time for a cup before you change for the theater. But first let me remove your shoes..."

Rory nodded, hugging one of the tapestry cushions to her as she snuggled deeper into the pillows at her back. As she always did, Edith removed the shoe from Rory's right foot first.

Just like the pretty shoes worn by countless young ladies, Rory's were often covered in material that matched her gowns. But unlike most shoes, which had identical lasts, Rory's were made to fit her left and her right foot individually. A master cordwainer, recommended by Professor Camper, had been making her shoes since she was a little girl. He took casts in plaster of Paris and made shoes that conformed to the twisted shape of her right foot; except for mules, she wore the latest fashionable footwear.

The shoes Edith held, as she covered Rory's stockinged feet with her white muslin petticoats, were purple satin slippers with low heels of white leather. Rory stared at the shoes and swallowed back tears. She barely heard Edith tell her to have a little doze while she fetched the tea, and turned her face to the window as the heavy curtains were drawn across the window seat. Snug in her little corner, it was only then that she realized tears were spilling onto her flushed cheeks.

Foolish! Stupid! Ridiculous creature! she castigated herself. *Stop feeling sorry for yourself this instant! Crying for no good reason. If you must shed tears, then do so for not telling Grand the truth. So last night was the most exciting night of your uneventful life? Be thankful it happened at all. You now have a memory to keep, and it is yours alone to cherish...*

"Rory? Rory? Are you there? May I come in?"

Rory dashed both hands over her wet cheeks just as the curtains parted and Grasby stuck his head between the hanging velvet. He looked sheepish, and was in undress, having shrugged a silk banyan over his white shirt and brown velvet breeches; a matching silk turban covered his short cropped blond hair. Rory nodded and gathered up her white muslin petticoats, sitting up against the cushions to give her brother space on the window seat's tapestry cushion. He needed no further invitation and eagerly scrambled to join her, quickly closing the curtains again, as if hiding them away from the rest of the world. For Grasby, he couldn't think of a more comforting place to lick his wounds.

"Remember when we'd hide in Grand's book room?" he said with genuine affection, back up against the wooden paneling. Following his sister's lead, he wrapped his arms about a tapestry cushion and hugged it to his chest. He was already starting to feel better. "We would giggle and whisper to each other to be quiet. Grand never said a word. He pretended he didn't know we were there behind the curtains! Even when he had meetings with those long-nosed fellows from the Foreign Department who came and went with all those papers. I don't think we ever fooled him, do you?"

Rory shook her head. "No. Not once." She smiled at a memory. "There was that time you tumbled off the seat and onto the carpet in full view of Grand and his visitors. They did not break sentence, and continued on with their meeting as if nothing was untoward. Even when I had to show myself to help haul you back up behind the curtain, not one of them said *boo*."

Grasby smiled crookedly. "I didn't fall, Rory. You pushed me out."

Rory widened her blue eyes. "Did I?"

"Yes, you did! Don't think you can pretend innocence. I know you better than that!"

They both laughed and then immediately fell into an awkward silence. Rory returned to gazing out the window, oblivious to the view of blue sky, green velvet lawns and a topiary garden that stretched to the river. Grasby anxiously watched her. He saw her cheeks were wet and knew she was upset. It wasn't difficult to figure out why. Despite his own sad and sorry state of affairs pressing down upon him, it said much for his brotherly devotion that he pushed those aside, concern for his sister's well-being overriding all else. Still, he avoided the topic uppermost in their minds for a little longer, enjoying just sitting with her, the world shut out.

"I thought I'd be turned away at your door; that you'd be dressing for the theater," he said in a rallying tone. "Whenever Silla makes ready for an outing, particularly if she knows important people will be in attendance—whoever they are, but Silla knows 'em!—her dressing begins straight after nuncheon. I dare not interrupt. Not that I would. After nuncheon I prefer a nap. I still manage to dress in half the time. I daresay that's because I don't have to be laced and buckled into panniers..."

"Edith is fetching tea... Then I'll dress..."

"Yes. I asked her to fetch me a cup, too. Have you decided on a gown? Didn't I hear you tell Silla you were wearing a gown of purple silk brocade worked with multi-colored flowers—

"I know I've been boring you and Grand to frustration with my enthusiasm for Sheridan's new play, and what I'd wear on the night."

"You never bore us, Rory, and Silla's been just as enthusiastic. Though... I suspect it was for the spectacle rather than the play itself. She still hadn't made up her mind on what gown to wear as late as yesterday..." He looked suddenly embarrassed. "But that's no longer a dilemma for her. She says she is too humiliated to attend Drury Lane; and never again in my company... Rory? Rory, did you hear me? Silla's staying home..."

Rory reluctantly looked away from the view. She had just caught sight of her grandfather and Major Lord Fitzstuart. They had strolled out of the shadows into the sunshine on the terrace, drinking ale from silver tumblers. Ale consumed, a footman took away the tumblers and the two men stepped off the terrace onto the gravel path. They were side-by-side, but the Major being so much taller than her grandfather had respectfully dipped his right shoulder, hands clasped lightly behind his back, an ear to the old man's conversation.

Such was the insistence in her brother's voice, Rory suppressed the desire to continue watching her grandfather and his companion and looked at Grasby.

"What is it? What's the matter, Harvel? You look so tired. Did you not sleep at all last night?"

"Not a wink," he confessed. "The chaise in my dressing room is lumpy, and the fire was let to die, so I froze." He shrugged. "Not the servants' fault. How were they to know I'd be in there all night? Still... Any lackey with half a brain could see how matters stood. I only had to poke my head into Silla's dressing room, and she threw a Meissen dog at my head. Can you believe that? She assaulted me, *her husband*, with porcelain!"

"Did it strike you?"

"No. Missed. Nice figurine, too. Gift for her birthday... She's got a good arm on her, Silla. Comes from being a keen archer. Thank God she didn't have her bow and quiver handy."

"Oh, Harvel! You poor lamb. Silla *will* forgive you... But best not to show yourself at her rooms for the next little while... She's had an upset."

"*She's* had an upset?" Grasby puffed out his cheeks, indignant. "Tell me one person who hasn't! I don't mind saying that my self-esteem is in shreds. Never more embarrassed in all my days as I was last night, being pounced on by the militia as if I were a common criminal! Damned cheek."

Despite her brother looking miserable, Rory couldn't help giggling. She put out her hand to him in sympathy. "But what were the soldiers to think when you ran across the studio without your clothes?"

"I was supposed to make for a door, but with Dair taking on the entire militia, and blows being exchanged left and right, I was disorientated. Turned in the wrong direction. An easy mistake to make—"

"Oh, yes. I agree."

"—so there was nothing for it but to high-tail it to the open window," Grasby continued, relief at being able to finally tell his side of the story, and to such a sympathetic ear, outweighing his consideration for the fact his conversation was wholly unacceptable for the ears of his younger sister. "I had almost made it to freedom, too, when the constabulary was alerted to my escape, and two of 'em threw me to the ground! Bones could have been broken! Mine! As if it wasn't galling enough to try and hide my-my *vulnerabilities* with one hand while making a dash across open space, a big brute sits on m'chest, leaving me no opportunity to cover anything at all! I tell you, Rory, if not for that brute, and me making a turnip of myself, Silla wouldn't have recognized me at all!"

"Oh?" Rory was all ears and wide-eyed attention. "I thought wives could easily distinguish their husbands without their clothes?"

"Much you know! Wives don't *look*. But I have this blasted birthmark, and when she saw it she fainted dead to the floor! I—"

Suddenly, Grasby swallowed his words, realizing that not only were they discussing a topic grossly unsuitable for the fairer sex, his audience was his little sister. He was so used to confiding in her, and she had always listened to his troubles, that no topic, until that moment, had been off-limits between them.

He had come to her rooms to apologize for his gauche conduct, and instead had merely confirmed that he was no gentleman. He was in every sense what Silla had branded him: An unmitigated, unfeeling ass! Yet, before he could construct a sentence of apology that would convey how deeply remorseful he was for his behavior, Rory further tied his tongue in knots with an acute observation that also set his ears aflame.

"Do you mean wives don't look because they choose not to and wish to be kept in ignorance? Or do you mean a wife merely *pretends* not to look at her husband unclothed because it is considered ill-mannered of her to do so? Because I cannot believe a wife would choose to be kept in ignorance, but as it is ill-mannered to stare in any social situation, I can readily believe the latter." She wrinkled her nose in thought. "That would explain why, when this topic is raised in conversation by wives at social gatherings, the gentlemen present are well out of earshot. There is a good deal of giggling behind open fans, about dimensions and estimates. And Lady Hibbert-Baker keeps a little betting book."

Grasby sat bolt upright. His face reflected his feelings. He was appalled and flabbergasted in equal measure. His voice pitched higher than usual. "Estimates? Dimensions? A *betting* book? I don't believe you! You're fibbing!"

"What reason have I to fib?" Rory argued, indignant. "Besides, I don't understand the half of what they are giggling about."

"No. No, you wouldn't," Grasby readily agreed with a grumble.

"I thought gentlemen were constantly making wagers about females?"

"But not about one's *wife*. Never about one's wife, or sister, or mother, for that fact. A man is not a gentleman if he did. It's bad form and not tolerated at the club to mention—"

"—but perfectly acceptable to mention one's mistress?"

"That's a different matter entirely!"

"How so? They are females, too. And whatever Society cares to brand them, they remain females with hearts and minds, desires and dreams..."

Grasby was unable to construct an intelligent rebuttal to his sister's acute observation, so burst out with frustration,

"One visit to Romney's studio and you're suddenly an expert on fallen women!"

Rory smiled, blue eyes full of mischief. "Oh? But I thought they were Opera dancers..."

"They are Opera dancers but—"

"Silly. Of course they are not only dancers. Particularly Signora Baccelli. Everyone knows she is the Duke of Dorset's mistress, even gilded caged birds such as myself. I just never thought I would meet a nobleman's mistress. It was such an enlivening experience... By the bye, when referring to females as "wagtails and canary birds," are such ornithological terms euphemisms for *whore*?"

"Hells bells, Rory! Silla is right. I am not only the most damnably bad husband, I am a wretchedly poor brother. You shouldn't know about such things as wagtails and canary birds, or be listening to those hen-witted wives and their-their—*tripe*."

"Easier said than done when they loudly discuss a particular wager as if I am not there at all."

"Here was I, thinking you were safe at these tea parties. Silla has the gall to accuse me of being the worse sort of brother, and she's taking my sister to dens of iniquity. I'll have a word to her—"

"You can't. She isn't talking to you, remember? Besides, I don't believe she has any idea what these wives twitter on about behind their fans. She's just not curious."

"Curious? That's one word for it. Eaves-dropper is another."

Rory pouted. "How can I not be when I am practically the only one at these tea parties who is unmarried? I am four seasons too old to be herded about with girls enjoying their first season, and far too young to sit with the pompous spinsters sporting ear-trumpets. And because Silla is kind enough to take me with her when she goes calling, her friends and acquaintances forget I am unmarried." She glanced at her brother and said with a shrug as she pulled the woolen shawl closer about her, "And once I am seated, it is not a straightforward thing for me to remove myself from the hearing of such conversations. I don't like to cause a fuss, and my stick—" She forced a smile. "Why is it that some people think that if you have a limp you must also be deaf? It is all so terribly embarrassing for the person shouting at me to be told by our hostess that just because I walk crookedly, it doesn't mean I don't have two perfectly working ears!"

"Rory—forgive me. I didn't think…"

"Oh, don't upset yourself on my account. They don't mean to be rude, and I have grown accustomed to such assumptions."

"That's magnanimous of you. Still, to be forced to listen to such distasteful conversations goes beyond the pale. And those wives call themselves respectable. Ha!"

"Oh, but they are. It's a harmless piece of funning, in its own way." She smiled cheekily. "As harmless, perhaps, as pretending to be an American savage for a bunch of dancing girls." When her brother covered his face with his hands, shame-faced, she added seriously, "I am unharmed and uncorrupted by the incident, so no hurt was done. And it helped clear up one matter that has been puzzling me…"

"Puzzling you?"

"Yes. The silly wagers written up in Lady Hibbert-Baker's betting book… I had an exceptionally limited knowledge of what a gentleman looked like without his clothes; all guesswork. But after last night, I no longer—"

"Oh. My. God. I have corrupted my own sister." Grasby groaned, a hand to his forehead, as if shielding his eyes and himself from any further frank confessions. "Hang me now!"

"To tell a truth," she said quietly, leaning into him and ignoring his melodramatic outburst, "I was more shocked to discover men have hair here." She placed a hand to her décolletage. "I was not prepared for that at all."

"Please, Rory! No more," Grasby begged, and dropped his head into the tapestry cushion. After a few seconds, he sat up again. Setting his turban to rights, he let out a great sigh. "It is times such as these that I do sincerely wish we had not been orphaned. Only a mother is equipped to answer her daughter's questions."

"Silla confided that Mrs. Watkins told her absolutely *nothing* about *anything*."

"Well that's at least *something*." He peered keenly at his sister. "Is that all Silla told you?"

"Most decidedly. Silla told me in a moment of weakness. I think she did so to warn me off, should I try to take her into my confidence, to seek answers to intimate questions she was not prepared to answer."

He sighed his relief. But no sooner did he allow his shoulders to ease than he had a sudden thought. "I don't—Rory... I don't have a hairy chest..."

"No. No, you do not..."

Grasby took a moment to digest this. In that moment, his sister's face blushed scarlet. He knew instantly whom she had been describing. It turned his frown of puzzlement into one of suppressed anger, and he gritted his teeth. When he could master his emotions he said flatly,

"Watkins said he found you unconscious behind the stage. He intimated you were back there with Fitzstuart for some time—alone. I threatened to knock his teeth out if he ever mentioned that circumstance again. Tell me the truth, Aurora. Were you alone backstage with Dair Fitzstuart?"

Her brother had only ever called her by her full name once, many years ago, and she could not recall there and then why he had done so, only that he had been furious with her—as furious as he was now. Oh dear, she was about to lie for a second time in as many hours, and she felt tears behind her eyes. But she would not give up the memory of the kiss exchanged with the Major. If she did, the kiss would be construed by others as something sordid and undignified, something of which to be ashamed. She was not ashamed, and regardless of how the Major and others viewed that brief intimate moment, she was intent on preserving the whimsy that he had enjoyed their kiss just as much as she.

"There is nothing to tell, Harvel. I said the same to Grand. I fainted at the first drop of blood. I have no stomach for men hitting each other. I am grateful to Mr. Watkins for carrying me to safety. It was truly frightening."

"Frightening? I don't doubt it! You should never have been subjected to such a God-awful sight. Never." Still furious, Grasby hit the painted sill with the side of his fist. "Bloody Dair, always playing the hero! Always getting himself into some scrape that has him beaten up at best, and almost killed at worse! Sometimes I wonder why I tolerate his damned heroics. *Bloody idiot...* Rory, he's my best friend, but you are my sister, and if I thought he had taken advantage of you— touched as much as a hair on your head—that would be an end to our friendship. I'd defend your honor, the consequences be damned."

"I know that, Harvel," Rory replied quietly. "I also know the consequences of such an encounter would be one-sided. He is a soldier; you are not. He has been trained to kill; you could not. And he would kill you..."

As if to underscore the truth of her statement, there was a burst of harsh laughter from the garden. Rory pressed her forehead to the window pane and saw the subject of their discussion. The Major had a firm buttock propped on a low stone wall, long booted leg swinging as he leaned into a lighted taper, held out to him by a footman, to bring his cheroot to life. Her grandfather was standing next to him holding a small porcelain basket. She knew the container. It held crumbs for the school of carp that lived in the pond surrounding a central fountain of leaping dolphins. The water to the fountain had been turned off to allow for routine cleaning, which was why their conversation, if not their words, was audible. The Major exhaled a stream of smoke into the blue sky and said something which made her grandfather laugh and shake his head.

Brother and sister observed the two men in silence, Grasby sitting back once his grandfather handed off the porcelain basket to a lackey to resume his stroll with Dair amongst the topiary.

"Forgive me, sugar plum," he said quietly, calling Rory by an old nursery nickname. "I have shamed myself doubly. Last night I acted the complete lunatic and today I'm swearing my head off. I am a disgrace, and have no excuse."

Rory slid down the window seat to embrace him.

"You are the best brother in the whole known world and I would not trade you for anyone. Yesterday I would not have thought you capable of swearing, least of all of running about an artist's studio naked, and you surprised me by doing both! Of course, such behavior behooves me to remove your halo and replace it with little horns and a forked tail. But I shan't love you any the less."

He shook his head with a smile, realizing she was trying to make light of his gross transgressions for his benefit, but he saw no humor in his ungentlemanly conduct. He pulled back to look in her blue eyes.

"Thank you. I deserve to have my halo confiscated. My brother-in-law now thinks me a lascivious freak. My grandfather shakes his head with disappointment, and my wife... Silla is so disgusted by my behavior she wants nothing more to do with me. She blames Dair and demands I cut the connection. That's her stipulation for a reconciliation between us."

"But... Surely she can see that the three of you were merely having a lark. There was no real harm done. And if we—Silla, Mr. Watkins, and myself—had not happened upon your mischief, then she would have been none the wiser to it."

"She is not as charitable with her forgiveness as you. She has never approved of Dair, though she cannot give me a reasonable explanation for her dislike. I had no idea just how much, until his return from the fighting in the Americas. This last six months she has taken every opportunity to revile him, and now her attitude has become something of an embarrassment. You're right. It was just a lark. And there was never any danger of me being unfaithful. So I told Silla. But will she listen to reason? No. She merely becomes hysterical and throws things at me! I told her she must accept my friends as they are. I will not give them up. Dair Fitzstuart is my best friend."

"But Silla is your wife, Harvel."

"So you see my dilemma. She must be made to understand. I will not be swayed. Until she does, we will remain estranged."

"Then we had best put our heads together to find a resolution acceptable to you both," Rory replied, glad the focus of their conversation had shifted away from her involvement in the Romney studio raid, yet disturbed that her brother's marriage was in such strife.

"And what better way to do so, than over a cup of tea?" she added in a much brighter tone, for the benefit of her maid who had made her presence felt with a slight clearing of her throat. "I'll pour, Edith. Thank you."

Edith had gently parted the curtains, and was flanked by two upstairs maids, one with the tray of tea things, the other with the silver teapot and its warming stand.

Grasby continued to brood, staring out the window while his sister fussed with the tea things. He watched his grandfather and his best friend stop at an intersection of paths. Here the old man counted off using his forefinger and fingertips, Dair nodding in response as he smoked his cheroot. He remembered Dair telling him once that soldiers smoked; officers dipped. He knew Dair was not partial to snuff, and had little time for those of his fellow officers who stayed well out of the line of fire, taking snuff in a striped marquee, while soldiers were being blown to bits on the battlefield. So he smoked in their company to annoy them. And he could annoy them. He, heir to an earldom, socially outranked most of them, who were the second and younger sons of noblemen and had no title to look forward to, other than the rank bought on commission.

But what annoyed these officers more than Dair's disregard for social rank, and his care-for-nobody attitude, was that the ordinary foot soldier would follow the Major headlong into battle, no questions asked. And so his fellow officers called him arrogant and foolhardy, and had no time for him or his heroics because it showed them up for what they truly were—painted papier-mâché fighters. One spark from Dair's cheroot and up in flames they would go.

Grasby smiled and found himself sipping hot milky tea before he realized he was holding a porcelain cup and saucer. He pulled himself out of his abstraction enough to say grimly,

"Truth is, Rory, I have no right to curse Dair for his reckless antics. He is the bravest man I know. With his family—his father in particular —holding him in little regard, is it small wonder he has little regard for his own safety? No, Rory. I will not abandon him. I cannot. It is Silla who must see why I cannot, or she will be miserable, and make me miserable into the bargain."

Rory had to ask the question. "Why, Harvel? Why risk your marriage?"

"If not for Dair Fitzstuart, you would not have a brother, Silla would not have a husband, and Grand would not have an heir to his title and estates."

TEN

WITH SUCH A WILLING AND SYMPATHETIC EAR, GRASBY WAS SOON confiding in Rory details and anecdotes about his best friend that, had Dair Fitzstuart been consulted, would have remained buried in the past, not to be repeated, and certainly not to the granddaughter of his mentor.

"Second year at Harrow was when Dair first came to my defense. I was being pummeled to a pulp by Bully Biscoe, a great big ape of a boy one year above us. Can't recall what for. I don't think he liked the color of my hair. Or was it my blue eyes? Whatever it was, it was not something I could alter about myself, even had I wanted to. Cedric did his best to pull the ape off me, but his chums got hold of Cedric, who had a pretty good fist on him, and held him down while Bully got to work on me. That's when Dair stepped in. In those days, he wasn't much bigger than me. But he could fight! Had Bully knocked cold before he knew who had hit him!"

"And so you became fast friends... You, Mr. Pleasant and Lord Fitzstuart," Rory stated to move the conversation along when her brother paused and shook his turbaned head at a memory. "When was the second time he defended you?"

"Second time?"

"You said Lord Fitzstuart came to your defense for the first time when you were at Harrow... So there must have been a second time."

"Clever! But it wouldn't be right of me to tell you the particulars. Suffice it for me to say I was staring down the long length of a blade, point held to my chest by a man who believed I had taken liberties with a—um—*female* under his protection."

"His sister? Wife? Not his daughter?"

"No! No! No! Not that sort of female or that sort of protection."

Rory's eyes widened, but she was matter-of-fact. "A whore. Please continue. Unless I am in the wrong and you need to correct me...?"

"No. No correction necessary. It was just before Dair headed off to join his regiment and Cedric and I were off to Oxford. We were celebrating the birth of his—well, that doesn't matter. We were out celebrating and ended up at a particular direction that welcomed young gentlemen. The man with the sword fancied himself in love with my— friend. I was not in a position to defend myself. He had every intention of spilling my blood. Dair got himself involved and to bring the story to its conclusion, he mortally wounded the man. It was a fair fight, with seconds, and a fair outcome. The man knew how to wield a blade, and if not for Dair, I would have been the one bleeding to death all over the floor."

"Then you do indeed owe him your life. Strange he did not go on to Oxford with you both, but instead went into the army. Not the usual route for the eldest son of an earl, is it? More tea...?"

Grasby held out his teacup.

"There's nothing usual about it! And nothing usual about Dair's family. Father deserted his Countess and three children when Dair was about ten years old. Went off to the West Indies and never came home. Dair said it was as if his father had died, but that there was no body to bury." Grasby dropped a sugar lump into his tea and replaced the silver tongs in the bowl being held out to him. "We may have been orphaned, Rory, but we had Grand to take care of us. Dair and his sister and brother were left to their own devices. The Countess shut herself away. Heartbreak sent her mad for a time—"

"The Countess of Strathsay? *Heartbroken?* Perhaps that explains why she is not a nice person."

"It don't explain why she's as cold as a frozen lake to everyone, including her own children! No motherly instincts, as far as anyone can tell. But she's Dair's mamma, so I won't say a word against her."

"Nor should you. But just because *she* is cold-blooded doesn't mean he is. His father must be warm-blooded, and Lord Fitzstuart takes after him... Perhaps that's why the Earl sailed off to the Caribbean?"

Grasby shrugged. "Possibly. Never asked. All I do know is that while the Earl lives on his sugar plantation with his dusky mistress and their two brats, his English estate falls into ruin. He won't spend a penny on its upkeep. Nor give his heir power of attorney to act on his behalf. So Dair plays a waiting game. Waiting for his father to die. Waiting to inherit. Waiting to be able to do something other than wait." He frowned. "It worries me that while he waits, his luck could turn. You can't be forever risking your life and not expect death to catch up with you in the end."

"Death catches up with all of us eventually," Rory said quietly. "But I don't understand why he tempts death. He seems to me..." she began, then instantly corrected herself before her brother realized her slip, "What I've heard said about him is that he has a zest for life. That he enjoys every moment of it."

"Well, you would, wouldn't you, if your next breath might be your last! What Dair should be doing is getting married and producing an heir. Then the Earl might consider giving him control of the estate. That's Grand's opinion. But since Dair went into the army against his wishes, Strathsay has refused to release a penny of his funds, or give him any responsibility."

"But if his father has not been in England for twenty years, who looks after his estates, if not his heir?"

Grasby sighed and looked blank for a moment. "Cousin, I think. Yes. Dair's principled second cousin, the Duke of Roxton. Holds the purse strings, and if any of the Fitzstuart siblings need funds, they have to go cap-in-hand to him."

Rory peered out the window. Her grandfather and the Major were nowhere to be seen. Only the gardeners remained, clipping hedges and raking gravel. She sighed and settled again amongst the cushions.

"He would hate going cap-in-hand to anyone... He would find it humiliating."

"Yes. Yes, he does. But it's not an unusual circumstance in itself. Plenty of sons live by handouts and IOUs until they inherit. I would be, if Grand hadn't given over the management of the estates to me when I married Silla. Now I have occupation, and still much to learn, but when I do inherit the title, Grand knows the estates will be well looked after. But few men are like Grand..."

"The Earl of Strathsay should be ashamed of himself! Not just for leaving his family, which is inexcusable, but for treating his children, particularly his eldest son and heir, with such contempt!" Rory said hotly. "Making them beg to a relative for their inheritance. Making his heir do likewise, when he should be head of the family in his father's absence... I take back what I said. The Earl is not warm-blooded at all. He is as cold and unpleasant as his countess. I'd say they were a perfect match. The wonder of it is that ice doesn't run in their son's veins, too!"

"Rory, there is no reason for you to upset yourself," Grasby said quietly, wondering why she was suddenly so passionate, though he knew her to possess great empathy. "This state of affairs has been going on since Dair was ten years old. It's nothing new."

"Then I am not the least surprised he has a reckless disregard for his heritage, his position in society, and his life! He is still being treated like a little boy of ten. He has no reason to grow up, has he? He might as well stay ten, for all the good it would do him to try and take responsibility for his family and his inheritance. While his father lives, and while he remains obdurate, Lord Fitzstuart can do nothing but wait. And everyone knows that boys who are without occupation and purpose will create mischief one way or another."

Grasby blinked. "By Jove, Rory," he whispered, adding in a much louder voice as her explanation took hold, "you've hit the proverbial nail! I've never thought about Dair's situation in that light. But you just might be right. In fact, it makes perfect sense. How clever you are!"

"Thank you. But I am not so clever," she smiled, yet dimpling at such praise. "His situation is not so different to that of females waiting to be married. Until we marry we have little purpose in life. We are just burdens on others, in every way. But once married, we have a position in society, a house to run, and God willing, children to raise and worry over. It must be the same for eldest sons, particularly those who are shunned by their fathers. They wait, too. At least unmarried females have fathers and brothers to look after them, and who they can look after in their own small ways. Although that too diminishes when brothers find wives…"

"You will never be a burden, Rory. I mean to look after you, always."

"I know that, dearest. I wasn't thinking of me, but speaking in generalities. I shall make an excellent aunt one day, and Silla will be pleased to have me. She will love your children, but I do not see her spending many hours in the nursery, do you?"

Grasby was about to say that the way matters were presently between him and his wife, it would take almost a miracle if the nursery received any occupants in the future. He was saved commenting when Rory continued, and he again found himself surprised by her naïve insight.

"I dare say army life was good for his lordship. Aside from the very real possibility of being killed or maimed in battle, the day-to-day discipline of a regiment does give men purpose. It may even keep them out of mischief until they are granted leave, and then perhaps they go a little wild…?"

"I can only agree with you," Grasby smiled. "Though I wonder how many officers you've engaged in conversation?"

"It is all observation and conjecture, dearest brother. I've seen soldiers on parade, not Lord Fitzstuart's 17th. It must take an inordinate amount of time and effort to shine all those buttons on their scarlet coats, and polish their jockey boots until they reflect the sun! As for keeping their white breeches whiter than white—whose idea was it to put soldiers in such an impossible color?"

"But it does make them look the part—all that scarlet and white."

"It does. And we have not touched on the hours that must go into taking care of their mounts. All that brass tack and leather, and the shine to their beautiful coats. To see the dragoons mounted is a sight to behold, is it not?"

"It most certainly is. Astonishing what a bit of spit and polish and a scarlet coat can do for a man," Grasby teased his sister, and then peered at her closely. "You've not fallen for a uniform, have you, Rory?"

"Certainly not!" she retorted, and to hide the heat in her cheeks threw her cushion at him, which he caught and threw back at her, laughingly.

"Good. Because I don't want you marrying a uniform. I found it difficult enough having my best friend go off and fight. I couldn't bear for you to worry yourself over a husband doing the same."

Rory giggled. "I do love you for thinking I might marry at all!"

"Why shouldn't you? I mean, you're pretty enough, and some men find blue eyes attractive."

"I'll take that as a compliment." Adding seriously, hoping her tone sounded offhand enough not to arouse suspicion, "So why did Lord Fitzstuart buy a commission?"

"Ah, well. He didn't have much say in the matter after he was discovered being foolish. I believe the decision was taken by the old Duke of Roxton, Dair's guardian at the time.

"My godfather? Why?"

Grasby gave an involuntary shudder. "The son is pompous enough, but the old Duke... Sinister doesn't begin to describe him! The times I've visited Treat, I half expected to see his ghost haunting the corridors of his palace. He was enough of a specter in life, with his beak of a nose, that menacing way he had of speaking, and those black eyes that missed nothing. I don't think anyone ever said 'no' to him his entire life!"

Rory shrugged. "Strange he should leave such an impression on you. He was always kind to me... I remember one particular time, when I was about six years old, Grand and I went to stay at Treat—"

"Where was I?"

"Harrow. Grand took me to see the baby. It was two months after Mme la Duchesse's lying-in with her younger son, and I was permitted to go up to her rooms... Her lady-in-waiting took me upstairs to the most magical apartments I have ever seen then or since! It was what I imagined a palace belonging to a fairy would look like, all golds and pinks... It smelled delicious and soft... But when I saw Mme la Duchesse suckling her baby, I forgot about my surroundings. I must have exhausted her with all my questions, because my godfather sat me on his lap and proceeded to divert me. Well I know *now* that was what he was doing. He told me a story about the old French King, his court and all the pretty ladies. Though I suspect it wasn't a story at all but his memories of his earlier life before he married my godmother."

"He was *there*? In the room? In the room while the Duchess was—while the baby was being fed?"

Rory giggled.

"Oh, Grasby, if you could only see your face! A suckling baby is the most natural sight in the world."

"Duchesses have wet nurses to take care of that sort of thing."

"Well don't be surprised if Silla decides to feed her own baby."

"Silla will do whatever is fashionable."

"Then she most certainly will feed her baby, because it is quite the fashion for Society ladies to breast-feed their own children. If I were to have a child, I would do so, regardless of the fashion. Just as Mme la Duchesse disregarded the fashion."

"Whatever that decision, it staggers me the old Duke was there as if it were an afternoon tea party!" He frowned. "Grand wasn't in on this baby-feeding episode, was he?"

"Silly! Of course not. When he had finished his story, the old Duke took me downstairs to where Grand was waiting." Rory grinned and hunched her shoulders. "And that's when I told him I liked his beaky nose."

Grasby's mouth dropped open. "You did no such thing! You told the scary old Duke of Roxton you liked his-his *beaky* nose? Well, I never! What did he do?"

"What do you think he did? I was only six years old. He laughed and told me that when I was older I could have it."

"You are the strangest girl, to be sure, Rory. Most little girls would say they liked a pretty flower or a diamond ring, or a pet parrot, but you tell an old Duke you like his beak of a nose!" He laughed and said jokingly, "If that's your criteria for forming an attachment, I'll have to see if I can find you a gentleman whose beak measures up."

Rory smiled in response, but she did not laugh, and felt her cheeks grow hot. She knew just the gentleman whose fine nose did measure up, but she kept this to herself, and asked her brother again why Lord Fitzstuart was bought a commission.

"I shouldn't confide this in you. But I know if I don't tell you, you'll just go and ask Grand the same question... And it possibly won't come as a surprise. It's been whispered about enough times that you may have heard it spoken of at one of those tea parties Silla took you to. Besides, Dair makes no secret of the fact he has a natural son, never has."

"Lily Banks' son?"

Grasby nodded. "So you have heard. Yes. Reason Dair was shipped off to the army. He and Lily tried to elope to Gretna; only place they could marry without needing all the legalities. He was just eighteen and she, well she was old enough to know better! Old enough to manage to get herself pregnant and hope the heir to an earldom would marry her!"

"But how could she manage to get herself pregnant? Isn't a child a blessing from God?"

"Not this sort of child, Rory."

Rory frowned and was instantly uncomfortable, not liking her brother's words at all. She left the window seat to fuss with the tea things, hoping occupation would soothe her emotions. She lifted the silver teapot and realized there was only enough tea for one more cup, so snuffed the candle warmer and replaced the teapot on its stand. She then stacked the tea cups and came back to the window seat where her brother still sat, watching her. Her thoughts collected into coherent sentences her brother would understand without becoming emotive, she said quietly,

"Harvel, it upsets me to hear you speak of a child in such a derogatory tone. A child is a child, and that is all he is. He comes into the world blameless, and yet he is immediately branded by others because of his parentage, or his characteristics, or his-his deformities, as being worth less than nothing—"

"Rory, I didn't mean you."

"I know that, dearest. But it doesn't lessen the pain I feel when I hear a child shaped into another's making. I have come to terms with my shortcomings. I have a privileged life that shields me from the ugliness in the world. But for you and others to condemn a child because its parents are not married... How easily you forget that our own mother was illegitimate!"

"I had not forgotten. Though I wish I could."

"Why? Because our parents' marriage was an unequal one? Even Grand admits their union was a happy one. For you to wish otherwise, is to wish away their happiness. It also condemns my existence, for in the eyes of many, I am God's punishment for my father marrying far beneath him."

"Anyone who says so isn't fit for dog meat!"

"So are those who condemn Lily Banks' son because he is illegitimate."

Grasby did not argue the point with her. He had never won a debate with his sister. Instead he said flatly, "His name is Jamie—James Alisdair Banks."

"Oh! I do like that name. And he gave the boy his Christian name, too…"

"Dair would have given him his legal name, if he'd been permitted. That was not going to happen, neither was a marriage. The old Duke of Roxton caught up to them and it was all sorted. Lily Banks had his baby and Dair went into the army. That was ten years ago, and a lot of water has flowed under that bridge since then!"

Rory scowled. "Meaning?"

Grasby could have bitten off his own tongue for his want of propriety. Still he answered her.

"Meaning, Lily Banks is married and has had four more children to her husband."

"So she isn't Lord Fitzstuart's mistress?"

"Mistress? I doubt she ever was in the true sense of the word. She was a pretty little thing when she caught Dair's eye. Five children later, do you think Dair would be interested in such a woman?"

Knowing Lily Banks was married and not Lord Fitzstuart's mistress cheered Rory more than she cared to admit, but it did not stop her saying, tongue firmly in cheek,

"Dear me, she must be old enough to have a toe in her grave! I can't imagine his lordship being attracted to such an old crone."

"Ha, sister dear! To own to a truth, I've no idea what Lily Banks looks like, only that her son by Dair is the spit of his papa. By all accounts, Mr. Banks is a fine fellow. They are cousins, and known each other since children, so Dair told me, hence the same surname. Makes for an easy transition, doesn't it? He's a botanist, or is he a plant collector for a botanist? Whatever, he's an adventurer who travels the world in search of exotic plants."

"Then that explains why they occupy a house next to the Chelsea Physic Garden… I wonder if Mr. Banks knows anything about pineapples… Harvel, I must dress now, or I shall be late. And Grand hates to be kept waiting…"

Grasby hopped off the window seat and shoved his hands in the pockets of his silk banyan. "I dare say Banks might know something about pineapples…"

Rory hooked her arm about her brother's and walked with him to the door of her sitting room. "Are you sure you won't accompany Grand and me to the theater?"

Grasby stopped on the threshold, the door opened for him by one of Rory's maids.

"And give Silla more powder for her cannon? Besides," he added with a guilty grin, "the theater is more your thing than mine. Silla's anger has just given me a good excuse not to attend… Oi! Hold on a moment! I never told you Lily Banks lived next door to the Chelsea Physic Garden. So how do you—"

But Rory had closed the door on her brother before he could quiz her further, already making plans to visit the Chelsea Physic Garden to learn what the gardeners could tell her about the cultivation of the pineapple. She might even be able to offer an exchange of information. She would take along her gardener, and perhaps she could coax Silla to accompany her and make a picnic of the day. And if she happened to wander close to the stone wall and peer over at the house occupied by Lily Banks and her family… It would be serendipity if she caught a glimpse of Mrs. Banks and her children, and most particularly the boy who was the image of his father. After all, had not the Major invited her to Lily Banks' house, no questions asked?

Rory would have been greatly surprised to discover that while she was thinking of Lily Banks and Jamie, Dair Fitzstuart was thinking about her and his promise to her grandfather, and what he could do about it.

ELEVEN

THE MORNING AFTER HIS VISIT WITH THE EARL OF SHREWSBURY, Dair arrived at the Hanover Square residence of his cousin just before midday, and found the house in the midst of a family celebration. He had no wish to disturb the gathering and so told the butler he would wait, not in an anteroom but on the steps of the main staircase. He stripped off his tan leather riding gloves and dropped them into the crown of his hat, permitted a footman to shrug him out of his gray woolen greatcoat, and gave up his sword and sash to the butler. Declining any sort of beverage, he asked for a taper to light a cheroot, then took up a position on the stairs that allowed him to stretch his long booted legs in their thigh-tight buff breeches as comfortably as possible. Here he lounged, smoking, both elbows resting on a step across the broad of his back, and staring at the full-length life-size portrait of a titian-haired beauty, his grandmother, Augusta, the first Countess of Strathsay.

But it was not his grandmother he saw in his mind's eye as he stared at the imposing canvas, but a young woman not much past twenty years of age, with pale blue eyes that held a twinkle of candor. She was not beautiful, but she was pretty. She was not plump as was the fashion, but delicate, like a fine Meissen figurine. Her hair was an indeterminate pale blonde, and while her mouth was perfectly formed, her lips were the palest of pinks. She was a female who, until the raid on Romney's studio, he would have passed in the street, or in a crowded drawing room, and not given a second glance. He certainly would not have sought her out for conversation or, for that matter, anything else. That was because his two-days-ago-self had always equated paleness with triteness.

But now he could not stop thinking about this pale beauty. After the raid on Romney's studio, while his battered and bruised body was being patched up, he was so consumed with going over in his mind every detail of their encounter that he failed to react to the blistering sting when Farrier applied linen bandages soaked in an antiseptic preparation of turpentine, alcohol, and aloe to his abrasions. This caused the batman to wonder aloud if his master had suffered an internal rupture that had left him numb to pain. To which Dair had ordered Farrier to stop fussing like an old maiden aunt and just get on with it.

While he toyed with the purple silken hair ribbon he had taken from her as a war trophy, he decided her pale prettiness was a subterfuge, just as snow blanketing a multitude of terrains left the landscape featureless. But he was not deceived. He caught the sparkle of mischief in her smile, and the humor in her eyes, at the outrageous situation in which she found herself, bound up with him in a curtain and then astride his torso on the floor at the back of the stage.

His *Delight* was no simpering miss, no fainting couch habitué. She confidently and playfully answered him back without artifice. Nor did she try to flirt with him. She was, quite simply, herself, and he found that fascinating. He was not good with words, but to him, for want of a better analogy, she was a star amongst a thousand twinkling in the night sky, unnoticed and unappreciated, until the fates had intervened. It was only then that she caught his attention, not unlike a shooting star streaking the black night sky, and in the most bizarre of circumstances. How could he ignore her after that?

God, he must be going soft in the head, waxing lyrical about blanketing snow and night skies filled with stars! What the bloody hell was wrong with him? One too many knocks about the ears on his last tour of duty could account for it. Or it could be that nick from a rebel bullet that had grazed his scalp. He knew of some men forced into restraining jackets, no longer able to cope with the endless bloody scenes that played over and over in their heads: Of limbs hacked off and heads blown to a meaty pulp; screaming death, and crying orphaned children; and rebel civilians who had no place on a battlefield, taking up arms only to be slaughtered in their thousands... Yes, all that could give a soldier a straw bed in Bedlam.

But had he truly survived nine years in the army, with all its attendant horrors, to lose his head over a female whom he now realized was so out of his reach that she might as well be living in Vladivostok?

When she had walked into Shrewsbury's study and dropped a book at his feet, the blood had drained from his face. Seeing her—no, hearing her voice, with that note of eager expectation—had him smiling before he even knew what she was saying or what she looked like. And then it hit him all at once, like a hard fist to his gut. Here was his shooting star and she was *Shrewsbury's granddaughter*.

Worse, two minutes before she showed up, he had given his word to forget all about the previous evening —to forget all about *her*. He felt he had been tricked out of something precious. Yet, he knew Shrewsbury was doing nothing less than he aught: Protecting his grand-daughter's unblemished reputation.

He had remained on his haunches, taking an inordinate amount of time to pick up her book before rising to his full height, hoping he had mastered his shock enough not to alert Shrewsbury. Trying his best to remain passive and in control—numb was a better word—he had held out the book, looking not at her but over her fair hair. He just wanted her to take it so he could get the hell out of there. Instead of doing so, she surprised him, not only by showing concern for his wounds, but more so because she spoke to him as if they were old friends. And what did he do in response? The only thing he could: Remain mute, and exhibit all the emotional depth of a log of wood. Callous idiot!

But it was when she touched him that he was forced to muster all his skills as a performer. She held his hand as if it were the most natural thing in the world for her to do so. Every fine hair, every square inch of skin on the back of his hand smarted, the sensation far more intense than the wounds already inflicted. He forced his mind elsewhere, as he had been trained to do in the event of capture and torture. And this was torture. Worse than thumb screws and flame.

One short sharp sentence and he escaped to the terrace. He was staring at clipped yew trees and boxed hedge rows set out in geometric patterns before he realized a footman had followed him out-of-doors. The servant offered him a tumbler of ale—he downed it in one and demanded another.

He had suffered a monumental shock. No. Two shocks. The pretty pale female he had playfully tried to seduce at Romney's studio was not a harlot, nor was her reputation remotely tinged with immorality. She was the Earl of Shrewsbury's granddaughter, and he was mortified. Had he known, he would not have acted towards her as he had. He certainly would not have said the things he did. But, to his abiding shame, he knew himself for a liar. He did not wish to apologize for his behavior towards her. He had enjoyed their banter, more so because it was honest and unstudied. Most of all, his overwhelming desire upon hearing her voice again was to take her in his arms and kiss her as he had kissed her when they were cocooned in a linen curtain.

Leading his first cavalry charge had been fraught with less terror than what he had experienced in Shrewsbury's study. He couldn't wait to set sail for Portugal.

With thoughts of Portugal and his imminent mission came the realization he had been sitting on the stairs of his cousin's Hanover Square mansion for at least twenty minutes. He was supposed to be on his way to Portsmouth, before anyone saw him out and about in London. After all, for all concerned, he was presently locked up in the Tower, while being investigated for aiding and abetting the traitorous deeds of his younger brother. The Tower was where he had sent Farrier, much to his batman's disgust. Farrier would be spending the next month as a guest of His Majesty. Dair had told him to think of it as a holiday. Farrier had told his lordship he could think of a few things to call his voluntary incarceration, but the word "holiday" was not one of them.

Dair was about to send a footman to the drawing room to disturb his cousin when the door opened and she came out into the passageway in a whirlwind of ivory satin petticoats with metallic thread embroidery, golden hair threaded with matching ivory satin ribbons, face flushed and radiant. Dair could not help smiling to see her so happy; a far cry from the widow who had mourned the loss of her beloved husband for three sorrowful years. The reason for her happiness followed her out of the room. Jonathon Strang Leven, newly elevated Duke of Kinross, was just as splendidly attired in dark velvet, his India waistcoat of gold and silver metallic threads dazzling against his brown complexion.

Dair realized then what the family celebration must be about, and he slowly rose to his boot heels to greet the noble couple and to offer up his congratulations.

JONATHON CAUGHT ANTONIA ABOUT THE WAIST, SPUN HER ABOUT and promptly kissed her. She laughed and went to put her arms up about his neck. But being so much shorter than he, she had to go on tiptoe, and her stockinged foot lost its satin mule. Always chivalrous, and mindful of the disparity in their heights, Jonathon effortlessly lifted her onto a chair up against the wall. This allowed her to look down upon him. He kept his hands to her silken waist and smiled up at her. She cupped his sun-bronzed face in her hands and brought her mouth to his.

Finally alone, after a morning filled with ceremony and family, their attention was wholly focused on each other, and they gave themselves up to a long leisurely kiss, punctuated with murmurings of eternal love and devotion in French, her native tongue, and the language they preferred when in private.

When they broke free, Antonia remained standing on the chair, arms about Jonathon's neck, fiddling with the black satin ribbon at his nape. She leaned into him, the layers of her ivory satin petticoats enveloping him like a cloud, and said with a pout, a playful light in her emerald-green eyes,

"I do not understand at all why it is our marriage it had to be at such an ungodly hour. Did you not want to stay in bed with me? Could not our marriage have taken place this afternoon? A more respectable time."

"But my darling wife—Ah! I do so love to call you that. *My* darling wife. *My* duchess. *My* love... Sweetheart, if it had been my choice we would have stayed in bed all day—got married there, for all I care—"

Antonia giggled. "Truly? But poor Reverend Jenkins, he would not know where to put his eyes!"

"—but for the sake of our family, most particularly your upright son, I thought it best to get the ceremony over with as quickly as possible. And in surroundings in which he would feel most comfortable."

"Julian? Comfortable? Did you not see his expression? He looks as comfortable as a cabbage about to be chopped!"

Jonathon gave a crack of laughter.

"Cabbage? Yes. Yes, he does look a bit sour. But don't take it to heart. He's an over-ruminator. Think how he must feel. Last night he goes to the theater to see a new play and what happens? The audience is less interested in what's going on up on stage than they are in the box in which sits his mother. Who, by the way, hasn't been to the theater in six years, and when she does, she turns up with a brown-skinned giant as her shadow. Worse, she kisses this unknown fellow in full view of the world, setting off a near riot into the bargain. And we know how much Roxton hates public attention of any kind. So the poor man is mortified when all eyes turn on him to see what he thinks of his mother's outrageous conduct. And first thing this morning, he has to front up to witness his mother marrying her kissing giant, who just happens to be not much older than himself. But with our signatures on that marriage document we are now legally and spiritually bound as one, and there ain't a thing he can do about it. Which means his mother is no longer a dowager duchess but Duchess of Kinross, and her husband is his new papa."

Antonia gasped.

"New papa?! That is amusing in the extreme! But not to Julian. Yes. When you say it like that, me I understand a little of his anxiousness. So," she added with a cheeky smile, "would it be rude of us to leave our guests and disappear to the book room?"

"Our guests, sweetheart, being your sons, your daughter-in-law, Roxton's chaplain and his godfather? I have invited them to stay to nuncheon." When Antonia scowled, he laughed and kissed her heartily. "As much as I would love to skulk off to the book room, our absence on this of all days would be noted."

Antonia dimpled and teased him. "But... Our marriage it must be consummated to be binding, yes?"

"And you think, with a houseful of people, the book room the wisest choice?"

"I did not say anything about being wise—or comfortable."

"Just outrageous?" Jonathon grinned. "You're so adorably wicked!"

"But that is why you love me, yes?"

"That and much more..." He went to pick her up off the chair only to place her stockinged toes back on the tapestry cushion. "Damn these hoops! How am I supposed to give you a proper embrace with that wretched device under your petticoats hindering my every move? You'll go in undress when we are at home."

"Married less than an hour and already His Grace of Kinross he is making demands of his wife's clothing!" When Jonathon frowned, Antonia pinched his square chin. "But of course. For you, and for my own comfort, I will wear as little as possible." She put a hand to his cheek. "But not today... Or tomorrow..."

"Perhaps we could scurry away, if only for half an hour..."

"Half an hour? I will not be cheated!"

This made Jonathon laugh heartily, the corners of his eyes crinkling. When he could master himself, he said seriously, "We only have today and tonight before I leave. Tomorrow your family may have you back until my return."

"Today you have made me the happiest of women, but tomorrow I will be desolate." She kissed his forehead softly, then set hers against his and looked into his dark eyes. "How will I bear it?"

"How will *I*?" he murmured, gaze never wavering from her.

Jonathon dared to wonder if it was not all a wonderful dream from which he would awake. But he had woken early that morning with this delectable creature, whom he loved beyond reason, snuggled into his arms. They had made love, as they always did, passionately and without restraint, knowing there were not many hours left to them before it would be months before they shared a bed again. He was off to Scotland to bury his ancient relative and take his rightful place as head of the Strang Leven family and laird of Kinross Castle on the shores of Loch Leven. His bride would return to the Roxton family estate, to her dower house, to tell her dearly departed Monseigneur news of her remarriage, to arrange her possessions for her new life, and to await his return.

They had been husband and wife for only an hour and he wanted nothing more than to scoop her up and take his wife back up to bed. But catching a few moments alone just outside the drawing room would have to satisfy them both. Family awaited them. He was about to suggest they return there when into his subconscious trailed tobacco smoke, pungently earthy, and with a hint of cherry. He instantly craved a cheroot. He did not need to turn to know who was nearby, nor did he take his eyes from his duchess, saying softly to Antonia,

"Sweetheart, we have a late arrival to our nuptials…"

DAIR WAITED UNTIL HIS FIRST COUSIN, ANTONIA, DUCHESS OF Kinross was returned to solid ground, and had slipped her stockinged feet into her satin mules, before going forward to greet and congratulate the newlyweds. He heartily shook Jonathon's hand and bowed formally over Antonia's outstretched fingers. And when she pulled him closer and presented her cheek, he kissed her diffidently, surprising Jonathon that he would be awkwardly shy in the presence of his cousin, a family member he had known all his life. If Antonia noticed, she did not react, nor did she acknowledge the grazes to Dair's knuckles, the healing cut to his lip or the dark bruising to his left eye.

Dair further surprised Jonathon by conversing with them in fluent French. He should have realized the lad could speak the language, like the rest of the Roxton family group. After all, Antonia spoke almost exclusively in French, though she could speak in English if necessity called for her to do so. An Englishman coming upon their conversation would surely have thought he had stumbled into a Parisian salon.

A short exchange of platitudes and it was obvious Dair wished to have a private word with Antonia. So Jonathon invited him to join the family for nuncheon, which was politely declined, as Jonathon knew it would, then made his excuses and returned to the drawing room, leaving the cousins alone at the bottom of the staircase. Antonia spread out her petticoats and sat on the stairs. Invited, Dair did likewise.

"I like your new duke," Dair stated, once again stretching out his long legs across several steps. "He's a good man." He smiled. "You wouldn't have married him otherwise. And he has made you happy."

"Yes. I am very happy—again."

"Not many are blessed with one good marriage, but to have two…"

"One day I hope you will be as happy as I am, Alisdair."

"But—Cousin Duchess—you don't even like me."

Antonia lost her smile. "That is a great piece of nonsense and it offends me!"

Dair politely inclined his head in acknowledgment of her status to say and do as she pleased, but as her first cousin he rudely shrugged a shoulder and inhaled on his cheroot. "You would be the first to chide me if I were not truthful with you."

"But you are *not* being truthful, you are making an ill-informed judgment about my feelings."

"Then forgive me. I am neither good with words, or with feelings…" He returned his gaze to the full-length portrait of Augusta, Countess of Strathsay. "I can't blame anyone for my lack of brains. Charles inherited whatever there was to dish out to the family. But I hold responsible that woman's son, my father, for my lack of feeling."

"If you wish to cast blame, then blame her our grandmother," Antonia stated, gaze also on the portrait. "She turned your mother against your father. She turned your father against Monseigneur. Your father he took a ship across the sea to be rid of her. But you cannot run away from yourself. Augusta she was a beautiful heartless woman, as cold as a serpent." Antonia gave a little shiver of revulsion. "Please. Let us not talk of her on this of all days."

"Why, if she was such a serpent, do you keep our grandmother's portrait on your wall? If I owned her, she'd be wrapped in a sheet and stuck in an attic, or consigned to a dusty corner of some picture gallery. Perhaps Roxton would like to have her?"

Antonia smiled but shook her head. "He cannot, even if he would be kind enough to take her off my hands. Monseigneur he has forbidden her at Treat. Her remains, they are not buried in the family mausoleum, but at Ely, beside her lover."

"But she doesn't have to be on your wall, surely?"

"That is true. But I keep her there… She is a reminder—a reminder that a beautiful façade does not always bring with it a beautiful heart."

"Strange… I mean, strange for you, considered the most beautiful woman of the age, in temperament and visage…"

"*C'est ce que vous pensez?* You think I do not have my bad days?"

They both laughed at this, Antonia adding seriously,

"Beauty is a gift from God and should not be abused or taken for granted. Those blessed with physical beauty cannot assume the appearance of goodness, they must *be* good and that requires *doing* good."

"On second thought, don't ship her off. What you need are some candles, incense and an altar. A papist shrine, if you will, to your archangel of beauty. Which, when you think on it, is fitting, given our grandfather was a papist general for the Old Pretender."

"It is important, is it not, that those blessed with great physical beauty have a duty not to abuse their gift?" Antonia continued, ignoring his quip. "To be a self-destructive care-for-nobody intent on self-harm is a great waste; it is also arrogant in the extreme."

Dair removed his gaze from their grandmother's portrait and slowly turned to meet Antonia's gaze, face devoid of his thoughts. He took the cheroot from his mouth.

"Thus lectured Duchess Beauty, whose first husband was in his day, and will always be remembered as, the most arrogant nobleman on both sides of the Channel."

Antonia smiled kindly. "Yes, he was. But Monseigneur he wore his arrogance with sublime confidence and force of personality, as one who owns the most exquisitely tailored frock coat in the room. He also had a high opinion of himself. He knew his self-worth and let others know it too. Which, for a nobleman in his position, was as it should be."

"And how do I wear my coat, Cousin? A little loose in the shoulders for your liking? A bit worn at the cuffs, perhaps? I dare say the cloth is not up to snuff either. Don't spare my feelings now. If I am to be served up a lecture for dinner, I want all twelve courses with lashings of humiliation!"

Antonia was silent a moment, and then she told him her thoughts, honestly and without artifice.

"This man you pretend to be, this conceited Adonis who abuses his body in fights and scraps with lesser beings, he is not a gentleman. He pretends not to care for anyone or anything. He whores and drinks to excess. He never refuses a wager and so carries out ridiculous dares for his friends to make them laugh, or rich, or for no good purpose at all. This man, I do not know him in the least. And I do not care to know him. But that does not stop me caring about him and worrying. Me I worry he will start believing in the façade he hides behind so that one day these two beings, they will merge, and then he will be lost to us, and to himself."

"I am what I am."

"No! You pretend. You act. But you have inhabited the role for so many years now, you cannot tell the difference between the two. But sometimes the real Alisdair Fitzstuart he emerges, and I think then that there is hope for you yet."

When Dair huffed and slowly shook his head in polite disagreement, Antonia put up her brows and said dryly, "So your marriage proposal to Sarah-Jane Strang, it was sincere and you are all desolation that she chose your brother—"

"Of course it wasn't sincere!" Dair growled angrily, finally taking the bait. "I didn't so much as put the question to the girl. All I had to do was seed the intent that I was about to ask her. All that required was confiding in my mother I was thinking of getting married. Quite frankly, if she knew me at all, she would know that thought has never entered my head! I knew she wouldn't approve of a merchant's daughter as the next Countess of Strathsay, whatever her dowry. And of course she ran crying to Charlie that I was about to ruin the family name! Charlie assumed the worst and when he saw Miss Strang and me walking alone on the terrace he decided to finally act. It was all the push he needed to get up the courage to reveal his true feelings to Miss Strang." He glanced at Antonia, still smoldering. "Staggers me my little brother had the nutmegs to be a traitor to his country, and yet, when it comes to asking the girl he loves to marry him, he acts the neutered tom! What else could I do but step in and hurry matters along?"

"Being in love can be terrifying—more terrifying than anything else, particularly if there is a doubt that love will not be reciprocated, or an impediment stands in the way of a happy outcome." Antonia rallied and smiled. "But my point, it is made. *Enfin*. So what is to be done with you, Alisdair? You who will be the Earl of Strathsay and head of your family one day. With your brother Charles branded a traitor for following his beliefs, he can never set foot on English soil and is excluded from his family's inheritance. You are the earldom's only hope of its continuance. So you will please promise me to stop trying to kill yourself in as many interesting ways as possible. This last, in a painter's studio, of all places."

"Cousin Duchess, I can promise you that if I do get killed it will not be because I wished to die."

He had been keen to make this interview with his cousin as short as possible. The parental lecture he could well do without, but he could see there was no stopping her once she was animated. Like a ferocious feline, she paced the black and white marble tiles at the base of the staircase, ivory petticoats swishing this way and that, and he had to concede that he was flattered she cared so much for his welfare. Indeed, that she cared about him at all. And on this of all days, her wedding day, which should have been joyous and carefree, not spent being concerned about him. He was astounded to realize that this was the first maternal lecture he had received in his eight-and-twenty years (his mother did not lecture, she merely suggested in a vapid irritating way or fell into a flood of tears). Rather bizarrely, he derived a certain satisfaction from Antonia's castigation.

"You think putting yourself in harm's way it is a laughing matter? Have you not been listening? You have an obligation, if not to yourself, then to others, to live up to your potential. No! Do not speak again. I have a few more words to say to you. Do not try and feed to me that ridiculous nonsense about *you* being a traitor because me I do not believe it in the least! And do not tell me this treason, which you did not commit, came from a need for funds. That, also, I do not believe. You would never sell your country for pecuniary gain. So that, too, is a big fat lie, and I am guessing from the mouth of Shrewsbury, who thinks me of little brain and himself as a modern day Machiavelli..."

This impassioned speech drew from Dair a reluctant laugh, and he found himself apologizing for his behavior rather than defending it, which had been his intention. Such an unexpected turn-around also surprised him and made it all the more difficult to put his request to her, particularly when it meant disclosing that he was again about to put his life in danger, and in a far more perilous way than a scrap at an artist's studio. So it was with an accompanying bashful smile that he withdrew a sealed packet and a small leather purse of guineas from an inner frock coat pocket.

"Do I have your permission to speak now, your Grace?" he asked quietly, looking down at her from the fourth step, and thus from a great height, because he had shot to his feet the moment she had. When she nodded and waved for him to sit again, she sitting on the step beside him, he placed the sealed packet and small leather purse between them and continued. "I would not have lied to you had you asked me outright about the allegations of treason. And thank you—thank you for believing in me... But it makes my request that much more difficult to ask. This," he said holding up the sealed packet, "I want you to keep in a safe place. You may never have to break the seal, but in the event of my death—"

Antonia sat up tall. "Your death? Alisdair, what—"

"Please, your Grace, I need to get through this without interruption. The packet contains my last will and testament, which is self-explanatory. Once my demise is made generally known, I want you to give it to your son. Roxton will know what to do." He put the packet back on the step and held up the leather purse. "For the boy's birthday. It's in a

month, but I might not make it back—back in time. There should be
sufficient guineas for a fine family feast and his gift." He smiled self-
consciously. "No idea what he wants. Last time he wrote, it was a musket
or a microscope. A soldier or a physician. He can't decide. But at ten
years of age, what boy truly knows what he wants to do with his future?
At that age I wanted to be a pirate. Ha! At least he doesn't have the
weight of birth on his thin shoulders, and is able to tread a path of his
own choosing." He glanced at Antonia then said, "If it were my choice, I
wouldn't have him follow in my bootsteps. His mother says he has a fine
head on his shoulders, so I am hoping he chooses the microscope. But in
the event you think the only place for him is the army. So be it."

Antonia blinked. "You are giving Jamie to me?"

"If anything were to happen to me, yes. Guardianship until his
twenty-fifth birthday, when he will get the bulk of his inheritance, such
as it is at the present. Were I in my father's shoes, and earl, I'd have
considerably more say in the distribution of the largesse... If you and
your new duke would keep an eye on him as he grows, I'd be eternally
grateful." Dair gave a lopsided grin. "You're the only two people I know
who won't look down on him because of his birth."

"Alisdair... Julian he, too, would never look down on your child,
any child, and perhaps he is a more fitting guardian, yes?"

"No. We are barely on speaking terms. And who can blame him for
that after what happened at the regatta? His son almost drowned and I
was distracted with the finish line at any cost... Jesu! What must he—
you—think of me...?" He inhaled on his cheroot and blew smoke
across his shoulder, away from Antonia. When she remained silent his
mouth twitched into a crooked smile. "Thank you for not asking...
Perhaps I'll tell you one day..." He rallied and added, "Even if we were
on the best of terms, he and Deborah have enough of a brood, and
another on the way. Besides, after all those years on the sub-continent
as a merchant, your new duke is far more open-minded to possibilities
and potential. I watched him around Roxton's boys; Frederick idolizes
him." Dair frowned on a sudden thought. "But if you would prefer that
I not—"

"No! No! Of course we will do as you ask," Antonia replied,
holding back tears. She laid her fingers over her cousin's large hand.
"Jonathon, he will agree with me. It will be an honor. Truly." She
sniffed and smiled when Dair drew up her hand and kissed it. "But it
will not come to that because you will return to us from wherever it is
you are going, and Jamie he will be able to thank his papa for the
microscope in person when next he sees you."

"I hope that you are proved right, Cousin Duchess. And thank you. My mind can rest easy now."

He stubbed the smoldering end of the cheroot on the sole of his boot, and dropped the butt onto a silver tray a quick-thinking footman held out to him. After helping Antonia to her feet, he gave her the sealed packet and the purse. She slipped these under the first layer of her satin gown, into one of two embroidered long pockets, tied about her waist between the layers of her petticoats.

"As far as the rest of London is concerned, I'm spending the next month in the Tower. You and Kinross may know it's Portugal for me. You'll be pleased that it's not a country we are presently at war with—a nice change. Shrewsbury tells me we have a trade agreement with the Portuguese and import barrels and barrels of port..."

"But you are not going for the port."

"No. And that's all I can tell you," he apologized. "I'll bring your new Duke and Roxton back a dozen bottles or a crate, whatever I can manage."

"Be safe, *mon cher.*"

Dair bowed over her hand, and because she was looking up at him with such worry he impetuously kissed her cheek. "I will do my absolute best to remain alive, *ma chère cousine.* Promise."

Antonia put her arm through his and walked with him a little way up the entrance foyer, turning a shoulder at the sudden burst of noise, of conversation and laughter, coming from the drawing room when the door was flung wide. Her younger son, Lord Henri-Antoine sauntered out, saw his mother and came up and grabbed her hand, a nod to Dair, who was buckling his sword sash.

"Fitzstuart! No one told us you were here. Zounds! But that bruise is a shiner; and your lip... Come tell us how it happened. I'll wager it was one heck of a mill. We're about to start a round of charades before nuncheon and you're just the fourth we need. Maman, you don't mind if Fitzstuart takes your place—"

"Henri-Antoine, please to be quiet. I think you have drunk too much of the marriage punch. Attend me. Alisdair he is leaving now and you will please forget you have seen him. Not a word. Not to Jack or anyone. *N'est-ce pas?*"

"If you wouldn't mind keeping it to yourself, Harry, I'd be much obliged," Dair said, a wink at his young cousin as he was shrugged into his greatcoat by the under butler. "His Majesty's business. You understand..."

Lord Henri-Antoine's dark eyes went wide as he watched his cousin take his hat and gloves from a footman. He tapped his long nose.

"Understood. Not a word." He kissed his mother's cheek and put an arm about her shoulders. "Then it is you, Maman, who are stuck with me, Jack, and the Reverend J—"

"Henri-Antoine? *Jenkins? Incroyable!* I leave the room for five minutes and me I am lumped with the chaplain?" Antonia was affronted. "Was that your brother's doing? He is a terrible player of charades, but Jenkins he is worse..." She allowed herself to be led back to the drawing room. "I have no idea as to what it is he is pretending to be! And me I cannot stop laughing behind my fan because he looks like a gasping *poisson*. It is most undignified."

"Who looks like a fish out of water, sweetheart?" Jonathon asked, putting a champagne flute into her hand. "Roxton wants to make a toast."

"The Reverend Fish," Lord Henri-Antoine whispered loudly, and skittered away before his mother could grab his arm. He blew her a kiss from the safety of the other side of the room.

Antonia smiled and blew a kiss back. A glance over her shoulder, just as the liveried footmen were closing the drawing room doors, and she saw the under butler securing the front door. Dair Fitzstuart had left the house.

TWELVE

Rory spent a fortnight campaigning her sister-in-law to accompany her to the Chelsea Physic Garden. She even co-opted her grandfather and Mr. Watkins to her cause. Both agreed fresh air, a picnic and different surroundings would lift Lady Grasby's spirits. Rory even tried to bore her witless, in the hope that incessant talk of pineapple propagation and the need for Crawford to consult with the gardeners at the Physic Garden would be enough to force Silla to say *yes* to the excursion. Lady Grasby remained implacable.

Rory's last line of attack was guilt. The visit to the Physic Garden had to be within the next three weeks. Rory and her grandfather were then off on their annual holiday to Hampshire, to the Duke of Roxton's estate, Treat. They would be away for a month. How could she leave her precious pineapple plants solely in Crawford's care if he had not been to visit the physic gardeners to know how to properly tend them?

Perhaps her grandfather would have to go to Treat without her this year? Although, this year was to be special because instead of staying up at the big house, the Duke and Duchess were giving them the use of the Gatehouse Lodge on the other side of the lake. The Lodge was at the end of the gravel drive up to the dower house, her godmother's delightful Elizabethan manor on the shores of the lake. She had been so looking forward to the swimming and the angling...

Lady Grasby would not be drawn out of her self-absorption, nor could she be made to have the slightest twinge of guilt. She took to having supper in her rooms, so as to avoid not only Rory's enthusiastic conversations, but also the conversations of the males of the household.

Everyone seemed to have forgotten not only the incident in question, but also the utter humiliation she had suffered at Romney's studio. Her humiliation was so great she was unable to venture beyond Talbot House for fear of being ridiculed. As for returning to the studio for the final sittings of her full-length portrait, that was now out of the question.

At the end of a fortnight not even her brother William, her stalwart defender, remained sympathetic. He grew weary of her continual need to relive the incident, and he went so far as to suggest that as an unmarried innocent, Miss Talbot's distress was far greater than what she had suffered. Lady Grasby had gaped at him, called him an unfeeling brute, and ordered him to leave her to her misery.

Lord Shrewsbury, who had little time for his grandson's wife as an individual, but valued her importance in the dynastic preservation of the Talbot line and the Shrewsbury earldom, took it upon himself to lecture her. He told her that exhibiting moral outrage because her husband cavorted with dancing girls was mundane in the extreme. It reeked of the behavior of the worst sort of Billingsgate fishwife. As the wife of a nobleman, she needed to get on with her only purpose in life: Producing an heir. Married almost three years and there was still no sign of a pregnancy, so what was wrong with her? His lordship's lecture was interrupted with the news his carriage awaited to take him to St. James's Palace. Which was just as well. Lord Shrewsbury fled his own book room to the sound of Lady Grasby's howling sobs.

The only member of the household who seemed unaffected by Lady Grasby's behavior was her husband. Aside from his altered sleeping arrangements, Grasby carried on with life as if the Romney Studio incident had never occurred. He spent time at White's. He dined out with Mr. Cedric Pleasant. He had meetings with his man of business, with his steward, and he was fitted for a new suit by his tailor. He knew his wife was being shamelessly self-centered and childish and it gave him pause to remember why he had married her in the first place: Not because he fell in love with her but because his grandfather said that with a dowry of fifty thousand pounds, she was the one he should marry. That she was beautiful certainly helped make up his mind. Part of him was flattered she was distraught by his behavior, it showed she cared. But he was as determined as ever not to give in to her demands to end his friendship with Major Lord Fitzstuart. That his best friend was languishing in the Tower accused of treason was of far more concern than his marital troubles. So was the fact his wife refused to accompany his sister to the Physic Garden, even though she knew Rory could not go without a female companion to an invitation-only all-male place of work and study.

But Grasby knew how to get his wife to bend to his will. Three years of marriage had taught him that much. While taking her supper alone, Grasby sauntered into his wife's presence and told her flatly that she was not to worry herself about being imposed upon to go anywhere. He would be taking his sister to the Physic Garden on the morrow, and her presence was neither required nor wanted, because the lovely Maria Hibbert-Baker had kindly agreed to be Rory's chaperone. If she wished to have the carriage, it was hers for the day, because he and his little party would be traveling by barge, an added treat for Rory and Maria.

His ruse worked. Drusilla instantly took exception to Maria Hibbert-Baker taking her place, as he knew she would. Had Grasby not married Drusilla Watkins, Maria was next in line to be asked. Later that same evening, Lady Grasby told Rory a leisurely sail down the Thames would be just the tonic she needed to clear her head. Perhaps while they were at the Physic Garden one of the apothecaries would be good enough to offer up the latest in herbal remedies for megrim.

Rory couldn't be happier the excursion was finally going ahead as planned. And because she was happy, so, too, was Grasby, William Watkins, and Lord Shrewsbury. For the time being at least, the Talbot household was at peace. And then it rained. There were unusual summer thunderstorms, and it continued to rain heavily all week. When next the sun shone brightly, ten days had elapsed and it was the day before Rory and her grandfather were due to set out for Hampshire.

Still time enough to visit the Physic Garden, in Lord Grasby's opinion. So off they went, in the Earl's private shallop, powered by eight beefy rowers in the Shrewsbury green and salmon-pink livery. The barge, with prow, stern and rail carved and gilded with fanciful sea creatures, was equipped with a carpeted indoor room with painted ceiling and gilded furnishings. A carpet was draped over this tilt, and there was even an awning of Plunkett blue cloth, providing shade from a summer sun that beat down fiercely for the first time in weeks, if one wanted to enjoy the cooling breeze off the river.

Rory had the most marvelous time strolling the Physic Garden, her party dutifully trailing behind her wherever she went. She could hardly contain her excitement and wonder at all she saw. She inspected various herb beds, listened attentively to the young apothecary-in-training who was their guide, and stared in awe at the only olive tree in England that had managed to thrive in the English climate. Though, she was not surprised that on such a hot day a native of the Mediterranean region was growing so well. For this comment she received such an enthusiastic response from the student apothecary, that when he took her and her party into the magnificent orangery, with all its glass panels and tub after tub of oranges, lemons and limes, he spoke almost exclusively with Rory. By the time they had moved on to the distillery and plant preparation areas, where medicinals were manufactured, he had lost his shyness and forgot all about the fact Rory was a pretty young woman.

Rory could not have been happier, particularly when the head gardener informed her he knew just the gentleman to discuss pineapple cultivation with her. He had taken the liberty to send word up to Banks House some twenty minutes earlier. Mr. Humphrey was an expert in bromeliads, and he lodged at Banks House, where he was presently enjoying his afternoon repast. He would send Mr. Humphrey to the barge, if Miss Talbot did not mind the inconvenience of having her nuncheon interrupted...?

It took mention of her grandfather's shallop for Rory to remember she was hungry, and that Grasby had come to fetch her ten minutes ago. He was patiently waiting by the imposing statue of Sir Hans Sloane, benefactor of the gardens. With mittened hand firmly about the ivory handle of her walking stick, she took her brother's crooked arm with the other, leaning on him a little heavier than usual. He scolded her lovingly for not taking the time to rest on one of the many benches dotted about the gardens, and said a straw hat was unlikely to provide her with enough shade on such a hot day as this. Where was her parasol?

"I gave it to Silla, who did not bring hers. You're right of course. I had quite forgot how ferocious the sun can be... Only now do I feel the ache in my ankle and hip—"

"Let's get you out of this heat... I sent Crawford off to eat his nuncheon with the rowers and the others who tagged along with us. We're all down at the south wall embankment."

"South wall...?"

"Where the shallop is docked."

"Oh! So *that* is the south wall." Rory tried to sound offhand. "Silly me! Always confusing my compass points."

"I decided the picnic was best had indoors or under the awning. It's far too hot out here in the open of the gardens. Besides," he added with a crooked smile, "Silla returned on board two hours after we set foot on dry land, citing the sun's rays as her enemy. So giving her your parasol was for naught." He sulked. "At least something else has upset her other than me!"

"Yes, at least," Rory murmured, distracted, "So the house—the one with the Jacobean chimney stacks on the other side of the wall—that must be Banks House…?"

Grasby wished he could see his sister's face, but it was hidden under the wide brim of her straw hat. Her innocently delivered question, however, did not fool him and he suspected it was accompanied by a blush.

"I wish we'd never had that conversation about Lily Banks. You're curious and you want to see her for yourself. And if I didn't know you better, and know that you do indeed have a keen interest in pineapples, I'd say this entire excursion is an excuse for you to go on tiptoe and peer over that fence to see what—"

"I don't need to go on tiptoe. And why shouldn't I be curious after what you told me about her?"

"I knew I'd regret confiding in you about Lily Banks. Dair doesn't talk about her, or his son, to anyone. But he just happened to confide in me the once. And now I've told you—"

"I have no intention of breaking your confidence, Harvel."

"But it hasn't stopped your curiosity, has it? There's really nothing more mysterious about her than what I told you. She's married and has had four more brats. What more could you possibly want to know?"

A great deal, in Rory's opinion. What did she look like? What was her nature? Was she a good wife and mother to her husband and sons? Did she still act as the Major's bawd? After all, he had invited her to Banks House and said Lily Banks would take her in, no questions asked. Did Dair Fitzstuart still care for her, and she for him? Perhaps her marriage was a sham, to cover her immoral relationship with the Major? Did their son truly look like his father? Was he worthy of his father, or was he spoiled beyond permission? Was it a happy household? Who lived at the house? Did they live in comfort? Was Mr. Banks accepting of his wife's child to another man? Did he love his wife? Was he a willing cuckold for his lordship? Was Mr. Humphrey just a lodger…? The list went on and on.

And until she saw Lily Banks and Jamie for herself, she was sure she would go on wondering and dreaming about them. Just as she dreamed about Major Lord Fitzstuart and that kiss, and why, in her grandfather's book room, he had acted as if he did not know her from a lump of sugar!

Her heart raced and she felt as giddy as a summer gnat trapped in an upended drinking glass, to think Banks House was within reach. All that separated the Physic Garden from this house was a low stone wall, built as a deterrent to four-legged beasts, not man, to stop them entering the Physic Garden and trampling and eating all the carefully laid out and tended specimens. There was even a closed, but unlocked, latched gate between the two properties, and a well-worn path that wended its way through the trees.

She was staring at the gate and wishing she could go through it, up to the house, on the pretext of introducing herself to the lodger, Mr. Humphrey, when, to her great surprise, a man appeared out from between the trees. He strode down the gravel path, then veered off it, crossed the small patch of grass covered in wildflowers wilting in the heat, and came straight up to them. Leaning a weathered forearm across the top of the low stone wall, he lifted his cap and smiled in greeting.

"Beggin' an interruption, kind lady and sir, but would you be the quality wishin' a word with Mr. Humphrey who lodges at Banks House?"

Grasby recoiled to be spoken to without giving the man permission to address him. Where was the servant's manners? One look at the rolled-up shirtsleeves and sunbaked forearms, the neckerchief tied about the red throat, and the gap-toothed smile in a sweaty face, and it was obvious that not only was the man an outdoor menial, he was at the base of that servile pecking order as well. But Rory stepped forward and lifted her chin so the servant could see her face.

"Yes, I am Miss Talbot, who wishes a word with Mr. Humphrey about his expertise in pineapples."

"I don't know anythin' about them there pine-whatsees, but the mistress sent me to apprehend if you would care to come up to the house, to have your word with Mr. Humphrey. The mistress also asked if you would care to join her in a cold cordial. It's fair wicked in this heat and there's shade in the garden—"

"Thank your mistress for her offer of hospitality," Lord Grasby enunciated coldly. "We have shade and refreshment enough on our barge."

"Where Drusilla and Mr. Watkins would rather we did not disturb them," Rory said behind her fluttering fan. "Besides, it would be rude to refuse the invitation—"

"—from someone we have never met? No, it would not be rude, it would save the embarrassment of having us foisted upon them," Grasby replied, not caring the man could hear every word. "Who sends a stable hand? Should be an indoor footman. Besides, it's not proper for my sister to make the introduction of such—*people*."

Rory again tilted her chin so the servant could see her face under the brim of her hat, and smiled at him. He had returned his felt cap to his balding head and was leaning his folded arms on the stone wall, patiently waiting a response, but at her smile, he lifted his cap again, seemingly unperturbed by his lordship's rudeness. She then turned angrily on her brother.

"Perhaps they do not possess an indoor footman? Perhaps the indoor footman is engaged elsewhere? Isn't it enough the offer was made, not how it was made?"

"It matters to me, and to any persons with manners," Grasby enunciated, nose in the air, the epitome of the arrogant nobleman. "There is a correct way of doing things, or better not to do them at all. And if persons don't know how to be correct, then they are mere knight and barrow pigs who aren't worth our condescension!"

"I never took you for a prig, Harvel. You are being petty-minded and obstinate to stop me going through that gate."

"What if I am! I am only thinking of your welfare. Best we remain on this side with our dignity intact, than on that side with who knows what kind of persons—spongers, smellfeasts and malaperts, for all I know!"

"That's just it. You don't know, do you?"

"I know more than you, and that's enough!"

Rory blinked. Perhaps her brother had been affected by too much sun and was not himself? She had never encountered him so rudely implacable, and, as far as she was concerned, without cause to be so.

"You call the Major your *friend*," she whispered fiercely, "yet you refuse to acknowledge *his* friends?"

"Ah, that's different, and he would agree with me. You're a female and my sister. You are a lady and shall remain one. I won't have your reputation—*or you*—corrupted by an association with persons of unknown lineage and dubious reputation. We already know one of their number has no reputation to speak of—"

"Reputation shredded by her *association* with *your* best friend! So that is hardly *her* fault, is it?"

"Ha! I told you. She was old enough to know better."

"I won't have you apportion *all* the blame on her. It takes two to make a baby. And I—"

"Steady on! Steady on!" Grasby demanded, taking a step away, shocked. "You've had a bit too much sunshine, sister dear—"

"—I have done the math," she enunciated. "He was only eighteen years old when his son was born, and she must have been younger. Not more than children themselves."

"You can't go declaiming loudly about the birds and bees," he said in a loud whisper, a significant sidelong glance at the servant, who continued to patiently lean on the stone wall. "Not before—"

"But according to you, Harvel, it doesn't matter what *we* say in front of our inferiors."

Grasby could offer no further argument, so he gave up and said on a sigh, "Come on, sugar plum, let's get you to the barge and some shade…"

"Harvel, we cannot refuse the invitation," she whispered. "We cannot. Mr. Humphrey has kindly offered to talk to me. When will I have another opportunity? Not for months. And the hostess of Banks House has offered us refreshment. These people are the friends of *your* best friend."

"Rory, to be honest, I don't know what these people mean to Dair. I certainly have not the least notion what Lily Banks means to him now. But one thing I do know, they are of inferior birth and not of our social circle, and as such we should stay well away."

"I do not agree with you, and I will not abuse hospitality freely given, from whatever quarter." When her brother threw up a hand and looked awkward she added, "Tell me this: Will sharing a cooling cordial with the occupants of Banks House and having a word with the Physic Garden's bromeliad specialist be any more of a corrupting influence on your sister than her sharing the chaise longue with the notorious mistress of the Duke of Dorset and her harlot friends at Romney's studio?"

"Oh, not you, too!" Grasby moaned with a roll of his eyes. He straightened, wiped a hand over his mouth, and let out a long breath of frustration. "I'm never going to hear the end of that piddling episode, am I?"

"No. Not unless you start treating people as you find them, not as your rank dictates you should." And before her brother could add anything further to the argument, Rory turned to the servant and accepted his mistress's kind offer with a smile. "We'll follow along shortly. I use a stick, so it will take me a little while to make my way along the path."

"Right you are, miss! I'll let Mrs. Banks and Mr. Humphrey know y'coming," the man replied with a grin, and with another doff of his hat, turned and walked back the way he had come, whistling as he went.

"I had a nice wedge of pheasant pie, a hunk of the best Cheshire, and a bottle of Bordeaux awaiting me at the barge," Grasby grumbled, opening the gate, then closing it again once Rory and he had passed through. "I hope you're pleased with yourself. And don't blame me when you get the shock of your life to find these people don't know the first thing about how to behave as they ought before the granddaughter of an earl!"

Rory let him see her cheeky smile of triumph. "Thank you, Harvel. But as *I* know how to behave as *I* ought, that's all that would matter to Grand."

He gave a grunt, offered his arm, and did not speak again until they were through the trees and at the edge of the lawn that swept left, down to a clump of willows along the river bank, and right, up to the house, a compact red brick Jacobean manor with ornate chimneys. A row of French doors that opened out onto a wide terrace were flung wide and secured against the outer brickwork by hooks, allowing ease of access into the house, and any breeze off the river to flow inside.

As the servant who had issued the invitation was nowhere to be seen, Grasby and Rory made for the terrace and the French windows. Here, in the shadow of the house, a carpet covered the tiles and set upon it was a dining table laden with a feast—a side of beef with all the trimmings, a leg of lamb, bowls heaped with vegetables, gravy boats and dishes of condiments, two large crusty loaves of bread, wine glasses and carafes. Dinner plates on either side of the feast held half-eaten meals, bone-handled knife and fork left atop the food. A child's frock coat was suspended from a chair back, and in another place, where the dinner plate should be, several wrapped packages were stacked and as yet unopened. Everything indicated a meal in progress. Yet, it was the chairs, pushed out and at every angle to the table, that told the story. It was as if the diners had left the feast in a great hurry. But why? What would cause more than half a dozen people to suddenly down knife and fork and flee?

Brother and sister looked at one another, mute, unable to provide a single plausible reason.

THIRTEEN

Lord Grasby was about to suggest to Rory they leave. It was beyond his comprehension why people would just up and abandon a splendid meal such as the one laid out before them. He saw no reason to wait it out and have his suspicions confirmed that the family were far beneath their touch. Besides which, staring at all that food just made him hungrier. If he didn't get back to the barge post-haste, to his pheasant pie and Cheshire cheese, he feared he would lose his mind to starvation, and help himself.

And then he instantly dismissed the idea of returning to the shallop. Rory's mittened hand was gripping his coat sleeve so tightly he knew it was only sheer force of will keeping her upright. The walk up to the house was twice the distance, and thus more than twice the effort it would have taken for her to reach the barge. She needed to rest and elevate her foot upon a stool. He would not have been at all surprised if there were blisters. And she needed refreshment.

Without asking, he picked her up and carried her to the closest chair, kicking it out wide from the table so he could sit her upon it. He then looked about for an empty tumbler amongst the dining table clutter. He found one at the far end of the table, where the child's coat and packages were, and also a jug of cordial. He filled the tumbler then stuck his nose into it and sniffed, before taking a sip of the cloudy bitter sweet liquid to taste if it was acceptable. Only then did he give it to Rory. When he told her to drink the lemon water because it was, in his opinion, perfectly acceptable refreshment, she did so without fuss. His precautions on her behalf to satisfy himself the cordial was suitable made her smile. He then went in search of a footstool, leaving her alone on the terrace as he crossed into the house.

Rory knew her right foot was blistered and taking a peek at her stockinged ankle, she saw that it was swollen. She itched to slip off her specially-constructed shoe and wriggle her toes. But she was not at home. With only herself to blame for wanting to visit Banks House, she was not complaining. She would not have missed this opportunity for anything. She cheerfully drank the rest of the lemon water and felt better. Sitting in the shade also helped, as did removing her straw hat, which she dropped into her lap. She prodded her coiffure with her fingertips then took up her gouache-painted fan that dangled from her wrist, unfurled it with a flick, and stirred the warm air across her flushed face.

When her brother did not reappear after five minutes, Rory became apprehensive. She hoped he wasn't giving its occupants a lecture on manners, or how to treat their social superiors. She was beginning to wonder if some of Silla's misguided ideas about her elevated station had rubbed off on him. Grasby had never cared for pernickety points of etiquette, claiming only dear old dowagers in their dotage were intent on enforcing rules that everyone in their circle knew practically from the cradle. But where were the occupants? Why had they left the table in a hurry? Where was Mr. Humphrey? What was so urgent everyone was required to be someplace else? What now had happened to her brother?

No sooner had she posed these questions than she was greeted by a great wall of noise. It made her jump. She was glad she had finished all the cordial in her tumbler for she certainly would have spilled it across the front of her glazed cotton petticoats. She turned from her view of the lawn and looked over her right shoulder to the French windows.

A great crowd of people spilled onto the terrace, or so it seemed to Rory. Men and women, both young and old, scampering boys, a crying baby in a basket, several loping dogs, and three young adult men deep in conversation and in no hurry at all. All were in high spirits and all resumed their places at the table, scraping in their chairs. Three little boys ignored Rory in their bid to satisfy their hunger, scrambling up onto their designated chairs with the help of the adults, and immediately taking up their forks to continue eating what food had earlier been put on their plates. The adults resumed their seats but did not eat, a smile of acknowledgement at Rory's presence, but seemingly too diffident to do anything more than nod mutely when she smiled in return.

Several maids followed the family onto the terrace, carrying even more dishes, and ice buckets holding bottles of wine which they placed at intervals in amongst the clutter. Next came a male servant carrying a footstool, and this was placed in front of Rory. The servant positioned it to her satisfaction and then took himself off, leaving Rory at a table of diners who knew she was there but treated her as if she was more specter than flesh. She breathed a sigh of relief when her brother reappeared, the sigh turning to a gasp when her gaze alighted on the dark-haired beauty at his side. She was grateful when a maid offered her a glass of wine. It gave her something not only to drink but to look at rather than stare at the woman who must be Lily Banks.

This was confirmed when they were introduced, Grasby coming to stand by her chair as Mrs. Banks proceeded to introduce the rest of her family seated about the table: Her grandmother Mrs. Clare Banks, her parents Mr. and Mrs. Harold Banks, her brothers Charlie and Eddie, and a cousin, Arnie, and four of her five sons. Clive, eight years old, wanted to be a soldier like his Uncle Fitz. Bernard, six, was going to sea to be a pirate. Oliver was three years of age and until two months ago had been the baby of the family, that is, until baby Stephen's arrival.

Rory had no way of knowing if the adult relatives were Lily's relations or her husband's, but it did not matter, nor could she hope to remember everyone's names, though she did her best to commit to memory the children's. The only family members not at the table were Lily's husband, who had departed on a voyage to the South Seas just two weeks ago, but who was home long enough to be at the birth of his fourth son, interrupted Grandmother Banks, which he had not been for the births of Bernard or Oliver.

"My eldest son, Jamie, is in the study setting up his microscope with the help of Mr. Humphrey, who knows about these things. Both should be joining us soon, unless," Lily Banks said with a smile, "they get so caught up in some scientific investigation that they forget the passage of time—"

"Which happens more often than not around here!" stuck in Father Banks with a grunt of laughter. "When he's preoccupied with somethin' or other, Jamie would forget to eat if we didn't put food in front of him!"

"Please, Lord Grasby, won't you sit?" Lily Banks asked. "There is plenty of food for an army, though all my boys but Jamie eat as if they are about to go into battle! Please," she insisted, and smiled when Grasby finally flicked out the skirts of his blue linen frock coat with silver lacings, and put his bony knees under the table. "We said grace earlier, so if you don't mind we shall continue with our birthday feast. Pass up your plates to Father Banks and he will cut you a few slices of beef and lamb."

Once Lily Banks was assured everyone at the table had what they needed, and were busy eating and drinking, the boys under the careful eye of their grandparents, she turned to Rory and Grasby and said matter-of-factly, "You must have wondered why the terrace was deserted, and so soon after I sent Old Bert with the invitation to speak with Mr. Humphrey here at the house. Please forgive me if I have separated you from your party. No sooner had Old Bert gone off to the gate than Mr. Humphrey tells me he saw you arrive by barge with a large group—"

"Don't concern yourself, Mrs. Banks," Grasby told her between mouthfuls with a smile, tucking in to the heaped plate of meat and vegetables put before him. "They were fatigued by the sun and are enjoying an afternoon nap, with little reason to think we are not amongst them. Isn't that so, Rory?"

Rory was amazed at how quickly her brother had adapted to his new surroundings, and how a kind smile and the attentions of a beautiful woman had done wonders to soothe any misgivings he may have had at sitting down to a meal with his social inferiors. And with a woman he had earlier intimated had the manners and morals so far removed from their own as to be considered unworthy of their notice. Regarding Mrs. Banks now, in her plain green linen gown and fitted jacket, black hair swept up and held by unadorned pins and one green ribbon, and no jewelry, she presented as any wife and mother of modest means and manners. It was her beauty that set her apart from her kinswomen, and from what Rory could deduce in all of five minutes of meeting her, she was modest about that, too.

She set down her wine glass, as if this had taken all her attention, and smiled at her hostess.

"As my brother says, it is of no consequence. Lady Grasby will be resting and completely oblivious to our truancy, though perhaps Mr. Watkins may be fretting as to our whereabouts. Perhaps we should send word...?"

"That won't be necessary—yet," Grasby stated, and, ignoring eye contact with his sister, said with a bright smile at Mrs. Banks, "You were about to tell us why the terrace was deserted..."

"Yes! We all went out to the front of the house to see the most magnificent carriage—"

"—pulled by six black high-steppers, with two outriders, and four footmen," stuck in Father Banks, slicing more beef for his grandsons' plates. "*All* in livery."

"And there was a coat of arms on the door—" began Grandmother Banks

"—belongin' to the Dukes of Roxton," finished Mother Banks. "Isn't that what you said, Arnie? Roxton? Here, Lily, pass the bottle up to his lordship. His glass is empty. And he's choked on his beef."

Grasby had swallowed and breathed at one and the same time at the mention of the Duke of Roxton. A glance exchanged with Rory confirmed they were thinking the same thing: What possible reason could the sixth Duke of Roxton, a proud nobleman of few words, have for calling at Banks house? It defied reasoning. And then their silent question was answered without the need to voice their incredulity.

"Imagine a birthday gift for our Jamie being delivered in such a carriage," Grandmother Banks declared with pride. "That's somethin' to remember for the rest of his days, ain't it?"

"It's not *that* hard to imagine, Granny, not when you know Jamie's father is—Argh! What was that for?" Charlie whined in a shrill voice, pulling back and rubbing his ear where his father had cuffed him.

"You know not to say it in company, Charlie," Father Banks warned, and went back to slicing more beef. "No one has the right except his lordship…"

"A'course we all had to see the carriage for ourselves," Grandmother Banks continued. "It's not every day—not *any* day—when a duke's carriage pulls up in front of our house! I don't think I've ever seen one so glorious. All black lacquer and gold paint. Do you remember ever seeing such a carriage, Eddie?"

Eddie Banks shook his head, a wary eye on his father. He wasn't going to put his tongue into the conversation and get his ear reddened. So cousin Arnie jumped into the conversational void to express the disappointment all the diners felt but had not voiced out loud.

"I only wish its noble occupant had stepped down from the carriage rather than have Jamie step up inside for a private word. Then we all could have seen her—"

"—and her fine clothes!" Mother Banks said on a wistful sigh. "Makes the gift-giving all the more special, don't it? To think our Jamie's the only one of us to have been inside a conveyance sat in by nobility. The inside would be lined with fine silks and brocades I imagine…"

"I doubt Jamie was thinkin' about the noble posteriors who've sat on those silk cushions!" Eddie Banks snorted, and received a similar cuffing as his brother; Charlie laughing loudly at his discomfort and thankful he wasn't the only one to embarrass himself before strangers.

"Poor Jamie was reluctant at first," Lily Banks confided to Rory and her brother, ignoring the activity at the far end of the table. "I couldn't blame him. To be summoned inside such a magnificent carriage all alone, and by a duchess! Any ten-year-old would be nervous."

"And not only a ten-year-old, Mrs. Banks," Grasby agreed. "I'd be shaking in my stockings to go it alone."

The young adult Banks brothers exchanged a wide-eyed stare before raising their glasses as one.

"Hear! Hear! That's what we said," offered Charlie and clinked glasses with his brother Eddie, both back in accord with each other.

Grasby put down his knife and fork, a glance at his sister. "So not the Duke of Roxton… It was Her Grace of Roxton who came calling?"

"Strange you should mention it, Lord Grasby," Lily Banks said, brown eyes equally wide. "I thought so too. But the liveried footman who delivered the summons that Jamie was to present himself at the carriage door, said a different name entirely—Kin-something…"

"Kin*ross*. Her Grace the Duchess of Kinross," Charlie announced with a superior smile. "Now may I mention the connection out loud, Pa? That footman did, so if the Duchess of Kinross owns to the connection…"

Father Banks gave a shrug of a shoulder and stuck out his bottom lip.

"It's up to your sister to say it or not. It hasn't bothered you 'til now, Lily, and it's not like we hide it. And Jamie has always known who his father is and what he is. His lordship acknowledges him as his own. But we got quality at the table today. Your past and his and the boy's parentage might not sit well with them…"

A small smile played about Lily Banks' mouth, and Rory held her breath, wondering if this was the moment for revelation, and if so, would she be able to detect if the lovely Lily was still in love with Major Lord Fitzstuart. Indeed, if they still had a connection, other than being the parents of an illegitimate son.

But when Lily Banks went to speak, Grasby intervened, and Rory could have kicked him.

"Not our business, why Her Grace of Kinross was here. If it's all the same to you, we'll just take it as read Her Grace came to speak to your son Jamie."

"If that is your wish," Lily Banks said calmly and returned to eating the rest of the vegetables on her plate.

"Pardon my female curiosity," Rory said into the heavy silence, Lily Banks' unquestioning submission to her brother's proclamation giving her voice an unintended edge, "but I have a great desire to know why the Duchess of Kinross came all the way from Westminster in the

Roxtons' magnificent carriage to give Jamie a gift. I presume today must be your son's birthday, Mrs. Banks?"

Lily nodded. "Yes. It is. He is ten years old today."

Rory glanced about the table, ignored her brother's significant look, and said as she cut her slice of beef into small chewable bites, "What a pity his lordship could not be here to share the day with his son…"

"Rory!" Grasby hissed under his breath. "You're playin' with fire, and I don't care for it."

"That's why the Duchess of Kin—*ross* came," Mother Banks volunteered, when no one else would reply after Lord Grasby's audible hiss. "She came with Jamie's gift because his father couldn't, and because Her Grace is Lord Fitzstuart's first cousin."

"Now, mother, you've gone and said it, and Lord Grasby here didn't want it to be said," Father Banks said with a shake of his head, though he didn't sound upset with her. "He possibly knows Lord Fitzstuart in his society. Still, I'm glad it's out in the open where it should be. Jamie is my grandson and it matters not a drop to me he was born on the wrong side of the blanket. I don't care who hears it or knows it! Not in this house. No offence, m'lord."

"None taken," Rory answered for her brother and rather too buoyantly for Grasby's liking. She looked about the table at the Banks family and saw that their attention was focused on her brother, who was cutting into this third slice of beef as if he needed to exert full force to ensure his meal was indeed dead. "Please. Won't one of you tell the rest of the story of the Duchess's visit…?"

All were willing to comply, and Grandmother Banks said,

"A footman pulled down the steps for Jamie to climb up inside the carriage, and another footman stood to attention at the open door, nose in the air as if he himself was a duke! Poor Jamie. He stood at the bottom of those steps peering up into the darkness as if it was a scaffold he was about to climb! But then Her Grace appeared in the doorway. What a sight she was! A real beauty. And wearing such heavenly silks and sparkling jewels befitting her rank. Though she needed none of it to improve what God has blessed her with."

"She was everything and more what you imagine in your dreams a duchess would look like," Mother Banks interrupted, eyes wide and voice full of awe. "Her petticoats were a lovely shade of soft pink, all covered in silver embroidery and spangles. And there was so much yardage that her petticoats filled the opening of the carriage! And I saw her shoe, too. A pointed toe and matching pink satin and silver thread. She was so lovely, she put out a gloved hand to coax Jamie up inside—"

"And we got to admire her heavenly bos—"

"—welcoming smile," Mother Banks interrupted her husband, giving him a swift dark look before again addressing Rory. "*Such* a beautiful lady. Of course my Lily is just as sweet-faced—"

"Oh, Mother!" Lily Banks laughed. "No one is as beautiful as the Duchess of Kinross. I'm sure Lord Grasby and Miss Talbot would agree heartily."

"Yes. Yes. Her Grace is said to be quite breathtakingly lovely for a woman of her age," Grasby muttered.

"And got the most admirable bosom I've yet set eyes on, too," Father Banks stated with satisfaction, a wink at Charlie, Eddie and Arnie, all of whom grinned from ear to ear. But what he said next turned their smiles into looks of abject disgust. He nudged his wife and said crudely, with a chuckle, "Not quite up to your sizable magnificence when you were at the height of your wet nursing powers, m'dear, but mighty close! What? Am I to beg everyone's pardon for sayin' what was before m'eyes?" he complained when not only his wife scowled at him, but so did his mother and his daughter.

He threw up his hands, got to his feet on a grunt, and made a bow before resuming his seat. "Beggin' your lordship and Miss Talbot's pardon for being so blunt. But I ain't used to speakin' before refined company. What I should have said, to put it in words my female family members would approve of is this," and he mimicked the awed wonder in his wife and mother's voice when speaking of their noble visitor, "The Duchess was wearing the prettiest embroidered bodice. Covered in tiny bows it was. So low-cut it was, too. Showed off her ample bosom to perfection. Well, mother, is that better?"

The entire table erupted into laughter at his mimicry that it took several seconds for everyone to calm down. Father Banks looked to his guests who were not laughing, but politely smiling.

"No offence but we do like a good laugh over our beef..."

"Please, Mr. Banks. You are not required to apologize at your own table," Rory replied. "We are *your* guests. Besides," she added, unable to suppress a smile, "I am all for plain speaking, and so is my godmother, Her Grace of Kinross. She will tell you so herself, she is not only famous for her beauty but for her—um—*décolletage*."

There was a collective sense of revelation and awe that the pretty young lady with the pale hair and fine features was the goddaughter of such a divine personage as the Duchess of Kinross. It was as if the Duchess herself had come amongst them and all had slack jaws of wonderment. The only person not impressed was Grasby, whose ears had turned bright red at Mr. Banks' speech. They grew hotter at his sister's confidence, though he was not at all surprised by her naïve truthfulness.

"Why his father saw fit to gift a ten-year-old boy a microscope is beyond me," Grandmother Banks stated to no one in particular, lifting a shoulder in dismay. "I thought his lordship might give him a pony of his own, or a cricket bat. That's more in keeping with what a ten-year-old boy should have."

"Granny, you know it is the perfect gift for Jamie," Lily Banks said mildly. "You saw his look of delight when he came out of the carriage, carrying that mahogany box as if it contained the most precious object in the world! He couldn't wait to go to the study, and he is still there with Mr. Humphrey. Both have forgotten that we are all here celebrating his birthday without him. But I do not wish to discourage his curiosity. Jamie wants to be a physician when he is grown," she confided to Grasby and Rory, and scooped up her crying baby out of its basket and cuddled him.

"Well, that's what he says today," stuck in Mother Banks.

"How splendid!" Rory enthused. "Then a microscope is the perfect gift. No doubt he and Mr. Humphrey are at this precise minute peering down the lens at a magnified beetle's wing, or at a flower petal. I'm sure he'll soon move on to more interesting matter such as a flea's leg and blood from a rat—Oh! Excuse me. That was not polite of me, was it?"

"My sister also has a keen interest in all things scientific," Grasby explained, hoping to turn the conversation to a more general topic that was more in keeping with the dinner conversation he was used to. "Her principal interest is in plants—pineapples to be specific. Which is why we are here to see Mr. Humphrey... Do you—do any of you know anything about the pineapple...?"

"No, my lord. We don't. But our lodger Mr. Humphrey I am sure will offer up an evening's worth of discourse on the subject! And there's nothin' to forgive, Miss Talbot," Father Banks stated as he scraped back his chair and stood. He pulled the napkin from the front of his waist-coat and dropped it on the table. "The conversations that go on at this table between my son-in-law, when he returns from one of his expeditions, and Mr. Humphrey, would turn your fair hair black, Miss Talbot. Full of rats, pestilence and pygmies! Still, got to be more civilized than hearin' about amputations and savages runnin' amok, which is what we get when Jamie's father and his batman put in a rare appearance. Now, my three monkeys," he said, rubbing his hands together as he addressed his grandsons, "if you have demolished all that is on your plates, I'd say it's time for that game of cricket I promised. Eddie. Charlie. Arnie. Which of you three is batting first?" he asked, as his sons and nephew scrambled to their feet. "Perhaps his lordship would care to join us in the game?"

Lily Banks' two eldest boys ran up to Grasby and stood by his chair. "Would you? Would you play cricket with us, sir? Would you? *Please.*"

"How can you refuse such eager little faces, Harvel?" Rory laughed at the resignation on her brother's face and said confidentially to the two little boys, "My brother is very good with the bat. But don't let him bowl. Put him in the outfield where he can take a catch."

"Thank you very much!" Grasby declared, reluctantly putting aside his napkin. "I have been known to take a wicket or two."

"Two. That's all you've taken!"

"So much for a lazy day on the river," Grasby grumbled with false resignation, but with a smile at the two little grubby faces eagerly peering up at him.

He shrugged out of his frock coat, Arnie Banks coming to his aid and laying the article over the back of Grasby's vacated chair, but not before covetously eyeing the cut of the cloth, the worked metal buttons and the delicate silver thread embroidery on the upturned cuffs and pockets.

Grasby removed the lace ruffles at his wrists and proceeded to roll up his billowing sleeves to just below his elbows. "Thank you for a most splendid repast, Mrs. Banks," he added with a short bow to Lily.

But when he straightened, Rory saw he was pale and she quickly grabbed her stick to stand, a natural response, but one that was not warranted when he turned and strode off in pursuit of Father Banks and his three sons. She soon realized the reason for her brother's lack of color when she accepted a cup of tea from Mother Banks. Lily Banks had untied the front of her linen jacket and had put her son to her breast, the baby suckling contentedly. Rory smiled, given the earlier conversation she had had with her brother on this precise topic.

It was on the tip of her tongue to enquire about the baby when the cascade of lace at her left elbow was unceremoniously given a tug. She put her teacup on its saucer and turned to find six-year-old Bernard standing by her chair. He had not followed his brothers Clive and Oliver down to the lawn with the men, but stood staring at her. When Rory smiled, he pointed to the footstool and said bluntly,

"Your foot is crooked. What's wrong with it?"

FOURTEEN

BERNARD! HUSH! THAT IS NOT A QUESTION TO ASK OUR VISITOR."

It was his mother and she was mortified.

"But her foot is all wrong, Mamma. Look!"

"Her name is Miss Talbot, and you are being discourteous. Please forgive him, Miss Talbot. He has always been the blunt one in the family, and the most inquisitive. He has to know about everything."

"It's perfectly all right, Mrs. Banks. When I was your age, Bernard, I would ask my grandfather so many questions he looked as if he was about to burst and his wig pop off his head." She smiled when the little boy giggled. "I will answer your questions, if I am able."

"Can you walk with your foot like that?"

"I walked here. In fact, I walked around those gardens on the other side of the wall, and then I walked up the path through the trees to your house," she answered calmly as she brushed her petticoats over her ankles. "I use a walking stick. Here. Would you like to take a closer look?" She held out her stick to Bernard. "Do you see the pineapple carved into the handle?"

Bernard readily took the stick and peered at it as if it was the most fascinating object he had ever seen, from the intricately carved ivory handle that resembled a pineapple fruit, down the length of its polished mahogany stem, to the worn end. He asked curiously,

"Do you need this to walk always?"

"Not always, but it is better to have it as not, so I don't trip and fall."

"Can you hop?"

"On my left foot, yes."

"Skip?"

"With great difficulty."

"Jump?"

"Up and down? Yes. But only if I am *very* excited."

Bernard smiled, then asked, "What about run? Can you do that?"

"No."

"Not even if a great big bear was chasing you?"

"No. Not even then. I would try, of course. But I'm afraid if a bear was chasing me it would catch me. Do you think if I asked it, it would dance with me?"

"Silly! Bears don't dance; not unless they're on a chain and been trained."

"You're right, of course."

"A bear would eat you as soon as look at you!"

"Bernard! How awful of you to say so," Lily Banks chastised.

"But true." Rory smiled at the little boy. "Don't worry. I will make certain to stay indoors if I hear there are any bears loose from Brookes's Menagerie on the Tottenham Court Road."

"Can you ride?"

"Yes. Riding makes it easier for me to get from place to place."

"You have boots?"

"Yes. Special ones."

"Can you get your foot fixed?"

Rory shook her head. "Sadly, no. This foot is with me forever, just as you will always have curly hair, except when it is wet. Then it is straight, isn't it? But my foot is the same, wet or dry."

Bernard had a thought and his eyes opened wide.

"Swim! Can you swim? Can you swim like a—like a—*mermaid*?"

It was his mother who laughed.

"Bernard! You do have silly notions. Miss Talbot needs her stick to walk; she can hardly use it in the river to swim."

"I beg your pardon, Mrs. Banks, but Bernard's notion is an excellent one," Rory countered, gaze remaining on the little boy who had flushed to be admonished before a stranger. She smiled and took hold of his hand and drew him closer. "I think you are very clever to think I can swim. I don't need my stick in the water, do I? The water keeps me afloat."

"Do you—do you swim like a mermaid?"

"I have never seen a mermaid, so I do not know how they swim. Perhaps my grandfather has seen one, because he was the one who taught me to swim, and I can swim very well indeed."

"With your arms; not your legs."

"Oh, you *are* clever! I do use my arms more than my legs, though I can kick with my legs, which helps me along." Rory took a sip of her milky tea. "Any more questions?"

Bernard shrugged. "No. If I think of more can I ask you?"

"Of course."

"Thank Miss Talbot for answering your questions—"

"Thank you."

"—and now leave Miss Talbot to sip her tea in peace," Lily Banks said firmly. "Off you go and play with your brothers."

Bernard handed Rory her stick with a shy smile then raced across the terrace, down the steps and out onto the lawn to join in the game of cricket. When he looked over his shoulder, Rory waved to him. He gave a wave in return and did a tumble on the grass for good measure. Turning to Lily Banks, Rory was about to say how much she was enjoying the afternoon and to thank her for sending Old Bert to invite them up to the house; she hoped she would see Mr. Humphrey and meet her son Jamie before it was time for her and Grasby to return to the barge. But instead of this calm speech of thanks, she said nothing at all.

She received a shock and lost the grip on the handle of her teacup. It clattered to the saucer and toppled. The drop of tea left in the cup splashed over the lip of the saucer and stained the blue satin riband nestled in the crown of her straw hat still resting on her lap. She was just grateful the tea had not found its way to her flowered petticoats. Still, she made a fuss with the hat, if only to regain her equilibrium and hope the heat in her face had faded enough for her to look at the new arrival.

First her book, and now her teacup. He would surely think her the clumsiest female in existence!

Out onto the terrace had stepped Major Lord Fitzstuart.

A MUD-SPATTERED GREAT COAT CONCEALED A DARK PLUM RIDING frock and buff breeches, and with his jockey boots similarly caked in mud, the Major looked to have been astride a horse all day, and in varying degrees of inclement weather. He still wore kid riding gloves, but had removed his black felt hat, revealing unruly shoulder-length black hair, damp from exertion or rain, or both. Gone was the bruising to his eye and the deep cut to his lip had healed, leaving a small purple scar. His skin had a healthy glow, as if he had seen many days of sun, and the dark, close-cropped beard gave him a piratical appearance. But it was at his eyes Rory stared without blinking. He was tired, as if he hadn't slept in a week, and he was staring at her in a way that suggested he wanted her to read his thoughts. Those thoughts were most discomforting, because she received the strongest impression he was not pleased to discover her at Banks House.

She was the first to look away, and fussed with her teacup and saucer, placing it on the table. She then inspected the stained silk ribbon as if it required all of her attention. In her forced preoccupation, the Major stepped forward and made his presence known to Lily Banks. Rory pretended not to notice, but out of the corner of her eye she saw him remove his gloves and place a bare hand lightly on Lily's shoulder. The grazes to his knuckles had also healed, and his hand, like his face, was sun-bronzed. He stooped, said something at Lily Banks' ear, kissed her cheek, then stood tall. That kiss, light and perfunctory as it was, had the power to make Rory blush, and with abject despondency. And when Lily Banks half-turned in her chair with an exclamation of delightful surprise, the baby still at her breast and a hand out to Dair in greeting, Rory's blush ripened into one of unwanted interloper.

Here was a couple pleased to see each other; a couple used to intimacy; a couple who shared a child...

For the first time since arriving at Banks House, Rory wished she had taken her brother's advice and returned to the barge. For a reason only known to her heart, she felt a great pressure in her chest. It was pain, the aching pain of affection not reciprocated or wanted. She was such a fool! He had never singled her out in the past, why, after a drunken kiss he did not remember, would he single her out now?

As if in answer to her question, he made her a small bow when Lily Banks mentioned her by name, though she was so deep in her thoughts she had no idea what was said. But it did not matter, the acknowledgment had been made and that was all that was required of him. He did not look at her again, nor did he include her in his conversation.

The oppressive feeling pressed down even further watching the interaction between the parents of Jamie Banks. Yet she could not dislike Lily Banks or feel any jealousy toward her just because the Major was at ease in her company. Lily Banks was no bawd. She did not flirt with him, or act in any way that indicated they were anything but friends of long-standing. Why was it, she wondered, that females who had children out of wedlock were instantly branded the lowest forms of life, incapable of constancy, honesty and decent behavior? And yet, their male counterparts were thought anything but immoral. She had always scowled at such uneven standards. Of course, Harvel branded her bookish and said she would be locked up as mad if she ever dared voice such thoughts in decent company. Silla had called her ruminations wicked and never to be repeated, certainly not in front of the vicar.

The general flurry of activity sparked by the Major's arrival allowed Rory to retreat into the background, to her usual place as observer at gatherings. In many ways, it was a relief not to have his eyes upon her; it helped quiet her heart, and permitted her to drink a second cup of tea without spilling a drop.

Servants scurried back and forth from the house. Great coat, gloves and hat were taken away. Dirty plates and empty bowls were removed from the table. A space was cleared for the new arrival. Clean plate and cutlery, fresh bread, a tumbler and a jug of ale were all placed before him. And the Major did not hesitate to fill his plate with the remnants of the birthday feast, saying in answer to Lily Banks' question, when his mouth was empty,

"You'd be famished too if you'd not eaten a good English meal in over a month!" He pulled a chunk of crusty bread from a fresh loaf and sopped up gravy. When he could speak again, he said with a grin, "Two slices of beef and I'm already feeling human again. No! Don't say it. I know. It will take a shave and a bath before I can present as human, but I wanted to get here as soon as possible." He looked out at the cricket game in progress. "I don't see Jamie. Where is my birthday boy?"

Lily Banks told him about the visit of the Duchess of Kinross and the presentation of the microscope, adding after she had tied and adjusted her jacket, baby put to her shoulder to gently rub his back to settle his stomach, "He's in the study with Mr. Humphrey, peering at all sorts of queer objects through a lens. Poor Miss Talbot has come to see Mr. Humphrey specifically, and Jamie has taken all his time, so has yet to show himself."

"Then get them out of there, Lil. I didn't gift him a microscope so he could monopolize your lodger's time and attention. Not when Humphrey is wanted elsewhere. And I don't want Jamie neglecting his food and his obligations. Did his brothers eat their dinner at the table with the rest of the family?"

"Yes, of course."

"Then why not Jamie?" Dair asked quietly.

"He did. We all started our meal, then were interrupted by the Duchess's carriage. But poor Mr. Humphrey did not have the opportunity to finish what was on his plate once Jamie saw what was in the mahogany box."

"Lil, he should have come back to the table. He's the eldest. He needs to set the example. And don't say because it's his birthday he can be shown leniency. He does it every time he can get away with it. He should not have had access to the microscope until after he'd finished his meal with the family. And he should have been made to wait until Humphrey had eaten his fill. That's just good manners. The poor chap's stomach must be growling!"

"Yes. Yes, of course. You're right," Lily Banks murmured and scrambled to her feet. "You know how he is when he gets distracted... He's so terribly clever. Much more clever than the rest of us."

Dair poured himself another tumbler of ale.

"Being clever is not enough. He needs to know how to use his cleverness in the right way. He still needs to be mindful of others. And he needs to spend time out of doors, enjoying fresh air, sunshine and cricket, like every other boy his age."

"He prefers the study..." When Dair made no reply and drank down his ale, Lily added quietly. "I'll have him fetched at once..." When she went to put the baby back in his basket he began to fuss, so she just stood there, flustered, wondering what to do with him.

Without a second thought, Dair put out his arm, took the grizzling infant and held him to his chest, a large hand spanning the tiny back to keep him firm and upright, the baby's wet chin resting on his shoulder. Sensing she was still there, he said quietly,

"Don't take it to heart, Lil. I'm tired... I'll stay the night, if it's not too much of an inconvenience—"

"Never. Your room is always made ready."

When he smiled and nodded, Lily Banks disappeared inside the house, leaving a heavy silence at the table. Rory wished the two older Banks women, who were seated at the furthest end of the terrace, heads together talking, would turn and notice the new arrival. She hoped Jamie and Mr. Humphrey were not long in coming. She put her teacup on its saucer and lifted her gaze to the sight of the small bundle cuddled against the Major's chest, while he continued to eat ravenously, using his fork as best he could, with only one hand free, to cut as well as scoop up the vegetables on his plate. He held the infant unselfconsciously, as one adept at doing so, and as if his embrace were the most natural and most comforting place to be.

There was something wonderful about a big handsome man holding such a tiny, vulnerable little being with one large protective hand. It brought inexplicable tears, tears Rory quickly blinked away. She mentally admonished herself for being sentimental, that even this small domestic scene involving the Major had the power to provoke such an emotional response in her.

She turned her gaze to the lawn and watched the cricket match in progress. Her brother, in the outfield, sleeves rolled to the elbow, had a hand up, shielding his eyes from the sun. One of the Banks brothers was batting. Another was bowling. The three boys were doing tumbles on the lawn with only a halfhearted interest in the game. Rory suspected the adults were completely dominating the match, so the children had lost interest. She looked away, to see if the Banks women still had their heads together. They did. She returned her attention to the table, and was startled to find the Major regarding her steadily. He must have had his eyes on her profile for some time, such was the intensity in his gaze, and when she did not look away he said flatly,

"Before you dare to ask what you are thinking, Miss Talbot, the answer to the burning question is no, this brat is not mine. Nor are his three elder brothers. They have a father and their mother is a devoted wife. Only Jamie belongs to me."

"Thank you for being frank, my lord," Rory replied levelly. Despite a heaviness of heart, she was affronted by his presumption. "But I do not thank you for thinking you can read my mind. It will surprise you to know that what I was truly thinking was what a wonderful job Mrs. Banks has done in raising her sons, mostly on her own; what with her husband the intrepid explorer, and you, an officer, leaving her alone for extended absences. I was also thinking how lovely it must be to have other family members around at such times. Not having uncles or aunts or parents, and only one grandparent, it was such a pleasure for Harvel and me to sit at a table with a large happy family group. It reminded me of the few times we visited my godparents at Treat—"

"Miss Talbot, I apologize if I offended—"

"My lord, you should wait until I have finished my diatribe before you decide if you owe me an apology or not," Rory interrupted, the sparkle back in her blue eyes when he promptly closed his mouth and glanced away. "As we are being frank, then let me be also. Even though it is none of my concern, if Jamie has a gift for science, and his natural inclination is to spend his time peering into lenses and classifying insects and plants, and whatever else catches his interest, then his mother is wise to let him do as he pleases, rather than force him to do what pleases you. I have never met your son—"

"—and yet you presume to know him?"

Rory smiled crookedly. She wanted to say that though she did not know the son, she was confident she understood the father's proclivities. Instead she said, a little less stridently than before, "No. Not him. But if you cast your mind back to your tenth birthday, as I have done, can you remember what you were eating? I surely cannot. But I am confident you remember what you were doing…"

Dair did not hesitate to answer. He shifted the baby to his other shoulder, again holding him there with a splayed hand, and said bluntly,

"I was outdoors skimming stones on the lake. I preferred—I prefer —to be outdoors. Anywhere but a book room. Such stuffy rooms give me the headache. Charlie and I were waiting for our father to join us. He was in his study; a place he rarely left. He'd been watching Charlie and me from his study window… When he finally joined us he gave me a birthday gift I will never forget. The next day he departed for London. We never saw him again. And before you make comment," he added with a thin smile, "I am not forcing Jamie out-of-doors because that is what I did at his age, or what I think he should be doing. He needs to be reminded he is one of five brothers, and on this of all days. Between you and me, his mother, his grandparents—even Lily's husband—all indulge him more because of who he is, rather than because he is clever. My great-grandfather was Charles the Second, so he has royal blood in his veins, however polluted, and one day I will be Earl of Strathsay. That's a heady mix for his mother's family, whose antecedents never rose beyond their position of servant these past three hundred years. But it does not remove the stain of his illegitimacy."

Rory cocked her head and said pensively, "Perhaps that bothers you more than it does them…"

This forced from him a reluctant laugh. "Yes, perhaps it does…" He glanced over at the two older Banks women. "Lil's mother was the family wet nurse, then nursery maid; her father was a gardener on the estate… That is, until the unthinkable happened—"

"You fell in love with Lily Banks."

Dair put down his fork, pushed his plate away and took up his tumbler. He drained the cup. She sensed he was about to confide something in her, but the sudden commotion at his back forestalled him and the moment was lost. He scraped back his chair, Lily Banks scooped up her baby, and a tall thin boy ran up to be crushed in his father's embrace.

There wasn't a dry eye on the terrace at this loving reunion between father and son; even Rory was quick to dab tears away before anyone noticed.

The hubbub brought the older Banks women scrambling off the wall and bustling to the table. They embraced Jamie's father. Mother Banks took Dair's handsome face between her hands and heartily kissed his forehead before enveloping him in a crushing embrace. Dair laughed when she scolded him for not alerting them to his presence, nodded obediently when she enquired if he had enough to eat, and grinned when she said it was just as well because she did not want him dying of hunger after surviving all those years as a soldier. She had a vested interest in his welfare. After all, she had been his principal source of nourishment from birth until two years. Whereupon Lily Banks told her mother to hush, and that she made the same observation every time Al (for that was what Lily called the Major) came to visit after one of his long spells away. And this last spell had been all of five weeks.

Dair took the attention in his stride, laughing and grinning and shaking his head at the women, before drawing his son to sit on his knee to tell him all about his birthday.

"I do always say it, too," Mother Banks confided to Rory as she eased herself onto a chair as a pinch-faced maid put a fresh cup of tea before her. "But I ask you, Miss Talbot, why shouldn't I say it? I'm proud his lordship has grown into a mountain of a man. What wet nurse wouldn't be? He was not a big baby. There was a time, just after he was born, when his father worried he wouldn't survive. But I told the Earl I'd get his heir through his first year, and I did. Truth told," she added in a confidential undertone, pulling her shawl closer about her round shoulders and leaning in to Rory's chair, "I'm not surprised he was such a scrawny baby. Starved, of nourishment and affection. The Countess was a cold woman *in every sense*. Loathed the begetting, the birthing, *and* the feeding of children. That's God's honest truth!"

"*Mother*! Miss Talbot is unused to such conversation. She is a *lady*," Lily Banks whispered fiercely, an eye to the Major, who was holding his son's hands and attentively listening to the boy's wide-eyed recounting of his visit with the Duchess of Kinross in the opulent interior of her carriage. "I dare say she is not only embarrassed, but offended, too. Poor Miss Talbot came here to speak to Mr. Humphrey about pineapples, not hear your stories about Al as a baby. Forgive my mother, Miss Talbot. Mr. Humphrey should be here directly. I don't know what is still keeping him…"

Rory smiled and swallowed and hoped her face was not the color of beetroot; Mother Banks' eye-opening revelations would have knocked her brother off his seat with shocked mortification. He certainly would have used them as a prime example of why he had not wished his sister exposed to the crude sensibilities of the Banks family. But watching the Major and his son interact, the obvious love they had for each other, indeed the entire Banks clan's great affection for Lord Fitzstuart, and his affection of them, was a balm to her finer feelings. For how could she truly be offended by Mother Banks' truthfulness when couched with the warmth of feeling she had for the Major? Besides, her own behavior was wanting, for if she had stared at Lily Banks' beauty when she first saw her, she stared twice as hard now at the beautiful boy with the mop of dark red curls who had his father's dark eyes. Oh, Jamie Banks would break hearts just like his father when he was old enough...

"Miss Talbot...?"

It was the Major. He brought her out of her abstraction, an arm about his son's shoulders. "Jamie, this is Grasby's sister, Miss Talbot. You remember Lord Grasby—he accompanied us to Mr. Pleasant's shooting box..."

"Grasby? Yes, I remember Grasby." The boy made Rory a quaint little bow and said solemnly, "How do you do, Miss Talbot?"

"I am very well, Jamie. May I call you Jamie?"

The boy smiled. "Everyone does."

"I should like to see your microscope one day, if you will allow me."

The boy's eyes lit up. "Would you? Mr. George Adams of Fleet Street made it," he said with awe. "He makes the best microscopes. It's brass and has *three* Lieberkuhn objectives, so I have both a compound body and a simple magnifier. And it all comes apart and fits into this big wooden case..." He looked up at his father. "May I show her, Papa? May I?"

"Of course. But not today. Miss Talbot must leave us now, and you need to eat the rest of what you left on your plate. But before you finish off your nuncheon," he added, picking up Grasby's frock coat, "please take this to Lord Grasby and tell him not to wait. I'll bring Miss Talbot to him."

Rory was about to enquire why his lordship was terminating not only her visit but her brother's involvement in the game of cricket, when the Major turned away to speak with a rotund gentleman in bagwig and spectacles who had just stepped onto the terrace from the house. Their conversation was brief and then the gentleman followed Jamie down the terrace steps to the lawn. Rory watched his progress and sat up when three figures on the edge of the lawn came into view. Jamie was still holding her brother's frock coat; Grasby had his back to the cricket game, hands on his hips, while the third figure was slightly bent forward with his hands clasped, as if in supplication, yet he was the one doing all the talking. It was one of the footmen from the shallop, and by his stance, and her brother's arms akimbo, she was certain the servant was giving Grasby an earful of complaints, courtesy of Lady Grasby.

FIFTEEN

Dair put out his hand to Rory. "Come. Let me help you up."

She removed her feet from the footstool and he kicked it out of the way with the toe of his boot. Helping her to her feet, he held her hand until she was steady and leaning on her stick.

"Did you come by carriage?"

"No. My grandfather's shallop."

"By river? How pleasant for you. The return journey should give you ample time to have a full and frank discussion with Mr. Humphrey about your pineapple flower—your first, I believe?"

"You remembered the flower?"

"You dropped a treatise on gardening at my feet, and you were so excited. If it is possible for blue eyes to shine, they were shining then. I gather the plant does not flower often?"

"Crawford and I have waited two years to see one. A flower means a pineapple fruit is not far away."

"Then it is rare and something to be animated about. I hope Mr. Humphrey's advice is useful. Now please give your stick to Mrs. Banks." When she hesitated, he smiled. "You'll get it back." Done as requested, he took a step away, still holding her hand, and looked her up and down, gaze pausing at the point of her beribboned bodice that highlighted her small waist. "If I'm not mistaken, under those fetching flowered petticoats are a set of light-weight panniers?"

"Yes. But—"

"No buts, Miss Talbot. I am now going to pick you up. As I do so, please bunch up your petticoats to collapse the panniers. It will make my task that much easier. Mrs. Banks will then return your stick, which you will hold without accosting me, and I shall then carry you to your barge. Understood?"

"Yes. But—"

He didn't wait to hear her excuses. He effortlessly lifted her and she quickly did as he asked, Lily Banks coming to her aid to brush down the layers of light cotton over Rory's stockinged shins. She was then handed her stick. Hurried farewells and thank-yous exchanged, Dair strode off across the terrace towards the trees that provided privacy between the south wall and the Physic Garden. But he had not gone more than fifty paces when he stopped under the shade of a spreading oak.

"Miss Talbot, if I am to deliver you to your barge without incident, you need to be supple in my arms. Not a plank of wood, for that is what I am carrying at the moment."

"I can walk!"

"You can. But not in your present state. Mrs. Banks mentioned you have blistered your feet. I'd wager you're stubborn enough to still walk, just to spite me. But don't think of yourself, think of your brother. In the time it would take you to walk back to the barge, I fear Grasby may have jumped overboard and be lost to the tangle of Thames reeds. I gather her ladyship is aboard your vessel?"

"Yes. And most reluctantly, too. Harvel and I left her and Mr. Watkins alone for quite some time…"

"Thank you."

Rory tilted her head to look at him. His face was so close she could see the individual hairs of the beard covering his cheeks and jaw. It was black, like the hair that fell across his brow… Like the hairs on his chest… With the light browning to his skin he did indeed look the pirate.

"Thank me? For what, pray?"

"For not bringing her ladyship and Weasel up to Banks House."

"Oh, they'd not have come within a hundred feet of the place! Oh! That was—"

"—the truth. I'm surprised Grasby gave you permission to do so."

"He didn't. But he could not stop me."

He chuckled.

She smiled, liking the sound.

"Of that I have no doubt. You're a determined little thing, aren't you?"

"I was invited—invited to Banks House…"

He did not hesitate in his response, and sounded surprised.

"Were you?"

"Yes. But… But I won't tell you who invited me because you would be more than surprised. You would be shocked."

"Would I? I am not a man easily shocked, Miss Talbot."

"That I believe. You must have had some horrifying experiences while in the army."

"Yes."

He set off again and had only gone a few yards when she said quietly,

"I hope I'm not too much of a burden."

"Not at all. I've carried wounded soldiers from a battlefield. Believe me, when men are dead or dying, they are twice their weight. You, Miss Talbot, are as light as a fairy's gossamer wings."

"I apologize."

"Apologize…?"

He tried to see her face but she looked away, a quantity of hair having escaped from an enameled hair clasp falling across her brow. He had no way of knowing her mood. What he did know was that he liked having her in his arms again, very much. Yet, the sensation was also oddly disconcerting, as if he had no right and no reason to hold her. There seemed to be nothing of her. She was delicately-boned, small-breasted, and he wondered if under the yards of glazed cotton she had any curves at all. Why did she befuddle him so? Why, when he had stepped onto the terrace, and discovered her sitting there in her pretty flowered petticoats, was he overwhelmed with the desire to scoop her up and kiss her?

Why did she feel she had to apologize? God, he hoped she wasn't going to mention the night at Romney's studio. If she did, he would have to lie to her again and plead complete drunken ignorance, as he had promised her grandfather he would. And that was another thing that bewildered him. He was uncomfortable with the thought of lying to her, of keeping up the subterfuge of indifferent dolt. For the first time in many years he had no wish to play-act. He just wanted to be himself; to be himself *with her*.

When she shifted slightly in his arms, interrupting his thoughts, he caught the faint perfume of lavender in her hair mingled with the scent of vanilla from her warm skin. It was such an evocative scent it shot a quiver of need straight from his nostrils to his loins, and nothing had stirred there since the last time he had held her. Alarmingly, his bewildered brain was not the only organ gone soft!

With just over a month abroad, and a bevy of curvaceous talent offering themselves to him each night, he had had ample opportunity to forget Aurora Talbot, to reassure himself he was still a fully-functioning male capable of satisfying any woman. So why had he elected to sleep cold and alone while in Lisbon? How had it come to pass that he had returned to English soil in the same emasculated condition he had left it, a non-functioning male; for all intents and purposes, a eunuch?

This shameful state of affairs could not be allowed to continue or he would go mad. And he reasoned there was only one cure. If he kissed Aurora Talbot again, he would be able to satisfy himself that the kiss shared at Romney's studio had been a whim and nothing special. He did not want it to be special; it could not be anything but ordinary. There was no room in his life for sentiment, particularly with a gently-bred female from within his own social circle. Sentiment carried with it the expectation of marriage, an institution he reviled. After witnessing years of his parents' hate-filled union, he had sworn never to succumb to the oxymoron that was "wedded bliss." It might do for his brother Charlie, but Charlie was younger. Charlie had not seen the violence and vitriol of two people trapped in a marriage neither could escape. Charlie was not the heir; not the one their mother had confided in, to whom she had pinned all her hopes and expectations; not the one their father played as if he were a marionette, using marriage as a lure and a penance for his own sins.

One kiss shared with Aurora Talbot and he would be satisfied that he was no more or no less attracted to her than he was to any pretty female who caught his wandering eye. One kiss, and his life would return to its previous untroubled state before the incident at Romney's studio, where he was able to fall into bed with a certain sort of female, make love with mutual abandon and satisfaction, then move on to the next beautiful nymph who gave him a come-hither smile—no questions asked, and no expectations of anything other than what it was, for either party.

So the sooner he kissed Aurora Talbot, the sooner his equilibrium would be restored.

Taking a moment to collect his thoughts, he cleared his throat as well as his mind, and said with mild disinterest to her statement of apology,

"I beg your pardon, Miss Talbot, but I see no reason for you to offer me an apology."

"Oh, I know there isn't a thing either of us can do to change the past. But just because we cannot change events, does not mean I cannot change my opinion. And it cannot stop me feeling the way I do, now that my opinion has altered. Does that make sense?"

"Perhaps you need to explain it to me more fully?"

"May I?"

"By all means," he replied blandly, thinking that if he allowed her to babble on it might help him ignore how she made him feel.

"Thank you... You see until you mentioned just now about carrying the dead and dying from a battlefield, I had not thought too deeply about what you and your brother soldiers endure in the army. Oh, I knew it must be wretched and too horrible for words, but I could never imagine what horrors you faced on the battlefield... But what you said just now, it was in such a matter-of-fact way that it instantly made me feel as if I was amongst the carnage—"

"Forgive me. It was not my intention to upset you."

"Oh, there is nothing to forgive. I am not upset. I just want you to know I would like—*like* isn't the right word—I would be *honored* if you ever wanted to tell me about your time in the army. Any of it. Grand tells me I am a good listener for a female, in that I do not interrupt or pry."

"I shall keep your offer in mind."

At that Rory gave a tinkle of laughter. "By which you mean you have no intention of telling me anything at all! No matter. My offer stands."

When he remained silent and continued down the path and out into the clearing, she allowed herself to put her head on his shoulder and snuggle into the softness of his plum velvet frock coat. Unbeknownst to her, she breathed in deeply and sighed her contentment, enjoying the masculine salty scent of him mingled with traces of bergamot and woody tobacco leaf.

"I've been traveling since first light," he muttered self-consciously. "I must be disagreeable to you."

"No! No, not at all. I like it—I mean—*you*—I mean your frock coat—Your *frock coat* is most agreeable."

He remained tight-lipped, square chin and dark eyes straight, but her panic of correction made him mentally smile.

They had come to the low stone wall that divided the Physic Garden from Banks House. Instead of opening the gate and passing through it, Dair carefully set Rory on top of the stonework.

"It saddens me you were forbidden to marry Lily Banks," Rory said conversationally as she set her walking stick by the wall. "I like her. She is quite lovely, and not just in her appearance. She has a good heart and a gentle soul. I like her family, too. They are all well-meaning personable people. They certainly consider you part of their family. And Jamie —it is obvious you love him dearly. All that truly matters is the deep affection you, Jamie and Mrs. Banks have for one another. In such circumstances, Society's good opinion is about as meaningful as a bowl of cold oats, is it not? Jamie has a great look of you, but, and you may scoff, he most resembles what I suppose your brother Charles must have looked like at the same age. Although, your brother's hair is rather more fiery…"

"Charles…?"

When he grunted his surprise, she said steadily, "It was not my intention to offend you, my lord."

"You did not, Miss Talbot."

With a short bow, he excused himself and walked a little way through the field of wildflowers, shrugging his shoulders and stretching his arms, as if to rid a stiffness in his muscles. He then walked on, hands shoved deep into the pockets of his frock coat.

He might say she had not offended him, 'but Rory thought otherwise. She was always too honest for her own good. Her thoughts came tumbling out without the circumspection her grandfather cautioned she needed. Her muddled speech was meant to reassure the Major that she was not judgmental about the Banks family, or offended he shared a son with Lily Banks, or even that he had a continuing relationship with Mrs. Banks, whatever that was—she was not precisely sure. Though, having now spent a few hours in her company, she was convinced she and the Major were not lovers, and had not been since her marriage to her cousin.

She watched him turn and come back to her, a hand through his mussed hair, and that's when it struck her. Why had he been in the saddle all day? And if he had, then it was no wonder he needed to stretch his limbs. He was tired and aching, and yet he had put himself to the bother of carrying her back to the jetty. And why were his face and hands lightly bronzed, as if he had spent days in a climate where the sun shone so brightly it could turn a man's skin caramel. Surely there was no place this side of the Channel where it had not rained in the past month, that would give rise to such a complexion. She concluded he must have been absent from England for at least four weeks. Was that why he had allowed a black beard to grow upon his face, as if he had not the time or inclination to shave in days? Or was it part of something more mysterious, a disguise perhaps?

The sun's brightness made her squint and place a hand to her brow, as he rejoined her at the wall. He moved into the path of the sun's rays, to block the glare from her eyes, leaving her in his shadow. She smiled up at him, removing her hand, and said blithely,

"I had always assumed an inmate of the Tower spent most of his day in a dark dank cell. It just goes to show that we on the outside know little about what occurs on the inside of His Majesty's premier prison for traitors…"

For one moment he had no idea what she was talking about. He'd forgotten he was supposed to have spent the past month in the Tower; though he had not forgotten his batman was still languishing under lock and key masquerading as him. He did not want to lie to her, but he wasn't going to give the game away, either.

"Why do you say so, Miss Talbot?"

"No doubt my grandfather could tell me. He knows the history of the Tower and its guests as well as he does the veins on the back of his hands. Perhaps inmates of the Tower are not permitted the implements to shave their beards for fear they might do themselves or others an injury. But I am certain inmates rarely go free with such a healthy glow to their skin as you have."

Dair put up a thick black eyebrow with studied surprise. "Is that so? Perhaps I was permitted more exercise time in the courtyard. I hate being cooped up, particularly in small spaces."

Rory's blue eyes narrowed and her voice held a note of triumph.

"Even were that the case, my lord, more time in the courtyard would have meant more time soaked through to your skin, and a possible cold caught for all your need of the outdoors. It has been raining on and off this past month—and at the Tower, too. Black clouds do not part for traitors, even if they are innocent and the charges a ruse for some higher purpose…"

For a moment he said nothing, and she wondered if he would refute her claims. But then he showed her a white smile, and shook his head.

"Bravo, Miss Talbot. Naturally, I cannot tell you where I've been or what I've been doing."

"Oh, I don't care about that! Oh! That is not strictly true. I care *you* are home safe, but as to what you've been doing and where you've been…" She pretended a moment to think on the matter, twirling a long lock of her fair hair between her fingers. "Not Paris. Not warm enough. And you have only been away for a little over a month… So you didn't sail off to the Caribbean and back… I would hazard you were somewhere down the Channel, towards the Mediterranean… The south of France? Spain, perhaps…?"

"With this beard, I would not blame you for thinking I had taken up piracy on the high seas, or smuggling the coves of Cornwall."

Rory's gaze locked on his fingertips lightly stroking his bearded jaw and she longed to reach out and do the same. She wondered what he would be like to kiss with a beard. Would it be just as delicious as that first time? Were the hairs on his face as soft as those on his chest? Would they tickle or annoy her?

Stop it, Aurora Christina Talbot! Your thoughts about this man are no longer delightfully wicked—they have turned ridiculously obsessive. He kissed you once and now you think there is some sort of connection between the two of you? There is not. Whatever you felt, it could not possibly be reciprocated. Stop being naïve, you little idiot!

So said the voice of reason. But she could not help herself, particularly with the man standing in front of her in all his piratical handsomeness. She so wanted to know what it would be like to kiss him with that beard. She swallowed and pressed her dry lips together and said with a nervous laugh and a shrug, in her best manner of appearing off-hand,

"Pirate. American savage. Officer in His Majesty's Army. Smuggler, perhaps… I wonder what other disguises you wear when you are absent from Society's drawing rooms…?"

"Your grandfather should consider employing you. Your observational and reasoning skills are second to none."

Rory beamed with pride at such praise. But she noted his voice was flat and he had skillfully avoided a direct response. Also, he showed not a flicker of recognition when she mentioned American savage. He was either an exceptional actor, or he had indeed been blind drunk the night at Romney's studio. Either way, her voice of reason dared to smugly confirm that such a lack of a reaction in him was proof she meant less than nothing to him.

"Not from want of effort, but learned over time," she said with a small unconscious sigh of defeat in response to her little voice of reason. "And from boredom. There simply isn't much to do at balls and the like when one is confined to a chair."

"You cannot dance—at all?"

She heard the note of concern in his voice, and it snapped her out of her preoccupation. That would serve her to rights for listening to the doubts expressed by her inner voice instead of concentrating on the here and now! The last thing on this earth she wanted from him was sympathy; the second last, to appear maudlin. She was rarely, if ever, self-pitying, and she never used her malformed foot as an excuse, or as a way of appearing interesting to others, or to elicit sympathy. She had been taught from a young age that to draw attention to herself in any way was the height of bad manners. Upon leaving the nursery and going out into Society, her grandfather had warned that it was her responsibility to put others at ease and to ensure they were not made uncomfortable in her presence. To do this she must be aware of her limitations. He said she was the most beautiful girl in the world and everyone else would soon see this too, if she was simply herself.

She believed her grandfather and did as he counseled. But what had never occurred to her, until she had set eyes on the very man who now stood before her, was to ask the question she now asked herself: Would she ever be desired for herself?

"You are right. Grand should employ me," she replied, ignoring his question as he had earlier ignored hers. "The tittle-tattle I could recount to him after hours of observing others over the rim of my teacup! But I don't need to tell you, do I? I suspect in your chosen occupation you need to be a master of observation. Though—in your particular case—you are accomplished at concealing your skills."

"Concealing my skills?" The corner of his mouth twitched. "I have more than one?"

She ignored his flippancy, breathing a mental sigh of relief that he did not pursue whether or not she could dance, and excited to have unmasked him. The more she thought about it, the more she knew her supposition to be correct. She recalled her unsettling impression of him the times she had watched him at balls and Society gatherings from the comfort of a chair and behind her fluttering fan: There was something about the way he played the big-headed Merry-Andrew a little too well. And it perplexed her that her grandfather quietly defended him whenever dinner guests dared to suggest Major Lord Fitzstuart was nothing more than an arrogant buffoon and a self-serving dullard, a disgrace not only to his royal heritage, but also to his august kin, the Duke of Roxton and his family.

She had always wondered what the connection could be between her grandfather and her brother's school friend. She assumed it was simply her grandfather keeping a fatherly eye on the Major, since his own father had deserted his family and his country. Possibly this was true, but she now believed there was nothing simple about their association. She could have kicked her own shin for not suspecting earlier that the Major was the Spymaster General's protégé. It made perfect sense, and the Major played the game very well indeed.

"Every spy hides behind a façade, or he would not be good at spying, would he?" she said matter-of-factly, and when his smile died she pretended not to notice, adding cheerfully, "Observation is an important skill. Not too many persons can do two things at once well, least of all observe a room full of people while pretending disinterest in his surroundings. And you are particularly skilled, because you are usually the center of attention, so it must be doubly difficult for you."

She cocked her head and screwed up her little nose in thought. "You have perfected the practice of blustering arrogance so well that you may call it your own, thus most people take you at face value—"

"Face value? You give me a great deal more credit than others who own to knowing me better."

She shrugged. "Why should your family, friends and acquaintances think you anything but what you present? Major Lord Fitzstuart can be dared to take on any wager, must win at all costs, and plays the big handsome buffoon so convincingly no one questions his performance. Society rarely looks beyond the superficial. It prefers to believe the most salacious answer is the correct one, and does not change its opinion once formed. That is how a sweet-natured female of good character can be branded a whore for all eternity, when, as a mere girl, she made the mistake of falling in love with a handsome boy out of her marital reach, and had his babe out of wedlock as a consequence."

He was surprised by her keen and succinct summation. He knew she was referring to Lily, and agreed with her, but all he said was,

"Thank you, Miss Talbot. You have made your point."

"I meant no malice in my reckoning, my lord."

He held her gaze, and she stared back at him openly and without guile. She was such a refreshing change from the majority of females with whom he associated. Whether in their beds, or amongst Society, even the women of the Banks family whom he trusted with his life, females told him what they believed he wanted to hear. But Aurora Talbot was incurably honest, and he doubted she could spin a lie even if she tried. Still, whatever her honesty, whatever she thought she knew about him, he had been on his guard for too many years now that he was not about to open up in any way, shape or form to a girl he had literally just realized existed, regardless of her good opinion of him. Besides which, the conversation was becoming far too serious and purposeful for his liking. So he said to tease her,

"Perhaps I missed my true calling? Should I be treading the boards…?"

"Oh, but you have the stage every time you step into a room. There isn't a head—male, female or powdered—that doesn't turn in your direction when your name is announced. And then your performance begins!"

He grinned.

"Aren't you the clever one!" And made her a sweeping bow. "If one is to perform, then an audience is a must, and there is none better than an adoring female audience."

She glanced down at the flowered cotton mittens that matched her dress, and smoothed out an imaginary crease, thinking of the enthusiastic reception he had received from the dancing girls at Romney's studio. Taking a deep breath she schooled her features into a smile, with a twinkle in her eye and a dimple in her cheek.

"You need not go to so much bother. You could stand in the middle of a room, say and do nothing, and your adoring female audience would still be more than satisfied. Much like a statue fashioned of marble, or a full-length painting by Sir Joshua or Mr. Romney. I pity the verbiage of the gentleman poet who attempts to compete with your visual feast."

At that he threw back his head and laughed heartily. When he could speak he moved to close the gap between them. Hands flat on the stone wall either side of her petticoats, he leaned into her, eyes level with hers and only inches away. He was so near she saw that his pupils had dilated, turning his irises coal black.

"My dear Miss Talbot," he purred, "I'll wager you a guinea that every time I strode into a drawing room, you itched to use your walking stick to trip me up."

"Why would you think me so mean-spirited?" she asked softly, gaze riveted to his unblinking obsidian stare.

"That's just it. I think you are the least mean-spirited person of my acquaintance." He gave a lopsided smile. "Having me fall flat on my face would at least allow some other arrogant blusterer the chance to take center stage."

"But to trip you up would deprive your adoring female audience. I could not be *that* mean-spirited to *them*."

"Touché, Miss Talbot."

"Though… I have a confession," she added hesitantly, and a little breathlessly because he continued to hold her gaze. "There was more than one occasion when I wanted to trip you, but—"

He held his breath, hoping upon hope she did not mention Romney's studio. Looking into her frank blue eyes, his defenses were crumbling and he was at the point of confessing all to her.

"—but my impulse was a purely selfish one, and I refrained from doing so."

He leaned in even closer. She unconsciously mimicked his action and inched forward. A hair's breadth was all that separated them.

"You should have been selfish a long time ago, Miss Talbot…"

SIXTEEN

RORY COULD HARDLY BREATHE. THE PRESSURE WAS BACK IN HER chest, as if her heart was too big to be contained in her ribs, and the tingling sensation had returned to her limbs. Did he have any idea how close his mouth was to hers? And then she felt his lower torso press gently against her legs. To her astonishment her knees parted of their own volition, allowing him to step right up to the wall.

She blinked and drew in a sharp breath, shocked. Yet, she did not shift to rectify her immodesty. She was scandalized into immobility, that he was standing between her open legs in the fresh air of a picturesque garden. For the sake of her reputation, and for propriety, she should shove him away as hard as she could, and bring her knees instantly and firmly back together. But as she had been in a far more compromising position with him when wrapped in a curtain, he naked but for a flap of leather between his thighs, to show outrage now would not only appear ridiculous but rather disingenuous.

So she allowed her response to be instinctive, rather than do what she ought. Her legs did indeed close, they closed around him, stockinged knees finding anchorage, hugging either side of his slim hips. And once fastened, her feet curled about the back of his thighs and locked, and would not let go. Her legs might be concealed beneath the yardage of her flowered petticoats, but there was no hiding the intimate proximity of their bodies. It mattered not that his hands remained flat to the stone wall and hers were clasped in her lap, or that they were fully clothed. From the waist down they were now joined and Rory knew of no other place she wished to be.

And now he would kiss her. That's what they both wanted, surely? She desperately wanted to kiss him, and if he did not take the initiative soon, she was sure she would faint with the anxiety of anticipation. She could not kiss him first. Females, gently-bred females, particularly virgins, did not take the initiative. To do so would lead to unnecessary speculation and conjecture. Gently-bred females waited to be kissed. They waited to be noticed. They could spend their whole life waiting, but wait they must.

But her *what if* voice dared to suggest she should just kiss him first. What if he was waiting for her to do just that? There she went again, with her *what ifs*! *Dolt*! Men such as the Major waited for no one and nothing. If he had any inclination to kiss her he would do so in the next minute or not at all. Perhaps he was merely trifling with her? It was possible he had orchestrated this intimate scene for the purpose of teaching her a lesson for calling him a big handsome buffoon and an arrogant blusterer. But surely he knew she had meant it as a compliment to his acting abilities?

So she continued to wait and ruminate, unaware that her breathing had become shallow and her face flushed with longing.

WHILE HE MIGHT NOT BE PRIVY TO HER DOUBTS AND WISHES, Dair was aware of her in every other sense. He wanted to kiss this delightfully pretty creature, with her pert little nose and large blue eyes, all over, starting with her exceptionally kissable mouth. He would then remove the gossamer modesty fichu covering the low square neckline of her bodice, to expose then suckle her divine breasts, drinking in the scent of her: A heady mix of soft vanilla and sweet lavender, but mostly the scent was uniquely her: Tender, honest, and adorable.

He was alert to the fact she had trapped him between her legs, legs opened wide and pressed against his hips, legs wrapped hard about his thighs, and he smiled to himself. All that was between him and paradise were the cotton layers of her floral petticoats. And to his utter relief the slumbering beast, which had spent three unresponsive weeks in Portugal, had finally woken, and threatened to transform into an excruciating hardness that would overwhelm his good sense, and all caution would be scattered to the four winds. He might keep his hands flat on the stone wall either side of her panniers, but what he yearned to do was not only kiss her mouth, but tug open the fall of his breeches, slide her petticoats up her silken bare thighs, and cure his troubling temporary impotence there and then. Once sated, he could then return to his preferred road of bedding beautiful women with lascivious abandon.

Yet, contrary to popular opinion, he was not a conscienceless lothario who seduced women with only his own pleasure in mind, and no thought to the consequences. The truth was that since receiving the life-altering news at the tender age of seventeen that he was to become a father, the possible consequences of satisfying his carnal appetites were never far from his thoughts. Thus only seasoned females, married women who had done their duty by their husbands, and those he paid and who knew how to prevent the natural consequence of a coupling, were permitted to share his bed.

It was this remembrance of his personal criteria for a suitable lover, and the terrifying fact here was a young woman with no experience whatsoever, that overcame his most base instincts. He had no intention of defiling the lovely Miss Aurora Talbot. A simple kiss would suffice. Of course, he realized that even a simple kiss shared with an unmarried spinster of good family and unblemished character would be frowned upon by his peers as thoroughly ungentlemanly. But he convinced himself that Miss Talbot was a sensible, clever female who would see their kiss for what it was: A fleeting springtime flirtation. Just as she had behaved sensibly after their encounter at Romney's studio, she would keep this kiss to herself, for which he would be eternally grateful.

He smiled into her eyes, anticipating their kiss, and when she smiled back, it was all the encouragement he needed. But unlike his behavior at Romney's studio, when he had mistaken her for a pretty whore in need of a new benefactor, and treated her accordingly, he was determined to show her he could be gentle and considerate and treat her with the respect that was her due as his social equal. Above all, he wanted her to enjoy the kiss as much as he did, and take away a pleasant memory from this brief encounter.

Deliberate in his movements, reasoning he had no wish to frighten her with any expectation other than treating her with gentlemanly reverence, he tenderly stroked her flushed cheek before gently tucking an unruly lock of her straw-blonde hair behind her ear. When he smiled into her eyes he saw her swallow. Whether deliberate or from nervousness, she ran the pink tip of her tongue along the rim of her upper lip, eyes on his mouth, and it was all the signal he needed he had her permission to press his mouth to hers.

Finally, he cupped her face between his large hands and kissed her.

RORY'S HANDS SLID UP THE SOFT VELVET FRONT OF HIS FROCK coat, around his neck to hold on tight, fingers in his shoulder length hair, head tilting in his hands to accommodate his nose as he pressed his mouth to hers. She was determined to savor every second of their kiss, and was delightfully surprised his piratical beard was not rough and spiky but silky and velvety soft, like the soft material of his frock coat. The black bristles of his beard brushed against her skin as they kissed, and in such a caressing way that it heightened her senses. She tingled all over. She liked his beard very much. But what surprised her even more was how gentle he was, and how tentative was his kiss.

This kiss was so unlike the one shared at Romney's studio she wondered if he'd had second thoughts about kissing her. The first time they had kissed, it was with all the enthusiasm of a man who found her desirable. Now the flicker of desire was barely alight. And just as she began to melt into his arms, he snuffed that flame by breaking off their kiss. Her cheeks burned with shame, that he must have come to the realization he was not the least attracted to her when sober. Yet, he did not pull away, but continued to stare down at her, as if requiring her to provide him with an explanation.

How was she, a novice to such a situation, supposed to respond? She had never been left alone with a man who was not a close male relative, least of all been kissed by one, until the handsomest man in London made her dreams come true. She recognized in this kiss that she was a willing participant, and yet with no experience of rejection and how to extract herself with dignity, she froze with indecision. Mortified by such weakness of character, she was on the verge of tears.

How could she be so incompetent? Why had she fallen in love with this man? The pressure in her chest and the quickening of her heartbeat whenever she was in his company told her so. Why did it have to be *this* man, whose nefarious history with women was well-known to her, and who clearly cared little for her above the ordinary? And now that he knew her for what she was, a passably pretty ingénue, who would never dance and never be an elegant lady of fashion, he had probably kissed her out of pity; and that made her sick to her stomach.

Slowly, she withdrew her hands from his shoulders and dropped them back in her lap. But when she began to untangle her legs, to release the pressure of her knees on his hips, face hot with humiliation to realize how low she had allowed herself to stoop, he startled her by grabbing her by the upper arms and not letting go.

Her gaze flashed up to his face, and she shivered at the intensity in his black eyes and the scowl to his mouth. What thoughts were swirling about in that handsome head? Was he struggling with the right words to offer her up an apology for his behavior? She did not want to hear it! She did not want his contrition, and she most certainly did not want his pity. Determined to maintain her dignity, she pressed her lips together and regarded him with candor, gaze unblinking and locked to his scowl. She said a silent prayer, hoping the tears welling up behind her eyes did not drop to add misery to her shame.

But he surprised her yet again by loosening his grip on her arms as his brow cleared. She watched as a look, difficult to decipher, passed across his features. It was as if he had experienced some sort of dawning revelation, something so profound that he had surprised himself with this newfound knowledge. Slowly, his gaze raked over her, and followed his hands as they slid down the length of her slim arms to the cascade of lace at her elbows, before continuing over her cotton mitts, to her fingers, and here he took hold of her hands. She saw his Adam's apple move, as he swallowed hard, then his jaw set hard, as if he had come to a difficult decision, but made it nonetheless. What that decision was she could not even speculate. She waited with shallow breath for him to speak. But when he did, he did not offer any explanation or apology, and he certainly did not provide her with a window to his thoughts.

He left her bewildered and adrift.

"Oh hell..." he muttered. "Hell and bloody damnation..."

FURIOUS WITH HIMSELF FOR VOCALIZING HIS FRUSTRATION AT AN inability to articulate his thoughts in any meaningful way that would convey the earth shattering nature of his revelation, Dair gave up the attempt. He might not be able to explain to her how he felt, but he could certainly show her. So he kissed Rory a second time.

Hands spanning her small waist, he pressed his mouth to hers, all reticence shattered.

ARDENT AND ALL-CONSUMING, THIS KISS LEFT RORY IN NO doubts as to his desire. And if she did breathe, she was not conscious of doing so. If she had a single thought, it was that she had dreamed of this moment, of this particular kiss, and with this particular man, since her thirteenth summer, when Alisdair Fitzstuart had called in his regimental uniform to take leave of her grandfather and brother.

Bereft of a sense of time and space, she was aware only of his mouth, the lingering insistence of his tongue, and the wonderful way he made her feel. She wilted, yet was more alive all over than she had ever been. She wanted him to pick her up and carry her to a shady spot under the trees and lie with her amongst the wildflowers. She wanted him to undress before her, so that she could again admire him naked, but this time all of him; and she wanted to caress him, everywhere. More than anything, she wanted him to make love to her as the couple in the temple tapestries made love, bodies unashamedly naked and entwined, and in the throes of an all-consuming passion.

But not here. Not on Banks House land. Not within walking distance of the house where lived his son and the woman he would have married, had it not been deemed an unequal match. Not with him being called from afar, so insistently, like a servant scratching at the door with some urgent purpose, and who would not go away no matter how many times ordered to do so. But... Old Bert was not one of her grandfather's servants... Why would he be calling out to her, and to his lordship...

That broke the spell.

With a hand hard-pressed to Dair's chest, she untangled her legs from their anchorage about his thighs, pulled her mouth from his and sat up. She flashed him a warning then bowed her head, hands back in her lap, fingers clenched tightly together. She did not know why she dropped her chin in such a cowardly fashion, because she was not ashamed of kissing him. It was an instinctive reaction, as if she had been caught out being terribly wicked, though this was not how she felt in the least. Yet she realized her actions must have signaled this to him because his hands loosened from her waist and he stepped away from the wall and from her, with an inarticulate apology she did not quite catch, such was her preoccupation with her own cowardice, though the sincerity of his apology was clear enough in his tone.

Had she been attentive, not only to the essence of his apology but the actual words spoken, she would have realized there and then that something momentous had happened, far beyond the kiss they had shared. He had called her *Delight*, as he had at Romney's studio. It was only later, when Mr. William Watkins and her brother arrived on the scene, that she recalled Dair's apology and his use of the moniker *Delight*, and it changed everything.

For now, sitting on the half-wall of stone between the Physic Garden and Banks House, Rory was too caught up in salvaging what dignity was left to her. She slowly lifted her hands and proceeded to the mundane task of smoothing and repinning her mussed hair, not a second look at the Major. Nonetheless, she was acutely aware of his proximity, that the masculine scent of him still lingered, and the salty taste of him remained on her tongue, and her face flamed to a guilty hue of pomegranate.

STILL GROGGY WITH DESIRE AND CAUGHT IN THE MOMENT, DAIR was slow to react to rejection. Breathing ragged, he stared at her, confused, not understanding why she had broken off such a perfectly wonderful kiss. Had he been too insistent? Should he have been gentler? She was young and inexperienced… that had to be it. He needed to take matters one step at a time. His ardency had frightened her. God, he was an inconsiderate loggerhead! Musing on this, he put a hand to his cheek and felt the hair under his fingertips. He pulled a face, but it gave him an idea. What if it was his beard that had made her baulk? She had not recoiled at Romney's studio, far from it, so why now? It had to be the facial hair. Damn it! He should have shaved at Portsmouth before heading out. But he had been too eager to get home to spend the day with his son on his birthday. And he'd not even managed to do that right! Great blunderhead that he was!

One too many times acting the part of Rodomonte, the boastful boisterous hero of Ariosto, had turned him into the same. For the first time in his life he was not only annoyed but also ashamed at allowing his desire and his gadso to dictate his manners. He had an overwhelming need to take her in his arms and console her, to tell her of his intentions, but now was not the moment; and she would hardly believe him, given his actions.

So he stepped away from the wall with a respectful bow, hand in his frock coat pocket clenching his silver cheroot case, and muttering an apology that was out of his mouth before he thought much about it. And that's when he, too, heard his name and swiveled about on a booted heel to discover Old Bert tramping across the open field, and holding aloft a wide-brimmed straw hat with blue silk ribbons trailing in the breeze. The old retainer was red in the face and puffing. He must have run most of the way.

When he reached Dair, Old Bert gave him the hat with a nod and then dropped his gaze to the grass, not a look at Rory. His furtiveness was evidence enough he had witnessed their intimacy. That he remained where he stood after being dismissed had Dair move a step closer, realizing the old man wanted to tell him something. He just hoped that with permission to speak, Old Bert had the wherewithal to remain as one blind, as all good servants were wont, and wasn't about to mention the obvious.

"Beggin' your lordship's pardon. There be a gentleman in yonder garden watching. I seen him from the trees, when his head popped out of the hedgerow. Reason for callin' out in the way I did. I meant no disrespect or offence."

"None taken. What's he look like?"

"Hatchet-faced. Small eyes. Fancy hair."

"Tall or short?"

"Short."

"Seen him before?"

Old Bert shook his bald head.

Then it wasn't Grasby. Not that his best friend was given to skulking in the shrubbery. Had it been Grasby, he'd have marched straight up to him, pulled his sister off, and rightly punched his nose. Grasby wasn't a coward, and he wasn't short. But he knew one of the party on Shrewsbury's barge who was both. He hoped his intuition proved him right. He itched to rearrange the officious weasel's neckcloth.

"This sneakup got any muscle to speak of? Do I need to brace myself?"

Old Bert gave a snort of derision and smiled a toothless grin. "Not on y'life, m'lord! He's a milksop as ever I seen one. Not that I seen one. But I'd know one if I did, and he's it! You'd only have to poke him with y'finger and he'd be to the ground in an instant, with his two hands over his head and whimpering like a girl!"

"That about sums up the Weasel. Good. I'll save the new skin on my knuckles. Is he still in the shrubbery?"

"No, m'lord. As soon as y'turned your back he showed h'self—"

"Did he indeed."

"—and went direct to your sweetling, where he be now in conversation."

Dair resisted the urge to turn around. He put up a black eyebrow at Old Bert's moniker for Miss Talbot, but made no comment. Fiddling with the blue silk ribbons of Rory's straw hat, he said flatly,

"Tell Jamie I'll be back up at the house within the quarter hour. And Mrs. Banks has permission to go through my satchels. There are a couple of bottles of port, a string bag full of oranges for the boys, and a mountain of laundry. And I need my razors sharpened."

"I'll do the razors for ye lordship!"

Dair didn't have the heart to refuse the old retainer. What Farrier would think of letting anyone else near his master's personal grooming implements he would deal with when the time came. For now he just had to get this beard off his face so Miss Aurora Talbot had no excuse not to kiss him again. And he would kiss her again, of that he was as certain as day followed night. And the next time there would be no excuses, no interruptions, and no weasel-like Peeping Tom in the shrubbery.

He watched Old Bert trudge back up to Banks House the way he came, the old retainer whistling as he went, thinking about the best way to deal with Mr. William Watkins and his perfidious propensities.

He might refer to Watkins by his Harrow schoolboy nickname Weasel, but the man was not a weasel, he was a snake. He was a back-stabbing sanctimonious coward who had slithered his way through school and had done the same to become the smug know-it-all-secretary to England's Spymaster General, and by virtue of his sister's marriage to Grasby.

The man didn't deserve to put his knobby knees under the desk of secretary to Lord Shrewsbury, where he had access to all manner of state and personal secrets; particularly the personal. There was no higher moral ground with Watkins. He was no selfless functionary doing his bit for his country. He was not motivated by a sense of duty, or the imperative to keep papal tyranny from England's shores, or the patriotic need to uphold the right of every Englishmen to live in the most liberal-minded country on earth. And he certainly had never offered to get his hands dirty by carrying out covert missions beyond the paper-work on his desk.

Dair had wondered how a man of Shrewsbury's masterful cunning and superior insight could employ such a self-server, only to be enlightened by the Spymaster that he knew exactly what type of creature he had employed, and that it was best to keep a snake close than to allow it to slither off into the tall grass not knowing its movements, and thus be unaware when it would strike.

Now, squaring his shoulders, Dair braced himself to play the arrogant blusterer. It never failed to put Watkins on edge, that at any moment he might be met with physical violence. But when he turned to saunter back to the wall, dangling the wide brimmed straw bergere by its blue silk ribbons, he was confronted with a most astonishing sight.

Mr. William Watkins was doing his best to keep hold of Miss Talbot's hand, while she was equally determined to have her fingers released. And when the man rose up off one bended knee to lunge at Miss Talbot, she thrusting out her arms to keep him at a distance, Dair's intended pretense evaporated like a popped soap bubble.

He broke into a stride, gripped by the primal urge to protect, regardless of the personal consequences to himself. It was an instinct first experienced upon the birth of his son, and most recently at Brooklyn Heights, when he had rescued a loyalist widow and her two small children caught in the crossfire of battle. But there was something new in the emotional mix this time, something he had never experienced before, and one that surprised and vexed him further. He was covetous—irately so.

No one touched what was now his—*no one.*

SEVENTEEN

How Mr. William Watkins came to be on bended knee before Rory, with a wrathful Dair Fitzstuart bearing down upon him like a wounded bull, could be traced to a conversation with Drusilla, Lady Grasby, an hour earlier.

Brother and sister had partaken of nuncheon in the opulent cabin of Lord Shrewsbury's shallop. The gold damask curtains were drawn together on those windows where the liveried rowers were eating their fare, while those cabin windows with a view of watercraft plying the Thames were cracked open to allow for a pleasant breeze.

There was enough food and drink for a party of six, but Lady Grasby and Mr. Watkins were the only ones to sit down to snap peas, salmagundi salad, terrine of duck, a variety of cheeses and the various fruits of the season. They ate in silence, and to the accompaniment of laughter and conversation from their servants, who had taken a picnic ashore under the shade of the willows along the bank. Such merriment merely underscored the irritation and embarrassment of brother and sister at being abandoned by Lord Grasby and his sister.

"I understand your continued annoyance with your husband for his behavior at Romney's studio," said William Watkins, pushing aside his empty Worcester plate, "but you must find it in your heart to forgive *and* forget. If you do not, there will be no heir, and you will find your-self divorced and both of us disgraced."

"*Divorced?*" Lady Grasby sat up, eyes wide with fright. She swallowed; fingers hard about the closed black-lacquered sticks of her chinoiserie fan. "I do not want to divorce Grasby. I like being his wife. I like him. I may even be in love with him… And I want to be Countess of Shrewsbury, William. I *must* be."

"Then give him a child, any child, boy or girl, will do for the present. That is how far you have fallen in Lord Shrewsbury's estimation. A child will show you are capable of breeding, and seal the breach. When the longed-for son arrives, you will be forever cemented in Grasby's heart and in his life. Nothing can touch you then. You will be Countess of Shrewsbury, my dear."

"It is all the fault of *that man*, William. If Fitzstuart had died in battle, Grasby could have mourned his friend, and our life without him would've been perfectly wonderful. It is unchristian of me to say so, but that is how I *feel*. I was so happy when he joined his regiment in the Colonies and left us alone. I prayed—yes, *prayed*—he would not return! The last thing I expected was for him to come back a war hero. *That man* has turned me into a bad person, William. Please, please tell me it is not my fault."

William Watkins glanced at the two mute footmen, whose chins remained up and their eyes staring straight ahead, and said gently, "We are in accord there. But he has the Devil's own luck, and there is little we can do to counter that." *Except have him poisoned, or stabbed to death in a bordello while he's sleeping off a night of drunken debauchery,* his inner claret-fueled voice told him. *But you're petrified you'd get caught. And you would, too. Even in death the luck would be with Shrewsbury's fatwitted favorite, Major Lord Fitzstuart.*

Mr. Watkins recalled the covert missions Lord Shrewsbury had entrusted to Major Lord Fitzstuart, and how he had survived each and every one, despite the danger and risk to life and limb. No wound to his athletic limbs, and the odd nick and scar to cheek and chin had only added to his Grecian good looks. He was convinced Fitzstuart had sold his soul to the black arts, and one day the Devil would come to claim it.

"I have given the dilemma of the Major's undue influence over your husband much thought and have arrived at a suitable solution which, I believe, you will approve of most heartily." William Watkins could not help smiling smugly. "Whatever the effect of Fitzstuart and his ilk on Grasby, it is countered by Miss Talbot's sensible and loving counsel. Careful nurturing, and the added influence of myself, in the more intimate capacity of husband to Miss Talbot, would wean Grasby off his friend's influence."

"*Aurora*? Aurora married to you…" Lady Grasby blinked her surprise. The idea had never occurred to her. But now the suggestion had been voiced, it made perfect sense. "William! Oh! Yes! *Yes*! It would make me so happy to have Aurora as my true sister! And Grasby does listen to her more than any other; more than he does me! And with you married to her—Oh please tell me you are serious. That this is not a whim. With your wealth and important position within the government, you could have married any woman of face and fortune. But to choose Aurora... I think I am about to cry with happiness."

He put up his hand in a gesture of self-effacement, though his grin was indication enough he was pleased with her effusive response, and beckoned a footman to set the crystal decanter at his elbow. It was such a hot day...

"My dear, your support pleases me greatly. I admit the prospect of approaching Miss Talbot, of seeking the consent of Lord Shrewsbury, makes me exceedingly nervous. Hence, I fear, I am full to the gills with claret. I know I am nothing above the ordinary. As my sister you have a duty to think so, but—"

"Oh, hush! That you are prepared to marry Aurora can only make Lord Shrewsbury eternally grateful. We all privately believed she would never receive an offer, even Lord Shrewsbury. As for Grasby's romantic notions, that one day a gentleman would come along who would love Aurora for herself, that is a great piece of fanciful nonsense. She has a pretty countenance and an excellent pedigree to be sure, but that vanishes from consideration, does it not, the moment she struggles to her feet and uses that wretched stick. But you—" She squeezed her brother's hand. "—you, dearest William, are such a *noble* man. You have always managed to cloak a natural uneasiness, as have I, with her ungainly ways."

William Watkins refilled his glass. His sister's enthusiasm for a match with Aurora Talbot was reassuring, but he was not the paragon she believed him. That she had a pretty face and gentle nature went a long way in his overlooking her physical infirmity and her headstrong character. But he was prepared to put up with a lot—the stares of pity from his peers, her passion for pineapple cultivation and a natural reclusiveness, not to mention her candid observations, all of it, however disagreeable—if it meant that through marriage he would realize his twin ambitions; of marrying into the nobility and being acknowledged the successor to her grandfather as Spymaster General.

"Your assurances warm my heart, Drusilla," he said with a thin smile. "It had been my intention to ask Miss Talbot this afternoon, and have her acceptance, then approach Lord Shrewsbury this evening. I realize this is an unorthodox method of seeking consent, but without the former I do not wish to pursue the latter."

Lady Grasby was up off the settee, and flung wide the French windows, a sweeping look about the barge and then out to the dry land, in search of her maid. She must make herself presentable for her husband's return, and that of his sister, newly-betrothed to her brother.

"What do I care about formers and latters?" she declared. "I just want you to marry Aurora as soon as possible and get my husband away from Fitzstuart! So go. Please go, and say whatever you have to, to get her away from those vulgarians. And on the return journey here, find a moment to rally yourself to ask her to marry you. Now, go, William!"

William Watkins dutifully followed his sister out onto the deck and instantly shut his eyes tight against the sunlight. Squinting, he opened an eye, made her a bow, and lurched towards the jetty. Glad to be off the barge, he was surprised when the feeling of dizziness did not subside, for he had assumed it was the gentle rocking motion of the barge that was making him sway. Now, he wondered if the claret was taking its toll on his tea-only brain. He stumbled onward, up the jetty, and made for the low stone wall. Glad to be on solid ground, and to have something to guide him onwards, he made for the gate he had seen earlier on his tour of the Physic Garden.

He was almost at his destination when he was confronted with the startling sight of Major Lord Fitzstuart carrying Aurora Talbot in his arms. The Major appeared as if from nowhere, out from under the canopy of a birch grove, and came striding across the open ground towards the wall. Thoroughly unprepared for such an eventuality, William Watkins panicked and did the only thing that came to mind. He hunched down, not wanting to be seen, scrambled across the graveled pathway, and flung himself sideways into a hedgerow to hide. But the unexpected vigor needed to ensure safe cover was enough to awaken a digestive system unused to alcoholic stimulation. His stomach was literally drowning in claret. William Watkins fell through bracken and leaves, hit the ground hard, promptly threw up, and passed out.

When he woke, which was a few minutes later, he had a moment of panic that the barge had left without him. But he dismissed this as mere fancy, picked himself up, brushed himself off, and hastily wiped his face and mouth with his handkerchief. Panic returned as he inspected his frock coat for signs of digestive stains and scuff marks. Satisfied he was presentable, he took a peek through the shrubbery. Startled by what he saw, and to convince himself he was not dreaming, he stuck his head over the hedgerow, and openly gawked.

Miss Aurora Talbot, the woman to whom he had pinned his matrimonial hopes and dreams, and the dissolute Major, were kissing! It was not any kiss. It was a fervent kiss. It was the sort of kiss reprobates and well-paid whores engaged in. Even then, degenerates did so under cover

of darkness or behind closed doors. It was a scene straight from a Hoga-
rthian etching, and it left William Watkins catatonic with rage and fear
in equal parts.

His matrimonial dreams were about to come to naught if he didn't
do something, and immediately, to haul aside a libertine, with more
muscle than brain, who was forcing his attentions on his chosen bride.
Dear God! Fitzstuart must have plied her with enough alcohol to make
her compliant, and too shocked and too fragile, she could not fight
him off.

He would stride over there and demand satisfaction. But a fat lot of
good that would do. The Major would rightly laugh in his face and
decline—they were not social equals. But as the Major was more brute
than nobleman, he would not have been at all surprised if his weapon
of choice were his bare knuckles rather than the nobleman's rapier. But
he did not want his facial features bloodied, so he sensibly decided to
put his own safety above any rash move to extricate Miss Talbot from
such a thoroughly compromising and immoral position.

Thus he bided his time in the hedgerow, wondering how best to
save a maiden from a fate worse than death, when an opportunity to
rescue Miss Talbot, without endangerment to his person, presented
itself. The Major, hailed by a yokel, had turned his back on his victim.
It was now or never to play the hero for Miss Talbot.

Mr. William Watkins parted the shrubbery and scurried across to
rescue his matrimonial quarry. His moment to shine had arrived!

EIGHTEEN

"MR. WATKINS! RELEASE MY HAND AND STAND UP THIS INSTANT!"

Rory looked about for her walking stick, but it was not against the wall where she had left it. It must have fallen into the grass while she and the Major were preoccupied. With Mr. Watkins determined to keep hold of her hand, gripping the wall with her free hand to remain upright was all she was capable of to stop herself toppling off to join her stick in the grass.

"Miss Talbot—*Aurora*—Please listen—"

"You do not have permission to use my name, sir. Again, I say, stand up! No good will come of this."

Balancing on the balls of his feet, and calf muscles aching from such an unnatural posture, William Watkins felt the sweat of uncertainty beginning to bead at his temples. Miss Talbot's reaction was not what he had expected. She was no shaking maiden, no terrified spinster, grateful for his interference, relieved to be rescued from the brutish arms of her seducer. Yet, he convinced himself she was not herself. That fiend had drugged her. It was the alcohol talking. And it was his own alcohol intake that fuelled his natural conceit, urging him to declare himself immediately or lose the opportunity. If he persisted and she was to hear him with a clear mind, she would jump at the chance to be Mrs. William Watkins. And so he persevered with his declaration, however unorthodox the delivery. This, despite the growing loss of sensation in his right leg.

"Miss Talbot, my greatest desire on this earth is to have you as my wi—"

"No! No, do not say it, Mr. Watkins," Rory demanded. "This is neither the time, and it certainly is not the place, for such a declaration. If you ask me, I shall be truthful, and I have no wish to embarrass you."

"Miss Talbot, when you are sober, you will see the merit in my proposal and give me the answer I want from—"

"When I am—when I am *sober*?" Rory gasped, affronted. "Mr. Watkins, clearly it is *you* who have been drinking or you would not dare suggest such an improbability! You have insulted me, and if you apologize, let go of my hand, and remove yourself from my presence, then perhaps I will forgive you."

"Forgive *me*?" His fingers tightened about her slender wrist as he rose up, unaware his right leg had gone to sleep. "Miss Talbot, I stand before you with an honest proposal of marriage. I will not remove myself until I have secured my present and future happiness, and that requires you to say yes, you will be my wife."

"Your...? *Your* present and future happiness...?"

Rory decided Mr. William Watkins was drunk, *very* drunk, and her anxiousness increased tenfold. Not so much for herself. She did not feel in any personal danger. If need be, she would slap his cheek, certain that would bring him to a sense of his surroundings, if not the impropriety of his behavior. What she feared for was the secretary's safety, should Major Lord Fitzstuart turn his shoulder from his conversation with Old Bert and catch the scene that presented itself. She was certain the nobleman would react first and deal with the consequences later.

If she had learned anything from her chair, as an enforced observer at functions, it was that gentlemen adhered to two fundamental types, to varying degrees. One was phlegmatic, given to drawling, and sauntering, and, no matter what the occasion, they appeared bored beyond tolerance. They were no doubt well-versed in sword play, but the preferred weapon of choice was the scathing verbal put-down, guaranteed to wither an opponent with maximum impact and minimum physical effort. The second type was not given to verbiage, and was far more tactile in every sense. Conversation in company was loud and uninhibited. Everything was done to excess—drinking, dancing, flirting, and no doubt whoring. Type Two relished every minute in the bright candlelight, and such was their infectious sense of fun that they attracted admirers as a flame did a moth. The Major most definitely belonged to this second group, and as actor and spy he had a knack of exaggerating these traits to his advantage. But there was no exaggeration in his physical size and agility. What made matters worse for Mr. William Watkins was that as well as being a warm-blooded vigorous male, the Major was fearless. He was also a trained killer.

Had Mr. William Watkins been any gentleman accosting her, she would not have hesitated to alert the Major to her situation and allow him to deal with him accordingly. But Mr. Watkins was her grandfather's trusted secretary. He was also Silla's brother, and that made him her brother's brother-in-law, thus he was part of the family. She did not want this episode to come between them and make life uncomfortable. He would also continue to come in contact with her, if not daily, then several times a week. It would be awkward from now on since he had made known his intentions toward her. Having the Major involved would vastly complicate matters, and if she were honest with herself, not knowing his feelings for her, she felt inadequate to the task of answering her grandfather's questions.

And so she tried one last time to reason with Mr. William Watkins.

"Mr. Watkins, please, I beg of you, release me and stand up." Adding with a bright smile she hoped looked genuine, "If you do as I ask I will listen to what you have to say, but not today. Tomorrow. When you have had time to reflect upon your intentions. Agreed?"

"Miss Talbot, tomorrow, or the day after that, or the day after that one, will not change my determination. I must and will marry you."

She did not doubt he was sincere, and for the barest of moments curiosity got the better of her. She put aside her anxiety, stopped struggling to tug her hand free, and allowed herself to engage with him.

"Why?"

"I beg your pardon?"

"Why do you wish to marry me?"

William Watkins blinked, sodden brain scrambling to remember and put into coherent sentences all the reasons he had formulated and written up in his diary as to why Miss Aurora Talbot, granddaughter of an earl, sister of a future earl, goddaughter of a duchess, would make him the perfect wife. But while his brain floated in alcohol and his bottom lip quivered, the only substance that came forth was a drool of spittle.

"Three little words, Mr. Watkins. No more. No less. Just three."

When he looked at her queerly, with no idea as to what those three words could be, Rory smiled crookedly. And when he thrust a hand into his frock coat pocket in search of his handkerchief to wipe his wet mouth, Rory saw her chance.

She gripped the edge of the stone wall so as not to topple backwards, then tugged hard. Her hand came free, but she was not free of William Watkins. Her sudden movement caught him unawares. He loosened his grip, but his alcohol consumption made him slow to react and take appropriate counter-action. Instead of staggering backwards, away from the wall, his unresponsive right leg stayed where it was. This meant his left leg over-compensated for this uncooperativeness by over-correcting, and after taking a step away, he stumbled forward.

This sudden change in direction made the secretary dizzy. With no control over his limbs, Mr. William Watkins pitched forward, right leg collapsing under him so that he landed heavily on his knee, arms flapping, and in search of anchorage. His chin came down hard against the corner of Rory's knee, and such was the force with which he landed that he bounced up and he came down again, face first, into the lap of Rory's disheveled petticoats. Here he remained in a state of paralyzed disbelief.

RORY'S KNEE WAS STRUCK SO HARD SHE GAVE AN INVOLUNTARY yelp of pain, almost lost her balance, and cried out again, this time with fright, as she toppled backwards into thin air before quickly lurching forwards to remain seated on the wall. She gasped her relief. But startled and in pain, she was shocked beyond words when Mr. William Watkins landed face down in her lap and there remained. She was torn between a desire to push him off and scramble along the wall to put space between them, and wondering if he were seriously hurt. She had no opportunity to do either.

As if by sorcery, William Watkins rose up, head and limbs hanging limp, and there he momentarily floated in front of her, before flying through the air to land, crumpled, amongst the wildflowers.

DAIR HAD WILLIAM WATKINS BY THE SCRUFF OF THE NECK. WITH a strength fuelled by unmitigated wrath, he hauled the secretary out of Rory's lap so high his buckled shoes left the ground. For a matter of moments William Watkins levitated. Dair wanted to throw the weasel into oblivion. Failing that, he would get him as far away from Miss Aurora Talbot as he was physically capable. He wanted to punish him, badly. Never again would William Watkins so much as put a fingernail to Aurora Talbot without fear of serious harm befalling him.

In the past he had resisted the urge to rearrange the secretary's supercilious smile, now he would not only rearrange it, he would permanently remove it. Nothing and nobody was going to stop him. But then, just as he made a fist and spun William Watkins to face him, he chanced to glance at Rory. He saw the distress writ large in her eyes, and he knew he could not do it, not here, not now, not in front of her. The last thing he wanted was to add to her anxiety. So he forced the violence back down within him and slowly unclenched his fist, flexing his fingers wide and straight.

He turned the secretary away from him, put a boot hard into the middle of his back, and shoved him into open ground, where William Watkins stumbled about, arms flapping wildly as he tried unsuccessfully to stay upright before falling, face first, into the grass.

Dair retrieved Rory's straw hat, dusted it off and came over to her. Whereupon, he gently settled it over her blonde coiffure and straightened out the blue silk ribbons, leaving them trailing either side of her face for her to tie. He then lifted her chin to look at her under the straw brim, gaze full of concern.

"Are you all right?"

She nodded, despite being close to tears, only because she was embarrassed to be caught up in such a piece of nonsense, and he there to witness it. What was William Watkins thinking? She had never given him the slightest encouragement, and he had never shown her any signs that he cared for her above the ordinary. What if the Major thought her a flirt, that she had somehow encouraged William Watkins? Surely not. Then again, she had kissed him, willingly and without restraint.

"Yes. Yes, I am fine," she added brightly, when he continued to stare hard at her. Adding, to put him at his ease, yet realizing after the fact she had probably made him uncomfortable when his response was brisk, "It must be the novelty of being accosted that has me flustered, unaccustomed as I am to such attention." She gave a little nervous laugh, a hand to her mouth. "There must be something in the fermentation of wine this Spring to make normally sober gentlemen drunk beyond reason. Hopefully Mr. Watkins will wake with a sore head and with no recollection of events."

"Did he hurt you?"

"I may have a large bruise to my knee, that is all. Though I wish he had hit my left knee rather than my right. That poor leg has enough to contend with without being knocked about! But it's nothing to worry about, truly, and-and—thank you," she added with a bright smile, because his frown of concern had dropped into a scowl. "Thank you for not hitting him. I know his drunkenness isn't an excuse for his behavior. He must have thought alcohol would give him courage. Though I have no idea where he got the notion I would ever—that he and I could ever—It's utterly absurd! And if I weren't so shocked—no gentleman ever looked at me sideways—that to receive the unwanted attentions from such a man as Mr. Watkins, my grandfather's secretary... Well, I dare say if my knee wasn't throbbing and he hadn't drooled all over my petticoats, I could find some humor in his behavior—"

She cut herself off, knowing she was babbling, but she hadn't been able to help it. The Major's scowl cleared as she babbled, and he was now looking at her in an odd sort of way, and with an odd sort of smile that she could not interpret, and which made her uncomfortably hot.

He raised an eyebrow in surprise she would know he wanted to put his fist into Weasel's face, but made no comment. What interested him more was the reason Watkins needed courage. He was about to ask her if the man had had the audacity to ask her to marry him. Why else would the Weasel need to guzzle wine, be on bended knee, and forcing his attentions on her? But he got no further than addressing her, and then her frankness truly surprised him.

"Miss Talbot—"

"Rory. It's Aurora, but nobody calls me that. I think we've gone beyond the formalities, don't you?"

He chuckled and was bashful. "Yes, I suppose we have—Rory. *Rory*. I like it. *Aurora* is quite lovely but Rory suits you. *Rory...*"

She felt a rush of heat to her face. The way he said her name in his deep rich voice, in an almost caressing lilt, sent a shiver across her shoulder blades. Yet, she surprised herself by managing to keep her tone steady and light.

"And you? I'd like to address you as something other than Major. Too stuffy."

"My friends and family call me Dair."

"Yes, but I would like to call you Alisdair."

He frowned at that, far from pleased.

"No one but Her Grace of Rox—Her Grace of Kinross, calls me that. I don't like her using it, but you know who she is, she is not to be denied. And she is my closest cousin; I would not refuse her." He smiled and tugged playfully at a silk ribbon of her hat. "Everyone calls me Dair."

But Rory did not want to be everyone. She wanted to be the only one to have permission to call him by his first name. She realized only mothers and wives, and beloved sisters, addressed their male relatives by their Christian names, and even then the practice was not universal, particularly if the husband had a title. Major Lord Fitzstuart might be the eldest son of a nobleman and inherit an earldom one day, but he permitted Lily Banks to call him Al. So if the mother of his son could be on such intimate first name terms with him, then she, who had now kissed him and had every intention of giving herself to him, could call him Alisdair. And if he refused her, then he was not as attracted to her as his kisses suggested. Her fingers tingled in anticipation of his response, but she was determined to find out one way or the other.

"Everyone calls you Dair. I prefer Alisdair. It suits you. So does—so does the beard…"

He let go of the ribbon and glanced over his shoulder, momentarily diverted by the sound of groaning. It was the secretary, attempting to pick himself up out of the grass. He turned back to Rory, and said more sharply than he intended,

"My father was the only one who called me Alisdair. I detest the man. I hate the name—have hated it since I was ten."

"Oh?" Rory was unperturbed, but her heart started to beat hard that he had confided this in her. "Then perhaps it's about time someone you like, other than the Duchess of Kinross, called you Alisdair? If you give me permission to call you by your name, then you give permission to lay those bad memories, or whatever it is you dislike about your father, to rest. So instead of thinking of your detestable father when you are addressed as Alisdair, you can instead think of—think about—"

"—kissing you?" He took the two silk ribbons dangling from her hat and slowly tied them in a bow under her chin, taking his time, as if thinking over her proposal. "I wish it were that simple… I will never change my opinion of my father." He shrugged. "Perhaps, in time, I may be able to lay those bad memories to rest, as you suggest." His mouth twitched with the hint of a smile. "Though… Hearing you address me as such, I cannot promise I won't grimace to begin with. It is an instinctive response after all."

"Thank you. No doubt, after a little while, you will stop frowning and learn to like your name as much as I do."

"I hope you are right. I know a way you can help guarantee I won't frown when you say my name."

Rory blinked. He could tell she had no idea to what he was referring and it broadened his smile into a grin.

"If you were to kiss me each time you said it."

Rory gasped, then laughed. Impulsively, she touched the embroidered front of his frock coat.

"Do you wish me to kiss you before or after I say your name? If it is before, I doubt I will get to say it, and that, I fear, is your intent, is it not? To stop me saying your name by kissing me? But I won't be tricked!"

"You, Rory, are too clever for your own good. I would like to kiss you again, now…" He looked into her eyes. "And I am not drunk…"

Rory swallowed and lost her smile. "That's different... *You're* different... I want—I want you to kiss me."

"Then say it. Say my name."

"Alisdair."

"Again."

"Alisdair."

He leaned in to kiss her.

"Again," he murmured, mouth almost on hers. "Say it, Rory."

"Alisdair... *Alisdair!*"

Her lips had barely brushed his when she jerked back, and repeated his name, this second time cried out in warning.

Dair's eyes opened wide. Seeing her safe, but with one hand at full stretch past his shoulder, as if to stave off evil, he knew there was danger at his back. Instantly, he swiveled on a boot heel. William Watkins loomed an arm's length away. His left arm was raised diagonally across his body over his right shoulder, both hands hard about the end of Rory's Malacca walking stick, its carved ivory pineapple-shaped handle high in the air. The secretary was wielding the stick like an axe, and in an act of sheer drunken stupidity, he was about to use this metaphorical axe to fell his nemesis across the back of the head.

Dair gave the man no quarter. He delivered one swift punch to the face.

NINETEEN

"*ZOUNDS!* WHAT A SPLENDID FACER! AND BRILLIANTLY EXECUTED, my friend! Quick. Precise. Perfect. Never in all my days did I expect to witness such a sight! By Jove, Dair, you could teach Jack Broughton a thing or two!"

It was the over-exuberant Lord Grasby. Such was his excitement at bearing witness to his best friend planting his fist into Weasel Watkins' face he hardly noticed his sister, mute and as still as a piece of ornamental statuary atop the stone wall. And he certainly did not gauge the mood of his best friend, who did not react to his presence, or turn his head to look at him, but kept his focus on William Watkins while flexing his fingers, knuckles smarting from the blow.

In fact, such was Grasby's delight in witnessing his brother-in-law get his just deserts after all these years, and at the hands of his best friend, who had always threatened to rearrange Weasel Watkins' facial features but had never delivered on this threat, that he quite forgot he was miserably angry, not only with William Watkins, but with Dair.

He was angry with William Watkins for having the audacity to think he was well within his rights to propose to Rory, and while fortified to the gills with alcohol. Grasby had returned to the shallop to a predictable berating by his wife, for abandoning her, and by the looks of him—he had taken a dip in the Thames on the way back from Banks House—he had had a lovely time of it without her. And in amongst her self-centered diatribe she happened to mention her brother's intentions, and how she thought it the most wonderful news. His response—that her brother could be the last man walking this earth and he still would withhold his consent to such a match—sent Lady Grasby into a flood of tears. Grasby left her prostrate on the sofa, and stomped off up the jetty in search of Rory before William Watkins got a paw to her.

But what met his gaze as he rounded a bend in the path, was not William Watkins pawing at Rory, but the startling vision of his best friend making up to his little sister! He was so taken aback he wondered if it was a trick of the sun, and he was witness to a mirage. Or was he drunk or dreaming? What he was, was as mad as hellfire. His best friend since Harrow had broken the cardinal rule of best friends: Sisters were strictly off-limits.

Sisters were married off to nice chaps who were boring clods; preferably a chap who was as close to being a virgin as was possible. Which meant one whose sexual history was unknown to brothers and friends alike. A chap who went off on the Grand Tour and sowed his wild oats abroad but did not do so at home. A nice chap who did not have any surprises lurking in cupboards, or as in his best friend's case, a Banks House with a past mistress and an illegitimate son, and a sordid sexual history known not only to himself, but to every member of White's and beyond!

It was one thing to brag and exchange tid-bits about his best friend's womanizing when the women were of a certain class and a certain type, but when it was his little sister Dair had within his sights, that was something altogether repugnant and unforgivable.

In fact, the sight of Rory and Dair as close as a couple could get without actually kissing, gave Grasby a severe jolt. He had never entertained the idea of his sister marrying at all. He liked the idea of her being a spinster aunt, living with him and Silla and the children. As for Rory being attractive to males, well, she was his sister, for God's sake! If he thought about it deeply, he was glad she had an infirmity because it meant she would never have a suitor, and could be left in peace. She would always be his little sister and not another chap's wife.

He might be irritatingly annoyed with Weasel Watkins' presumption, but William Watkins' motive was transparent. He did not love Rory, he wanted to marry her for the status it would bring him. At least the Weasel was obvious, whereas he had no idea what game Dair was playing. Possibly a whim of the moment, but one he should have resisted. The last thing on this earth he wanted was his sister falling in love with Dair Devil Fitzstuart. Only anguish and heartache could result, of that he was convinced.

So when he saw Rory sitting on the wall, and his best friend standing so close to her that it was clear he was going to kiss her, shock and anger quickened his stride. He marched up to the wall about to demand that Dair unhand his sister, when to his amazement, William Watkins jumped up out of nowhere brandishing a stick, his intention clear. Grasby's anger instantly vanished, replaced by incredulity. He was just about to shout out a warning when Rory did that for him, and his best friend dealt swiftly and violently with the situation.

Caught up in the moment, his angry purpose was forgotten in his admiration for Dair and his great satisfaction at seeing his brother-in-law finally get his comeuppance. He couldn't wait to tell Cedric and the lads at White's. He was confident a great many wagers would be settled, and a pile of debts cleared and made on the strength of that one punch.

Still, he did have a twinge of conscience watching the Weasel stagger about with a hand to his fractured nose, eyes blinded by tears of pain. When all was said and done, the man was his brother-in-law, and he knew Silla would fall all to pieces when she discovered her brother had suffered an injury, and, to his cost, at the hands of Major Lord Fitzstuart. He predicted bliss, domestic or otherwise, was about to become unobtainable within his household. And that reminded him of his sister, and Watkins' marriage proposal, and his sympathy vanished. But before he had a chance to go to Rory, Dair called out to him, and Weasel Watkins found his voice in amongst his cries of pain.

"My nose! My nose, it's-it's broken! Dear God, you've *broken* my nose! You bloody bastard, Fitzstuart. You bloody brainless lout! You've broken it! Do you know what—"

"Button the language, Weasel or I'll break your jaw as well."

William Watkins gave a snort of laughter that saw blood spurt from his nostrils and splatter the front of his exquisitely embroidered silk waistcoat. Despite the stabbing pain between his eyes he found the mental energy to snigger a reply.

"Language? What would you know about that? You can't cobble two sentences together that make sense. I doubt a fatwitted numbskull like you can write more than your name—Dear God in Heaven, my n-nose!" He wiped his eyes free of tears, though they continued to water, and then ran a finger tentatively across his nostrils, saw the blood, then the blood on his clothes and collapsed cross-legged into the grass. "Jesu—I'm bleeding to death! The pain! I'm *dying*!"

"No, you're not. Your nose is broken, and broken noses bleed—a lot. If you want to know pain, ask my batman. Having your mangled hand amputated, that's pain. Four sentences and one conjunction, not counting this one. Grasby!? Give me your flask."

The word *conjunction* had William Watkins turning his head to stare at the Major. As if seeing him for the first time, he had to wonder if, after all these years, he had read him wrong. But he quickly decided the quantity of wine drunk at lunch combined with the hell between his eyes had made him delirious. And when Dair winked at him with a twitch of a knowing smile, he knew it must be so.

"Grasby? Flask! The one full of cognac you always carry in your frock coat poc—"

"Hold on a dashed minute!" Grasby interrupted, a finger pointing at the Major. "You've grown a beard!"

Dair rubbed his cheek.

"There wasn't much else I could do. Prisoners aren't permitted shaving implements. They might use them for other purposes."

"What other purposes?"

"Murder and suicide come to mind…" Dair murmured.

"Hold on to the reins! You've been let out of the Tower!"

Dair grinned. "Yes."

"Good God, it becomes clear to me why the two of you are suited!" William Watkins burst out between groans, unable to listen to another minute of such inane conversation.

"Should I keep the whiskers?" Dair asked Grasby, ignoring William Watkins.

He glanced at Rory, but as she had her chin down, he wondered if she was doing her best to suppress a fit of the giggles at her brother's remarkable lack of awareness. To goad her into lifting her head, he added, "I've heard ladybirds like a piratical beard. What do you think, Grasby?"

When Grasby looked to give the notion serious consideration, William Watkins shuddered with uncontrolled exasperation, the blood gurgling in his throat.

"*Think?* With a walnut-sized brain, and it located between your legs, I can't imagine you think of anything else!"

"Walnut-sized?" Dair lifted an eyebrow.

"There's nothing walnut-sized about him!" Grasby confirmed. "Brain or-or—Egad!! Is he supposed to do that?"

Grasby had saved himself from embarrassment when William Watkins started coughing uncontrollably. The secretary dropped his head between his knees, and blood started pouring from his nose into the grass.

"Give me your handkerchief. Mine won't be enough," Dair ordered, and was about to turn away to attend to the injured William Watkins when his gaze locked on Rory. She had been watching him, and she did not look away. "Are you all right, Miss Talbot?"

"Y-yes. I will be fine directly, once you help Mr. Watkins."

A moment, not ten seconds had passed between them, but Grasby caught it, and while he was not usually quick on the uptake, he was this time. He had a foreboding that his first summation upon coming round the bend in the path was the right one. Dair had been kissing his sister, and perhaps Watkins had caught them, attacked Dair and been punched for his efforts.

"Here," Dair said to Watkins, going down on his haunches beside him and holding out one of the handkerchiefs. "The blood will stop soon, and then you can take a swig of Grasby's cognac. The sooner you get back to the barge, and apply a cold compress to the swelling, the quicker it will subside. The bruising will take much longer."

Watkins snatched the handkerchief and tentatively dabbed at his nose, eyeing the Major with loathing. The man was a gorilla-sized buffoon but he had to concede he could see why females fell into bed with him. Well, there was one woman he was determined to keep from his bed at any cost.

"I give you fair warning, Fitzstuart. Keep away from Miss Talbot. She is mine and I mean to marry her."

Dair threw his head back and laughed. He gave William Watkins a shove, half playful, half forceful.

"You? Warning *me*? You and whose army? And to think I dared hoped I'd knocked some sense into you!"

"Don't think I didn't not know your game!"

"Dear me, Weasel, a triple negative, and you call *me* the language fatwit." He unscrewed the cap and held out the flask. "Take a swig. You'll feel better for it. Though why I should concern myself with you…"

The secretary took a mouthful of the cognac, swilled out his mouth and spat. He then took a sip, swallowed, and thrust the flask back at Dair.

"Molest Miss Talbot again and I'll go straight to Shrewsbury with what I know about you—"

"You never fail to be predictable! You were a tale-bearer at School, too."

"—you and your-your *perverse pleasures.*"

"Perverse pleasures? Kissing a pretty girl a perverse pleasure?" Dair gave a huff of dismissal. "Fat lot you know about perversity! In fact, fat lot of nothing you know about pretty girls!"

A hammer banged behind his eyes and he could feel his face swelling, but for all that William Watkins was determined to wrest the upper-hand from this bearded baboon. With an over-inflated sense of his own cleverness, and an under-appreciation of the Major's intelligence, he took it upon himself to inform his lordship, without spelling it out word-for-word, that he was well aware of the long-standing wager that dared the devil to tup a cripple. If such a repugnant wager was to become generally known, it would be the end of the Major's social acceptability. For while absurd wagers were the order of the day, there were some areas that were off-limits, even to the most base, hard-hearted gambler; the insane, the deformed, and the very young being top of the list.

"I know why you've taken a sudden interest in Miss Talbot," William Watkins said, looking past Dair's shoulder, to the wall, where Lord Grasby had retreated to speak to his sister, the siblings in quiet conversation. He brought his gaze back to the Major. "It must have taken all your powers of deduction to finally realize there was one of *them* on your doorstep. And there's none finer than Miss Talbot, that when she is seated, one can almost forget her—*disadvantage*."

"One of *them*?" Dair interrupted, at a loss to know what the secretary was babbling on about. He concluded the man must be concussed. "One of *what*?"

"Oh, come now, Fitzstuart!" William Watkins scoffed. "You're stupid, not blind! Miss Talbot is a *cripple*."

Dair's jaw set hard and his hands clenched.

"And you have brown hair. Neither requires further discussion."

William Watkins blinked. His eyelids felt heavy and huge. "She has a deformed right foot and is lame in one leg, which makes her a prime victim for your perverse wager, wouldn't you say?"

Dair grabbed the secretary about the throat, high enough to close his jaw. He gritted his teeth and hissed in the man's ear. "I'd say you're about to add broken teeth to your list of injuries, if you don't keep your bread hole shut!"

He then threw him off, rose to his full height and strode away, leaving the secretary spluttering for breath, mouth opened wide to take in air because his fractured nose was clogged with dried blood.

"He's all yours!" Dair barked at Grasby. "Get him to his feet. His legs can't be as useless as the rest of him."

"But what about my—"

"I'll take Miss Talbot as far as the jetty."

"No. I don't think that's a good idea," Grasby stated, coming away from the wall. "I'll take Rory—"

"Your sister has blistered feet and cannot walk, and you cannot carry her the distance." He pulled Grasby aside, saying in his ear, "If you leave me with him, I'm likely to beat the maggot to a watery pulp. Want that on your conscience?"

"Certainly not!

"Good! Then my way it is!"

Anger was one emotion his best friend rarely, if ever, exhibited, so Grasby made no further objection. He watched Dair stride over to where his sister sat, silent and observant, hands in her lap, an unsettling feeling making his stomach tighten. William Watkins' persistent coughing made him reluctantly turn away to offer his brother-in-law his assistance. Which was just as well, because there was no mistaking the emotion writ large on Rory's face when the Major handed over her walking stick he found discarded in the grass.

DAIR HAD SCOOPED UP THE STICK AND WAS ABOUT TO OFFER IT to her, when Rory lifted her head so he could see her face under the brim of her hat, and all the anger instantly vanished. He was so taken aback by her expression that he stopped dead in front of her, speechless. He had meant to apologize, for his violent reaction to Watkins' behavior, for her having to bear witness to such an unseemly sight, and for leaving her sitting in the sun. But all those words, already formed but yet to be said, were swallowed back down his throat and forgotten.

She was smiling at him, but it was not just any smile, it was a joyful, loving smile, and it was the last thing he was expecting from her, given present circumstances. It was the most beautiful smile he had ever seen. It made him smile in return without even knowing he was doing so.

"You do remember me," she whispered, so only he could hear her. She took her stick from him and laid it across her lap, then held out her hand. He took it without a second thought, and she drew him closer. "When you apologized earlier for kissing me, I heard what you said, but I wasn't listening. If that makes sense. But now, sitting here and thinking about that kiss—which was a nicer way to pass the time than watching poor Mr. Watkins' bleed into the grass—"

"I regret hitting him in front of you, but not that I hit him."

"—I recalled what you said to me earlier. You said: *I'm sorry, Delight.* That is proof, is it not, that you do remember me from Romney's studio! You weren't drunk at all, were you?"

He picked her up without a word, and carried her through the gate and along the path.

"You've had a touch too much sun, Miss Talbot."

"And you, my lord, cannot tell a fib after you've kissed me! Admit it!"

He strode on.

"Miss Talbot, would you be so kind as to look over my shoulder and tell me if you can see your brother and the Weasel."

"Call me Rory or call me Delight, but I am done with you calling me Miss Talbot! You are being stubborn because I found you out!"

"Can you see your brother or not?"

She lifted her chin, looked over his shoulder and shook her head.

"No. There are trees and they must be out of our line of—Oh! *Alisdair*! What-what are you doing?"

He had ducked into the shrubbery. Behind a hedgerow, he slid her to her feet, pulled her tight to his torso, and before she could straighten her hat or her petticoats, or knew what to do with her walking stick, stooped under the brim of her hat and kissed her on the mouth. It was only one kiss, but it was enough to bring the smile back into his dark eyes and lift the corners of his mouth.

"Now I feel much better. Thank you—*Rory*."

She dropped her stick and put both hands about his neck and went up on tiptoe to kiss him. "Was it Grasby who told you not to remember me from Romney's studio?" She smiled shyly and looked through her lashes. "I remember you—all of you…"

"You, my Delight, are a baggage! No. Not Grasby. Your grandfather."

"Oh! That makes much more sense. Grand must have wanted to spare me the shame of such a predicament." She giggled. "Or wanted to spare you and Grasby the shame of yours! Will you kiss me again?"

"Not here. Not now. Not with your brother breathing down my neck."

Rory pouted and pretended disappointment. "But you will kiss me again, won't you?"

"Yes."

"And with those whiskers?"

"Ha! So you truly do like my piratical beard?"

"I am not a ladybird, but I do have a sense of discrimination. And all I can tell you is that I am yet to determine which incarnation of you I prefer: American savage or pirate… But I will let you know after due consideration."

He laughed out loud and then quickly stifled his mirth by clapping a hand to his mouth, though the laughter still danced in his eyes. When he could speak he said huskily, "You are incorrigible!"

"And you must be sorely missed at Banks House," she said and scooped up her stick. "I feel dreadful for taking up so much of your time when you should be spending it with your son, and on this of all days."

"Knowing Jamie, he is preoccupied with his new microscope, and when I walk into the book room and make my presence known, he will look up and smile and think I have been there all along. You may think he looks like my brother Charles, but he has his mother's sweet nature, for which I am profoundly grateful." He went to pick her up again, then hesitated, and said with a frown, "Do you mind—about Jamie—about—the Banks family?"

"Mind? I don't know what you mean."

He scooped her up again and rejoined the path.

"No. No, I suppose you don't. I will have to rectify that before I—I think it is important I tell you, about them and about me, before we take this any further."

Rory held her breath, wondering what he wanted to confide in her, and equally interesting, what he meant by further... Take *what* further?

"If that is your wish," she said calmly.

He nodded. "Good."

And that was the last word he spoke on that subject, as they had come to the jetty. Here he put her to firm ground just as Lady Grasby came out onto the deck of the barge. She gave such a start that Rory thought her sister-in-law about to faint, and breathed a sigh of relief when a quick-thinking footman pushed a chair under her before she collapsed. Her personal maid produced a fan to cool her mistress's heaving bosom. But a glance over her shoulder, and Rory realized it was not her return which had caused her sister-in-law such distress, but the sight of William Watkins with an arm across Grasby's shoulder and a bloodied handkerchief up to his nose.

"I fear your journey home is not going to be as uneventful as the one here," Dair said at Rory's ear as he bowed over her hand in farewell. "I just hope you can ignore the high drama and find a quiet corner to discuss pineapple cultivation with Mr. Humphrey, uninterrupted."

"Oh! Is he here? On the barge?"

"Yes. He should be aboard awaiting you. I thought it only fair you have the opportunity of Humphrey's undivided expertise for a few hours, given Jamie monopolized him while you were at Banks House."

"That was thoughtful of you, my lord. Thank you." She dimpled. "I will have to think of a suitable way to repay you."

Dair raised an eyebrow and said blandly, "No need to think too hard. I am but a simple soldier, thus my needs are equally simple." He bowed again and said just as Grasby and William Watkins arrived at the jetty, "I look forward to dining with you and Lord Shrewsbury at the Gatehouse Lodge in the coming weeks, and having the mysteries of pineapple cultivation explained to me." He nodded to Grasby, and said to the secretary with tongue firmly in cheek, "I do believe I've added character to your face, Weasel. Don't thank me now. Later, when the swelling has gone, will be soon enough." He then turned on a boot heel and wandered off, back up the path, hands shoved deep in his frock coat pockets.

Rory watched him go, gaze lingering on his back longer than was polite. To her shame, pineapple cultivation was the last thing on her mind.

TWENTY

TREAT, HAMPSHIRE: THE ROXTON DUCAL SEAT, JULY 1777

DAIR CAME OVER THE RISE OF MANICURED LAWN AND STROLLED down to the jetty that jutted out into the lake, where bobbed several moored skiffs. The sun was high in a bright blue sky, with no clouds and no breeze. It was the perfect weather for a swim. Not for the first time did he gaze enviously out across the sparkling water of a lake stocked with fish and dotted with islands. How he wished to strip, dive in and cool off. But such longing was quickly overtaken by dread. He squared his shoulders, drew back on his cheroot, and ignored the heat under his stock. He also ignored the woman at his back, who had followed him from the Duchess's summer pavilion.

He had found her there, alone with her needlework. She was waiting for her young mistress to return from her swim. A basket by a squat table had been emptied of its afternoon tea contents and was laid out on a linen table cloth. The silver teapot on its pedestal and the necessary attendant tea things he knew had come courtesy of the Elizabethan dower house up on the hill. The Duchess of Kinross was due home any day; so the housekeeper had told him when he had arrived unannounced on the doorstep the night before, with his valet and his portmanteaux.

He had just spent a trying fortnight at Fitzstuart Hall in Buckinghamshire, his family seat. He meant to stay only a week, but felt obliged to remain because his widowed sister Lady Mary and her daughter Theodora arrived the day before he was to depart. They were so happy to see him he could not, in good conscience, offend them by not extending his stay. Besides, he was genuinely fond of Mary and his

tomboy niece. Teddy begged her Uncle Dair to take her riding and
hawking, anything to keep them outdoors, so she could escape her well-
intentioned mother's attempts to fashion her into a young lady. He
could not refuse her, and it gave him the excuse he needed to avoid the
indoors, too.

But staying on meant enduring more of his mother's overly
dramatic lamentations about his brother's socially unacceptable and
disastrous (in her eyes) elopement. Never mind Charles was a traitor to
king and country, that was as nothing compared to the unsuitability of
his choice of bride. Dair made no comment. What was the use when
there was only her point of view? He was also required to lend a sympathetic ear to his sister's predicament. Mary vented her humiliation at
the terms under which she was now forced to live, courtesy of her late
husband's despicable will, and the man (Mary called him a fiend and a
tyrant) who was charged with administering the estate until its heir, Sir
John Cavendish, reached his majority.

When Dair ventured to point out she was extremely fortunate not
to be evicted from a house and lands to which she no longer had any
claim, Mary's response was to accuse him of being an unfeeling brute,
who had no notion of what it was like to go cap-in-hand to a functionary for every little thing required to make a woman's life bearable.
As Lady Mary was wearing a gown of the most costly silk embroidered
with gold thread, matching mules and mitts, and was able to change
her gowns twice daily, Dair suspected that the "tyrant," whose name he
knew but at that moment escaped his memory, was generous to a fault.

And when Dair made the observation that he did indeed know
what it was like to be financially beholden to another, and that she had
all his sympathies, Lady Mary instantly and tearfully apologized, well
aware her brother had no control over his inheritance and all decisions
regarding the estate were made by their cousin, the Duke of Roxton.

The Countess's response was to sigh tragically and bemoan her
eldest son's continued unmarried state. All that was required for Dair to
take control of what was rightfully his and end the family shame of
Roxton's rule over them, was for him to marry.

That was the end of his patience, and cemented his resolve. Not a
truer word had his mother spoken. He apologized for not taking her
advice sooner. And with that he excused himself and went off in search
of the steward. Whereupon he shut himself up with the old retainer for
two days. He then departed Fitzstuart Hall, his relatives none the wiser
as to his motives and intentions, leaving the steward with a long list of
requests and requirements he couldn't wait to put into immediate
effect.

Dair rode into Hampshire more content with life than he had ever been.

His cousin Antonia was one of three people who had brought him to the Roxton ducal seat, Treat. Lord Shrewsbury was another. He needed to debrief him about his mission to Portugal. But it was the third person he most wanted to see, and it was she who was presently enjoying the refreshing waters of the lake.

When he had offered to fetch her mistress, so the maid could remain in the coolness of the pavilion, the woman had vigorously shook her head and declared that she, and all the servants, had been given strict instructions Miss Talbot was not to be left alone. That had raised one of Dair's black eyebrows, for surely Miss Talbot was alone now, in the lake. The maid had blushed and corrected her pronouncement: Miss Talbot was not to be left alone with any gentleman other than her grandfather or her brother. Dair made no comment, turned on a boot heel and off he went to find Miss Talbot, her maid on the skirts of his cream linen frock coat.

He was almost at the jetty when he caught sight of Rory. Well, part of her. He heard a splash, was quick to look to the right of the skiffs and glimpsed bare flesh. Her round derriere bobbed up in the water then disappeared with a kick of her legs below the water line with the rest of her. He glanced over his shoulder, saw the maid huffing, a hand to her brow to shield her eyes from glare, and said casually, pointing over to a clump of willows on the embankment,

"Go sit in the shade. You will still be in line of sight of the jetty and can say with confidence you did not leave Miss Talbot alone —with me."

The sun's summer heat decided the maid, and she was gone to the shade, leaving Dair to approach the jetty, something he did with cloaked trepidation, and without looking down between the wooden boards to the water below. He had all the outward appearance of calm confidence, but the long fingers which brought the cheroot up to his mouth twitched. He cursed his Achilles' heel; cursing his father more for inflicting it upon him. But most of all, he cursed himself for not being able to overcome such a weakness, for he knew it was all in his mind.

Such bitter thoughts evaporated on spying Rory's walking stick and a pile of clothes at the end of the jetty. Using the carved amber handle of the walking stick, he prodded the clothes and picked up each article for inspection. He was well-versed in female attire and its underpinnings, and the diaphanous garments told him Miss Talbot was, quite sensibly, wearing as few layers as possible during this unusual hot spell.

She had given up wearing stays under her light muslin gown, went barefoot, though there was a pair of white stockings scuffed with grass stains on the foot, and perhaps worn for modesty's sake. And unless he was much mistaken, she had eschewed a linen bathing costume as well. He set the walking stick against a fat bollard, and with the cheroot between his teeth and his right hand shielding his eyes, he searched out across the water for any tell-tale breaks in its glassy surface.

"Hello! What are you doing here?"

The voice was behind him. It was cheerful and held no anxiety— that he had come upon her swimming naked in the lake. He turned but did not look down at the water but out over the skiffs to the embank- ment. It had nothing to do with propriety, and everything to do with calm water. Still, he managed to sound offhand, removing the cheroot from between his teeth.

"I've come to kiss you."

When she gurgled with laughter, he grinned. But still he did not look down at her.

"You kept your beard."

"Yes."

"Did you keep it for me?"

"Yes. Much to my mother's chagrin. She says I present as a swarthy vagrant. I will have to shave before I return to—"

"But you just got here—"

"—Fitzstuart Hall."

"Oh… You can look, y'know. Most of me is hidden behind a boat."

He smoked his cheroot, doing his best to remain calm and in control, and to forget that just a few feet under his boot heels was reed- filled still lake water. It never ceased to puzzle him that he did not have the same reaction when boarding a ship to set sail on open ocean. He would have thought vast stretches of sea water, with the constant rolling motion of the waves, the salt air, and the lack of land in any direction, would have held more fear for him. But no. It was the glassy stillness of a lake, the black pit nothingness, and the inevitable entanglement in the grasping tendrils of reeds, that set his heart racing. It also sent his mind hurtling back to his tenth birthday, when he was held under water until almost drowned, lungs filling with water as he flailed about, desperate for air, his brother's screams and his father's fury ringing in his ears, as he was brought to the surface and dunked time and again. His father meant to teach him a life lesson. All it did was make Dair hate him all the more.

"Down here, at your feet," Rory called, waving an arm above her head to get his attention.

The movement broke Dair's distraction with the past and he shook himself free of such melancholy, dark eyes finally locking on her.

Rory had anchored her elbows over the side of the skiff and rested her chin on her hands, so that all he saw of her was her bare arms and face. She smiled up at him, hair plastered to her scalp and falling about her shoulders in long, dripping coiled tendrils. In turn, he rested a buttock on the bollard and returned her smile.

"Farrier warned me the lake was inhabited by mermaids, but I did not believe him. For one thing, mermaids are sea creatures."

"Farrier…?"

"My batman since before the war in the Americas. You may have seen him about recently, fishing from a skiff, or casting a line from the weir. He is on a fortnight's angling holiday, his reward for spending a month cooped up in the Tower in my place. He has the Duke's permission to catch as much trout and game as he can eat, to sleep under the stars wherever he pleases, and to observe mermaids at his leisure."

"Is he a bald gentleman with a scar to his cheek and a silver hook for a hand?"

"That's Farrier."

Rory shook her head. "I've not seen him, but Grand described him to me, and warned me the Duke had a guest using the lake."

"And still you swim naked…?"

Rory pouted and was suddenly uncomfortable.

"It's obvious you've never had to swim in what amounts to a bed gown. Hideous article! More a hindrance than a help, and likely to drown its wearer." She dimpled. "Without it, I am an exceptionally good swimmer; practically a fish. Not surprising your batman thought he had seen a mermaid."

He let his dark eyes flicker over her slim arms and shoulders, and down the tangle of long wet hair that framed her heart-shaped face and disappeared to dip in the water. She did indeed present as a beautiful mermaid. He wondered if not only her narrow back but also her round buttocks were visible above the waterline, and for the first and only time begrudged Farrier his well-earned holiday. His batman was in his skiff, halfway between the jetty and the island, with a line in the water. But if he was angling, Dair would eat his boot. The man was directly behind Rory, with the best seat in the house. Dair made a mental note to order Farrier to remove himself as far as possible from the dower house jetty and its resident mermaid for the rest of his little angling adventure.

He pointed the end of her walking stick over her fair head in the direction of Farrier's skiff.

"If you do not wish to be caught on the end of his hook, I suggest you come up to the pavilion for nuncheon."

A glance over her shoulder, and Rory took in the small boat and its occupant. When the angler dared to doff his hat, she gave a squeal of revelation and disappeared below the water line to Dair's laughter. She resurfaced on the other side of the jetty, hidden from Farrier's line of sight but now in full view of her shocked maid and, had Dair peered over the side of the wooden planks, in full view of him, too. He swiveled to face her but remained where he was.

"I shall head back to the pavilion so your maid can help you dress. I suspect being a mermaid makes you ravenous."

Rory remained silent a moment, then said quietly, so quietly he came across to the edge of the jetty to hear her,

"Perhaps you'd like to take a swim first? It is so warm... You must be hot in that frock coat..."

"Thank you for the offer, but I—"

"Oh! Oh, I won't stay. I didn't mean you take a swim *with me*," she quickly corrected, embarrassed at being rejected. "You can have the lake all to yourself. And men don't need to strip to nothing. They can swim in their breeches. I wore Grasby's cast-offs to learn to swim, so I know how easy it is for men to—Or not," she added quickly, because of the way he was looking out across the water, but not down at her. "You don't have to swim in your breeches, if you don't want to. You can—"

"Rory. There is nothing I would like more than to swim naked with you."

It was the truth. There was nothing he desired more. Correction. There was one thing, but that could wait. And if there was ever a moment to overcome his dread of lake water, this was it, and with her. But instead of seizing the moment, because the moment would have to wait until he knew how matters stood between them, he politely declined, saying gently,

"I will keep your offer for another day. I'm going to send Farrier away now, so you can dress. I'll be up at the pavilion waiting. I have something important to discuss with you."

"What is so important?" she asked him half an hour later, coming up the steps to join him in the shade of the Duchess's pretty pavilion.

She had dressed in haste. Her bodice was damp in patches where she had improperly dried her skin, most notably at her bust line, and her hair, though scraped back off her face and tied up with a satin ribbon at her nape, still dripped. But that was not a bad thing. With no breeze, even the shade of the pavilion afforded only minimal relief from the summer heat.

Dair had stripped out of his frock coat and was in his sleeveless silk waistcoat and shirtsleeves, booted legs sprawled out across a line of tapestry cushions, a hand under his head. He was staring up at the painted ceiling. He had almost dozed off when Rory's question brought him to life. He sat up and offered her the cushions opposite him at the squat table laden with a modest nuncheon: A wheel of Cheshire cheese, a jar of chutney, a loaf of fresh bread, slices of cold beef, pickled onions, and a salad of greens. As well as the silver teapot on its stand and tea things on a tray, there was a jug of pear cider, once sitting on ice, now melted to cold water, in a porcelain bucket. It was at the jug Rory looked at in puzzlement as she set aside her stick.

"Courtesy of Cousin Duchess's kitchen, just like the teapot," Dair said, pouring her out a tumbler of cider. "Tea is well and good, but in this heat, it is best to start with a cold drink. Are those really necessary?" he added sternly, when Rory's maid Edith came forward with a pair of ankle boots.

Rory shook her head and Edith retreated to resume her seat between two fat columns by the pavilion steps. She picked up her needlework, one ear to the conversation.

Rory took her place at the table, tucking her stockinged feet under her cotton petticoats, and gratefully drank the cider.

"Are you lodging at the dower house?"

"Yes."

"Why not up at the big house with their Graces?"

Dair went about filling a plate with a variety of what was on offer on the table.

"Roxton is an excellent host, and he still owns me as family, despite my despicable behavior at the regatta. But we are barely on speaking terms." He passed her the laden plate, holding her gaze. "And, it is but a short stroll from here to the Gatehouse Lodge, and you…"

Rory felt her face grow hot and she smiled unconsciously. His admission of staying at her godmother's house to be close to her made her tingle all over, and she could not have been happier. Yet, she remained pensive at his mention of the regatta. That had been held on the estate two months ago. Rory remembered the boat race well indeed. How could she, or any other guest forget that day?

During the boat race, one of the Duke's five-year-old twin sons fell out of a skiff into the lake and almost drowned. His little life was saved by the efforts of the Duke of Kinross. The race had all but been abandoned. Yet, the Major had rowed on and won the race, to great fanfare and bravado on his part. The Roxtons remained tight-lipped about the entire incident. And as no one could believe a war hero capable of

ignoring a plea for help, there had to be a perfectly reasonable explanation as to why the Major had rowed on to win the race.

Rory might not know the reason behind Dair's behavior but she
believed she had more insight than most into the episode. The best
vantage point to see the boat race was from a marquee pitched at the
highest point of the rolling lawn. And here Rory watched the Major
cross the finish line under the arch of the stone bridge, the first of three
boats to complete the race. And while the unwitting crowd cheered
wildly to have a victor, Rory caught sight of two more boats close
together, making slow progress towards the bridge, clearly no longer
competing. It was only much later that she came to hear of the near
tragedy on the lake. But before that, before the shocking incident
became general knowledge, the Major and his party of followers,
including a clutch of young beauties hanging on every word the
dashing Major uttered, burst into her tent in search of refreshments.

The Major was in fine voice and fine form. He had an arm about Mr.
Cedric Pleasant's neck, not because he required his friend's support to
remain upright after such physical exertion, but as an affectionate
acknowledgement of Mr. Pleasant's backing him to win. Recounting the
finer points of the race with his boon companions, Rory was certain the
adoring females in his party, particularly the Aubrey twins—two sylph-
like beauties with large brown eyes—heard only one word in ten, too
preoccupied, as Rory was herself, in admiring the Major's handsome and
powerful physique. His head of unruly black hair fell damp across his
brow and into his eyes. The usual billowy linen shirt was wet through and
thus adhered to every muscle of his torso; likewise, his clingingly tight
cream breeches, displaying to advantage the contours of his taut thighs.

Rory resorted to fluttering her fan, suddenly giddy to be in close
quarters with such potent masculinity, and because the space within the
marquee was suddenly hot and heavy, crammed as it now was with an
audience eager to be part of the Major's victory celebrations. When Mr.
Pleasant shoved a jug of ale into the Major's hand, it was downed in
one gulp, and to appreciative shouts of encouragement. Finally, the
Major was swallowed up by the crowd of admirers, leaving Rory
looking up from her chair at the backs of frock coats, and the intricate
rumpled creations of the ladies' polonaise petticoats.

Ignored and feeling invisible, Rory snatched up her stick, eager to
seek fresh air and solace on the lawn. But it was no easy task for her to
rise from her chair. She was hemmed in by a crowd too caught up in
the moment. But not five minutes later the crowd parted, to allow the
Major, a footman at his shoulder, to move to the back of the marquee.

He stopped short of Rory's chair, gaze fixed at some point over her head, unaware she was there. Here, the footman shrugged him into his embroidered silk waistcoat.

Rory's gaze never wavered from his face. She, who always sat in her quiet corner, the observer but never the observed, saw what others could not, and what he did not want others to see. The moment he turned his back on everyone else, the devil-may-care mask he wore in public fell away. Gone was the twinkle in his eye, and the self-assured grin. His face dropped with sheer relief—from what, she had no idea, but it was as if he had been given a task he was sure he would fail, only to miraculously do well. He took a deep breath and briefly closed his eyes, perhaps in thanks for having come through what surely must have been quite an ordeal, gauging by the extent of the reprieve writ large on his handsome features.

Rory instinctively knew it had everything to do with the boat race, just as she knew now, as she sat across from him in the shade of the pavilion, he wished to confide in her. So she took her time to formulate her words, pulling at the soft center of the chunk of bread on her plate. She ate it before saying, as conversationally as she could muster, a flicker of a glance across the squat table where he sat cross-legged on the cushions, piling a slab of bread with slices of beef,

"You gave quite a performance at the regatta…"

"Performance? Ha! It was one of my best. It had to be or I was destined for failure. But the word failure is not in my lexicon. So from the moment I stepped onto that jetty and into the skiff, until I stepped out of it over the finish line, I put in the performance of my life. I am relieved I don't remember any of it—the rowing; what happened during the race; the shouts of encouragement from the shoreline. I looked neither left nor right, and I did not stop, for anything or anyone. I cannot…"

"So you rowed on when others may have needed your help?"

"Yes. But my brother assured me my help was not needed."

"Surely you would have stopped had they shouted for your assistance?"

"Truthfully?" He held her gaze, despite feeling the heat suddenly burning his throat. He wondered if it was possible to see a man's blush under a full beard. "I cannot answer that. I just rowed like bloody hell, determined to cross the finish line and get to dry land in the shortest time possible."

"You could have declined to enter the race," she said, then immediately answered her own question. "No. Of course you wouldn't. Dair

Fitzstuart does not refuse a wager. If he did, that would be strange indeed, and your friends would ask questions…"

"Yes… I have small consolation in knowing I was too far ahead in the race to be of any use had I been called back; so Charles confided. Little Louis was overboard and sinking fast and Kinross dived in and had him rescued before even Charles or Roxton had time to react."

Rory continued to tug at the bread without eating it, leaving a hollowed crusty shell and a pile of crumbs on her plate.

"I believe that had your brother called out to you, you would have instinctively gone to his aid, all other considerations secondary."

"Thank you for your belief. It means the world to me…"

She smiled shyly at such praise, but did not drop her gaze from his.

"You gave no thought to your own safety when you rescued that family from the battlefield at Brooklyn Heights, did you?"

"Battle is different. I know how to handle myself and my men on a battlefield. And that was on terra firma."

"But surely in battle your primary goal is to secure victory at all costs?"

Dair gave a lopsided grin. "We may not have secured victory recently, but victory was ours in the Long Island campaign. Washington and his rebels would have been captured, too, had they not slunk away in the middle of the night."

"But near the Jamaica Pass you rescued a woman and her two children from a burning house; a house deliberately lit by colonial militia believing the woman was harboring the King's general. The rebels gave no thought to sacrificing those lives if it meant they could flush out and secure the bigger prize of General Clinton. And yet you went into a burning building, with musket fire all around you, and the enemy at close quarters, and saved not only those three lives, but the General's life, too."

"I see you keep abreast of the war in the Colonies, and read the newssheet reports on that little skirmish," he replied with a self-effacing smile. "But no mention was made in those reports of General Sir Henry Clinton's capture. To do so would not have been good for public morale."

Rory lost the furrow between her brows as her blue eyes widened and she mouthed the word "Oh". When Dair mimicked her actions, she dimpled and confessed.

"As the Spymaster's granddaughter I am privy to some tid-bits not generally known to the public. Of course, I would never reveal my sources, but you are in my grandfather's confidence, too, so I do not feel I have betrayed anyone."

"Rory, you do realize there are those on both sides of any conflict who would not think twice in using innocent lives as a means to an end?"

He was thinking specifically of Lord Shrewsbury. But he would never mention him by name to her, and shatter her loving view of her grandfather. Lord Shrewsbury was a cunning and ruthless Spymaster General, with no conscience when it came to winning at all costs. For him, any price was worth it. Not for Dair. Children were innocent regardless of the actions of their parents, and sometimes in spite of them. Enough of a reason why he could never take Shrewsbury's place, and would decline the offer if it were made to him. But that conversation was for another day, and with his mentor. He pushed aside his plate, saying flatly, "You may find this hard to believe, but not all women are innocent bystanders of war."

"Oh, I do not find that hard to believe at all," Rory contradicted earnestly. "Our sex does not preclude us from taking sides in a conflict, and acting upon our convictions."

"The husband of the woman I saved was a rebel, but she was not. She was a loyalist and a spy for us. I had to save her. I could not let her fall into enemy hands. She knew too much. But that is not why I saved her. I could not deprive her children of their mother."

"Of course you could not," Rory replied with a smile. But then her brow furrowed. "If my husband were a rebel soldier, or one of the King's men, I could not betray him by being a spy for his enemies. I would support him, help him in any way I could. Isn't that the nature of marriage? To be supportive of one another in good times and bad?"

"But what if you did not believe in his cause?"

Rory gave a little laugh of incredulity at the very idea.

"Silly. Why would I marry a man whose cause I did not believe in? I should hope that before we married we would know each other well enough, love each other enough, esteem one another, that the ceremony is but a formality. There would be no surprises, no uncertainties. We would be in accord, if not in all things, but certainly in matters of great importance to our union. If this not be the case, well, I-I—I might as well marry a *bedpost*!"

Dair had it on the tip of his tongue to quip that marriage to a bedpost was preferable to marriage with Mr. William Watkins, but he had no wish to spoil their *tête-à-tête* by mentioning the Weasel, so he said as casually as he could manage,

"So what does Miss Talbot consider of prime importance in a marriage?"

Rory shrugged and lifted a hand in a gesture that suggested the answer was self-evident.

"Love. Respect. Friendship. Honesty. Trust…"

"Physical compatibility?"

"Of course. Surely it follows that if there is love, respect, friendship, honesty *and* trust in a marriage, there will also be physical compatibility?"

His lips twitched into a brief smile.

"There can be physical compatibility without marriage…"

Rory's face flooded with color, with embarrassment, and anger. His smugness and that twitch annoyed her, and more than it should.

"That is something different entirely. That is like-like—stealing food from another man's table!" she said in an angry rush. "It may satisfy a temporary need but at what cost to self-esteem and the guilt that follows? Such couplings are surely unsatisfactory for they lack the qualities I spoke of that make physical love between husband and wife so satisfying. While I am well aware men have mistresses and females take lovers, I could never betray my husband in that base way. For him to take a mistress…" She took a deep breath, aware she had said more than she should, and stole a look at him, up into his eyes to see if he was laughing at her, for her naïve pronouncements about a matter in which she had no experience. "If my husband were unfaithful, then it stands to reason that those qualities that first brought us together no longer existed. I could not remain married to such a man."

"But there is no way out of a marriage for a female."

Rory held his gaze.

"Hence the importance of making the right choice, or no choice at all, before marriage. Though why we are speaking of marriage, I do not know, because I am completely witless on that subject and-and of-of— anything else. Thus my opinion is worthless—"

"No, that is not true. Your opinion matters, it matters a great deal —to me. I apologize for making you uncomfortable. I merely wished to express the idea that while it is possible to have physical compatibility outside of marriage, it is impossible for a marriage to flourish if physical compatibility is not present. But I take your point. If love, respect, honesty, trust *and* friendship exist, then there is no reason why a husband and wife should not enjoy physical intimacy. And if they do not, then surely the fault lies with the husband, who is the experienced partner. Although, in some rare instances, both parties may be ignorant—"

"Surely not?" Rory found the notion absurd, particularly in present company. But when Dair did not disabuse her, she lost her incredulous smile, wondering to whom he was referring, for he must have someone or some couple in mind. "Then should not both parties work equally at finding a solution to their—to their—*conundrum?*"

He laughed out loud. "*Conundrum?* Oh, Delight, I do so love your choice of words! *Conundrum.* A perfect euphemism!"

His laughter was infectious. She giggled and was about to make an inappropriate quip when they were interrupted by what sounded like a wounded mouse. It made her lose her train of thought and look over at her maid, for that was where the noise had emanated. But there was no mouse, no small wounded animal at all. Just Edith, sitting tall, with her hands grasped tightly in the lap of her gown, eyes wide and staring at Rory, mouth shut tight, so tight the tendons in her neck were visible.

With her ear to the conversation, every word marched the couple toward an intimacy that was inappropriate between a bachelor and a spinster. And when talk turned to the wholly inappropriate topic regarding the intimate relations between a husband and wife, and then onwards to the scandalous notion of lovemaking outside the vows of marriage, Edith was unable to hold herself in check any longer. But instead of ending such inappropriate talk with the excuse it was time to return to the Gatehouse Lodge, and pointing to the pony and trap awaiting them under the shade of the large spreading Linden tree across the rolling lawn from the pavilion, she expressed her disapproval in a most unintentional manner. All her suppressed words came out from between her lips in a thin high-pitched squeal of alarm that sounded as if a mouse had been pounced on by a cat, or, to Dair's ears, that of a cat's tail caught between sill and window sash.

Yet, the noise had the desired effect of bringing the couple to a sense of their surroundings. And while it highlighted the unsuitability of their conversation, it did more to make them aware of how comfortable they were in each other's company. This was evidenced when Rory glanced at Dair from under her lashes and he winked at her. They exchanged a conspiratorial smile, as if caught out collaborating in something utterly wicked. Still, they respected the maid's unspoken edict, and dutifully turned their attention to their respective plates and the food on offer. They consumed the rest of their meal in silence, Rory picking at her food while Dair ate ravenously, as always. She wondered if large vigorous males had bottomless pits for stomachs. Despite the swim in the lake giving her an appetite, with him, she was now curiously not hungry at all. When he drank down a tumbler of pear cider and refilled hers, she asked in a whisper,

"Why must you row like—like—*bloody hell?*"

He gave an involuntary smile at her hesitancy to swear and had an overwhelming urge to leap across the table and kiss her lovely mouth. He curbed this desire and finished off the rest of the bread piled with slices of beef and smothered in chutney, saying when he was replete,

"You won't believe me—No, that is not true. *You*, more than any other, will believe me, because you see through the performance. You see *me*, do you not, Delight?"

She nodded and extended her hand across the table between the empty plates and dishes, hoping Edith had returned to her needlework, for if her maid had considered the table conversation inappropriate she would surely disapprove of the couple holding hands. But Rory was beyond caring what her maid or anyone else thought. She was light-headed with happiness, but perhaps that was because she had not eaten? No! Surely this was how people felt when they were in love? Light-headed, unable to eat, so full of joy they wanted to run out onto the lawn and share their feelings with the world. And she knew it was so when he entwined his fingers with hers, and a warm sensation not unlike pins and needles—she did not know how else to describe it—flooded up her arm, invaded her body and settled in her chest. It was as if she were suddenly immersed in a bathtub full of warm fragrant water. But it was when he smiled into her eyes and made his frank admission that she knew in her heart that he felt as she did.

"How is it I did not see *you* until recently?" he asked with a note of wonder. "How could I have been so blind…?" He shook his head at his own amazement, and grinned sheepishly. "I am not the most perceptive of men, particularly when I am inhabiting the guise Society expects of me. You said yourself I am a fine actor. I am good at hiding my true self and intentions from others. A spy must be an expert at disguise, in feelings as well as form." He rubbed his cheek then his ear lobe between thumb and forefinger. "I grow a beard, put in a gold earring, tie a red kerchief about my neck, and I can walk amongst the natives of Portugal as a privateer, undetected and unbothered. I have worn the uniforms of my enemies, faced battle for His Majesty as a dragoon without fear… Yet, when it comes to rowing, or swimming in blackened water where reeds grow thick and strong—" He leaned into the table, smile gone, and not wanting to be overheard, "I am—I am a-a *coward*."

Rory's fingers convulsed in his on the word *coward*, realizing the courage it had taken him, a soldier, who had risked his life upon many an occasion for king and country, to confide his fear to her. She cleared her throat of emotion and found her voice.

"A war hero is no coward. *You* are not a coward. It is as natural to fear drowning as it is to breathe. How many of us can swim or care to learn? Our sailors are not required to know how to swim, and they spend most of their lives at sea."

"Rory, I can swim. At least, I think I still can. I have not been called upon to do so in many years. I was taught as a boy. I presume it is much the same as learning to ride a horse. Once it is learned, it cannot be unlearned. You will think me doubly foolish when I tell you I have no qualms about going to sea. Sailing on the high seas does not trouble me." He shrugged. "Mayhap it is the smell and taste of the salt in the air, or the motion of the waves, or both, that quells my dread of large bodies of water? Whatever it is, it is fortuitous, or I would've had a damned awful time of it sailing to and from the Americas with my regiment."

"So it is only still water that bothers you?"

He smiled. "Thank you for using the word bother. Yes, it *bothers* me. It bothers me greatly."

She looked at their fingers knotted together, and was surprised how small and thin hers were compared to his. He was a bear of a man, and it was difficult to comprehend that with such size there could be a fear of anything, least of all the cool, calm waters of a lake where she spent so many happy hours swimming, feeling graceful and completely alive. She truly did like him with a beard. Close-cropped and as dark as the hair on his head and chest, it suited him. Somehow it made his eyes darker and his smile brighter. What a pity the fashion was for clean-shaven faces.

She was procrastinating, wondering how best to ask him what had happened in his boyhood to make him fear swimming in a lake. It must have been something monumental, something appalling that had scarred his mind, for he was a soldier who had faced death time and again, and was in every other way fearless. She heard herself ask the question.

"Why does still water bother you, Alisdair?"

"Because, Delight, on my tenth birthday my father drowned me in a lake."

TWENTY-ONE

HE DID NOT SAY *TRIED TO DROWN*. HE SAID *DROWNED ME*. RORY was more appalled than she thought possible. So many questions crowded her thoughts that she considered it wise to say nothing at all. He would tell her in his own good time, and in his own way. She did not want to say anything that might forestall him. Yet, the presence of Edith bothered her, possibly more than it did him. It was not right her maid should hear his intimate and clearly harrowing confession, so she sent her away quietly, with a few words, up to the dower house to fetch a footman to clear away the nuncheon things. It must have been her stricken look, for Edith complied without a word of protest, gone from the pavilion with a quick curtsy.

Rory wondered if Dair even noticed Edith's departure, such was the faraway look in his eyes. Yet, no sooner had her maid disappeared down the stairs and out onto the lawn than he grabbed her fingers a little more tightly than he intended and said flatly,

"It was my tenth birthday. Charles and I were waiting for our father to join us by the lake. He was to watch me sail my model sailing ship, my birthday gift. Well, boys will be boys, particularly boys who are forced to wait such a long time that they forget why they are there waiting in the first place." He flashed a smile up at Rory, from where he had been focused on their fingers entwined. "Before long, we'd stripped out of our frock coats, removed our shoes and stockings, and rolled our breeches up over our knees so we could wade into the water to launch my ship. Any other day, we would have been down to our drawers. But we'd been given the lecture that we had to stay clean because our suits were new."

Dair shrugged.

"To be honest, the details still elude me. All I know is that Charles and I started splashing each other, the ship's mast snapped in our tomfoolery, and I blamed him. We got into a tussle. It was nothing serious. I was big for my age even then, and Charles was a good head shorter. I'd not have harmed a copper hair on his head... But as younger brothers are wont to do, they scream twice as loud and as long. I dunked him for his whining. He breathed in water and started coughing. Instead of being sympathetic, I laughed. And the louder his wails, the louder I laughed. Father had joined us by this time, but we hardly noticed. Charles accused me of trying to drown him.

"I don't blame him for saying so. He was only eight years old, and we both feared our father more than we feared monsters under our beds! He was a rigid, cold man who had no time for children, particularly no time for me. He couldn't fathom why I preferred the outdoors and doing things, *anything*, rather than sitting still over a pile of dusty old books. I spent my lessons gazing out the window at sheep, and got the birch more times than I care to remember! My lack of aptitude and application frustrated him far beyond his limited patience. He had one view of what his heir should be, and I was not it."

He smirked and shook his head.

"Ironically, Jamie is exactly the sort of son of whom he would have been proud: Scholarly, reserved of temperament, and can spend hours with his nose buried between parchment."

"And you are proud of him just the way he is."

"Yes. But I have a sense of self-worth. I appreciate the value of difference; the value of *him*. My father was an insecure, bitter man who harbored long-held resentments. He wanted to fashion me into what he should have become and did not—But back to my tenth birthday...

"Father said I needed a lesson. He said I needed to know what it was to drown, so that I never again set upon my younger brother. He took me by the back of the head... He held me under water... My face... I remember the tangle of reeds... I didn't feel the cuts to my flesh... My last conscious moment was black water rushing up my nose...

"When I woke from the blackness I was on the bank... I was coughing up a lungful of water, and with the water was blood. My face was lacerated from forehead to chin... There were people and shouting. My sister—Mary—she told me the rest. She had come out onto the terrace, saw what was happening and screamed for our mother. By the time they reached the lakeside, I was out of the water and breathing, saved by Banks, the head gardener.

"That's right," he said with a smile when Rory's fingers moved in his, "the same Father Banks you met at Banks House. At great personal cost to him and his family, Banks intervened. He pulled my father off, got me to dry land, where he slapped the water out of my lungs. Later, I found out my father was too stunned to do anything about Banks' intervention. But once I was breathing, he struck Banks hard across the face for interfering. Banks did not retaliate. How could he? For striking a nobleman he'd have been strung up, at the very least transported. As it was, he lost his position, so did his wife, my old nurse, and their family were all cast out with no references and nowhere to go…"

"How did the family come to be at Banks House?" Rory prompted. "Did they have relatives at the house who took them in?"

Dair shook his head.

"No. They spent a year living off charity. With no place to go, and with no character references, they drifted, unable to find steady work. And then Monseigneur—the old Duke of Roxton—he found them, housed them, found Banks employment at the Physic Garden."

Surprised the old Duke had involved himself in this traumatic episode in Dair's life, Rory could not help but interrupt. "My *godfather* found the Banks family a home? He found Mr. Banks employment?"

Dair looked at her as if there was nothing unusual in this circumstance.

"Of course. He not only helped the Banks Family, but when he discovered what Father had done to me, Monseigneur called him to account, to explain himself. I do not know what was said in that interview but, not long after, Father went off to the West Indies to inspect the family's sugar plantations, and he's never come back. Rumor is, he was ordered to go by the Duke, and I believe it. I was sent off to Harrow, which was the best thing that ever happened to me at that time, and I got to spend a couple of my school breaks with the Banks Family."

He suddenly looked sheepish, and again Rory was rewarded for her silence when he said bluntly, "No doubt had he been able to foretell what would happen during one of those breaks, the Duke would have thought twice about allowing such visits."

"You fell in love with Lily Banks and she fell pregnant with your son."

"Rory, that is the second time you've stated confidently I was in love with Lil. I was seventeen; she was sixteen. What happened between us should not have happened, but it did. I cannot say I wished it had not, because I now have Jamie. We have a great affection for each other, but we never fell *in love*. Lil is in love with her husband, which is right and proper, and I—I had to grow up fast. There was to be no Grand Tour for me. The Duke gave me no alternative. He bought me a commission in the army and two months after Jamie was born, Lil married Daniel Banks, and I went off to join my regiment. But I have no regrets, about Lil, about Jamie, about my time as an officer."

"I do not doubt that at all," she answered with a smile. "You have a wonderful boy, and he is being brought up in a loving home; Mrs. Banks is a good mother to him, and to all her sons. But," she added with a frown of puzzlement, "I do not understand why the Duke of Roxton involved himself in the affairs of your family... How he managed to have your father, who it seems was not at all a pliant and biddable man, banished. Indeed, he seems to have had a fierce temper and a limited understanding of children, of people in general. Such men are best left alone to their books, and possibly should remain life-long bachelors! I hope I have not offended—"

"Not in the least. Your summation is to the life. But surely you realize why the Duke of Roxton intervened on my behalf, why he got himself involved?"

When Rory blinked at him, still mystified, he explained.

"My father brought dishonor not only to his immediate family, but to the wider family connection, and most importantly, to the head of *his* family. By casting out the Banks Family to fend for themselves, retainers of good character and service, a family whose ancestors had served mine since the time of James the First, Father irreparably tarnished his good name. He might be an earl, but even *he* is required to answer to a higher family authority, to the head of his family."

When Rory's brows remained drawn together with incomprehension, Dair smiled and sought to patiently explain a matter he had long considered self-evident.

"We all belong to an extended set of family connections. That's how it works for people like us; that's how the nobility remains powerful and in control of the kingdom. Unlike the French nobles, who bow and scrape to their sovereign, we have the Magna Carta. Even your grandfather must, when required, bow to the wishes of his head of the family."

"I understand we are all connected in some way or other, but surely Grand, as Earl of Shrewsbury, answers to no one but himself?"

Dair so far forgot himself that he caught up Rory's fingers and kissed the back of her hand.

"He would love to hear you say so! And have you, and everyone else, believe it. As Spymaster General he certainly has more power than

most. But in family matters, when it comes to personal and family allegiance and alliances, his lordship is as compliant as the rest of us. Not
that the head of our family regularly intervenes or interferes, only when
there are disputes, or, in the case of my father's treatment of the Banks
family, when the family's honor and reputation are at stake."

"To what extended family does my grandfather owe his allegiance?"

But as soon as she said this she had an epiphany. The look of
dawning wonderment on her face widened Dair's smile into a grin; he
found her adorable. He let her say it.

"The Duke of Roxton is the head of Grand's family, and yours. We
—you and I—we belong to the same extended family but different
branches?" When he nodded, she smiled. "Oh, that is satisfying! It
explains why the old Duke agreed to be my godfather. How could he
refuse Grand, even when he probably wanted to, *then*. Though perhaps
it was the Duchess who persuaded him...? She has such a kind and
loving heart, and I know how much they loved one another. He would
not refuse *her*."

Dair frowned. "Why would he refuse? Why would Cousin Duchess
need to persuade the old Duke to act as your godfather?"

Rory blushed in spite of herself. She did not want to say it out loud,
but did.

"Because I was born—Because of what I am," she said quietly.
"Because—because I am a cripple."

Dair's brow creased with anger and his mouth thinned to a line. He
looked as angry as Rory had ever seen him—like black thunder rolling
in over distant hills. She tried to remove her hand from his, but he
would not let go. She wondered what angered him more—that she had
accused her godparents of being petty-minded, or that she had called
herself a cripple out loud and thus made him feel awkward in her
presence.

"Balderdash! That is not what you are, you little idiot! You are so
much more than that, and if you think their Graces hesitated to
become your godparents over such a trifle of a thing, then you do not
know them at all!"

"I did not say they regretted being my godparents," Rory replied
quietly, though she blushed at his spirited defense, wondering what to
make of it. "But when I was born, the physicians told my grandfather I
was crippled in mind as well as body. Before I was able to walk, and
before I could speak and show them I had a functioning mind, it must
have been difficult for Grand to ask the Duke and Duchess to be my
sponsor. But I see now why my grandfather wanted the head of the family

to sponsor me. By becoming my godparents, the Duke and Duchess were not only giving me their blessing, they were silently telling others that I was under their care, too. It had always been a wonder to me why I was readily accepted at Roxton gatherings; why others in the wider Roxton circle invited me to balls and parties, when surely, had I not been the Duke's goddaughter, the invitation would not have been extended at all."

"You undervalue yourself, Delight," Dair told her gently, all anger evaporated. "A few minutes in your company is enough to cement a person's good opinion. Besides which, you are quite the prettiest bloom in any ballroom bouquet, all other considerations aside."

"A shame then that I've been consigned to the ballroom vase since my first season. If only I had been on the ballroom floor with the other pretty petals," she quipped with a sigh of disappointment, though the dimple in her cheek told him she was pleased with his assessment. "You may then have noticed me sooner."

"I'm grateful you remained in your vase while I was away fighting wars," he said and kissed her hand again, this time looking up into her eyes as he did so, "otherwise you'd be married to another and have a couple of brats by now."

"Married to another? That implies there is someone else out there for me…"

He cocked his head. "So you believe each person has only one true love?"

She did but she could not bring herself to say so, not when he had asked her with a note of skepticism. It was just as well, because his next confidence made her swallow down those words and banish the idea he could believe in the notion, too.

"My parents thought so, in the beginning. That was before they married; before they spent their first night together as man and wife."

"Your parents did not find a solution to their—to their *conundrum*?"

Dair tapped the side of his nose, signal she had hit the proverbial nail on its head.

"Precisely. I suspect his inexperience, and hers, meant a solution was unlikely."

"If they were truly in love, if they were meant to be together forever, they would have worked harder at finding one."

"What a romantic you are!"

Rory pouted. "You say it as if it is a bad thing."

"Not at all. But there is something to be said for being practical, particularly as marriage does mean forever. My parents had never even shared a passionate kiss before the exchange of wedding vows. Remarkable."

"You cannot hold that against them. It is not unusual for a well-bred girl and a gentleman intent on upholding her virtue not to kiss until married. Grasby and Drusilla did not share a kiss until they were man and wife."

"Just because they hadn't kissed each other, doesn't mean they hadn't kissed others, does it?"

Rory's blue eyes widened with shock. "Oh! You are *wicked*. Grasby, yes, of course. But Silla? No! She was a maid when she married, of that I am convinced."

Dair made no further comment, and Rory had the suspicion that he knew just who Silla had kissed, where and when. She did not care to know. Though she was inclined to think it was Dair her sister-in-law had kissed, and perhaps he had then rejected her. That would explain why her sister-in-law loathed him.

Rory had a sudden devilish thought and decided to test her supposition.

"I am so pleased we had this discussion. I can now make it my business to kiss as many gentlemen as possible before I settle on the one I marry. It seems experience is required—"

"No you don't!" he interrupted, and finally decided the table was a barrier between them that could no longer be tolerated.

But instead of joining her on her side of the squat table by means of walking, as any sedate gentleman would do, he leapt across it. He vaulted over the clutter of their shared meal, across the array of glasses, porcelain dishes, plates and cutlery, and managed to miss scattering it, all but for a tumbler which he knocked with his knee. The silver tumbler spun on its side and shot into midair to land on the marble flooring with a loud clatter.

Rory let out an involuntary shriek at the sudden noise, startled because her whole concentration was on Dair's wild leap, hoping he would not hurt himself, or her, or break something by his impetuousness. She squealed with laughter when he landed beside her, only for the momentum to cause his feet to skid out from under him, and he land on his side, on a cushion, legs sprawled out sideways. She half rose up on her knees, and her hand shot out and grabbed the billowy sleeve of his white linen shirt, as if this would bring about inertia. It did not. It sent her after him, and she landed against his chest, in amongst the pile of cushions now scattered around them. He threw an arm about her waist to hold her close, and there they lay sprawled on the cushions on the marble floor, both of them laughing without restraint. And when he held up a gold and pink silk tassel, come free from one of the many cushions, and dangled it before her eyes with a big silly grin, as if it was some prize he had captured on his mad venture across the table, they both laughed harder.

When they were still and quiet, Rory found herself nestled against his chest. Dair had one hand under his head that lay on a cushion, and was staring up at the painted ceiling of the pavilion, while his right hand played with her damp hair.

"Not as elegant or as dramatic as my entrance to Romney's studio," he commented, "but I have achieved the desired result. You are back in my arms, where you belong."

Rory smiled contentedly and rested her chin on his chest.

"But where are the dancing girls to offer your lordship applause and praise?"

He lifted his head slightly to look down his long nose at her upturned face. Her blue eyes sparkled with mirth, her lovely mouth had curved into a cheeky smile, and there was a delicate flush to her cheeks that heightened the flawlessness of her porcelain skin. She looked radiant. At that moment and forever more she was the most beautiful creature he had ever set eyes on.

"I don't want their applause, just yours…"

She sat up on an elbow.

"You have that, Alisdair. Always…"

He shifted onto his side.

"Then why are we wasting precious time? We are alone and I came all this way into Hampshire just to kiss you. But first you must promise me—"

She put a finger to his lips to stop him talking. Then caressed his bearded cheek.

"I know, and I will," she said gravely, but the sparkle was still there.

"You have no idea what I was going to ask you, minx!"

She nodded and pressed her lips together to stifle a smile before saying flatly,

"You were going to ask me to refrain from kissing any gentleman but you."

"Well, yes, that was what I was going to ask you, but—"

"—such a request, you will agree, is grossly unfair."

He scowled. "It is?"

"Of course. Particularly after you just argued that inexperience before marriage is not an ideal state for husband and wife."

"I said no such thing. What I meant is that you and I—"

"—should kiss as many persons of the opposite sex as possible so that when we kiss each other, we know exactly what we are doing. And as you are vastly more experienced, I have a lot of catching up to do if you expect—"

She got no further.

"What rot!" he growled and crushed her mouth under his, the rest of her ridiculous argument forgotten as her mouth melted into his in one long luxurious kiss. "Catching up to do, indeed," he murmured as they came up for air. "Your kisses are perfectly wonderful without the need for experience..."

"Oh, but I shall be a much better kisser if I were to kiss as many—"

"No! No, you don't. You don't need to kiss another man, ever. Just me, you wicked creature. And don't pretend you thought I meant otherwise! And don't twist my words," he sulked, gently running a large hand down the middle of her narrow back. "You're much better with words than I, but I've always thought it best to show rather than tell," he added, leaning in to kiss and nuzzle her neck, hand coming to rest on the gathered petticoats at her waist. "What is that scent you are wearing? It could send a man—me—mad..."

She giggled, and shuddered, tickled by the soft bristles of his beard brushing against her throat. She turned in his arms so that she was now the one lying on the cushions, he above her. "Silly! Soap. But more likely pond water since I've just been for a swim."

"No soap on God's earth smells that good," he murmured, continuing to drink in the scent of her, soft kisses progressing to the swell of her breasts all but exposed by a low square neckline. "And if the lake water smells this intoxicating, then I am willing to sacrifice myself to whatever perils await me out there in the deep..."

His fingers deftly set about finding and tugging undone the tabs that held the bodice to the skirts. He then gently slid the light cotton material with its little lace edge down off her breasts giving his mouth access to her nipple. He smiled to himself, rediscovering she was not wearing stays. He had forgotten that. And when he gently suckled, then teasingly scraped the very edge of his teeth against the delicate pink tip, Rory gasped, back arching in pleasurable response. Her hips began to undulate under him, and she held fast to the sleeves of his shirt, signal enough she liked very much what he was doing and did not want him to stop.

Caught in the moment, he allowed his hand to stray further. Slowly, he gathered up the many light layers of her cotton skirts, exposing her feet, then her ankles, and then on up her long slim stockinged legs. Her petticoats were bunched over her knees, where her white silk stockings were held up by pretty pink silk garters, and he let his fingers stray over one of those garters, before gliding up the silken flesh of her inner thigh. She had such shapely long legs... That's when she baulked. His delightful exploration was over within a blink of an eye, leaving him alone, propped on his elbows, bewildered and wondering.

TWENTY-TWO

Rory scrambled away from him, to the table, hastily brushing down her petticoats. She needed to cover her legs, most importantly to hide her feet. She also did her best to close her gaping bodice across her breasts; only now realizing all the tabs had been deftly undone. How was she to tie them up again without Edith's help? She felt foolish for her behavior, and more so when tears of frustration pricked her lids. She was overwhelmed with conflicting emotions: Of wanting him to continue pleasuring her, yet not ready for him to touch her foot. Not that he had, and that made her wonder if he had deliberately shied away from doing so. His caresses were so gentle, his kisses so passionate, that she craved more and yet, having shunned him, she was left with an aching loss, and wholly dissatisfied.

Dair stayed where he was, on the marble floor, one long booted leg drawn up, until his ardency had cooled sufficiently that he was no longer an embarrassment to himself. And then he sat up and watched until he could no longer bear her failed attempts to tie the tabs of the bodice without assistance. He silently joined her at the table and took matters in hand. At first she did not want him and pushed his hands away. When he persisted, when he caught up her fingers before she could slap his away again and pressed his lips to the back of her hand, her shoulders slumped with acceptance. She offered no further resistance.

After her bodice was secure, he set about tidying the cushions, picked up the errant tumbler and put it back on the table, then returned to sit opposite her. All the while he was moving about the pavilion he was aware she was limp, head bowed with her hands in her lap, and no doubt with her pretty head full of all sorts of emotional castigation. He reminded himself that she was still young. Her experience of the world was limited to her grandfather's house and a handful of society functions amongst relatives, however distant. She was always chaperoned, always surrounded by others when not in the familiar surroundings of her home. Even in her own home he was sure she was never left alone with a man save her grandfather or her brother.

And here he was lifting her petticoats the moment her maid's back was turned! What must she think of him? He knew precisely what her grandfather would think, and that's why he was determined to speak with him that same night. And yet there remained a kernel of doubt to his determination, a small, niggling worry he should dismiss as nerves usual for a man about to embark on a life-altering path. The worry persisted because it had been with him since he could remember; at least since he had discovered the root of the problem with his parents' marriage. He had resisted marriage, particularly a marriage of convenience for the sole purpose of producing an heir. The notion made him recoil. He wanted no loveless match, and yet for a man in his position marrying for love was surely a foolhardy venture?

Looking across at Rory, he did not now think so. He had known almost from their first meeting, though he had tried to ignore the notion of fate and falling in love at first kiss. Oh, but that second kiss at the stone wall at Banks House, that had undone him! He knew then there was no turning back, that what he felt for her was much more than just lust. But what surprised him most of all, what sealed his determination, was that she saw beneath the façade and yet was comfortable with him in whatever role he cared to present to the world. She doubted him less than he doubted himself. With her there was no artifice, no second-guessing, no wondering if she were interested more in his earldom than in him. And when all was said and done, her values, what she wanted from a life's companion, matched his own.

Yet, that kernel of doubt lingered, brought to the fore by her reaction to his caresses just now. He realized he had taken matters too quickly. But if she was as ardent, if she had been in the moment just as much as he, surely she would not have pulled away? He dreaded the thought they might not be well-suited. What if the physical expression of love repulsed her? His mother had been young and innocent and thought herself in love, and yet she had so abhorred the sex act it was only duty to produce an heir that had made her endure the marriage bed.

And so his father had told him, not to his face, man-to-man, but in a letter, sent some years ago, while Dair was fighting for his country and his life on the other side of the Atlantic. What a revelation! It would have provided some light relief from the bloody business of war had it been any other couple but his parents' marriage laid bare in black ink. His father had not blamed the Countess for the breakdown of their marriage, but his own failure as a husband. And why, after all these years had his father taken it upon himself to confess his sins? Dair had wondered, and then been told in the next paragraph. His father had fallen in love and was living openly with his mistress, and this mistress, this Monica Drax, was his wife in everything but name, and had been for a number of years.

And because his father was in love, and, so it seemed, for the first time in his life, he now felt a great burden of guilt and shame at how he had treated his legal wife and legitimate heirs. He had been a terrible husband and a worse father. He explained that because Dair and his brother were conceived out of duty, and in the most despicable of ways (he stopped short of using the word *rape,* but Dair could read between the lines), he had not loved them. They reminded him that his marriage was loveless and a prison from which there was no escape, and that he was a monster. He now asked for his sons' forgiveness. A similar confessional had been sent to Charles.

In the very next line his father went on to mention that the love of his life, this Monica Drax, had borne him two dear sweet children, twins. No two children could be dearer to him or as perfect as Barnaby and Bernadette. And because he loved them dearly, he had changed his will so that fifty percent of the wealth derived from his sugar plantations would now go to his natural children by Monica Drax, the other fifty percent to be his. He hoped he would do his duty by his sister and brother, and provide for them out of this inheritance, too. He was sure Dair would see the fairness in this arrangement. After all, the income from his estates in England, the Jacobean mansion in Buckinghamshire, the townhouse and the various rents from properties in London, all were to be Dair's when he succeeded to the earldom of Strathsay. And, his father added, with an illegitimate son of his own, Dair could hardly object, now could he?

Dair did not object. But he wanted none of the income derived from the ill-gotten gains of slavery. As far as he was concerned, the Drax twins could have it all.

His father concluded his revelatory epistle with the proclamation he would not be returning to England; life suited him exceedingly in Barbados. He had written to his attorneys in London, instructing them that the moment Dair married, all rights and responsibilities to his

English estates, and the management of the considerable income held in trust by His Grace of Roxton, would revert to him. He wished he could hand over his earl's coronet and ermine to him, too.

So did Dair. He learned later that both Mary and Charles had replied to their father. He did not ask either one what they had said or if they had offered the forgiveness their father sought. He did not reply. He set the letter alight with the burning tip of his cheroot and watched it until it had turned in on itself and to ash in the camp fire.

He shook his thoughts free of his contemptible father and his last letter, poured out the final drops of pear cider and put the tumbler before Rory, saying as conversationally as he could manage,

"Should we have tea, too? It would be a shame not to use Cousin Duchess's teapot…"

Rory looked across at him then, and such was her despair it took all Dair's willpower to remain inert and not rush to her side to take her in his arms.

"I-I apologize," she said glumly, a catch to her voice. "You must think me woefully childish."

"What I think is that you have never before been in a situation such as this, and you were momentarily frightened by the unexpected. That is perfectly natural."

"Is it? How many other whey-brained virgins have you had to reas-sure—No! I should not have asked—"

"Only one. Lil. And she, like you, is not whey-brained. Though I possibly was, and am. We were both virgins when we embarked on our springtime romance. Since? None." When she frowned, he smiled to himself, adding gently, "You did say it was important to be truthful."

"Yes. I did. Thank you for telling me."

"But of course, being truthful doesn't make it less hurtful…"

"I am not hurt by that knowledge. I would have been surprised had you confessed to bedding virgins. And, to be perfectly frank, disgusted. I never took you for a man who preyed on the innocent for sport. I had always assumed you conducted your affairs with females who knew what they wanted and could give you the same pleasure in return."

He inclined his head with a smile, but volunteered nothing further.

Rory clasped her hands tightly in her lap and forced herself to look into his brown eyes.

"I apologize, but none of that is reassuring to me—here."

"Rory, we are in this together. You have nothing to apologize for. I am the one at fault. I should have realized—"

"No! Don't! Don't *you* apologize for my behavior. I wanted you to kiss me. I wanted to kiss *you*. I want us to make love. It's just that I-I don't want—I don't think I am ready for you to-to—"

"Rory, if you are not ready for me to touch you *everywhere*, then you are not ready to make love."

The calm even tone of his mellow voice should have reassured her. All it did was make her feel even more awkward and unsure of herself. He was right. Perhaps she wasn't ready... Oh, but the way he made her *feel*. The way her body reacted to his touch... When he kissed her; when his hands were on her skin; when he suckled her breasts... The throbbing between her legs had been almost unbearable, and now, just thinking about making love with him made that sensation return. Her face flamed with embarrassment, and she drank down the pear cider in one gulp, unaware of its taste or that she had drained the tumbler and set it down without thinking.

Perhaps he was right. She needed a cup of tea. It would settle her nerves. It would be best to talk about something—*anything*—else until she could find the words to explain herself... And then she sat up tall, as if struck forcefully by an idea, and she looked at him with narrowed eyes and a mutinous puckering of her mouth. How had it come to this? They had been discussing *his* fear of still water, and now, by some trickery, he had managed to turn the subject, and before she had satisfactorily concluded their discussion on how best to help him overcome his vexatious childhood memory.

She was confident she could help him, even if it was merely to enable him to row a boat without being anxious by such an innocuous activity. She smiled to herself. She was certain she knew the place where she wished him to row. It was only a short distance from the jetty. A man of his strength could row there in minutes. It was the most magical place, a place where she could forget her own shortcomings, and where she always imagined she would make love for the very first time: The temple grotto on Swan Island.

Her mutinous expression was replaced with a dazzling smile as she formulated her plan.

"I can help you overcome your dread of still water, if you will let me."

Dair smiled doubtfully.

He was enchanted by her confidence, and not insensible to her adeptness at returning their conversation to an episode in his childhood that he still found difficult to discuss. His embarrassment at having confided his weakness to her—after all, soldiers did not admit to having any fears—made him sound supercilious.

"Let me hazard a guess," he drawled. "You intend to lure me to the jetty and when I'm not looking, push me in, hoping I'll be instantly cured?"

She ignored his flippancy.

"If it were that simple, I would do it. No. Promise to meet me at the jetty tomorrow morning, and I will tell you then what I propose."

"Perhaps we can help each other?" he suggested, extending his hand across the table. When she smiled shyly and took hold of his fingers, he added with a smile, "I'll be there, but you have to leave your shadow behind."

"Edith?" Rory let out a small sigh of sympathy. "Poor Edith. She is under orders never to leave me alone for a minute. Grand has turned positively medieval since you punched Mr. Watkins in the nose. He is recovering, by the by, but his nose will never be straight again. Thank you for asking after him." She dimpled when he laughed out loud at his own lack of interest in the fate of Weasel Watkins' fine nose. "Grasby told Grand everything, of course, and now Grand is furious with Mr. Watkins. Yes. I thought that would please you. But you can stop looking smug that no one caught you kissing me! I am certain Grasby suspects, but it is not the sort of conversation one has with one's sister."

"Thank you for the warning."

"Oh, I wasn't warning you. You can look after yourself, and Grasby will forgive you anything. Indeed. He took your side and not Silla's regarding the whole Romney Studio imbroglio, which has sent her into a farouche. Nothing and nobody can lighten her mood."

"I am not surprised. Grasby should not have taken sides. And he should be loyal to his wife, always."

"I thought you had no time for Silla…?"

"I don't. But I'm not married to her. Grasby is. That means he must do his duty by *her*, not me."

Rory regarded him for a moment, blue eyes keen, and said what was on her mind.

"Interesting you say that now. I'd wager fifty pounds that at the moment you and my brother dropped through that window into Mr. Romney's studio, you didn't give a tuppence for Grasby's marriage, or any other gentleman's marriage, truth told—" She paused when he shook his head and laughed, then continued in the same blunt tone. "All you cared about was your performance, and causing an almighty hullabaloo amongst a clutch of shrieking, barely-dressed dancers, worthy of newssheet ink."

He smiled thinly with a raise of an eyebrow, as if punctuating her assessment with an exclamation mark. She was dead on the mark, and he wondered if she had any idea that if he and Grasby had not dropped through that window, they would not now be having this conversation. Did he believe in fate? Before that night he would have rejected the notion as fanciful. Now, he was not so dismissive, particularly since Miss Aurora Talbot was the catalyst that had made him question his world view. He now saw it through a whole new lens. It was as if his life had been smeared across one of Jamie's small glass plates, just like a drop of blood, and slid under the lens of a microscope for intense scrutiny. And just as he had peered through the eyepiece of his son's birthday present and adjusted the lens, a whole other world appeared before his eyes, one he never knew existed or thought possible. It thrilled and alarmed him.

Rory had the same effect on him. With her, his life came into sharp relief. She made his heart beat a little too hard and his chest to ache. He was not one for deep thought or rumination, but he was confident this young woman seated across from him with the light of triumph in her eyes had forever changed the way he viewed the world. He could think of no one else with whom he wished to share his life's journey.

"Wager?" he managed to calmly enquire. "Be careful, Rory. Have you forgotten my moniker?"

Rory laughed. "Not at all. And I advise you not to take up the offer because you'd lose!"

"Yes. Yes I would."

"I have no idea why Grand thinks my virtue needs guarding *now*," she prattled on because he was looking at her intently, the look in his eye new and unsettling. "Two months ago he gave no thought to leaving me with Mr. Pleasant unattended in the Pinery for a whole afternoon. Admittedly Cedric was helping me prepare pineapple pots ready for embedding in troughs of tanner's bark. Not even Crawford was there..." She cocked her head and grinned, wrinkling her little nose. "I suppose Grand thought having our elbows deep in horse manure was not conducive to a romantic interlude."

"It wouldn't have stopped me kissing you."

"Now who is being the romantic!" she teased.

"Did the manure stop Cedric?"

The serious tone of his question surprised her. She was incredulous.

"Don't be a silly head, Alisdair! Mr. Pleasant kiss *me*? Me kiss *him*?" She gave a little shudder. "Cedric is a dear heart but I consider him a second brother."

"I am sure a sister is not what he considers you; besides, he already has eight of those."

Mr. Cedric Pleasant's feelings for her was news to Rory, and it sounded in her voice as she shifted along the cushions to the end of the table where the teapot rested on its pedestal, a lighted candle under the base to keep the water in the pot at the correct drinking temperature.

"Truly? How odd that I never thought so…" She dimpled. "Then again, I never thought of *you* as a brother… Please stay seated and allow me," she ordered when he rose up off the cushion to assist her.

He had been determined to lift the teapot from its stand for her, a job normally performed by a butler or footman because of the heaviness of the silver, particularly when filled with hot tea. But he did as requested and resettled on the cushion.

"I may not have the same strength in both my legs, but I do have strong wrists and arms, and that is from the swimming I do at home, in the Thames, and here, on the lake," Rory told him as she arranged three Sèvres porcelain cups on their saucers. "Grand insisted I learn from a young age, determined I strengthen my body and prove the physicians wrong. I cannot take exercise in long walks or dancing, and though I use a sidesaddle, I find that long rides do not agree with my ankle. But swimming—"

She lifted the silver teapot and expertly poured tea in each cup without spilling a drop and set the teapot back on its stand.

"—I love to swim! I wish I could do so all year round."

She next used the silver sugar tongs to select a small sugar lump from the porcelain sugar bowl that was in the same pattern and color as the tea service, and dropped this into one of the teacups. Placing a silver spoon on the saucer she stood there for a moment holding the teacup and smiled down at him. "

"When I was a little girl I desperately wanted to be a bird, so I could fly free. I observed that birds with a broken foot, or with only one foot, were still able to soar high into the air. But swimming is an excellent substitute for flying. When I am in water, I feel free and-and *graceful…*" She gave a tinkle of laughter, shrugged and said teasingly, "Perhaps I am a mermaid after all? Perhaps when I am in water my legs transform into one long fish tail. You'll just have to wait until tomorrow morning to discover that for yourself. No, Edith. Please stay where you are. I will bring the tea to you. You look to have run all the way back from the house, and in this heat need something to revive you."

Dair's head snapped round, just as surprised at seeing Rory's maid, as Edith was of being noticed by her young mistress.

EDITH HAD COME UP THE PAVILION STEPS PANTING, AND adjusting the pins in her disheveled hair, from running most of the way

down the winding path that led up to the big house. She was late but
full of news. The dower house was a hive of activity. The servants were
buzzing from room to room, arms full of linen, trays of polished silver
and glassware, carrying endless buckets of water up stairs, and firewood
was being set in every fireplace ready for the cool of the evening,
though that seemed unlikely given the unusually stiflingly hot weather
over the past week, day and night. The large kitchen was heavy with the
mingling of delicious smells, of cooked pastries and breads, of roasted
lamb being turned on the spit. The French chef was shouting Gallic
obscenities at his two busy assistants (Edith was sure the words were
unfit for a female's ears, for why else would he be yelling in French?).
No one had a minute to spare for Edith, a maid from the Gatehouse
Lodge, who was an interloper and in the way with their illustrious
mistress returned home.

Edith followed a group of upper servants to the wide-open front
door, and stood just inside the portico in time to witness a large traveling coach, black-lacquered doors covered in dust and pulled by six
grays, now spent, come to a halt in the circular gravel drive. Four
liveried outriders who had accompanied the carriage dismounted and
stripped off their riding gloves, stable boys rushing to their horses'
heads. A second carriage with a further two outriders followed. This
carriage was almost as splendid, but was weighed down with luggage,
strapped to its roof and stacked inside so high that hatboxes and parcels
blocked the view from one of the windows. Four upper servants piled
out of this carriage, shook out their crushed petticoats or the skirts of
their frock coats, and immediately went indoors, leaving the occupant
of the big carriage to be attended to by her lady-in-waiting, who had
made the journey with her mistress. So, too, had two spirited whippets,
one black, the other white and tan, who were taken in hand by a footman, who snapped leads to their diamond-studded chokers and led
them away.

Edith knew she had now left Rory alone too long with the handsome Major, but she could not tear herself away until she had seen the
mistress of the house, the Duchess of Kinross, a noblewoman known to
her only by reputation, and by the thread of connection with her young
mistress. She was not disappointed.

At first she mistook the smartly-dressed lady in the brocade gown
and upswept coiffure as the Duchess, then realized the woman was too
young, and she was not pretty enough. The Duchess was said to be
breathtakingly beautiful, a feast for the eyes, and in every way a
duchess. This must be the lady-in-waiting. She knew it was so when the
woman stepped to one side of the carriage steps where a line of upper

servants, from housekeeper to butler and those privileged enough to have access to the Duchess's private apartments, had gathered to greet their mistress.

A footman at the opened carriage door offered up his gloved hand, and out onto the top step appeared a fairylike creature not much above five feet in height. Her bright blonde hair was swept off a sweet face that was still exquisite. Most of the weight of curls fell about her shoulders and down her back, tied up with satin ribbons that matched her open robe gown of soft green silk with underskirts of lace. The matching silk bodice had a delicate lace trim and displayed a magnificent décolletage, where nestled a three-strand baroque pearl and diamond necklace. Slender arms were adorned with gold bangles and a pair of embroidered silk mules were just visible under the hem of her gown. Edith was more than satisfied she had indeed seen a duchess this day, and that this particular duchess measured up to expectations. She tried to take in her every detail, from her unusual almond-shaped eyes to the pretty silk hair ribbons, down to the Dresden lace of the underskirts, convinced she would never again have such an opportunity.

And then, as if by magic, the careful storage of these memories evaporated the moment the Duchess put an expensively shod foot to solid ground. She suddenly came to life, and she was mesmerizing. Clutching a handful of her delicate petticoats, she swept up to the servants, proclaiming how glad she was to be back in Hampshire, speaking not in English but in French. Fluttering a delicate fan and commenting that the heat was unbearable for this time of year, she spoke to each servant, asking questions and listening attentively to each response. And when she reached the head of the line where stood the housekeeper, who bobbed a curtsy, and the butler, who bowed his head, the Duchess took hold of the butler's hand, and then the housekeeper's, and engaged them in quiet conversation for three or four minutes, the housekeeper dashing a tear from her eye. And then the Duchess was gone inside. Her lady-in-waiting and the rest of the servants followed, each and every one of them smiling, leaving Edith, who had ducked to the other side of a grandfather clock to be out of sight, awestruck. To have been privileged to be in such close proximity to a noblewoman of the highest rank and of such dazzling beauty was not likely to happen again in her lifetime, and Edith vowed to remember always the homecoming of Antonia, Duchess of Kinross.

AT THE PAVILION, EDITH'S NEWS, AND THE MESSAGE TO BE
delivered to the Major, entrusted to her by a footman as she left the
house, were forgotten in her surprise at being proffered a cup of tea.
With her head still full of images of the Duchess of Kinross's arrival, she
also forgot the requisite thank-you. Her state of confused preoccupation was compounded watching Rory move about the pavilion in her
stockinged feet and without her walking stick. In the absence of her
special shoes and a stick to lean on, her awkward gait was at its most
pronounced. This circumstance in itself was of no surprise to Edith,
who had cared for her mistress since she was in her teens. It was that
Rory chose to allow the Major to see her at her most vulnerable, a situation that was avoided at all costs, even with family members.

Obediently, Edith took the cup of tea and went to the spot on the
marble bench between two fat columns where her needlework lay. She
stirred the sugar lump and once dissolved, sipped at the sweet black
brew, grateful for the hot drink, a wary eye on her mistress.

Rory returned to the table and fussed with the tea things. She
placed a cup of tea, the milk jug and the sugar bowl before the Major,
and then set the remaining cup of tea at her place, but did not immediately sit. She was well aware of what she was doing. She knew Dair's
gaze remained fixed on her the whole time she was chatting away about
sidesaddles, flying like a bird and swimming like a mermaid. She could
hardly believe she was prattling on like a shatter-brain. But it was
nerves, pure and simple. She knew also that his eyes never left her while
she poured out the tea and took a cup across the pavilion to her maid.
That was a last minute stroke of evil genius. Out of the corner of her
eye she had seen Edith come up the stairs and stop to catch her breath
on the top step. Taking her a cup of tea would give her a reason to walk
the length of the pavilion, without her shoes and no stick. It was not
that she was worried about spilling the tea, or tripping, or making a
fool of herself in that sense. She readily went about in her stockinged
feet in her own apartments or out in the garden on a summer's day, if
no one was about.

What filled her with trepidation, what made her nervous, was that
she had put the Rory no one saw on show, for him. The lame Rory with
a turned right foot and an ungainly gait. The Rory who loved silk and
satin embroidered gowns and robes, and all the feminine fripperies that
went with an outfit, and could convince herself when standing before a
long looking glass that men would find her attractive. That is, until she
took a step away from her reflection. Her right foot would not obey her
left foot and point forwards, nor would it lie flat. It turned inwards and
the weight was on the ball of the foot, compressing her toes; it gave her

a limp. She tried to blame the underpinnings or her gowns and the spangled silk embroidery for exaggerating her impediment when she walked. But the truth was, nothing changed when she was stripped to her chemise, or in her nightgown. She would always walk in this manner. There was no escaping the raw physical facts that when she moved about on land she would never be graceful, elegant, or pleasing to the eye.

She took small comfort in the knowledge that at least today she was dressed in a simple cream muslin gown, without stays, and with her hair an untidy damp mess down her back. Perhaps his eye would stray from her gait to find fault with her plain gown and bird's-nest hair…

If ever there was a moment for him to change his mind about making love to her, this was it.

Taking a deep breath, heart thumping in her ears so loudly she thought she might go deaf, she finally turned to look across at him. And what she saw, or more to the point, what she did not, was of no comfort. She could not fathom his reaction. Reflected in his eyes was something altogether unknown to her. She held his gaze, and with each passing second the heat intensified in her throat and cheeks. She would not speak. She waited for him to do so. And she waited for him to move time on, and in the direction of his choosing.

When he did, he did so in a wholly unexpected manner. It was so unexpected that Edith's teacup slid from her hand. The hot black tea splashed and stained the hem of her skirts, as the teacup smashed on hard marble, splintering into a hundred tiny shards across the floor of the pavilion.

TWENTY-THREE

DAIR KNEW WHAT SHE WAS TRYING TO DO, AND WAS HAVING NONE of it. Just because he wasn't bookish didn't mean he couldn't read a person's emotions and motives. If by this display she was trying to turn him away, break his resolve, make him realize how thoroughly unworthy she was of him, then she did not know him at all. But he suspected it was her lack of confidence that made her flaunt her physical weakness so openly. It must have cost her dearly to do so. In the eight weeks (had it only been eight weeks?) since he had scooped her up into his arms off the platform in Romney's studio, she had only ever walked in his presence with the assistance of her walking stick.

He was a little hurt she needed to test his sincerity in this way; that she possessed a scintilla of doubt he might be shallow of character; that he would not desire her, esteem her, love her, all because of a tiny flaw of God's making. Again, he reasoned her doubt came from her youth and inexperience. Her grandfather had kept her sheltered, and that was not such a bad thing. Only time would see her lose the self-doubt and strengthen her self-belief about how truly lovely she was in character and form. And he had every intention of spending that time by her side, kernel of doubt be damned. He knew in his heart they were compatible in every sense. If this walk across the pavilion had shown him anything, it was to take a good hard look at himself, and how he had allowed his parents' loveless marriage and his father's vile bitterness to determine his own outlook on life for far too long.

Here was a young woman who, through no fault of hers, lived with an impediment every day. It was a circumstance out of her control, and yet she had not allowed it to rule how she viewed the world. She was not bitter. She did not blame others. She was joyful and full of optimism. He needed that in his life. He needed *her* in his life.

He joined her by the teapot stand.

He wasn't entirely sure how to conduct himself at such a momentous crossroads in their lives. He was as nervous as she was hesitant. In fact, he was so nervous the skin on the back of his neck prickled. He thought for a moment he might lose consciousness. Why did time slow upon such life-altering occasions? It was the same the moment before the infantry drummer set his sticks to the skin of his kettle and started to beat, or the trumpeter sounded his bugle, signal to charge into battle. Terror mixed with the relief of getting on with it, and getting through it, to live another day, sent him at full gallop. But as many times as he had made the charge astride his mount, he had never done this before, and knew he never would again.

It was only later that night, lying naked under a sheet in the big four-poster bed with the windows thrown open to allow for a cool breeze, both hands under his head, and smiling up into the darkness, that he recalled what he had said, and her response.

He took hold of Rory's hands, smiled into her eyes, and gently kissed her forehead. He then let go of her right hand and, still holding the left, went down on bended knee. He looked up into her face and for an instant he smiled. He could see by her expression she had no idea of his intent. That settled his nerves enough for him to say in a steady voice,

"Rory, I love you. Will you—Will you—Miss Aurora Talbot—consent to marry me?"

When she merely blinked down at him, as if he had spoken to her in some foreign tongue only known to himself, and touched his bearded cheek, he smiled nervously and turned his head in her hand to kiss her palm. For the second time he was glad he had grown a beard; he knew he was blushing. He rose up off his knee but kept hold of her hand.

"Rory, I want you to marry me… I have never wanted anything in my life as much as I want you to be my wife, but—but only if you want to…"

Rory's blue eyes widened. She clapped a hand to her smile, as if in disbelief and shock at his offer. And then she began to laugh and cry at the same time. Her series of small nods were acceptance enough for him. She threw her arms around his neck and he gathered her into a tight embrace and laughed along with her. She clung to him, murmured that she loved him too and nothing would make her happier than to be his wife. They stayed that way, joyous and reassured, tremors of relief coursing through their bodies, until involuntarily parted when Edith dropped her teacup and it smashed into pieces on the marble tiles.

After that, time raced forward, and too fast for him to remember all the words spoken and the promises made. It seemed within a blink of an eye of his proposal and her acceptance, he was watching his newly-betrothed go off with her maid in the pony trap back to the Gatehouse Lodge. Two things he did remember: They agreed to keep their betrothal to themselves until Dair formally spoke with Lord Shrewsbury; he would meet her at the jetty in the morning to row her across to Swan Island. As he drifted off to sleep, he couldn't decide which held more dread for him.

HE ARRIVED AT THE JETTY IN HIS SHIRTSLEEVES, LIGHT LINEN frock coat slung over a shoulder, to find Rory waiting for him.

He was late.

He had risen early, as was his usual practice since his time in the army, and taken breakfast in his rooms to write three letters: One to his father; one to his father's bankers; and one to his brother Charles. All three letters informed their respective recipients of his betrothal. The first two letters he knew would be delivered without being diverted to Shrewsbury's secret post office, where all suspect letters were opened, read and expertly resealed, usually with the recipient none the wiser to the trespass. But his letter to Charles, a known traitor, would land in the secret post office. The wax seal with the impression of the Fitzstuart coat of arms left by his gold signet ring would be expertly removed, and the contents of the letter pored over in every detail. Which is why he wrote it in the cipher his brother had used to pass on vital information through the French to the American rebels about English troop numbers and deployment.

There was nothing traitorous or of interest to the Secret Service in the letter. It simply informed his brother of his betrothal and expressed the wish that under different circumstances he would have greatly desired Charles to bear witness to his nuptials. He hoped his brother and his new wife had settled into their life in Paris, and to expect a wedding present from him soon. He signed off with the firm belief that one day in the not-too-distant future they would be reunited.

Although the letter's contents were innocuous and far from traitorous, he knew the double agent within Shrewsbury's secret service could not take the chance the letter didn't hide some important piece of information vital to the American war effort. Why else would the Major write to his brother, and in code? Dair hoped mention of a wedding present would be construed as code about the English army's movements in North America. It was a ruse, and he would wager his future inheritance on the traitor ensuring the letter made its destination without anyone in the secret post office, and most importantly, Shrewsbury, knowing of its existence. Now it remained for him to set the trap and wait for the traitor to walk into it, trip more belike.

He was convinced the traitor was William Watkins. But proving it would not be easy, and he feared the trap he had set would not be sprung in time for him to avoid the upcoming interview with his cousin the Duchess. His contact in Portugal would not wait forever, and it was vital the man's identity be confirmed, and only the Duchess could do this. The gentleman could then be given safe passage and immunity to return to England in exchange for evidence and the name of the traitor in Shrewsbury's midst. The interview, William Watkins, and the gentleman waiting in a Lisbon tavern were forgotten as he caught sight of Rory on the jetty, and he lengthened his stride.

She was in her stockinged feet, the hem of her light cotton glazed petticoats just skimming her ankles. She wore a matching low-cut short jacket that laced in front, and a light gauze shawl draped across her shoulders and crossed over her breasts for modesty. Her fair hair was in undress, falling forward over her shoulder in one long thick plait that reached to her waist and was tied off with a pink satin ribbon. Both hands gripped the curved handle of a wicker basket that contained a large loaf of bread peeking out from under a linen cloth. There was another larger and heavier basket by a ladder that dropped over the side of the jetty into the water, where a skiff was moored.

Seeing Dair striding across the lawn, she put the basket at her feet, where her walking stick lay beside her discarded shoes, and waved excitedly. He waved back, face splitting into a grin at her enthusiasm. He was so looking forward to spending the day with her that any nerves he felt at boarding a rowboat on a still lake were pushed back down out of the way. He was determined to row across the lake to Swan Island for her, terrifying childhood memories be damned. And being in charity with the world since she had accepted his proposal of marriage, he was even prepared to accept with equanimity Rory's maid as chaperone on their adventure. He was surprised then, taking a tentative peek over the side of the jetty, to find the skiff unoccupied.

"Edith is bedridden with a megrim, so cannot join us," Rory told him matter-of-factly, and without a hint of a smile, so that he almost believed her. "And I did not have to tell Grand an untruth because he left the house well before I did. He has business with the Duke. But I did tell Ernest, Grand's majordomo, I was taking the trap to see my godmother… Which was a half-truth because I visited the dower house before coming here to pick up these supplies." When Dair raised a questioning eyebrow, she had to suppress a smile, and could not look at him. "The main thing is, I didn't lie…"

Dair peered beneath the cloth covering the wicker basket at her feet, and then under the one by the bollard. Both were filled with enough provisions to feed a party of four. He draped his frock coat atop the bollard.

"Are we going away for some time? Should I have left a note?"

"Silly! I just thought—after all that rowing—you—*men* need sustenance after physical exertion…"

Dair ignored her muddled explanation and blush of embarrassment, saying matter-of-factly, as he rolled his shirtsleeves to the elbow,

"How thoughtful and clever of you to obtain such a feast by half-truths."

She was smug. "Pierre thought nothing of it, truly, because the food for the Gatehouse Lodge comes from the dower house gardens. So do our bread and pastries. He was obliging, and happy to see the dinner he had prepared for the Duchess not go to waste. And he offered two of the kitchen hands to load the baskets and the *nécessaire de voyage* onto the skiff." She frowned suddenly. "You dined alone, not with my godmother, last evening?"

"She did not come downstairs, but kept to her apartments. I sup with her tonight, if she is well enough. And then I have an appointment with Lord Shrewsbury."

"Strange that she is ill. I hope it is nothing serious." She looked up at him with a hesitant smile. "You are—you are going to speak to Grand today? He should be returned after dinner."

He smiled to himself at the hesitancy in her voice, and chucked her under the chin.

"What a doubting beauty! I suppose you woke this morning and instantly thought you had dreamed my proposal of marriage?"

Rory gasped.

"Oh! How did you know?"

He burst out laughing and shook his head.

"Oh, Delight, your lack of guile fills me with joy." He affected a frown. "Or perhaps I should be offended you think me a fickle fiend?"

She was suddenly shy and shook her head. When she went to pick up the lighter of the two baskets, he was quick to do this for her. He followed her across to the ladder.

"No. But I am certain there will be many a young lady and her match-making mamma who will wish it was a dream when they discover the swoon-worthy Major Lord Fitzstuart is betrothed, and to me, of all the young ladies paraded before you each Season."

"Paraded before me? I hardly noticed. You don't give yourself enough credit, Rory." He put the basket down and cocked his head. "Am I swoon-worthy?"

"Do you doubt it? Did you not believe me when I said every time you walk into a room female hearts—Oh! You *are* a fiend!" she gasped when he grinned and winked at her. "You are funning with me again!"

But he lost his grin peering over the side of the jetty, down into the skiff.

"I presume you want these baskets, and me, in that boat?"

"Yes. I will pass them down to you… Or do you want me to get in first, and you can pass them to me?"

He put the basket at his feet and took his frock coat off the bollard to rummage in a deep pocket. Finding what he was looking for, he removed the contents from a small velvet-covered box, then put the empty box back in his pocket and laid the frock coat across the top of the larger of the two baskets. Rory wondered if he was delaying the inevitable and was about to put her plan into effect when he asked her to hold out her right hand. He cleared his throat, and said after taking a deep breath then breathing easy,

"Before I make a complete ass of myself, faint and fall off this wretched jetty and drown, I want you to have this."

On to her ring finger he slipped a thin gold band set with an octagonal-cut pale lavender sapphire. He turned the ring to check the fit, and was relieved that though her fingers were slim and her knuckle small, the ring fit snugly and could not slip from her finger.

"This was given to my mother by my father upon my birth, in celebration for giving him an heir. She never wore it, and gave it to me on my twenty-first birthday on the understanding I present it to my betrothed. Now," he added with a crooked smile, "when you wake, you will have tangible evidence our betrothal is not a dream. And proof," he added, looking into her eyes, "of my love—and devotion."

She stared at the ring, almost disbelieving, unconsciously moving her fingers so the sunlight glinted in one of the eight octagonal facets. The pale lavender sapphire changed color in the light. It was the most wondrous ring she had ever seen. Tears misted her view.

"Silly. You are not going to drown," she said in a small voice, overcome. "It is—It is *very* beautiful. Thank you, Alisdair... I want to kiss you but—"

"I understand. We are standing out in the open and there are eyes *everywhere*. Quickly! Let's get to that island so we can kiss there!"

They both laughed. He was only half-joking. Before he could pick up the baskets, she threw her arms about his neck and kissed his bearded cheek.

"Damn and blast those eyes!" she declared hotly, casting caution to the breeze. She tilted her chin up to him and received a gentle kiss on the mouth. "Yes. Let's get to the island," she added quietly. "I can thank you properly there. And I have a surprise waiting for you. Something you will enjoy..."

It was then, with her caught up in his arms, he realized not only was she without her stays but the tabs that kept her petticoats about her waist were tied loosely indeed. He let her go before he gave in to desire and unraveled every bow, and tugged a finger in the lacings to open her jacket. He picked up the basket.

"Did you dress yourself this morning?" he asked, desire making him sound gruff.

"How else was I to dress? Poor Edith has the headache. Oh, did you think I made that up? No. Events of yesterday, and the secrecy of our betrothal, were too much for her. Of course, knowing we were off to Swan Island today only made the pain in her head pound all the more. So of course I had to dress myself, just as I am now undressing myself, and to good purpose."

While she was talking she was doing precisely what he wanted her to do, but never dreamed of her doing it here, out in the openness of a jetty. She slid her cotton petticoat down off her hips and stepped out of it. Next she unwound the gauze shawl from around her shoulders. Lastly, she unlaced the jacket, pulling the lacings away from the final eyelet so the two sides of the jacket fell open to reveal her breasts covered by a thin linen chemise. Having pulled her arms from the elbow-length sleeves, she scooped up the petticoat and shawl, and pressed all three feminine articles to his chest.

He mechanically held her clothing, gaze riveted to her standing before him in nothing but a thin chemise and white stockings. If there were eyes out there watching them, all were riveted to her, and no wonder! Rory's chemise skimmed her embroidered garters secured just above her knees. She might as well have been naked. He had not blinked from the moment she started undressing. His eyes were void of moisture, just like his throat, which was parched. He swallowed hard and tried to clear his throat of yearning.

"Rory—Are you—are you *mad*? What—what are you about?"

He tried to return her clothes but she pushed them back on him, a sly smile curving her lips. If she'd thought about it for a moment, she would have found his reaction to her nakedness amusing. After all, here was the Dair Devil himself, shocked by *her* behavior. But she knew what she was doing and she had faith in her ability to take him by surprise, leaving him disconcerted and baffled, and hopefully so preoccupied he would forget what lay ahead. By these means she was confident of getting him in the skiff and rowing across to the island before he knew what he was about, and where he was.

"Put my clothes in the skiff, with everything else," she ordered mildly. "I'll have need of them later. *Au revoir.*"

He had no idea what she was talking about. He turned to look down at the skiff, one arm holding a basket, the other full of her clothes, and at a loss to know what to do with either, despite her directive. Then he heard a neat splash and realized what had just happened. His head snapped round to where she had been standing. Sure enough, she was no longer there. She had dived over the side of the jetty into the lake.

He called out to her, and without a second thought scrambled down the rusted steps of the iron ladder, her petticoat, jacket and shawl bunched up under his arm and the basket in one hand. He was halfway down the ladder before he glanced over his shoulder, down at the water. He was just in time to see Rory surface from the depths of the lake near the bow of the bobbing skiff.

"Don't forget the other basket!" she yelled, pulling herself up out of the lake, chemise heavy with water and adhering to her curves like a second skin. "And remove the rope from the bollard, too!"

"*Jesu…*" Dair almost lost his grip.

Rory hung there, half out of the water, leaning her frame against the outer shell of the boat, arms extended and gripping its side to keep herself upright. Here she balanced, waiting for the water to drain off her so most of it wouldn't end up in the skiff with them. She then scrambled up over the side and into the boat, onto the curved polished burden boards.

Dair didn't take his gaze off her for a moment. But once she was safely aboard, he turned and scurried back up the ladder to do as she had directed, descending the ladder again in what would have been record time, had records ever been kept of such feats.

Rory scampered up into the stern, to haul in the rope, and to take the baskets from him, one by one. She stowed them with various other items the kitchen assistants had brought on board earlier and stacked in the bow: A small shagreen-covered *nécessaire de voyage* containing all they needed in the way of porcelain plates, bowls, cups and saucers, as well as cutlery, glasses, serving implements and a small silver teapot. A waterproof leather satchel held a bundle of candles and a tinderbox. There were also a couple of towels, and a quilted blanket to sit upon and spread out their feast.

Dair was numb to it all as he dropped onto the thwart where the oars were secured in their oarlocks. He could have been carved from stone, such was the tightness in every muscle, now that he was aware of being on water. He was conscious only of the rocking of the unmoored skiff as Rory scampered about, and that all there was between him and the murky black water full of reeds was a thin wooden hull. He just wanted to scramble out of the skiff, up the ladder, and make a dash for firm land. There wasn't even a wager in place to force him to remain or lose—not only face, but his moniker of Dair Devil, and the admiration of his fellows. But such intangibles all seemed rather trivial to him now.

He heard Rory suggest he remove his striped silk waistcoat, it was such a warm day. He did so without realizing he had, and it disappeared as if by magic, Rory folding it and putting it aside. He even removed his stock, and undid the two small horn buttons of his shirt at his throat, though he had no recollection of either, or why his neck and chest suddenly felt cooler.

It was only when Rory settled herself in the stern opposite him that he forgot about the thin wooden hull, the tangle of reeds and the murky water. His whole concentration fixed on her, as if his life depended on his gaze not faulting for a second. And in a way that was true. Watching her calmed him considerably. He was able to take hold of each oar, though he gripped the shaft so hard he lost sensation in his fingertips, and prepared himself to break the water's surface with the blades.

Rory had one of the towels and was using it, not to put around her shoulders or to cover her bare legs, but to dry her face and squeeze the moisture out of the thickness of her hair. She froze momentarily, shot a glance at her right hand, then breathed easy. The pale lavender sapphire was still on her finger. Finally she laid the damp towel across her lap, as if she had just remembered her modesty. But she did nothing to cover her breasts, which, for all intents and purposes, might as well have been bare, such was the clinging wetness of her chemise. If she was aware, she gave no indication.

"What a wondrously sunny day for our adventure!" she enthused. With a sigh of contentment, she closed her eyes and tilted her face up to the warmth of the sun, and settled in. "Alisdair, I think we should make a start, don't you?"

He did. With his gaze locked to her wet and clinging chemise, he began to row. He rowed, not in the frenzied way he was used to doing, but in long, even and powerful strokes that had the skiff gliding through the water like a hot knife through butter. He rowed effortlessly, and as he continued to row in such an easy manner he began to relax, and enough to wonder about their destination, the mysterious Swan Island.

TWENTY-FOUR

S<small>WAN ISLAND WAS THE LARGEST ISLAND WITHIN THE LAKE SYSTEM</small> on the ducal estate, and had been off-limits since Dair could remember. It was said to be inhabited by a mad old hermit, or was it a pack of wild dogs? Whatever was living on the island, it was nasty and dangerous. It certainly wasn't swans! Swans, water fowl and ducks glided past, but he had never heard of, or noticed, flocks of birdlife gathering on or near the island's foreshores. He was told as a boy, and it was often repeated, watercraft were to stay well clear. As for setting foot on the island, that was strictly forbidden. By ducal decree, no one but a handful of servants went there. Who knew what they did, but a gamekeeper went with them. This seemed to suggest there was something worth shooting. None of the servants who went there ever spoke of it; all were sworn to secrecy. As far as Dair was aware, this arrangement had been in place since the fifth Duke had ascended to the title over fifty years ago, and his son, the sixth and present Duke had yet to rescind his father's decree.

Not that Dair had taken much interest in trespassing. After all, it was an island, surrounded by lake water. He hadn't wanted to go near it for love nor money. The only occasions he remotely got close was when participating in the regatta, which required he row past the island as part of the course. That is, until today...

As they neared the island, Rory directed Dair to row towards what appeared to be an impenetrable wall of forest that went down to the water's edge. It was, in fact, a dark narrow channel, hidden under an arch of tangled elms. Within a dozen row strokes it magically opened out into daylight and a small secluded cove. Here was a pebbled beach, and beyond the strip of beach, a wall of dense forest. The water was deep enough to anchor the skiff close to the beach, so that with only a few swimming strokes, Rory and Dair would be in water shallow enough to wade ashore. With his height, Rory expected Dair could walk the entire distance from skiff to shore. And the water here was invitingly clear.

Dair only became aware he had rowed into a clear water cove when Rory quietly told him it was time to put up oars and weigh anchor. He realized then that while he had kept his gaze on her as he rowed, her gaze was similarly locked to him. And by the small secret smile hovering about her mouth and the twinkle in her eye, she had not been admiring his rowing technique as much as his rowing physique. Well, he would give her more of him to admire.

His shirt was damp with sweat, so he pulled it up over his head and dropped it on the thwart beside him. He then stretched his arms to loosen his muscles and expanded his wide hairy chest with a deep breath of fresh air, not the least tired or spent. He did as she asked, and with the sandbag secured to the mooring rope, he dropped it over the side, surprised and delighted to see the water so clear. He turned about, ready to take next orders and winked down at Rory. When her gaze immediately shot to the boards beneath his booted feet, he chuckled.

"Don't be shy, Delight. It pleases me more than I can tell you to find you desire me as much as I do you."

"Forgive me. That was foolish," she said with a sigh of annoyance. "I looked away out of habit, not because I wanted to. Well-bred young ladies, maidens in particular, are forever counseled by their governesses and married female relatives that to openly admire a beautiful male body is the height of wickedness. Which is utterly absurd, when we can admire paintings and statues of men as art without a word of reproof." She dimpled. "I did not look away when you were an American savage. Though, thinking back on it, I was in such free and easy company that night I did not feel constrained to do what was expected of me, rather I did what I wanted to do, even if it felt utterly wicked at the time."

"Oh, I have high hopes of us being utterly wicked together... When the time is right."

She hunched her shoulders and smiled as if she was keeping something from him. When he put up an eyebrow she giggled and said cryptically,

"Then we are in the right place!"

He had no idea what she meant, and wasn't given the opportunity to ask. Just as she had done on the jetty, she surprised him. She scrambled over the side of the boat and disappeared under the water. This time he did not panic nor did he hesitate to look overboard. The water being clear as the ripples disappeared, he was rewarded for his calmness when Rory's lovely round derriere came into focus just below the surface, her chemise tangled up around her waist. She kicked her legs out as a frog does to propel forward, and made wide circles with her arms to help pull herself through the water. He marveled how effortlessly she swam and definitely agreed that a bathing gown would have hampered such fluid movements.

He was just wondering how far she could swim before needing to surface to take a breath when she appeared close to shore and stood up, the water now just above her knees. She turned to face him, hands running up her face to clear her eyes, then over her hair and down her long plait, the water pouring off her, single droplets caught in the twinkling sunlight. He had never seen anything so utterly bewitching. If mermaids did exist, they looked like her.

He suddenly had an urgent need to tug off his jockey boots, strip out of his uncomfortably tight breeches and throw himself overboard; he hoped the water was as cold as ice.

"How old did you say you were when you discovered this cove?"

"Fourteen."

"And you've been coming here every year since then?"

"Yes."

"And it never troubled you the Duke has made this island off-limits to all?"

"No. And it doesn't bother you either, or you wouldn't have rowed me over here."

"I rowed you over here regardless of my cousin's decree. That doesn't mean I am not bothered."

She stopped on the narrow path that lead through the dense forest to the clearing and turned to look at him; Dair following up behind, laden with the supplies from the skiff.

"Why?" she asked, curiously.

"I can look after myself. Tackle a wild dog, a bloodthirsty ogre, or a mad old hermit brandishing a rusty knife, if it came to it. But you, you are made of much finer porcelain, and should never come here alone —again."

"But I've been coming here for seven years now and never once felt in any danger."

"I wasn't only thinking of danger… But what if an accident befell you. What if you twisted your good ankle? What then? How would you summon aid? Who would know you were here?"

A mutinous light came into Rory's eyes. "I won't be put on a mantelshelf!"

He blinked. "Shelf?" Where had that sprung from? "What shelf? I just want to look after you—"

"I won't be treated like one of those fragile females who are forever languishing on fainting couches and requiring burnt feathers thrust under their noses. They never exert themselves, and yet expect their husbands or their brothers to run after them for every little thing just because they are female!"

"Of course not. I wasn't suggesting—"

"I've seen it happen often enough and it's shameful. Silla uses it to great effect on Grasby—"

"I don't doubt it," he muttered.

"—and it's not right!"

"No, it isn't."

His quiet agreement made her pause. She glanced up at him and was suddenly annoyed with herself, and pouted.

"Forgive me. You were only being protective in a nice way, and I was being overly sensitive."

"Yes."

"I never thought about getting into real difficulty and not being able to call for help. I've always been self-sufficient. Grand says that was the best way to learn to live with my-my shortcomings."

"It is. But you must also be practical. So you will promise me not to come here, or any place, alone…"

He stared down at her as if his promise was non-negotiable.

She sighed, as if in defeat, and said with feigned annoyance, "I suppose when we marry, as my husband, you can order me to do as you please, so I might as well promise."

"That is not the sort of promise I want," he stated, rising to her bait. "And if that is the type of husband you think I'll be then you had best give me back that ring!"

Rory whipped her hand behind her back, as if he truly meant to take it from her, but then stuck out her tongue like a spoiled brat. He gawped, then laughed heartily.

"You-you—actress!"

"Brute!"

They both laughed and she leaned in to him, a hand to his bare chest, and lifted her chin to receive a kiss. He did his best to oblige her, though he had to squat to do so because his right hand was balancing the heavier of the two baskets on his shoulder, while under his left arm was tucked the *nécessaire*, and his left hand held the second basket.

"Thank you for wanting to protect me," she said quietly. She kissed him again. "I've never had a champion before."

"You'll not need another."

She caressed his bearded cheek. "I have never wanted another, ever. Just you…"

He rose up to his full height and they continued on their way, he saying conversationally,

"So no wild dogs, beasts, or threats of any kind for me to vanquish while I'm here?"

"None. It is a peaceful place full of birdsong and the occasional duck."

"Not even a mad old hermit?"

She laughed at his disappointment. She was confident he would have enjoyed taking on any threat that came his way.

"Sadly, not even the old hermit. But I can show you his cottage, and where he is buried."

"Ah! So there *was* a mad old hermit!"

"Geoffrey was not mad, he just preferred a solitary life. Here we are!" she announced with excitement. "So what do you make of my secret paradise?"

The forest had opened out into a broad, flat clearing, tall trees on all sides, and looming large in the background the steep slope of a bluff. But what dominated the immediate landscape was man-made, a circular Greek temple, a *tholos*. It sat proudly in the center of the clearing, elevated on a series of graduated plinths, giving it eight shallow steps. Its fluted colonnades soared twenty feet into the air, each Ionic column made from sectioned marble. There was no roof and it was open to the elements, but hanging off one end of the *tholos* was a smaller and more intimate rectangular temple, with an internal room surrounded by columns. It had a domed roof that allowed light to penetrate through a glass oculus, and was accessible through the main round temple.

Rory was sure that when Dair was given the time to fully appreciate this smaller temple he would see, too, what she only came to realize a couple of years ago: That it was a scaled replica of the Roxton family mausoleum atop Treat Hill. But the temple here on the island did not honor past illustrious family members, nor was it a place to mourn. It was something else entirely. It was this temple and what it symbolized she wished to share with Dair.

For now though, she was content to join in his excitement at seeing the clearing and its temples for the first time. He looked as awestruck as she imagined she must have been when she made the discovery on her island wanderings, and Geoffrey the hermit caught her trespassing.

The clearing might only be a five-minute walk through forest from the cove, but Dair's immediate thought was they had somehow stumbled back in time to the age of mythology. It had a daydream, castles-in-the-sky feel about it, and he wondered if they had walked onto the canvas of a grand mural displaying Mount Olympus, the home of the Gods. He was so excited and intrigued, he dumped his cargo at the base of the steps in the shade of a spreading elm and ran up them and inside the circular temple.

Rory did not follow but stayed in the shade, to take the pressure off her foot. For although she had managed to walk the distance without her special shoes, and completely ruined a pair of white stockings, there was pain in her ankle and in her toes. But it was of little consequence. She was just so happy to join in Dair's wonderment of a new-found place of discovery. And when he called out that there were statues inside the temple, as if she would not know this, she did not deflate his enthusiasm but called back asking if all eight were present and correct. There was a delay of seconds and then he shouted the affirmative, which made her stifle a laugh, lest he think she was mocking him.

When nothing further was forthcoming from him, she set to shaking out one of the cloths and opened up the *nécessaire*. She took out one of the etched glass tumblers to fill with water. She was parched. But that was not surprising, and she only had herself to blame, traveling in a skiff without her parasol, and in only her chemise and stockings. She would quite possibly wake tomorrow to find her white skin the color of ripe strawberries.

She had unpacked most of the crockery and cutlery from the *nécessaire* before Dair reappeared from the temple. He had been gone a good five minutes or more, and there was a look on his face, hard to read, that made Rory wonder what there was here to unsettle him. Before she could ask he said quietly,

"I'm an unthinking ass. I should have helped you. And you're thirsty. Where can I fetch water?"

She pointed beyond the steps at the front of the temple.

"See the bathing pool. It fills with water from a spring. But the freshest water is to be had from the water fountains—from the lions' mouths. It is also the coolest. You can't see them from here. See those

large vases atop two pedestals either side of the steps? The fountains face
into the bathing pool, so the water gushes from their mouths and into
the pool. The pool isn't deep, and has a tiled floor, so you could—What
—What is the matter?" she asked suddenly. She had been looking
towards the bathing pool as she spoke, but when she turned she found
him not looking at the bathing pool but staring down at her intently.
"You look to have seen a specter." She blinked and gave a little gasp.
"Not—not the ghost of Geoffrey the Hermit?"

"No. No ghosts. I went into the second temple... At what age did
you say you first started coming here? Fourteen? Did you go into that
second temple when you were fourteen?"

She did not immediately answer the question, saying instead with
a smile, "Isn't it lovely? Such gorgeous tapestries, and the carpet so
thick underfoot, and the gilding on the wood paneling is exquisite. It
is so cozy with a fire in the grate and the sun shining through the
stained glass oculus." She frowned in thought. "It must be a trick of
the furnishings, because it seems much smaller on the inside than
expected; the size of an intimate salon. No doubt it's the tapestries
that run floor to ceiling on three of the walls, which draws the room
in... How do you suppose they got them across to the island? By
barge?"

"The same way, I expect, they shifted marble, stone and wood
across to construct the temples and the bathing pool. Though I suspect
the temples were built before the land around here was flooded to make
the lake."

"Oh, yes! That makes sense. I forgot the lake isn't a natural feature,
though it looks as if it has been here since forever. Bullock teams could
have been used to drag the marble across... But the tapestries are not as
old as the island. They—"

"Rory, it matters little how they got here. It's those tapestries—that
room—"

"Wait until you see it with the wall sconces lit and a fire. There's
something more intimate and beautiful about it in candlelight."

"Intimate? Beautiful? Ha!"

"Alisdair, what is it?"

He wiped a hand over his mouth and took a deep breath. He wasn't
sure how to put into words what he wanted to say, so he just blurted it
out. Of course, his declaration made him sound angry, angry with her,
which he was not. He was embarrassed by what he had seen on the
walls of the small temple because she had seen it too, and at a much
younger age than his first sexual experience. His reaction had shocked
him more than he thought possible.

"Rory—those tapestries—that room—they are not fit for a young girl's eyes."

"I thought—I don't understand… That was to be my surprise for you."

"Surprise?" he blustered, folding his hands across his bare chest but not meeting her eye. "It was that, and more!"

"You don't like them?" she asked, disappointed, and got to her feet. "Why? What's wrong with them?"

He looked at her then and saw only studious enquiry. It only increased his discomfort. He dug a larger metaphorical hole for himself.

"Wrong with them? You want me to say it aloud?"

"Yes. Yes, I do, because it is now obvious to me that the temple, the tapestries, the room itself, has greatly upset you and I do not understand at all why it should. Particularly to a man of your worldly experience."

He walked away from her, hands through his dark hair, and then returned.

"And in your unworldly opinion, what did you think the naked couples in those tapestries were up to? No! Don't answer that. The question was asinine, like me!"

"There is only one couple," she said quietly. "One couple in many different—*situations*."

"Situations?" he said doubtfully. Rory thought he looked smug. "I was in that room less than five minutes and believe me, I know an-an orgy when I see one."

"I am sure you do. But you are wrong."

"Rory, that's not what I—"

She cut him off.

"You think because I am a virgin I should not look upon those tapestries. You possibly believe all females must be shielded from such expressions of love?"

His black brows contracted over his beak of a nose. "Love?"

"Yes. Love. Just because I have never *made* love does not mean I do not appreciate the joy physical love must bring to a couple who are *in* love. So please do not address me as if you are speaking to an ignorant fool—"

"I was not—"

"I am well aware, despite my lack of tangible experience, that there are those who indulge in venery for its own sake—"

"Aurora!"

"—which is altogether different from making love. And it is the latter which is represented in those tapestries. You cannot persuade me otherwise." She looked up into his flushed face and stated bluntly, "Making love frightens you."

When he stared at her, horrified, she knew she had prodded the raw nerve of truth.

"Oh, I know you are a wonderfully considerate lover. I have heard the stories, about your—abilities and your-your—attributes. You would be surprised what women gossip about behind their fans, particularly when they think they cannot be overheard. But those exploits are not what I am talking about, nor do I care to know more about them than I do already. What is of importance to me is this situation we now find ourselves in. It is unique to both of us."

"It is?"

"You have never made love to the one you love, and neither have I. So in that way, we are both inexperienced and—" she smiled shyly, "—more than a little bit *apprehensive*."

"I suppose when you put it like that..." His shy smile mirrored hers. "But even you cannot deny my experience puts the onus squarely on my shoulders to make you happy."

"Oh please do not negate my responsibility, just because I am a virgin," she responded earnestly. "I want to give you just as much pleasure as you give me, I assure you."

He gave a deep chuckle and shook his head.

"As God is my witness, Delight, if someone had told me three months ago I would be having such a brutally frank discussion about the marriage bed, with a pretty blonde virgin whom I love and adore, I would have condemned him as a Bedlamite!"

She was momentarily concerned.

"I hope I am not being too brutal?"

"With me? No. Not at all. I like it."

"Then you won't mind me saying, if all that is required for you—*for us*—to be completely comfortable with each other is to make love, then what are we waiting for?"

He could not hide his astonishment, or stifle his laughter. But he was not shocked; there was truth in her words. When he had mastery over himself he said,

"I don't deserve you, but I refuse to give you up. You know just what to say to make me realize I have a head full of unfounded fears and doubts, and only you are capable of banishing them." He stroked her cheek. "I will never be able to thank you enough for rescuing me from myself."

She dimpled. "You can but try, by letting me show you those tapestries."

He pretended offence.

"You want me to go back in there, into that den of iniquity, with you? And here was I thinking love was unconditional."

"Alisdair James Fitzstuart, you are a prude! For a man who can parade about a painter's studio in a loin cloth, putting on a show for a gaggle of giggling dancers—"

"Show. It was a *show*. I was acting. I am good at *acting*."

"Not an excuse I am willing to accept!" She pouted. "Five minutes' cursory inspection of that room, you will agree, is as nothing to the hours I have spent—"

"Hours?"

"—studying and admiring those tapestries. They tell a story—"

"A story?"

"—about a marriage, a loving marriage. And because it is a loving marriage, it is quite natural for the couple to make love, many times, and on all three tapestries. Each tapestry represents a different stage in their mar—Oh! You have outwitted me!" she declared when he started to chuckle. "You are being prudish to annoy me! Admit to it."

"I admit to nothing, only that I adore you all the more, if that is possible, when you talk so ardently on a topic that is of interest to you. I can't wait to hear all about pineapple cultivation."

She pouted. "Now you are mocking me."

"Never! I am sincerely interested in pineapple cultivation."

"I do not believe for one movement of the second hand of your pocket watch that you have the slightest interest in pineapples! Alisdair!"

She squealed with fright when he suddenly scooped her up into his arms.

"What—what are you doing?"

"What am I doing?" he repeated, carrying her lightly down the temple steps to the edge of the bathing pool. "It's time we gave ourselves up to this paradise and went for a dip. *And*, I promised to fetch you a glass of water half an hour ago."

The surface of the bathing pool shimmered and rippled like a length of white satin caught up by a breeze, water pouring forth from the open mouths of two large lion heads set in enormous pediments either side of a set of broad stairs that descended to the tiled floor. Dair went down these steps without hesitation, the water refreshingly cool on such a warm sunny day, he and Rory taking a shallow intake of breath as the cold water snapped at their warm skin.

"Let me tell you just how serious I am about pineapple cultivation, wife-to-be. I have engaged Bill Chambers to design a pinery for Fitz-stuart Hall."

"Chambers? *Sir William* Chambers? The Swedish architect? To build a—a *pinery*? At your family home? For-for *me*?"

He waded into the middle of the pool with Rory still in his arms, the water level at its deepest rising to just above his navel.

"Soon to be *our* home," he corrected. He frowned. "You do want a pinery, don't you? I thought it would make an excellent wedding present. It may take a year or two to build, but a wedding present it shall be."

When she clung to him, when she muffled unintelligibly into his neck, he took it as a sign she was pleased with his wedding gift. He tried to unhook her arm so that he could see her face, to reassure her and to kiss her, but she remained fastened to him. So he did the most natural thing in the world, something every good swimmer would do, but something he had not done in a large body of fresh water in many years. He slipped out from her hold on him by ducking under the water. And once underwater, and seeing how clear it was, he swam away to resurface by the steps.

Rory waved to him from the middle of the bathing pool, and he waved back before diving once again under the water and disappearing. She followed his lead and dived, too, knowing they were now engaged in a watery game of cat and mouse. She couldn't have been happier. Her happiness had nothing to do with his wedding gift of a pinery.

TWENTY-FIVE

It was inevitable they would make love.

Two people deeply in love in a secluded paradise would have required the combined willpower of all the mythical Gods to resist giving in to the overwhelming need to physically communicate such love. All other considerations were unimportant. Custom, family expectations, and societal norms, dictated they wait until they were legally and spiritually one before consummating their union. And their betrothal remained a secret, and had yet to receive the blessing of either family, in particular Dair's mother, the Countess of Strathsay, and most importantly, the sanction of Lord Shrewsbury, Rory's grandfather.

These considerations were mere formalities. Blessings and sanctions were a foregone conclusion for two young people from within the same social circle, who were distantly related, as all the nobility were in some form or other, dating back to the Conquest. Their union would surely be seen by all as the epitome of social, political and economic acceptability. But to the happy couple, and in this place, none of that was important.

There was something about the forest clearing, its isolation, even from the rest of the island, with its tall deep curtain of trees, its fanciful temples and its enchanted bathing pool, that rendered the lovers, at that moment in time, invulnerable.

The handful of hours leading up to the couple falling asleep in each other's arms under a coverlet in the small temple was burned into their collective memory. They made love twice in the very room Dair had railed against, but it wasn't the first time or the only setting. The consummation of their union occurred under the shade of an ancient elm, on the picnic rug by the bathing pool. Dair had been prepared to wait, whatever his private misgivings, given his parents' disastrous wedding night, for her sake, because he loved her. Rory had other ideas, though she'd had her heart set on the temple as the perfect setting to give herself to him. But when in the throes of an all-consuming passion, reticence and the best-laid plans are irrelevant. Nothing else mattered except their love for one another, and in this paradise, the shared experience of mutual physical pleasure.

Much later, Dair carried Rory into the small temple, built a fire in the grate and boiled water for tea. While he lit a cheroot she made tea, both silent, words unnecessary to express the joy and relief both felt at discovering they shared a healthy enjoyment of making love. It went unspoken that the bridal night now held no fears for either of them. They could go forward into their new life together, confident and full of optimism. And while they drank tea on the coverlet spread out over the thick rug in front of the fire, Rory told Dair the story of the couple woven into the three enormous tapestries covering three walls.

She confessed that the tapestries held more meaning for her having listened to Geoffrey the Hermit's fairytale. No, not here in this room, she quickly reassured Dair. It was on her first visit to the island, when the hermit had found her trespassing in the round temple. In exchange for allowing her to come and go on the island whenever she pleased, he made her promise not to set foot in the small temple until her seventeenth summer. Despite her overwhelming curiosity she promised, and he took her at her word, though he warned her he would be watching to make sure she kept true.

And because he could see she was a good girl with a kind heart, he offered to tell her a fairytale connected with this island, about a dark-haired sprite and his golden-haired fairy nymph, and three magic carpets. How could she resist? It was only years later, when she finally viewed the tapestries (what he called magic carpets) that she realized the fairytale was true, woven in silken thread into the three large tapestries. It made the hermit's simplistic telling of the couple's life story that much more poignant.

Geoffrey the Hermit had been living on the island for ten years or more when one day a couple appeared at the round temple, as if by magic. They stayed two nights, and then disappeared. He had watched them from the safety of the forest, fearing they might be evil sprites, come to do him mischief. But as he watched them splashing in the bathing pool, chasing each other through the round temple, and all the while laughing and being playful with each other, he knew they would never do him a harm. Every year for the next twenty-three years they returned to the island, for two nights, to splash in the bathing pool and to chase each other through the temple.

He could tell that they loved each other beyond reason.

A week before the couple's second visit, workmen came to prune the trees and bushes about the temples, to clean the pool of leaves, and to dust and rid the small temple of cobwebs. And so it was that the hermit knew precisely when the sprites would return to the island each year.

Just before their seventh visit, the workmen brought with them a magic carpet. This they hung on a wall of the small temple. When the men left, Geoffrey went to gaze at it, and it was truly magical, woven with brightly colored silks and gold thread and as dazzling as a sunny spring day. Woven into the carpet were his two friendly sprites, and he saw that there was a small sprite, a son. He also recognized the palace across the lake from the island, and now knew where his sprites lived for most of the year, and who they were. They were in truth the king and queen of this domain, and when they set foot on this island, magic turned them into sprites. He knew this because they wore no gold coronets, brought no servants to serve them, and cooked their own food. Their clothes, however, were of silk and velvet, when they chose to wear clothes, which, being sprites, was not often at all.

From that day forward, every year he gathered flowers and vines and wove them into crowns for the sprites to wear on this their fairy island kingdom. He left them as offerings in the small temple just before they arrived. He knew his flower crowns pleased the sprites because he saw them frolicking about in them.

The second magic carpet arrived just before the couple's fifteenth visit to the island. This carpet was as brightly colored as the first, and was all about families. There were four panels to the carpet. The first showed the sprites being as friendly as ever with each other. In the second they were with their son who had grown tall. The third panel showed the sprite family with another couple, who also had a son, and finally, in the fourth panel a third family with a mother but no father and three children, two boys and a girl had joined the sprites and their friends with the one son. Everyone was happy and holding hands.

And on this fifteenth visit, Geoffrey was surprised to see that the female sprite was heavy with child. The couple went swimming as they always did, but they did not run about the colonnades of the round temple, but spent most of their time shut away in the little temple. He could see the smoke from the temple chimney from his cottage. And when there was no more smoke, he knew they had left the island to return to their palace.

Two days before the couple's twenty-third visit to the island, a third magic carpet appeared on the wall of the temple. The male sprite no longer had dark hair, but a mane of pure white, and he walked with the aid of a stick. But the female sprite was just as beautiful and as full of life as the first day he had fallen under the spell of her beauty. This visit was to be different from all the others, and the most memorable for Geoffrey. On dusk of the second night, there was a knock on the door of his tiny cottage. There standing before him, much shorter than his estimation but more beautiful than he thought possible, was the fairy queen. She had the most mesmerizing green eyes, and was wearing his crown of flowers on her long golden hair that flowed past her waist.

She asked if she might enter his cottage, and he gave her his only wooden chair to sit upon near the warmth of the fireplace. He set a mug of dandelion tea before her, which she drank in tiny sips. She thanked him for the flower crowns, which were always so welcoming upon their arrival. She thanked him, too, for being the guardian of their island paradise. She was smiling, but he could see she was inconsolable. Her green eyes told him so. He asked her what he could do to stop her sadness. She said there was nothing to be done; it was in God's hands. She told him in a brave but halting voice that this would be the last visit to the island by her and her one true love. She told him not to concern himself, that he would always have a home on the island. And when his time came, he could be buried on the island, and she would see to it he had a headstone and his name would be carved over the mantel of his fireplace, so that he, the guardian of Swan Island, would never be forgotten.

With no smoke from the temple chimney, Geoffrey knew the sprites had returned to their kingdom and he would never see them again. Rory had asked him to describe what was on the third and last magic carpet. It was a map of the island, and it was filled with all the wondrous things to be found there, and the wonderful times enjoyed by the two sprites. They were there, the king with his white hair, the fairy queen with her flowing golden hair, both wearing his crowns made of flowers, and they were being as friendly as ever with each other. But what pleased Geoffrey the Hermit, what brought tears to his eyes in the telling of it to Rory, was that woven into the island map was his little cottage, and looking out of the only window, there he was, smiling with his long beard and whiskers and a flower behind his ear.

Dair had then gone over to stand before the third tapestry, to study it and to find the cottage. There it was, on the other side of the clearing from the temples, in a bed of wildflowers, and woven into the flowers was the hermit's name: Geoffrey Swan. Still gazing at the tapestry, he then quietly asked about the fate of the hermit. She told him. Two years ago she visited the island as usual, but could not find Geoffrey anywhere. He often found her. She went to his cottage. It was empty, and by the cobwebs and dust it had not been lived in for some time. She found his grave not far from the cottage, in a sunny, open spot. It was marked by a fine headstone and covered with wildflowers. By the headstone was a large urn filled with beautiful, exquisitely-wrought porcelain flowers of every color and variety. Rory imagined it had been placed there so that every day Geoffrey the Hermit, guardian of Swan Island, would have flowers on his grave, whatever the weather.

THE COUPLE WERE DISCOVERED ASLEEP IN EACH OTHER'S ARMS, under the coverlet before the fireplace in the temple; the irony not lost on Dair. If figures woven in tapestry had the ability to mock him for being a hypocritical prig, they were doing just that as he pulled on his drawers and followed Farrier through to the cool of the circular temple and into the afternoon light.

"Beggin' your lordship's pardon for wakin'—"

"Why are you here, Mr. Farrier?"

"There's a cottage over yonder. Neat and tidy and with a comfortable bed. I reckon it belonged to the guardian of Swan Island, Geoffrey the Hermit, cause that's what's carved into the mantel over the fire."

Dair raked the unruly hair out of his eyes and accepted the cheroot his batman offered him.

"I don't mean here, here on the island. Here, bothering me. Don't you have a few days left to your angling holiday?"

Farrier gazed out through the temple columns to the forest that ringed the clearing, the leaves against the sky now tipped with the orange glow of an afternoon sun. A curl of smoke rose into the clouds and seemed to touch a flock of ducks as they flew past in formation. The batman kept his profile to his master and puffed on his cheroot. He didn't answer the question and he couldn't hide his smirk.

"This little glade is a paradise, ain't it? Private and out of the way... No one would know y'here... Thing is, today of all days, a gamekeeper and his two thumpin' great lads came ashore. They heard what they thought was a wild beast, but instead of headin' straight here, as luck would have it, they saw smoke and came to reconnoiter the cottage first. Got me to state m'business. And then we got to smokin' and havin' a nice mug o' tea, and I kept 'em occupied until—well, until it went quiet again. Don't reckon your lordship would be interested in knowin' that every bird song, every snapped twig, echoes out into the forest—"

"I'm not," Dair retorted. He drew back deeply on the cheroot, as if he hadn't smoked one in a week, and with a lift of his heavy chin blew the smoke into the air. "What do you want?"

Farrier came straight to the point.

"There's a flotilla out lookin' for your golden-haired mermaid. Seems she left her shoes and somethin' else on a jetty that she can't do without, and that's made 'em think there's been a misadventure—"

"Damn!"

"—and so the gamekeeper and the lads were sent to see if she was here."

"What did you tell them?"

Farrier glanced at his master and said smugly, "Told 'em squat, like I always do. Not my business, is it, if yesterday's dish was breast of opera singer and today's is rump of mermaid. Your tastes are anythin' but pedestrian. But y'beard has me flummoxed. Though, in this woodland setting, and making the beast with two—"

"Stow it, Mr. Farrier!" Dair growled, the ferocity of the order making the batman recoil, stunned. "This isn't one of my brainless pranks, and I'm not here on some idiotic wager, or lust driven whim! Got it? She's—Frankly, she's none of your God-damn business!"

"Very good, Major," Farrier stated, saluting his superior officer. "Consider m'self cautioned, m'lord."

Dair flicked the cheroot to the ground and the batman instantly extinguished it underfoot. Dair sighed heavily, and lifted a hand in resignation.

"Look, Mr. Farrier, I don't want—"

"My stick," Rory interrupted, coming forward. "I left my shoes and my walking stick on the jetty. Silly of me to forget them. That's what they must have discovered. I don't remember putting either in the boat…"

Rory had been standing a little way off, the coverlet wrapped around her as best she could manage it, held closed at her breasts, the excess material gathered up over an arm so she did not trip. Her fair hair fell around her face and about her shoulders down to her waist like a curtain. She had heard most of the conversation between master and trusted servant, waking just after Farrier had gingerly poked Dair out of a light sleep.

To Farrier, she appeared less the mermaid and more the ethereal medieval maiden he'd seen in stained glass church windows. She was prettier than he had expected of a fair-haired beauty, with dark lashes framing deep blue eyes, and she had a lovely dark pink mouth. But she was not as beautiful nor as voluptuous as the Major's usual preference in female bedfellows. And she was a good many years younger, which instantly made the batman wonder at the arrangement between his bearded master and this girl. He did not have to wonder long because he had his answer when Dair turned at the sound of Rory's voice. A light came into his dark eyes, his features softened, all anger and annoyance extinguished. Farrier knew then the significance of this female in his master's life and he mentally gave a low whistle and dropped his gaze to the dusty toes of his boots, where they remained.

The couple smiled shyly at each other and when Dair went over to Rory and gave her his hand, she took it and he drew her to him. He kissed her forehead, saying gently,

"I had best get you back before your grandfather works himself into an apoplexy, and your maid is compelled to divulge her fear something far more distressing has happened to you."

"Than drowning? Surely not." She smiled and leaned against his bare chest with chin tilted up. "He may think my loss of virtue a fate worse than drowning," she continued in a whisper. "But I do not. I was never more happy of such a circumstance in my life."

He brushed the hair from her cheek. "Let's get married here, at Treat, this week. I'll have Roxton get us a special license."

"Oh? Will it take a week?"

He laughed and pinched her chin. "If I had my way we'd marry tomorrow. But archbishops require some notice, to ponder and to be important... But Cornwallis is a congenial fellow. Roxton won't have any problem there."

"A week will be time enough to have a gown fetched from home... And Grasby must be in attendance—"

"Yes. I'd like Grasby there, too. Then it's settled." He gently kissed her mouth. "I can't wait."

"Nor I... Now I must dress so you can return me to the dower house... But first I need to-to bathe—"

"Of course," he interrupted quickly, to save her any embarrassment. "I took the liberty of setting out your stockings and clothes down by the steps of the pool, in readiness."

"Oh! How-how thoughtful. Thank you," she replied, heat intensi-
fying in her cheeks. "I-I don't know when you-you found the time…"

"I've packed up most of the nuncheon things, too, but left out the
strawberries and there is a peach…"

Her awkwardness, rather than abating, grew more acute with his
tactical interruptions. To think he had gone to the trouble of arranging
her clothes, knowing she would want to bathe. But of course he would
know that. This wasn't the first time he had made love. For some ridiculous reason only known to her heart, she felt suddenly awkward and
stupidly gauche in his presence, which was far from how she had been
when they were naked in each other's arms.

She recalled how, when they had finished playing hide-and-go-seek
in the bathing pool they had dried off and then together gone about
setting out the nuncheon things. They were both hungry, and after a
leisurely nuncheon and a bottle of wine between them, had lain replete
on the picnic rug and stared up at the sky, at the clouds. She wasn't sure
of the precise sequence of how they ended up making love. Some
moments were more vivid than others… How he had gently removed
her stockings, tugging the little silk bows undone that held her garters
in place and her stockings up over her knees. Rolling each damp
stocking down her leg and off her foot, he had kissed her instep,
favoring both feet equally, all the while telling her how much he loved
and desired her; and she had not flinched. He had been so patient, so
gentle when required. She trusted him utterly.

He loved her as much as she did him, and it was a wondrous thing.
She had learned things, extraordinary things about herself and her own
body, and his. Oh! His body was so gloriously masculine, his reaction
to her kisses and caresses of exploration most extraordinary of all. She
was still in awe of what had just occurred between them. And having
shared the most intimate experience in the world with the man she
loved above all others, she had crossed a bridge from which there was
no turning back. She was now spiritually bound to him forevermore,
and she couldn't be happier. All that remained was to celebrate the legal
union for their happiness to be complete.

So why, with her body cooled and her mind at rest, did she feel
there was still a shadow cast over their happiness. Her heart told her
making love with her beloved was the most natural thing in the world.
Yet, there was a small niggle of doubt, of guilt, that pressed against her
heart and troubled her greatly. She could not help it. From girlhood she
had known that a female's maidenhead was her most prized possession.
It was not to be given away lightly, and not to just any man, and never,
ever, before marriage; to do so would be the beginning of the end of her

moral decay. And while she believed this, she never seriously thought she would marry, least of all make love in a magical grotto with the handsomest man in England.

He had given her a ring pledging his commitment before they had made love... And he said they would be married by special license by the end of the week... That was all the reassurance she needed —wasn't it...?

Dair sensed Rory's uneasiness and noticed how her fingers unconsciously fiddled with the unfamiliar pale lavender sapphire ring, turning it back and forth on her ring finger. But he had no idea what was troubling her or the extent of her inner turmoil. He thought perhaps the presence of Farrier was making her uncomfortable, so he put an arm about her shoulders and led her to the bathing pool and away from his batman, who stood staring at the ground as if it had all his attention.

When he returned, leaving Rory to bathe in private, Farrier had moved inside the little temple and was making himself useful by dousing the fire, and tidying the room. Dair tugged on his breeches and threw on his shirt and waistcoat, but had yet to do up the buttons. He held his jockey boots and stockings.

"Mr. Farrier! A hand, if you please."

"As it so happens, I do have one of those I can offer your lordship."

Dair smiled. "One is all I require."

Comfortable again with each other, Farrier felt free to ask,

"May I cut short m'anglin' holiday and return to your service, m'lord?"

Dair looked up from securing a breeches buckle.

"Are you sure? It's not necessary... On second thought, yes! Please do. I need to shave, and this afternoon. Reynolds is a fine valet in most respects, but he can't shave me, or take proper care of my razors, and he hasn't the foggiest notion of how to prepare a whetstone."

Farrier shook his head with grave concern.

"'Tis no wonder you're wearing a woolly face then, m'lord. I'd not want Reynolds slittin' me throat! And he has two good hands with which to do it, too. Leave it to me... There!" he added with satisfaction, now his Major was booted and dressed. "If you don't have need of me, I'll head back to the cottage to collect m'kit. My skiff is moored in the cove, too."

"Mr. Farrier—Bill..."

The batman stopped in the doorway of the temple and turned back into the room.

"Yes, m'lord?"

Dair looked him in the eye.

"My life has taken an unexpected but welcome turn since you were locked up in the Tower."

Farrier couldn't have agreed more. To his mind, the Major's confession was a colossal understatement. When Dair did not elaborate, Farrier nodded and left. He was confident they were headed into interesting times... By nightfall, even he could not have predicted just how interesting.

TWENTY-SIX

ANTONIA SLOWLY ROSE UP OFF THE TAPESTRY CUSHIONS ON THE chaise longue and put her stockinged feet to the carpet. She did this without opening her eyes. And with her eyes still closed, her toes searched out her embroidered turquoise silk mules, which she had kicked off earlier. Despite it being late afternoon, she had yet to change out of her morning *déshabillé*, a soft brown silk gown *a la Turque*, loose-fitting but for the wide sash of turquoise silk around her waist. And given the way she was feeling, she had no inclination to dress for dinner, and this despite having her cousin to dine. How she would get through the meal, she knew not. Food was of no interest to her.

Her body did not crave sustenance and, for some reason also known only to her body, it was easier to cope with the waves of nausea with her eyes shut to the light. Michelle had offered to close the curtains, but she wanted—no, she *needed*—to feel the light breeze that came in off the lake. And with the sun behind the dower house, the windows were thrown wide, the view of jetty, lake and Swan Island bathed in a glorious golden glow of late afternoon light.

It just so happened that an hour earlier she had been standing at the window as two boats glided in to moor at the jetty. They were met by half a dozen men, some of whom had been out on the lake earlier as part of a search party. Her first reaction was one of relief, that her goddaughter was safe and well. The second was one of extreme interest in the company Rory was keeping. Her interest intensified to discover the young woman had been out boating on the lake with her cousin the Major.

She watched the men offload the cargo from both boats and go about their business, one handing Rory her walking stick. The Major and Rory then slowly made their way up the sloping lawn towards a pony trap waiting to return Rory to the Gatehouse Lodge. It was at the trap, more precisely, what happened behind it, that made Antonia sway and grip the window sill with two hands, her maid thinking her about to faint. Did the couple seriously think no one would see them kissing with an Elizabethan manor house looming large over them? But by the manner of their kiss, Antonia recognized that the couple were not thinking at all. They were so wrapped up in each other they were oblivious to all else, particularly their surroundings. There was only one conclusion to reach about her goddaughter and her cousin the Major, one that was met with mixed emotion. For while their kiss curved her mouth into a smile, it also filled her with a disquiet she could not shake.

She was reminded of that kiss when Michelle interrupted her thoughts with the announcement that the private dining room was ready and only awaited her guest for the dishes to be brought up from the kitchen. Did Mme la Duchesse now wish to change for dinner? Antonia shook her head, and in a rare fit of impatience grabbed the end of the sash about her waist, opened her eyes and blurted out,

"If all I need do is change out of this and into a new gown and different shoes, to change the way I-I *feel*, do you not think me I would do so? *Mon Dieu*," she muttered to herself, "what is wrong with me?"

Michelle could have told her mistress but she kept her opinion to herself. With a jerk of her head at the curtained opening that led deeper into the Duchess's private rooms, she sent away the two personal maids, who knew by the lady-in-waiting's look that the clothes they had selected and set out for their mistress were to be pegged and boxed for another day.

"Mme la Duchesse, would you prefer I sent word to his lordship you are unwell, and—"

Antonia shook her fair hair. "No." She looked up at Michelle, who had come to stand before the chaise longue. "That, too, it will not change how I feel. Perhaps first bring him here. And me, you can fetch a pot of tea. No milk. And perhaps a slice of bread. No butter. That may help settle the queasiness…"

Her gaze flickered over the expanse of deep carpet between her and the fireplace, littered with documents, tidied into neat piles and from left to right, in order of importance. There were legal papers, boundary maps, house plans, bills and receipts, the trade cards of a multitude of tradesmen and merchants, and correspondence from the same. As well as piles of well-ordered papers, there was *The Gentleman and Cabinet-Maker's Director* bookmarked at various pages, textile swatches, paint color swatches and numerous wallpaper samples. There were even several detailed drawings from a carriage maker for a new traveling coach and a town carriage. And at the end of the chaise longue, on top of a pile of books she had brought down from the house in Hanover Square to read at her leisure, her appointment diary. It was open, and told her the painter, Mr. Joseph Wright, would be arriving in the next week or so, traveling down from Derby at her request, to spend a fortnight making preliminary sketches for a new portrait. When completed it would be sent up to Leven Castle, to hang beside Wright's commissioned portrait of the newly elevated Duke of Kinross.

All of it, from the smallest tradesmen's account to her appointment diary, was connected with her new life as Duchess of Kinross, and the four houses of which she was now mistress: The dower house, now part of the newly-formed Strang Leven estate; the Hanover Square mansion, to be renamed Kinross House; Leven Castle, the sixteenth century French chateau on the shores of Loch Leven in Scotland; and a townhouse in Edinburgh. Her duke had given her dominion over them all, because he trusted her judgment implicitly, and, she suspected, to keep her occupied during his absence north of Hadrian's Wall.

But how could she think of taking charge of one house, least of all four, as well as order two new carriages and provide guidance to the Duke's new man of business on a number of administrative matters pertaining to his estates, when she could barely concentrate to read the most recent newssheet, least of all make critical decisions. And without Jonathon to share the decisions with her it was all rather strangely unimportant. But she would do her duty by him, and, though she had yet to come to terms with it herself, the tiny life now growing inside her, heir to his estates and wealth, and the Scottish ducal coronet.

IT WAS WHILE ANTONIA WAS SIPPING FROM HER CUP OF BLACK TEA and nibbling on a slice of soft plain white bread, that Dair was admitted into her cluttered pretty sitting room with its view of the lake. He was dressed formally, which was a surprise. And even more so when he was usually seen in a frock coat made for comfort, the habitual jockey boots, and with his thick black hair indifferently tied back off his face. Today he wore an elegant midnight blue linen frock coat, embroidered on short skirts, tight upturned cuffs and pocket flaps with silver sprays of flowers and spangles, and a pair of matching thigh-tight knitted breeches. Both were adorned with shiny silver buttons that matched those of a cream silk waistcoat. And for the first time in many years, his large feet were encased in plain black, low-heeled leather shoes with unadorned silver buckles. His shoulder length hair was neatly dressed and combed off his face, tied at the nape with a cream silk ribbon.

Most surprising of all, he no longer wore the close-cropped black beard Antonia had seen him with just that afternoon. In fact, his heavy chin and jaw was the smoothest it had been in many years. He had always carried some stubble, even to the most formal of occasions, as if he couldn't be bothered or didn't have the time for an exacting shave. Antonia always assumed this an affectation, like the untidy hair and the jockey boots. Props taken from his performer's bag for the benefit of his admiring female audience and, she suspected, to annoy his mother; the Countess was a stickler for convention in form and correct dress.

It was not the calculated devil-may-care cousin with the arrogant swagger who bowed over her outstretched hand in greeting but an affable young gentleman with a smile that bordered on shyness. It had Antonia sitting up and peering at him keenly. She said to tease him,

"A month in the Tower and you are a changed man, Alisdair."

He put up an eyebrow.

"You and I both know, your Grace, I spent that month in Portugal."

"Ah, so not incarceration but sunstroke sees you forsake your boots, *hein*?" She put aside her teacup. "This cousin you present to me looks a good deal more serious than the other one. But you should go without jockey boots more often. White stockings they show off your large calves to better advantage. And the beard, it had a certain appeal, but you are far more handsome without it."

"Thank you, your Grace—"

"Your Grace? I compliment you and you go all formal on me? And now me I have you blushing! Who would have thought it possible. But I am not telling you anything you do not already know."

Dair grinned. "No, your—No, Cousin. But I will take the stockings and shoes on advisement."

"Julian he knows you are here and has invited you to a concert this evening perhaps?"

Dair shook his head. "No. After I sup with you, I have an appointment with Lord Shrewsbury." When Antonia's eyebrows lifted imperceptibly, he added, "To debrief him about my trip to Lisbon. But before I can do that, I need to discuss an important matter with you—"

"With me?" she interrupted, recalling the passionate kiss she had seen him share with her goddaughter. Offering him the wingchair adjacent to her chaise, she apologized for the untidy state of the carpet when his large feet found it difficult to pick their way through the piles of papers. When he was seated, she added with a smile, "Naturally, I will help you in any way I can. You know that, *mon cher*."

He nodded and, suddenly overcome, easily slipped into her native French tongue. "Yes. Yes, I do know that, *ma chère cousine*... Jamie loves his microscope, and your visit to Banks House has provided the family and their servants with enough to talk about for weeks, as well as a certain notoriety in their little corner of the world. I suspect you knew the outcome before you drove out to Chelsea in state...?"

She gave a little tinkle of laughter, and then was serious.

"People in our position we have a responsibility to live up to the expectations of others, particularly those whose circumstances or position do not allow them the opportunity to come close to our social circle, least of all mingle within it. How could I not drive out in the big black traveling coach, with outriders, and me in one of my best gowns, looking every inch a duchess? What a disappointment had I turned up looking like this!"

Dair laughed and shook his head. "Never a disappointment, Mme la Duchesse. Whatever you say to the contrary, you are *always* every inch a duchess; the attire an inconsequential detail."

"Me I hope that remains true in the months to come..." Antonia murmured, and braced herself to stand without feeling nauseous, prompted by the appearance of a footman in the doorway of the anteroom that connected the sitting room with the private dining room. "You do not mind if first we dine before we discuss this important matter? Pierre he will tear out what hair is remaining to him if I do not at least taste the dishes he tempts me with. I am only too pleased you are here staying with me," she added with a smile, when Dair offered her his arm, and they walked through to the dining room and a table set with silver, fine crystal and Sèvres plate. "Your appetite at least makes my chef feel he is valued..."

While the cousins dined on lamb loin with a breaded mushroom crust, salmagundi, carrot puffs, stuffed cucumber and potato pudding, the conversation remained topical but not personal. They discussed the infirm Lord Chatham's surprise visit to the Lords in his sedan chair, and the defeat of his motion to end hostilities in the Americas, by a vote of

76 to 26. They both agreed that the publication of Macpherson's General History, condemning the first Duke of Marlborough's avarice, was needless abuse, Macpherson having no right to cast a stone at Queen Anne's great general. Both were intensely interested in the recent raids by American privateers on the Scottish and Irish coasts, Antonia expressing the hope the crates of her personal belongings from her old Parisian home made it to the safety of an English port without being confiscated by traitorous pirates. Dair was quick to bite his tongue and not comment that those traitorous pirates were being aided and abetted by her kinsmen, the French, who continued to hide their treacherous two-faced cowardly dealings with the colonists behind a cloak of cordiality with the English. He knew open war with the French had to be just around the corner, months at most.

Antonia was not so distracted by her nausea or the present conver-sation that she did not notice the sudden tightness in her cousin's strong jaw at mention of the French, so she skillfully steered the conver-sation away from the war with a mundane observation Horace Walpole had made to her in one of his letters. It had to do with the present folly of Society to keep later and later hours in London. She told Dair how Lord Derby's cook had given his lordship warning he would be killed if he had to dress suppers at three in the morning, to which his lordship had asked him coolly how much he would have to pay to kill him!

They both laughed and cordiality was restored, so much so that by the time pudding arrived, Antonia, who had managed to keep her nausea under control by eating very little, was able to indulge in a scoop of pistachio ice accompanied by a thin barberry-flavored wafer. And Dair forgot why he was dining with his cousin, and instead poured forth his feelings for Miss Aurora Talbot.

Antonia masked her incredulity and listened without comment. But as she finished off the last spoonful of pistachio ice in the tall crystal glass, she believed in his sincerity utterly. Now the change in him made perfect sense. It was not so much that he had changed as that he had become the man he was always destined to be. If she was privately astounded her goddaughter was the woman who had brought this about, and in whom Dair had invested all his hopes and dreams for the future, it was not because she did not see the potential in Rory to be the love of a good man's life. It was that it was her cousin, who had been within Rory's orbit for many years, had finally noticed, and fallen irrevocably in love with her. She could not have been happier and natu-rally assumed this was the important matter he wished to discuss with her.

They returned to the sitting room for tea and macaroons, the deep-

piled carpet before the fireplace miraculously cleared of the paraphernalia pertaining to the organization and refurbishment of four homes,
and neatly stacked in piles on a long mahogany table up against one
wall. It was with the tea things before her and the butler going about
the business of pouring out into porcelain cups, that Antonia enquired
if Dair's secret betrothal was the important matter he had wished to
discuss with her.

The Duchess's innocent enquiry brought Dair out of his reverie
with a heavy thud, and he returned to the real reason he needed to
speak with her. If it were possible, he was even more reluctant to do so.
The newfound intimacy of understanding between them made it that
much more difficult to broach the subject of the identity of his contact
in Lisbon. Yet, it was unavoidable. Confirming the identity of the
double agent meant the man could return to England, and in so doing
could pass on all he knew about France's dealings with the American
rebels and expose the double agent within Shrewsbury's own Secret
Service.

Antonia was naturally puzzled when her cousin returned the
conversation to his secret visit to Portugal.

"You wish to speak to *me* about your business in Lisbon?"

She became alarmed the matter was serious indeed when, after
accepting the cup of tea, Dair shifted from the wingchair to perch on
the end of her chaise longue.

"The principal reason I went to Lisbon was to meet a contact, an
important agent, a double agent in fact, working not only for France,
but more importantly, working for us against the French. He has vital
intelligence—information—that could save the lives of thousands of
our troops. He also knows the identity of the traitor within Shrewsbury's own service."

Antonia held out the sugar bowl and watched Dair use the silver
tongs to drop a small lump of sugar into his milky tea.

"Did you ask this individual if your brother he is the traitor Shrewsbury says he is?"

Dair heard her note of censure and took a moment to stir his tea
before saying levelly, "He believes, as I do, Charles is an intellectual
idealist whose ideals were played upon by forces loyal to *le Roi* to
further their own ends."

"I see. So this individual you met, he must think he knows Charles
well, as well as you, to make such an observation, *hein*?"

"Yes, Mme la Duchesse," Dair replied. He asked she put aside her
tea dish, fearing that in her surprise she might spill her tea given what
he was about to tell her.

She did as he asked, the use of her title, and the look in his dark eyes, setting her heart racing. Before he could say anything further, she said in a whisper, "Your brother... Is Charles... He is-he is *safe*?"

"Yes. Yes, of course. He and Sarah-Jane have settled in a house in the town of Versailles, just outside the palace grounds. According to Charles, it has a lovely walled garden and is close enough to the palace he can stroll across there when required."

Antonia nodded and breathed easy. "Yes. Yes. Me I had a letter from Sarah-Jane. She and Charles they are happy in their new house, which pleases me and her father very much." '

"The agent I met in Lisbon calls himself M'sieur Lucian, M'sieur Gaius Lucian. Although, that is not his birth name. I admit when he told me his true identity, I was unconvinced—No—I was floored. You could have knocked me out with a feather! But we spent several days together and by the end I had to admit there were echoes about his person which reminded me of the young man he once was. So he could well be who he says he is, but I am not the man to make that determination.

"After all, it is more than ten years since I last saw him, and if it is he, he is much altered. My memory of him is not favorable. I always wanted to plant him a facer for his posturing insolence. It was only Julian's intervention that stopped me acting violently towards the prancing twit! Flitting about in heels higher than any female wears, and with an irritating laugh that should never be uttered out of the mouth of a man. And he had this irksome conceited habit of carrying his viola with him wherever he went. He'd strike up some discordant composition, usually within my hearing, that made me want to smash the instrument over his powdered head to shut him up."

Antonia patted Dair's hand that had balled itself into a fist on his knee.

"I know whom you describe, *mon cher*, and me, I understand your irritation. I loved him dearly because he was the son of my dearest best friends, and my nephew. But me too I wanted sometimes to rap his knuckles with my fan. It was all one big show, you realize?"

"Yes. Yes, I do now. But my younger self could not see through the outrageous performance." He laughed harshly. "Imagine that? Me, the most accomplished performer in the Secret Service, oblivious to his own cousin's subterfuge!"

Antonia let out a little sigh of sadness. "It is too sad... A whole family lost... I console myself that he Evelyn did not live to see both parents and Monseigneur leave us in the way they did..."

Dair frowned. "But the person I just described to you, the cousin whom I had no time for over a decade ago, he *is* the gentleman I spent time with in Lisbon; or so he aimed to convince me! M'sieur Gaius Lucian purports to be Evelyn Gaius Lucian Ffolkes, your nephew and heir to the earldom of Stretham-Ely."

Antonia shook her head. "No. No. No. This man, he is a liar! Evelyn, he was lost to us many years ago. He eloped with a most unsuitable girl who died a few years after they were married, in Florence, I think. And after that—" She lifted her hands in a gesture of helplessness, "—we lost all contact with him. Monseigneur, he spent a small fortune searching for him. His sister, Evelyn's maman, as you may imagine, was distraught with grief; first at his elopement, and then when he disappeared. He was her only child. Never a day went by when she did not burst into tears at some moment, thinking about him. It was too, too sad for my sister-in-law and her husband. And that is why, when word reached Monseigneur from Krakow, that his body— Evelyn's body—it had been fished out of the Vistula River, it was some closure for his poor parents. Of course, we, none of us, believed he was truly gone, and there was a grain of hope that the body it was not his because it was so badly mutilated. But when his signet ring it reached us, and his father identified it as belonging to his son, we knew then he was truly dead. So this man, this M'sieur Lucian, he is a liar, Alisdair."

Dair had listened without comment or reaction to the Duchess's argument. Had he not spent time with this M'sieur Lucian, and been convinced by him that he was who he said he was, he would have been the first to agree with her. But all that she told him, he already knew, and it had been countered by Gaius Lucian. And so he persisted to convince her otherwise.

"What if I told you the body in the river was not his? What if I said the signet ring was sent to finally convince the Duke and his parents he was indeed dead, because at that point in his life he wished himself dead, and he did not wish to be found? Is that not plausible?" When Antonia gave a little shrug but did not dispute this, he put aside his empty tea cup, and continued. "I am sure there is much more to his story than what I was told, but my time was limited, and it was not my place to be this man's confessor. I was to make contact with our double agent in Lisbon, find out certain particulars, and return that information to Shrewsbury. But, it seems, our agent has his own ideas of what he is prepared to divulge, and when. He will only do so when given safe passage to England, and once in the country, immunity from prosecution. So it is imperative I believe he is who he says he is, and that Shrewsbury does, too. Only then can we trust the information he gives us as the truth."

"You want me to say I believe this man to be my nephew, back from the dead? But I cannot, and will not believe it. Not until he is standing before me and I look in his blue eyes. Then, perhaps, I will give such an assurance."

"Believe me, cousin. I was no more astounded or skeptical than you are now that this man is who he claims he is. After all, he is nothing like the prancing pony I remember. He can't even play a viola. Well, at least I do not think it possible. He is missing two fingers from his left hand. I reckoned his age to be nearer to mine, but he looks ten years older—"

"If he were alive, he would be turning thirty."

"This man looks forty if he is a day. His neck and hands carry the scars of torture. He is wiry and gaunt, as if he had gone a long time without proper sustenance. He does have blue eyes—"

"Small consolation."

"—and everything he told me—and I do mean *everything*—about his family, his boyhood spent in Paris and here, at Treat, about Monseigneur, you, his time at Eton with Julian, teaching the Duchess to play the viola, even events that included my father—all of it is correct."

"Imposter! He could have told all these stories to a close friend, a servant even, and it is that sinister person who pretends to be my nephew. All to make a grab for the inheritance, me I do not doubt it!"

Antonia waved a hand in dismissal and groped for her folding fan. Suddenly, she needed air. Why had the windows been shut and the curtains pulled? At her bidding, two footmen rushed to pull back the curtains and push out the windows to their full extent. And where was Michelle? Or for that matter, any of her four attendants. She looked about, at the chinoiserie painted six-paneled screen in the corner of the room. It hid from view a commode and a wash stand that held a water jug and porcelain basin. She wondered if she could make the dash to the basin in time should the wave of nausea she was riding prove over-whelming. Usually Michelle, or any one of her attendants, was close, ready to thrust the basin at her should she require it. That they were not in the room increased her panic. And it was this panic, this feeling that she may suddenly need to run behind the screen and be ill, that made her sound irritated with her cousin.

"Why do you not bother Julian with this matter? He could tell you the same. He was close to his cousin for many years, until he ran off with the Farmer-General's daughter and they lost contact. I am certain he could also put his hands on the letters his father wrote to many

agents on the Continent seeking information about Evelyn. I am sorry,
Alisdair, but this M'sieur Lucian he is a fraud."

"I wish I could be as certain as you, Mme la Duchesse. I wish I did
not have to disturb you, and could resolve the matter with Roxton. But
that is not possible."

"Why? Why not speak to my son?" Antonia demanded. She had
managed to get herself to the window seat and put her face to the cool
breeze that came in off the lake. "Do you not agree it is strange this
M'sieur Lucian he would want you to bother me and not my son?"

Dair remained silent, bracing himself for what he had to ask her to
confirm, made all the more difficult if his suspicions about the origins
of his cousin's lack of appetite proved correct. He had watched her turn
up her nose at foods she had readily eaten in the past. Most telling of all
was her aversion for her favorite beverage, coffee, and her new-found
preference for tea, a drink she usually abhorred. It was as glaring a sign
as any that she was suffering from morning sickness. And while he was
mildly shocked that a woman of his cousin's age was with child, he
knew it was not unusual. He was also secretly elated for her and her
new duke. A baby was always welcome, and he knew this one would be
all the more precious to the newly-married couple, particularly as the
Duke of Kinross was without a male heir.

"If I could disturb the Duke with this, I would. But the piece of
information M'sieur Lucian entrusted to me, to prove his identity, is for
your ears only. He does not want it mentioned to the Duke, and when
you hear what I have to say, you will agree it is best kept between us."

Antonia sat back in the window seat and regarded Dair with her
clear green eyes. She remained silent a moment and then lifted her
hand off her silken lap, as indication he could continue with whatever
it was he had to say; she would no longer offer any protest. If all that
was required was for her to verify or dispute this M'sieur Lucian's story,
then so be it. The sooner the better. She was sure she was about to be ill
at any moment.

"Only five people are aware of the details of this disturbing incident
—six now, counting me. Two of those six are no longer with us:
Monseigneur, and a Mr. Robert Thesiger. The others, Roxton—Alston
as he was known then, M'sieur Lucian and, quite obviously, you, were
the only family members present on the night of Harry's birth."

Mention of her sixteen-year-old son Henri-Antoine had Antonia
sitting up, face suddenly white, but she remained mute, and so Dair
continued.

"I won't distress you by going into detail about the incident,
although I can, if required. M'sieur Lucian expressed the regret that he

had not gone to your aid, at the very least dragged Alston away. But he, like his companions, was very drunk. Despite his impaired faculties, and the passing of the years, he was able to give me a vivid account of the events of that night. He described to me the shocking behavior of your eldest son, who accused you of being a whore and that the baby you had almost carried to term did not belong to his father. He dragged you out of the house and into Hanover Square whereupon you went into an early labor, and it was only the Duke's timely return from White's that saved you and the baby. The nature of Harry's early birth is the reason he suffered crippling episodes of the falling sickness when younger—"

"*C'est assez! La mémoire est trop douloureuse!* I cannot. Please. Alisdair. You will not say another word about it. Now—or ever. *C'est compris?*"

Dair was beside her on the window seat and had hold of her hand before she had stopped speaking, but not before the tears began coursing down her white cheeks. He quickly fished out his clean linen handkerchief from his frock coat pocket and gently put it into her hand.

"Never. I give you my word. I would not have distressed you for the world, believe me, but I could not confront Roxton with—"

"No. You were right to come to me. Julian he must never know that you know. He has lived with that night and its consequences every day of his life. Me I still think he has not forgiven himself, even if his father and me we did so a long time ago. He still blames himself for his brother's early malady. But who is to say Henri-Antoine might have suffered from the falling sickness regardless of the circumstances of his early birth. The physicians cannot. But still he Julian blames himself." She grabbed Dair's hand hard. "You will not say a word to Shrewsbury. Promise me."

"Not a word. I only need to verify the identity of M'sieur Lucian with you, and Shrewsbury will be satisfied with that."

Antonia let out a sigh of relief and nodded slowly. "This M'sieur Lucian, it must be Evelyn... I—I am pleased he is alive but... How could he be so cruel and unfeeling as to allow his parents, Monseigneur, me, his family, to think him dead all these years? Does he know his parents are both dead? That Monseigneur, too, is no longer with me?"

"He does. He told me a little of his history. He asked that I pass this on to you, in the hopes that you will have a better understanding of him and perhaps one day forgive him—"

"He is an imbecile! Why would I not forgive him? He is my nephew."

Dair laughed and then became serious again, saying quietly,

"He did not tell me how this came about, but he spent many years incarcerated for crimes against the Russian Imperial state. He lost all contact with the outside world. When he was finally released, he was a broken man, and then had no wish to make contact with anyone, particularly his family, on whom he had brought great shame. He believes his parents were better off mourning him than knowing what he was and what he had endured at the hands of Empress Catherine's secret police. But that and much more is for him to tell you in his own words, and in your presence, once he is returned to England, and has your permission to contact you."

"But of course! Again he is an imbecile. Why would I refuse him? Julian too, and Deborah, they will welcome him home, I am certain of it. And please, you will allow me to break the news to them, *n'est-ce pas?*"

Dair pressed her hand and made her a bow.

"Of course. M'sieur Lucian will be overjoyed at the news. And now I will leave you in peace. I am already late for my interview with Lord Shrewsbury—"

Antonia's moist eyes lit up. "To seek permission to marry my goddaughter, yes?"

Dair nodded, strangely overcome with emotion at her enthusiasm.

"To discuss your nephew's return to England, and," he couldn't help blushing, which Antonia thought delightful, "to ask for Rory's hand in marriage. I admit I am more than a little nervous at the prospect."

"*Eh bien!* But, *mon cher*, it is surely a mere formality as Rory, she is of age."

"Formality, it may be, but it makes the task no less difficult. Rory loves her grandfather dearly, and thus his approval is necessary."

"He will not refuse you! How could he? *Why* would he?"

She hopped off the window seat and put her arm through his. Halfway across the carpet she turned and stuck out her hand in farewell, and when he bowed over it, she pulled him down to kiss his forehead and to touch his cheek.

"You will come and see me later, after your return, and tell me all about it, yes? I will be awake, I assure you."

How could Dair say no to such enthusiasm? Nor could he wait to share with Rory how happy her godmother was with the news of their betrothal.

"Mme la Duchesse, M'sieur le Duc, he has come," the butler inter-rupted, and sent two footmen into the sitting room, one to clear away the tea things, and the other to put in its place a heavy silver tray holding coffee pot, coffee cups and saucers, and a plate of almond biscuits.

One whiff of the heady aroma of rich dark coffee was all it took.

Antonia clapped a hand across her nose and mouth to stifle a heave, snatched up a handful of her silk petticoats, and dashed across the room to disappear behind the folding screen.

TWENTY-SEVEN

THE DUKE WATCHED, JAW SLACK AND GREEN EYES WIDE, AS HIS mother ran from him, two of her attendants in her wake, to disappear behind the folding screen in the corner of her sitting room. Her lady's maid then proceeded to berate the two footmen, not caring who was in the room. The servants turned frock coat tails and fled back from whence they came, cups and plates rattling on their silver trays. The butler watched, just as astounded as the Duke, but in a different way. His face above his white cravat was puce, aware he had just committed a faux pas from which he was certain he would never make a recover. Michelle raged at him and called him an idiot, for had she not told him coffee was now banned from Mme la Duchesse's presence? The butler tried to argue he had no choice. After all, it was M'sieur le Duc who had ordered the coffee, and who was he to deny a king in his own domain? Michelle retorted she did not care if it was Louis King of France wanting a café au lait with her mistress, he could go hang! It was only with these words out of her mouth that she realized the Duke was standing beside her, and with a quick curtsy and mumbled apology she, too, turned and fled behind the screen.

Used to living in an environment that was disciplined and predictable, with well-mannered, soft-footed servants who acted accordingly, whether they were in his presence or not, and where his word was law, this chaotic environment was incomprehensible to the Duke. He had never understood his mother, and he found her at best a tiny whirlwind of impulsive gaiety. For a heartbeat, he wondered if she had slipped back into the melancholia that had gripped her for the

three years since his father's passing, what with her new Duke of a few
months absent north of the border. And his instantaneous and harsh
reaction was to wish Kinross had taken her away with him to Scotland,
rather than leave her here within his dominion. The instant this was
thought, it was banished, replaced by such guilt that before he knew
what was happening he was three rooms away, in a small anteroom off
the private dining parlor his mother used as a library.

Dair had taken his cousin by the elbow and led him there. Unlike
the Duke, he had found the whole episode amusing, particularly
Roxton's look of total confusion watching his mother flee his presence,
and the dramatic reaction of her loyal servants to her predicament. And
before the Duke asked the question, he stuck his head out into the
corridor and had a footman fetch back the silver tray with the coffee
things, reasoning there was now enough distance between them and the
Duchess. The Duke looked in need of a strong cup of coffee, if not
something stronger. Dair then opened the two windows above the
window seat, hoping fresh air would dissipate the strong coffee aroma
before the Duchess found her way to them.

"I just set Shrewsbury down at the Gatehouse Lodge, and thought
I'd come and see how maman was settling in," Roxton said for want of
something to fill the silence and cover his awkwardness. "I know she
only arrived back yesterday—You were welcome to stay up at the big
house. Deborah and the children would love to see you."

"*Merci, mon cousin,*" Dair responded in French, and was not
surprised when the Duke frowned in puzzlement, having no idea he
had spoken to Dair in his first language. "The Duchess was kind
enough to put me up," he continued in English. "It is close to the
Lodge, which suits Shrewsbury's purpose."

"He told me you had matters to discuss… Your recent visit to
Portugal…?"

"Yes," Dair said but did not elaborate, and was glad for the interruption when a footman returned with the coffee pot.

He declined to join the Duke in a cup, itching to take his leave. Yet
he did not want to appear hasty or rude, so he waited a few more
minutes, reasoning the Duchess would show herself, or the Duke
would be called to attend her in her sitting room. Either way, he could
then escape to the Gatehouse Lodge and get done the harrowing business of asking for Rory's hand in marriage.

"Has… Has everything been all right with your stay…?" Roxton
asked, hoping his tone was light.

Dair realized that what the Duke was actually enquiring about was
his mother. Knowing his upright cousin would have no idea as to the

Duchess's condition, and would never expect in a thousand years such an eventuality to be possible—such was the nobleman's temperate disposition—Dair decided he needed a little mental push in the right direction. He was also being a little mischievous; wanting to see the nobleman's face when his brain turned a cog and realized the woman who had given birth to him over thirty years ago, and who had recently remarried, was with child by her new younger husband.

"Perfectly all right. Of course I don't have to tell you," Dair said conversationally, "what with four children and another on the way, you must have a perfect understanding of how it is. No doubt the Duchess has had bouts of morning sickness. It is often the way with females in the first few months of breeding, that they inexplicably develop an aversion for those flavors and scents they love most..."

The Duke blinked his incomprehension, but when Dair just stood there grinning knowingly at him, he staggered back, as if he had been struck, such was his shock. Then, without a word, he turned on a heel and strode off to his mother's sitting room, as if he'd just been told the house was on fire. Dair followed.

"Roxton! Julian! Wait up! Your cup! Give me your cup!"

The Duke stopped, looked down at the coffee cup in his hand, thrust it at Dair, and then yanked aside the brocade curtain, disappearing into his mother's sitting room. Dair was still smiling at the look of utter disbelief on his noble cousin's face to the news of his mother's pregnancy when he was admitted into the small entrance hall of the Gatehouse Lodge twenty minutes later.

Rory was sitting on the next-to-last step of the stairs waiting for him.

THE PRESENCE OF THE BUTLER PREVENTED THE COUPLE FROM being anything but politely civil. Dair nodded and Rory, who had a hand to the polished banister, bobbed a curtsy. Yet, the look and smile which passed between them said it all. They were ecstatic, and tense with excitement and heightened anticipation. Both had dressed carefully, wanting the moment to be accorded its proper due. After all, it was not every day a couple got engaged, and in the wider Society in which they mixed, it was rare for that couple to be deeply in love.

When the butler disappeared into the study to see if his lordship was ready to receive his guest, they had a few moments alone. Both seized the opportunity. In two strides, Dair was at the foot of the stairs. He caught Rory to him and she threw her arms about his neck.

Dair could not remember a day when he had been as happy as he was on this day. All his past fears about marriage, about ever finding the right woman to share his future, least of all finding a soul mate, had evaporated, and all because of this divine creature in his arms. He had no doubts whatsoever. He hoped the same was true for her. So he was alarmed when, after they had shared a kiss, the smile on Rory's flushed upturned face dropped into a pout.

"Is—Are you—Is everything all right?"

"I am not sure...You need to kiss me again. I am not convinced I like you without whiskers."

He stifled a laugh and instantly relaxed, whispering near her ear, "And here was I affording you the opportunity to kiss a different gentleman... You could then tell me which one you'd prefer to take on your honeymoon."

She gasped and then giggled.

He held both her hands and took a step backwards to look her up and down. He liked the outfit she was wearing very much. Over a chemise of the finest cream linen, with a wide flounce at the hem and a similar flounce to both sleeves, was a pink-lavender open-robed gown of shimmering silk. It hugged her lithe frame, from small breasts to tiny waist, and opened out over her hips, to display the cream linen underskirts. Her waist-length straw-blonde hair, too, had been carefully dressed, swept up off her face and loosely piled atop her head, pinned, beribboned, and the weight allowed to fall down her back. And her shoes, of course, matched her gown. All in all, she was beautiful and radiant, and just how he imagined a bride looked on her wedding day. He wished they were about to go up before the vicar.

He swiftly kissed the back of one hand, and then the other, as he heard the door behind him open, and let her go, saying softly, "You look so beautiful. Don't send for another gown. Wear this one to our bridal. The color perfectly matches the sapphire I gave you."

Rory beamed with happiness, so much so, her blue eyes filled with tears. All she could do to answer him was smile and nod when he asked,

"Wait for me here...?"

As Dair followed the butler into her grandfather's study, she sank back onto the step, to wait, unaware she was toying with the unfamiliar, but reassuringly present, pale lavender sapphire betrothal ring.

The meeting took much longer than Rory anticipated. More than once the butler enquired if she wanted him to fetch her a glass of wine or a cup of tea and a biscuit. But Rory was too nervous to eat or drink. She tried not to listen for sounds, and it was impossible to hear voices or conversation, but once or twice a loud burst of laughter penetrated the oak-paneled door. Then there was nothing for the longest time that Rory began to drift off to sleep. It was now very late, and she had had such a big day, a momentous one, spent on Swan Island, that with the darkness of a late night, it was almost as if she had dreamed it.

She was asleep, slumped against the banister rail, when in her dreamlike state, the door to grandfather's study was suddenly yanked wide and the man she loved strode out into the hall. On his frock coat skirts followed her grandfather. Why couldn't she wake up? Her head was so heavy. Her grandfather spoke to her, and although she heard his words and instinctively did what he asked, she could not remember exactly what he said. She rose up and he offered her his arm. But when he moved away from the stair, there was her husband-to-be. He was standing in the middle of the hall, and the front door was wide. She wanted to cross the small space that separated them but her grandfather kept her at his side, his hold on her arm vise-like. It was then she realized she wasn't dreaming at all. She was wide-awake, and nothing and nobody was making any sense.

ALMOST AN HOUR EARLIER, WHEN THE BUTLER HAD ANNOUNCED Major Lord Fitzstuart to his lordship, Lord Shrewsbury had greeted his best agent as he always did, with affable good humor. He was always genuinely pleased to see the young man, and relieved he had survived his latest assignment unscathed. He knew most of what had occurred in Lisbon from Dair's coded report, sent as soon as he had disembarked at Portsmouth. He also knew that the most crucial pieces of information would not be in ink but reported verbally. What he most wanted was the name of the double agent within his own Secret Service; a name the Major had gone all the way to Portugal to retrieve.

So he was bitterly disappointed when Dair told him bluntly that he could not supply the name, but that he could supply the person who could give him the name, but that there were conditions attached. When wasn't there? Shrewsbury conceded.

The two men sipped fine port from crystal glasses; port brought back from Lisbon in crates by the Major, as Dair related all that he had been told by his contact, M'sieur Lucian. Shrewsbury was most surprised and intrigued to discover this M'sieur Lucian was in fact back from the dead, heir to the Stretham-Ely earldom, and the Duke of Roxton's closest cousin. He was even more interested that the lost heir had himself been a spy, and wondered what information, if any, he could offer him about the court of the Empress Catherine. Of course he agreed to the man's terms for his return to England, and told Dair he would have Watkins arrange for M'sieur Lucian's immediate safe passage home.

Mention of William Watkins steered the conversation away from Lisbon and back to England. Out of politeness, Dair asked after the Weasel's broken nose, to which Shrewsbury laughed heartily and said it was about time his secretary got knocked off his high horse and returned to where he belonged, the back room amongst a mountain of papers where he could do least harm. For a second Dair felt sorry for the secretary, but that evaporated remembering why he had punched him in the face in the first place. Shrewsbury was having the same thought, and surprised Dair into thinking he could read minds when he said bluntly,

"I'll have you forget why you broke Mr. Watkins' nose. Best if people believe it was two men falling out over a wager of some description—I don't care what—as long as my granddaughter's name is never mentioned."

"It never will, sir."

The old man continued to stare at Dair, as if he expected him to be more forthcoming about the incident, but Dair remained silent, and Shrewsbury said in a low voice,

"Grasby told me all about what happened at the Physic Garden. He also told me he must have been mistaken in thinking he saw you in close contact with my granddaughter. Of course we both agreed this was nonsense. Grasby said it must have been a trick of the sunshine in his eyes..." Shrewsbury looked Dair up and down and visibly huffed. "You might be a womanizing lothario with dancers, whores and other men's wayward wives—and the best of luck to you—but one thing we both agreed you are not is a seducer of young—"

"Sir, I—"

"—innocent females of good birth—"

"Sir, I—"

"—particularly the sisters of your closest friends, whatever Watkins might try and convince us to the contrary. My secretary has always had you pegged for a brainless libidinous muckworm, and I would hate to think his estimation had any basis in fact. But you've never let me down in the past and I know you won't now. You quite rightly forgot all about that incident at Romney's studio and I know you'll do the same now, about Watkins' idiotic attempt to ask my granddaughter to marry him." Shrewsbury shook his head. "The sheer idiocy of the man defies my intelligence. What did he think would happen? What did he think my granddaughter's response would be? How did he ever convince himself he was worthy of her?"

These were obviously rhetorical questions not requiring a response, so Dair remained silent. When Lord Shrewsbury held up the decanter, Dair shook his head and watched him refill his glass and put the decanter back on the tray at his elbow. He reasoned it was best to let him have his say, in the hopes that once he had let off steam about Weasel's pathetic behavior, he would be more conducive to Dair's proposal of marriage. And after all, he and Weasel were chalk and cheese in every way, shape and form!

"It's a damned shame I need his expertise in constructing and deconstructing ciphers, or I'd have got rid of him as soon as I learned of his reprehensible behavior," Shrewsbury confided, still warm to his topic. "Grasby's brother-in-law he may be, but that doesn't give him the right to even *think* of my granddaughter in any way whatsoever! And even if I wanted a husband for her, the last place I'd look is Billingsgate! His grandfather was a fishmonger, for God's sake! Whereas hers—*me*— is an earl! If his sister hadn't come with a fifty thousand pound dowry she'd still stink of fish, too! Speaking of my dear granddaughter-in-law, my grandson and his dear wife are due here tomorrow. I told them not to give Watkins a seat in their carriage; he deserves to be left out in the cold. Justifiable punishment for his gross presumption. Besides, if there is to be a celebration, it will be for *family only*."

The old man's eyes lit up and he gleefully rubbed his hands together. He couldn't keep the excitement from his voice.

"Grasby has some news... News! He wouldn't put it in ink. He says he must announce it to me in person. I can tell you, my boy, I pray to God it's that his wife is breeding—*finally*! I'm not getting younger, and neither is my grandson's wife! Three years married and nothing to show for it. Now, if you were to marry, my guess is you'd have your wife with child within the month, if not the week! You've already proven you can breed. But I don't blame Grasby. I blame her. Flighty, nervy creature... If you'll take my advice, marry a widow with children. A pretty little widow, but one with children, so you know she can breed. If I'd given it more thought, and not let that fishmonger's ransom addle my brain, I'd have found a nice fertile widow for my grandson..."

When the Spymaster General paused to sip at his port, Dair gauged it was the right moment, and Shrewsbury in the right frame of mind, for him to broach the subject of his own marriage.

"As it so happens, sir, I have rather important news of my own to share with you."

The old man sat up, all attention, and Dair found himself clearing his throat. Still, he managed to keep his deep voice steady and impassive.

"I've decided it is time to follow in Grasby's footsteps and marry."

Shrewsbury's face split into a grin and he smacked his silken knee in delight.

"By Jove, but this is excellent news indeed, my boy! *Excellent* news!"

"Thank you, sir. Your support means the world to me—*to us*. I've written to Lord Strathsay, and to his man of business, giving them my news, and requesting the necessary arrangements be made for me to assume management of the family estates. And my mother has been advised of my intentions and the need for her to quit Fitzstuart Hall and take up residence in the dower house. Of course, not at once, but arrangements need to be made so my wife can take up her position as lady of the house."

"So marriage is more than a new thought? You've been contemplating the notion for some time?"

"That is difficult to answer. Had you wagered me upon my return from the war that I'd marry within a twelvemonth, I'd not have risked coin on the possibility." He shrugged and smiled self-consciously. "But life, thankfully, is not ruled by the betting book, is it, sir? Which leads me to request that I be released from my obligations to the Service. I am sure you agree I cannot, when I have a wife and family, and estates to manage, continue to act as a free agent."

"No. That is entirely understandable. Marriage comes with a set of obligations and responsibilities, particularly for a man in your position, who will one day inherit his father's title. It pleases me no end you are taking the institution seriously. There are some within our ranks who treat marriage with less than the dignity it deserves. Not that I'm advocating you take your vows literally. You don't have to become a plaguey priest upon marriage; far from it. But I do advise you not to waste time or seed on your mistress until your bride is breeding. Once you've accomplished the deed, you can return to your mistress, or what filly takes your fancy, with a clear conscience in having done your duty. If your bride is a sensible, compliant creature —and I do not doubt you've chosen one who is—she'll be relieved to be left alone. Who is the—"

"I beg your pardon, sir, but I want to assure you I have every intention of taking my marriage vows seriously, for what is the p—"

The old man waved a hand in dismissal at Dair's assiduousness.

"Young men mean well, but let me tell you from experience, it rarely, if ever, happens that we remain faithful. It's not in our natures to do so. Frankly put, why should we? Females bear the burden of growing our seed and so it is they who need to be damn well faithful to us! It's the way God made Adam and Eve, and there's an end to the argument."

"Sir, that is not the sort of marriage I intend to have. The Duke of Roxton is a faithful husband, like his father before him. They are my yardstick for what constitutes a good husband, a good father, and a marriage worth having."

Shrewsbury was dismissive.

"Aberrations, both! And let me tell you, before he fell under the spell of that divine creature he married, old Roxton was a libidinous goat! There was a reason he was called the noble satyr, my boy, and I should know. He was mounting every pretty skirt that caught his eye since our Eton days." He leaned forward in his wingchair, as if not wishing to be overheard, and chuckled knowingly. "From what I've heard of your bed sheet escapades, you easily fill old Roxton's breeches. So unless you've found yourself a rare and magnificent beauty such as your Cousin Antonia to marry, which I very much doubt, I'd not lose sleep over a trifle of a thing as fidelity. Trust me, neither will your bride." He sat up. "So who is the lucky creature? An heiress, I don't doubt. One of the Spencer girls, or a Cavendish relative of Deborah Roxton? Or have you preempted my advice and gone and got yourself a fertile young widow. No need to prove yourself, is there? How many brats has that mistress of yours given you now? Four or is it five? All healthy sons, too. Knowing your luck, you'll have the new wife pregnant before the sun rises on the night before!"

"I have one natural son, sir," Dair said in a measured tone, gripping the upholstered arm of the wingchair to maintain calm. He was furious. "His mother has been faithfully married for almost nine years. Her four younger sons belong to her husband."

"Yes. Yes. If you say so, my boy. I'm not one to quibble over bastard offspring. If it gives her husband comfort to think the brats are—"

"Sir! My lord! Mrs. Banks is no adulteress, and I am no liar!"

Dair had shot to his feet. It was only the esteem in which he held the Spymaster General that had kept his anger in check for this long. He had not wanted to offend him. Now, he could not care less.

"I did not come here to be lectured on the institution of marriage, or how I should conduct myself as a husband. I don't need your advice, nor do I care greatly for your good opinion, because it seems you have no good opinion of my character as it is!

"I was an eyewitness to my parent's hell on earth, so I am well versed in how *not* to conduct myself as a husband and a father. But I also know a loving union when I see it, and with the help of the woman I love, I intend to have the sort of marriage, be the sort of husband and father, that will make my wife and children proud. I love your granddaughter with my whole heart and I would never do or say anything to ruin her happiness, or our marriage. There is your assurance. I give it honestly. It is for Rory's sake I seek your blessing to our union. I hope you will give it freely and make her happy. She is waiting outside in the hallway. Shall I fetch her in so you can tell her so yourself…?"

Lord Shrewsbury slowly rose out of his wingchair by the fire while Dair was in the midst of his earnest discourse, surprised by the young nobleman's uncharacteristic fit of temper, but prepared to forgive him for the same reason; the boy had never before been so discourteous. But what he was not prepared for was to hear Rory's name trip so familiarly off the Major's tongue, and he fell back into his wingchair, in shock.

Not in a thousand years would he have suspected his granddaughter to be romantically linked to *any* man, least of all this man. Why had he not seen this coming? Why had he not been wary of the warning signs of a clandestine attachment? Why had none of his servants, his agents, her own brother, seen it too, and warned him? The only person who had hinted at Major Lord Fitzstuart's interest in Rory was William Watkins, and stupidly he had dismissed the man's insinuations as ridiculous, and fueled by jealousy.

He was incredulous and disbelieving.

Why would a man of action, a decorated soldier and a spy, a man who risked his life as if it meant nothing to him—a man whose masculinity had the effect of causing some females to faint at the sight of him—why would such a man be interested in his granddaughter? His beloved Rory was a naïve cripple who had rarely strayed beyond her family's garden gate. She was pretty in her own way, with her mother's Norwegian fair hair and his deep blue eyes, but she was not so beautiful as to catch the roving eye of the hot-blooded Major Lord Fitzstuart. She was no Antonia Roxton Kinross, no voluptuous beauty who could heat a man's blood with one look.

It just didn't make any sense to him, and so he told Dair in as many words, though his speech was halting and garbled at times. Nonetheless his incredulity was blatant, as was his opposition to the couple's betrothal. He forbade it. He would not give it his blessing. In his opinion, Rory was not mentally or physically capable of marrying anyone. The idea of this lusty lothario bedding his innocent granddaughter made him feel physically ill. As far as he was concerned, Rory would remain a virgin, spend the rest of her days as his companion, and die an old maid.

Dair was just as incredulous by Shrewsbury's violent opposition, not only to Rory marrying him, but to the very idea of her wedded at all. It soon became apparent the old man had suffered such a severe shock that it was pointless arguing any further with him that night. But he expected Shrewsbury to put on a brave face and not disappoint his granddaughter. Regardless of what he thought of the betrothal, Dair was going to marry Rory, with or without his blessing.

"After all, she's two-and-twenty and doesn't need your consent," Dair stated flatly. "We can marry without your blessing, but for the sake of her happiness, I would rather have it as not."

Shrewsbury was not to be appeased. Shock gave way to anger and resentment. He thumped the arms of his wingchair and shot back up to his feet and stayed there this time.

"I'll not give it! Now or ever. You can't seriously expect me to believe you want to marry her? Ha! This is some sort of joke! A damned awful one, but a joke nonetheless! How much money have you got riding on the outcome of seeing me bamboozled? Eh?" When Dair pulled a face of revulsion at the idea, Shrewsbury let out a harsh laugh. "That's your best piece of acting yet, Fitzstuart! But I'm not fooled! I know all about your revolting wager to tup a cripple. Watkins told me—"

"I beg your pardon? I never—"

Dair stopped himself. He could not refute Shrewsbury's outlandish claim because it was true. He had accepted such a wager, but he had been blind drunk and it was years ago. He tried to recall the exact circumstances under which he had agreed to such a despicable dare. He was with a group of fellow officers at a Covent Garden bordello, or was it a Turkish Bath? Was he nineteen or twenty years old? No matter, all he remembered was they were so idiotically debauched he would have accepted any wager put to him, no matter how devilish and unlikely. All because he could not disappoint his army fellows. Somehow it had got written up in White's betting book. He suspected William Watkins had something to do with that. But it was all so long ago…

"That has nothing to do with the here and now," he blustered. "I deeply regret having agreed to such a preposterous wager, but if you knew the circumstances—"

"Don't make a fig of difference. You bragged about it before witnesses and that's all that matters. Whether you meant to carry it out is neither here nor there to me. I couldn't care less, but it will mean a great deal to my granddaughter."

Dair was too horrified to speak.

Shrewsbury looked supremely smug at his response.

"Call off this ridiculous betrothal and she'll not hear about the wager from me…"

Dair made one last attempt to make Shrewsbury see reason.

"Sir, I love Rory with every fiber of my being. I want to marry her, take care of her, cherish her for the rest of my days…"

The old man was unconvinced. He did not understand couples marrying for love. His wife had been chosen for him by his father, and he had chosen who his grandson would marry. Parents knew what was best in a mate for their children. His son had foolishly married for love and that had been a disaster for everyone concerned. Rory was the most precious thing in the world to him and he would never subject her to the pain and heartache of a love match, nor would he give her up. And so he told Dair, unmoved by the young man's open and honest declaration of his feelings.

Dair sighed his incomprehension and threw up a hand impatiently.

"One day I will be Earl of Strathsay, and she my countess. Surely, that must mean something to you, even if nothing else I've said does?"

"It does. That, too, works against you. She is not equipped to take the stage in Society as the wife of a nobleman. Enough heads turn as it is when she limps into a room, and not in a good way. Imagine her on *your* arm. What a spectacle! What a-a *farce*. She can't even dance, for God's sake! You'll make her a laughing stock and I won't have it. It would break my heart, and hers."

Dair shook his head in disbelief.

"You have so little regard for her, and of what she is truly capable, that you fail to see beyond the obvious. She is not some flawed diamond to be kept in a velvet box for fear a tiny imperfection is all that will be noticed. She is a magnificent unique jewel whose true worth should be allowed to shine. Let her take her place at my side, and watch her sparkle. She deserves nothing less of life. And that life is with me."

Shrewsbury was incredulous at this young man's presumption. To be lectured to about the person he loved most in the world turned his face purple with rage.

"Shine? Poppycock!" the old man spat out. "She won't shine, she'll wilt and die as sure as you'll return to your whoring and your devil-may-care ways once you've had your fill of her! God knows what perverted lust demon drives you to want to marry a creature who can no more climb the stairs on the other side of that door, as fly! I know about men like you. No one suspects but deep down you have unnatural desires, inclinations and urges that if allowed to bubble to the surface wreak untold damage that can never be repaired! I won't let that happen again, and not to her. Find yourself a lame female elsewhere. There's a cathouse in Covent Garden that caters to such perversions—"

"Enough!" Dair growled, spinning away from the fireplace, where he had his head lowered, gripping the mantel to stop himself from grabbing Shrewsbury by the throat. "I've heard enough of your salacious drivel! If you weren't her grandfather, I'd shut your foul mouth with my fist!"

He took a deep breath, reminding himself Shrewsbury was seventy years of age, and it was the love he had for his granddaughter making him lash out with irrational and absurd statements. In such an emotionally charged state, it was fruitless to continue arguing with him. He decided the old man needed time to come to terms with his proposal. He hoped that with the dawn, Shrewsbury would see that what was best for Rory's future happiness was to give his blessing to the match. If the old man proved immoveable, then the marriage would take place without him, and the sooner the better.

There was nothing left for him to do here tonight. Yet, the thought of walking out of the study and seeing Rory on the stair, smiling with happiness, blue eyes full of expectation, was almost too much for him to contemplate, and he wished he could scramble out a window and make off across the park, like a thief in the night. Still, he was no coward. But how was he to allay her natural distress when she learned her grandfather had rejected his proposal? He must give her a word or a look before being shown the door, so she knew he was determined to marry her, and would brook no opposition.

"I'll say goodnight," he said calmly. "But I will return tomorrow morning—"

"That would not be wise or welcome."

"I will come anyway."

"No. You won't."

"You cannot stop me."

Shrewsbury sneered his superiority.

"No? Some time ago I requisitioned that particular betting book from White's in the national interest. I will show Rory the offending wager if necessary. But I hope it does not come to that. You must understand I will do whatever it takes to preserve her innocence and her happiness. If that means locking her up, I'll do it. Regard me, Fitzstuart: I am deadly serious."

Dair believed him. But two could play his game, and he fully intended to return at sun up and kidnap Rory if need be. With nothing left to say, he bowed civilly to the old man and followed him out of the study and into the hall, where the butler waited by the front door.

And there was Rory, curled up on the stair, head resting on her arm, blonde hair falling across her flushed cheek, asleep.

Dair took a step forward, to go to her, but Shrewsbury put a hand on his linen sleeve to forestall him. He then brushed past him and, like a sentinel, stood between the couple, blocking Dair's view. The old man jerked his powdered head at the butler and the front door was opened on the night air.

Dair hesitated, hands clenching and unclenching in frustration. As much as he wanted to go to Rory, take her in his arms and leave this place with her, he could not do so, knowing the old man was fully capable of creating a distressing scene. So he turned on a heel and left.

He calculated there were less than eight hours until dawn.

TWENTY-EIGHT

WHEN ANTONIA FINALLY REAPPEARED FROM BEHIND THE PANELED screen, Alisdair Fitzstuart was no longer there, and the Duke was perched on the window seat looking out on the view. She had splashed cold water on her face and tidied her hair, catching up the waist-length tangle of fair curls with a cream silk ribbon. When her attendants followed her across the room, she waved them away, a nod to Michelle to also leave her alone with M'sieur le Duc. She then resumed her seat on the chaise longue as if there was nothing untoward in her behavior, a sideways glance at her silent son before saying conversationally in French (the language they always used when alone),

"Was there something in particular you wished to speak to me about, Julian?"

Roxton turned from the window.

"Nothing in particular. I had Shrewsbury over to the house for the day and just now set him down at the Lodge. So I thought I'd ride on and see how your journey was from Westminster."

Antonia shrugged a shoulder. "Uneventful. Thank you for asking."

Roxton suppressed a smile. "Surely not as uneventful as every other journey home?"

"I do not understand your meaning."

"I thought perhaps the motion of the carriage may have been disagreeable upon this occasion? And that you had more frequent stops than usual…?"

Antonia frowned. "How did—" Then quickly changed the subject. "How are the children? May I see them soon?"

"Constantly asking after you. I told them they could resume their bi-weekly afternoon teas with you, which set them all off screaming with delight around the Nursery! I've never heard the like before. Nurse's ears were still ringing an hour later." He cocked his head. "But perhaps their visits should be postponed until you are feeling—"

"No. No. Do not do that. Let them come. This feeling it will pass, I know it. How is Deborah?"

The Duke could not suppress a grin.

"Well indeed. She thinks she may be carrying twins again."

"*Mon Dieu.* That is something not to be grinned at, Julian. I could not bear it!"

The Duke lost his smile.

"You do not have to bear it, Maman. And Deborah she is just as thrilled. We both want a large family."

"Yes, of course you do. That was uncharitable. Forgive me. I am not myself." She darted another sidelong look at him then stared down at her hands clasped in her silken lap. "I blame it on the-the—*weather.*"

The Duke stared at her long and hard, and then he did something most uncharacteristic when in her presence. He burst into uncontrollable laughter. At first Antonia was affronted, but then she began to giggle. Mother and son laughed until their eyes watered.

"Oh, Maman! Do not ever change!" Roxton declared when he could finally speak, wiping dry his eyes. "I do love you so very much."

Antonia took a few staggered breaths and then burst into real tears, overcome by his heartfelt declaration. When she had mastery of herself, she patted the space next to her on the chaise longue and the Duke willingly sat beside her. She then rang her little handbell for Michelle, who was sitting just inside the next room at her embroidery, and had her fetch the smaller of two tortoiseshell jewelry cases that always traveled with her.

Antonia unlocked the case with the little silver key hooked on her gold and enamel chatelaine, and took from it a small carved ivory box. This she placed in the palm of her son's hand and told him to open it. One look at the contents and he glanced up at her with a frown of enquiry.

"I have been meaning to give you this, but when the time it was right," she explained with a gentle smile. "The ducal emerald it should have been yours a long time ago. Always it has been passed from one Duke to the next. That is the proper order of things. Your father he would want you to wear it. I know now why Monseigneur he did not give it to you but into my safekeeping. He possibly told you so himself..." When Roxton nodded but was too overcome to speak, she was not surprised. Of course Monseigneur would have confided his intentions in his son. Still, she said it out loud. "He worried, did he not, lest I was not strong enough to carry on without him. He made me promise to give the ring to Frederick on his twenty-first birthday. In that way, he knew he had prevented me from doing something —*idiotic*. Your father he—he was thinking of me—right to his—right to his—last breath."

"Yes, Maman."

The Duke slipped the ring on a finger of his right hand and marveled at how well it looked. He knew it well, remembered his father was never without it. The square-cut emerald on the slim gold band was large and the same color as his mother's beautiful eyes, the same color as his own.

"You have your father's long elegant fingers, *mon chou*," Antonia said, as if reading his mind. "It looks well on you I think." She gave a little sigh of happiness. "May Frederick be old and gray before it is his turn to wear it, yes?"

The Duke embraced her then kissed her hand.

"Thank you, dearest Maman. I will never take it off…" He kept hold of her hand and said with a crooked smile, "Is there something in particular you would like to confide in me?"

Antonia put a hand to her cheek. She was suddenly forlorn.

"I do not know if me I have come to terms with the matter to confide it in anyone. I have not said it out loud, as if saying it will somehow make it more real than it already is. My women know, of course they must, and sometimes I catch them looking at me as if I am witless. But me I want to ignore it because it is quite shocking for a woman of my age. I am nine-and-forty. I can hardly believe it myself. It is *incroyable*, yes?"

"I grant it is not usual, but it is not unheard of for a female to bear a child at such a *great age*."

Antonia sat up tall, eyes wide with affront.

"Great age? Do I look in my dotage, Julian?"

"Far from it." The Duke smiled. "Then again, you have always been unique in every way, Maman. So, tell me: When will you inform *the weather* of your wonderful news? Kinross will be over the moon with joy."

Antonia could not help dimpling.

"Jonathon he was adamant we would have a child, and me, I thought him mad. Now, it seems the wretched man he is right. And where is he when I have such momentous news to tell him? Hundreds of miles away! He should be here, with me, to see what I am going through to give him an heir. No! That, too, is uncharitable. I know it. But what I do not understand is that one minute I am happy that we are to have a child. The next, I am miserable, because Monseigneur he is not here to share in my happiness. But how could that be? Is that not a ridiculous notion?"

The Duke shook his head, eyes on the large ducal emerald ring he now wore.

"No. Not at all," he said softly. "Father would be pleased for you— for both of you. All he ever wanted was for you to be happy—again."

Antonia took a deep breath and heaved a great sigh. Then she rallied and said with a little laugh,

"I must visit and tell him my news, and you know what he will say? That me I am a wicked woman and that is what comes from marrying a much younger man." She shrugged a shoulder. "It is so strange being *enceinte* again. But my *bébés* they came fifteen years apart, and so, too, now this one on the way... Please, Julian, you are not to say a word, to anyone, until I am certain the event it is to occur. A fortnight and then the danger it will be over, and the baby it will be here to stay. Then I will write and tell Jonathon he is to be a Papa."

"Not a word. But I will share your news with Deborah."

Antonia covered her son's hand and looked up into his eyes.

"I am sorry to be a burden to you both. Now you have two pregnant women to worry about, *mon cher*."

The Duke kissed her hand again and smiled into her eyes.

"The best kind of worry to have, Maman. What of Henri-Antoine? Shall you tell him? He and Jack are on their way here. I have had their old apartments made up, but if you would prefer they stay with you—"

"Julian, *mon cher*, you must do as you see fit. Do not second-guess what I want or think. It is most appropriate the boys they stay in the big house with you and Deborah. What would they do here with me, particularly while I am suffering this wretched morning sickness? The big house has always been their home and you are their guardian. And if you want the truth of it," she added with a sad smile, "since Monseigneur's final illness, you have been Henri-Antoine's papa—"

"Maman, please, I—"

"It is the truth, I tell you! And your father, he would agree with me. I am certain Henri-Antoine he believes it too. So no more consulting me, unless of course when it is time for him to marry, and then, me I will want to know all about the girl well ahead of the engagement!"

"Very well, Maman. Now you will excuse me. I have a desk covered in correspondence. And that reminds me. The crates arrived from Paris yesterday; the crates with your personal effects from the Hôtel. I will store them until you come across and go through them and decide which are to be brought here, and what objects and books are to go up to London and on to Leven Castle."

When his mother merely nodded, otherwise preoccupied—he had expected her to clap her hands with joy to finally be reunited with her personal effects from the Hôtel Roxton—he went to take his leave of her, standing and kissing her forehead. But it was then that she caught at his hand and said, as if he had not spoken about the crates at all,

"Julian, you are to write to Frederick Cornwallis tonight requesting a special marriage license, and tell him you need it at once; within the sennight. Send a courier to fetch it if need be."

The Duke flicked out the skirts of his brown velvet riding frock and patiently resumed his seat on the chaise longue. He tried to sound offhand.

"Another Special License? His Grace the Archbishop will begin to wonder if I am on-selling these licenses. This will be the second in two months. But I doubt Cornwallis could be more surprised than when he signed over a license to marry you to—"

"This is no time for levity, Julian. It is my cousin Alisdair who is to marry my goddaughter Aurora, and as soon as possible."

"*Dair* and-and Miss *Talbot?*"

"Yes. That is what I said. And I tell you in the strictest confidence, and no other, not even Deborah, that after having dinner with Alisdair, and knowing they spent the afternoon on Swan Island—"

"*Swan* Island?"

"Yes, Swan Island. He rowed her over there."

"To Swan Island? But it's strictly off-limits."

"Nevertheless, that is where they went."

The Duke set his jaw. "He must know he does not have permission to go there, and still he went!"

Antonia counted to five then said patiently, "Julian, did you not as a boy, perhaps with Evelyn, sneak over to Swan Island and take a peek, to satisfy your curiosity, or in Evelyn's case, just to be naughty?"

Roxton was offended. "While Papa was alive? Of course not! I gave him my word never to trespass on the island. I do not break my word."

"You have always been a good boy," Antonia said with a laugh and kissed his cheek. "Thank you for keeping your promise. Your papa he would be proud of you; he always was." She tried to sound light-hearted. "You have been to the island since-since Monseigneur he left us, yes?"

The Duke was made momentarily uncomfortable, and when he could not meet his mother's gaze, Antonia realized he had not only been to the island but into the little temple and seen the tapestries. She knew he was aware she and his father spent two nights of every year in celebration of their marriage on the island, and was certain the bacchanalian setting of temple, bathing pool and tapestries would be a sore trial on her son's prudish temperament. Yet, she made him even more uncomfortable by waiting for him to answer her question.

"Yes. Yes, I have. I went with the surveyors," he said, returning the conversation to less intimate matters. "It seems—and I was going to discuss this with you and Kinross upon his return—that before the surrounding lands were flooded by the fourth Duke to make way for the lake, the boundary separating the Strang Leven lands and the ducal seat of Treat cut through the high ground that became Swan Island. Thus half the island is part of the Treat estate, the other part of the Strang Leven land attached to this house, which is now part of the Kinross ducal inheritance."

Antonia dimpled and said mischievously, "I do hope the temples are on my side of the boundary...?"

The Duke failed to hear the playful note in his mother's voice, such was his discomfort discussing the island at all, that he flung up a hand and said bluntly, "As far as I'm concerned you and Kinross are welcome to it all! And so I told the surveyors, when drawing up the new boundary. So it will be up to you and Kinross to decide if the island is to remain off-limits to the likes of Fitzstuart and Miss Talbot, not I."

"Thank you. That island, it means a great deal to me..."

Roxton nodded and smiled. "Yes, Maman. I know. I am happy for you to have it."

Antonia gave a little sigh.

"But I do not think even if I were to retain Monseigneur's edict and keep the island off-limits that Alisdair he would heed the warning. Some people—no, that is not so—*most* people are not like you, *mon chou*. They see warnings and edicts as guidelines not absolutes. And our cousin Alisdair, he is of the temperament that would see such an edict as a challenge rather than a barrier."

"Reason why he gets himself into all sorts of scrapes!" Roxton replied with irritation. "If he's not breaking into the studios of a respected painter, he's breaking the nose of Lord Shrewsbury's secretary! And now I hear he has the impudence to row Miss Talbot over to an island that is forbidden to all but the Duke, and that's me!"

"Of course it is you, Julian. And yes, he rowed her to the island," Antonia repeated, hoping he would soon realize the significance of their cousin taking to open water in a rowboat. She smiled when the Duke looked at her askance.

"*He* rowed her over there?"

"That is what I said. He rowed her over there. So you see how serious it is for them."

"*He* rowed her? He went out into open water with no other incentive than to row Miss Talbot over to the island?"

"Julian, is it a hearing-trumpet you need?"

"Certainly not!"

"Then attend me! Yes, he rowed her over there of his own free will. That is what I said, and that is what he did. That is not all. They went swimming in the bathing pool."

"*Swimming*? Alisdair went swimming?" Roxton would not have believed it but it was his mother telling him. "Together? They went swimming together in the bathing pool? He told you this?"

"He told me they went swimming," Antonia replied with a sly little smile. "It does not take a sharp mind to deduce it was together."

"Good God! What will Shrewsbury think if he discovers his granddaughter—"

"Julian, what will a proud man like Shrewsbury care other than his granddaughter is to marry the heir to an earldom! Now you must go and send that request to Cornwallis. I am expecting Alisdair to return at any moment from seeking permission of Shrewsbury to marry Rory."

"Then his intentions are truly serious."

"Yes. That is what I am telling you. But I do not think they need to wait the three Sundays necessary for banns to be read. That is most inconvenient—

"—but most proper. And Shrewsbury, he might want—"

"It is not what Shrewsbury wants that matters in the least. And as you have the power and the wealth to get the Archbishop of Canterbury to do your will, and give you a Special License, why must the young couple wait?"

"Maman, what is three Sundays—"

"Julian, I am so proud of you, and Monseigneur he could not have asked for a better son to succeed him as Duke, but sometimes me I wonder at your capacity to seize the moment. The couple they are in love, they spent the afternoon alone on Swan Island and went swimming together. Must I spell out the rest for you?" When her son's eyebrows drew in tightly and he blushed, she swiftly kissed his cheek and said with a little laugh, "Methinks your wish for a houseful of babies it will come true, and by Christmastime!"

A<small>NTONIA</small> <small>WAITED</small> <small>UP</small> <small>FOR</small> <small>HER</small> <small>COUSIN</small> <small>TO</small> <small>RETURN</small> <small>FROM</small> <small>THE</small>
Gatehouse Lodge. When he did not come, and because she could not
sleep and it was a warm night, she went for a moonlit walk down to her
pavilion by the shores of the lake. A footman with a flambeau lit the
way for her. Michelle followed, a woolen wrap over her arm, refusing to
let the Duchess go alone. What if Mme la Duchesse needed something?
What if she twisted her ankle on the stone stairs? M'sieur le Duc d'Kinross would never forgive her for not doing her duty by his duchess and
his *enfant*. *I am sorry, Mme la Duchesse, but even if you will not say it, I
will, because, by my calculation, it is fourteen weeks not ten since you had
your last menses, and that was just a fortnight before M'sieur le Duc he first
made love to*—Antonia stopped her there. She had heard enough and
forbade her lady's maid to utter another syllable. Michelle was easily
silenced. By voicing aloud such intimate particulars about her mistress
she had shocked herself mute.

Antonia had the footman and Michelle wait at the base of the stairs
and ascended the steps into the pavilion alone. There was enough
moonlight to see the way. On the top step, a frisson of memory made
her stop. It was the pleasing aroma of a lit cheroot, and it so reminded
her of Jonathon that she experienced a stab of loss so acute it was as if
she had lost him as she had her first husband. But she quickly shook
the melancholy off. Her second husband, her second duke, was very
much alive, healthy and as strong as an ox. He would return to her
within a handful of months, of that she was certain.

Lost in thought, she hesitated, long enough for a familiar male
voice, deep in the shadows, to offer to stub the cheroot. She shook her
head.

"No. This scent, thankfully, it still pleases me. It reminds me of my
husband…"

When Dair did not reply, she went towards the sudden red glow as
the tip of the cheroot came alive, and found her cousin in his shirtsleeves, a shoulder leaning against a marble column. His face was
turned away from her, she assumed so that he could exhale smoke. But
when he did not face her but continued to gaze out on the silvery light
across the still surface of the lake, she drew closer and said quietly,

"You did not come and see me, Alisdair…"

Finally, slowly, he turned. As he did so, the moonlight sliced his
face, illuminating his dark eyes. They were bright and glassy, the light
striking them in such a way that she saw they were brimful of tears. He
looked away, swallowing hard, and puffed on his cheroot. Shocked at
the change in him since dinner, Antonia kept her composure and

waited for him to speak, wondering what had gone wrong with his visit to the Gatehouse Lodge.

"You told me once that I hide behind a façade; that I have inhabited the role of blustering care-for-nobody for so many years now, that I cannot tell the difference between the real and the imagined me. But you are wrong, Cousin," he said, looking down at her again. "It is because I know exactly who I am, where I have come from and what I must become, that I chose to hide myself away. It was the only means I knew how to bear my father's—your uncle's—bitter disappointment I was not the bookish heir he wanted. It was how I endured my parents' hate-filled marriage. This façade—this mask—you derided helped me survive many bloody years in the army, and it got me through more than one perilous scrape as an agent of the Crown. But never did I lose sight of who I was or what I wanted from life..." He quickly turned away and put his face in his shirt sleeve to wipe dry his eyes, then turned back to Antonia with a crooked smile. "You'll be surprised to learn that what I have always wanted from life is what you had with M'sieur le Duc, and what Roxton has with Deb, and what I never thought I would ever have—a happy marriage, wed to the love of one's life, and with children of my own to nurture. Is that too much to ask?"

"No. No, it is not."

"Do you remember telling me on the stair at Hanover Square that being in love can be terrifying?" When she nodded he continued. "You said that being in love can be more terrifying than anything else, if doubt exists that love is not reciprocated, or if there is an impediment to a happy outcome... Do you remember saying that, Cousin?"

"Yes, *mon chou*. Of course. I stand by what I said."

Dair nodded and took a great shuddering breath. He glanced down at the smoldering cheroot between his fingers then at Antonia's face, partly concealed in shadow, and fixed on her green eyes. Antonia did not look away. When he finally spoke, he was barely audible, but Antonia heard his torment as if he had shouted it from the rooftop.

"Cousin... I am—I am *terrified*."

TWENTY-NINE

DAIR WAS SEATED ON A WOOLEN SHAWL ON THE TOP STEP OF THE entrance to the pavilion, with a cheroot—or was it his second—between his fingers, and pouring forth his heart to Antonia, before he realized where he was or what he was doing. His anguish was all-consuming and he saw no clear way out of his predicament. Antonia did not interrupt his revelatory self-castigation, and her servants were acute enough that one look and a sign from their mistress and they went off and returned with hot tea for her and a bottle of something much stronger for Major Lord Fitzstuart.

His hands were shaking and his throat dry. Spying a tumbler of spirits on the step below the toe of his shoe, he snatched it up and drank it down, the fiery liquid barely registering on his tongue. He set aside the crystal tumbler, and out of the shadows stepped a footman who refilled it before disappearing back into the night.

Antonia listened without comment, criticism or question until Dair drew breath and reached again for the tumbler. It was only when he declared he had no other option but to kidnap Rory and make for Gretna, that she decided it was time to intervene.

She could see his distress was such that he was incapable of thinking rationally. His only thought was to get Rory away from her grandfather long enough to vindicate himself. He needed time to explain to her he was no libidinous monster, no seducer; that his intentions were honorable and sincere.

To anyone other than Antonia, his desperation to allay Rory's fears about his intentions would have been mystifying. After all, he had proposed and she had accepted, and there was the pale lavender sapphire ring as tangible proof he meant to marry her. Both were of legal age, and could marry, whatever Shrewsbury's objections to the match. But Antonia knew the couple had spent the day on Swan Island. It was an island for lovers, a mystical yet sensual place where she and Monseigneur had been free to enjoy each other in every way without interruption. Now, for her, the island was a sad place, full of happy bygone memories and another life. To row over there now her beloved was no longer with her would surely unravel her peace of mind. But to a young couple deeply in love, the secluded island with its fanciful temple grotto, bathing pool and small tapestry-lined temple, was a magical place to make love and be loved.

Of course Dair and Rory had made love on Swan Island, Antonia was convinced of that. This was why her cousin was distraught beyond reason. Justifiably so. If Shrewsbury told Rory about the ridiculous wager, doubt would surely be cast in Rory's mind as to Dair's true intentions, and more importantly, as to his true character. What sort of man was capable of accepting such a loathsome wager?

An unthinking, arrogant and foolish boy, was Antonia's firm belief. The despicable wager was in no way a reflection of the man who sat next to her with head bent. The wager was not worth the paper it was inked on. But as easy as it was for her to dismiss such a wager, it would be difficult for Rory to do so. Particularly when she had given Dair her virginity before marriage, which surely must be pressing on her conscience. It would be natural for her to then ask herself what sort of man seduces his bride before the wedding night, if he truly intended to marry her? With her grandfather adding gravitas to the wager, and his opposition to a match with the notorious handsome rogue Major Lord Fitzstuart, Rory's carefully-constructed worldview of the loving man she thought she was marrying would inevitably start to crumble.

Antonia could hear the old man now, filling Rory's little ear with all sorts of distressing tid-bits about the man she loved, to cast doubt, to engender distrust and misery, and all to make certain Rory remained unmarried and by Shrewsbury's side for the rest of his days. Well, Antonia was having none of it! Her cousin and her goddaughter were in love and deserved their happily ever after. She would make it happen, even though it would mean invoking a secret Monseigneur had entrusted to her, only to be used in the direst of circumstances. She knew he would understand and forgive her. When she visited the mausoleum on the morrow, she would explain everything to him, and tell him the all-important and startling news she was to have a baby in the new year. But that visit would be after she called on England's Spymaster General.

Dair was convinced the only solution to his predicament called for action: Kidnapping Rory out from under Shrewsbury's nose. So when Antonia told him kidnapping was unnecessary and not to worry, all would be set to rights by tomorrow afternoon, his immediate response was incredulity, and to tell her insolently that stamping her pretty foot at Shrewsbury would be an interference he could do without. She ignored his rude dismissal. After all, she was not going to make plain her thoughts or her methods, and he was under considerable emotional duress. Instead she said cryptically, as she got to her silk-slippered feet and shook out the folds of her satin embroidered banyan,

"All men have secrets, Alisdair. Even spymasters. And this spymaster, he has more to hide than most. But that is all I will ever tell you. Now you must go to bed and try to sleep. Tomorrow after breakfast I intend to call on Shrewsbury unannounced. You will come too, but wait in the carriage until called." She smiled up at him as he rose slowly to his feet after stubbing the cheroot on the heel of his shoe. "Tell your man to pack up your belongings and take them over to the big house first thing in the morning. That is where you must stay until the wedding—

"Wedding? You want me at the big house?"

"Yes. Under no circumstances must the bride and groom stay under the same roof until they are married, and as Rory will be here with me—"

"Rory is coming here? To-to stay with you?"

"Yes. Until you are both married in the chapel over at the big house. Tonight I will write and invite your mother and your sister—"

"Write to Mary? And to my mother?"

Antonia let out a sigh. "What is it about the hearing of young men these days? Do you all need hearing-trumpets? No! Do not answer that, and do not interrupt me again. Just listen—"

Dair grinned and made her a little bow, suitably chastened.

"Yes, Mme la Duchesse—Forgive me—I am more than a little dull —Ah! And I have interrupted you again."

"Yes, you have, but it is of no matter," she responded gently, watching the cloud lift from his brow, and liking to see him finally smile. "To tell you again: Your wedding it will take place in the Roxton chapel. Until that is arranged—and believe me, arrangements are already underway—you will stay in the big house, as will your mother and your sister. Charlotte she will expect nothing less of her son. And I am sorry, Alisdair, but me I cannot abide Charlotte to stay with me.

Even more so with Rory staying here." She dimpled. "It is for the best if your bride she spends as little time as possible in the company of her future mother-in-law, yes? It is to my son and his wife you must give your thanks for-for—

"—everything," he interrupted softly, dark eyes bright and wet. "But mostly to you…" He grabbed her hand and kissed it, before looking into her eyes and saying with a catch to his voice, "If you are able to bring about this miracle, I will be forever in your debt. I can never thank you enough—"

"Attend me, Alisdair!" Antonia interrupted brusquely, because her green eyes were also filling with tears. "*Naturellement* I would do anything for you. Does not the same blood run in our veins? Are we not first cousins, descendants of the great Stuart king Charles the Second? Do we not have a duty to give our royal ancestor the legitimate heirs he did not have himself, so that he may live on through us?" She laughed then and touched his flushed cheek. "How full of self-importance I am! But your grandfather, whom you never met, but whom I lived with in the last years of his life, he was proud to be the son of Charles the Second, of having royal blood in his veins. His one regret was that he was not made a duke as his royal father had made his other natural sons. But that was the fault of his mother, and a story for another day.

"Now I have letters to write, and you must go to bed," she added with forced cheerfulness. "Tomorrow morning after breakfast, you and I we will call at the Gatehouse Lodge and everything it will arrange itself."

They retired for the night, neither saying what was on both their minds: The hope Shrewsbury had allowed Rory an uneventful night, and they would arrive at the Gatehouse Lodge before the Spymaster had the chance to shatter his granddaughter's hopes and dreams. As it turned out, they were almost too late.

ANTONIA ENTERED THE GATEHOUSE LODGE, ANNOUNCED BY THE butler, into a drawing room where the tension crackled louder than the fire in the grate. Why there was a fire on such a warm day, she could only wonder at, as she stripped off her silk half-gloves and shrugged bare shoulders out of a pretty India shawl. Both articles were mechanically handed into thin air, and swiftly taken by her lady-in-waiting, who had accompanied the Duchess with her own task to perform. At the first opportunity, Michelle was to slip away and seek out Rory's maid, to have Miss Talbot's personal belongings packed up and ready to be transported up the hill to the dower house.

Antonia swept across the threshold in a rustle of petticoats, noble host come to see the occupants of her Gatehouse Lodge. She was dressed more appropriately for an evening soiree at her son's palatial mansion, than for a morning visit on a country lodge. Her robe à la française was of luxurious India-glazed cotton, with matching shoes affixed with diamond buckles, and the décolletage was cut so low across her ample breasts that every man in the room affixed his admiring gaze on her legendary bosom.

There were three men, Lord Shrewsbury, Lord Grasby, and Mr. William Watkins. It was at this tall lanky gentleman Antonia paused to study, her arched brows lifting slightly at sight of his bent nose, and both eyes ringed in fading bruises. The only female present was the pretty auburn-haired Lady Grasby, and it was she who was cut off mid-sentence upon the butler's announcement Her Grace the Duchess of Kinross had come to call.

Antonia was not certain but it seemed that it was Lord Grasby and his grandfather who were most tense. She wondered if it had anything to do with Rory, and later had this confirmed. But for now, whatever the disagreement between the two men, it was put aside in her presence.

Everyone in the room was instantly on their feet, to bow or curtsy, and then politely remained silent waiting for the Duchess to speak. After an exchange of pleasantries and a few inane comments about the weather, Antonia asked lightly, looking about the cozy room for added effect,

"I do not see my goddaughter. I trust Rory she is well?"

"Very well, your Grace," Shrewsbury replied quickly. "Would you care for a dish of coffee? We have just had a pot and it would be no trouble to have another fetched…"

Antonia closed her eyes at the thought and waved a hand in refusal.

"Apparently my little sister has taken to sleeping late in the country," Lord Grasby offered, his tone suggesting he did not believe it for a moment. Antonia saw his gaze dart to his grandfather as he added, "I thought she would be up and awaiting our arrival, particularly when my letter hinted we have an exciting announcement we wished to share with her—"

"Lady Grasby has made us all the happiest of men," Lord Shrewsbury announced proudly with a wide smile. "I am to be a great-grand-father in the new year, Grasby a father, and Mr. Watkins a proud uncle."

Lady Grasby gave a light laugh behind her fluttering fan and needlessly confided in Antonia.

"I thought it was the intolerably hot weather making me peevish. But then I realized I have not been myself for some months now. And a visit by the physician confirmed what I had hoped for, but did not dare to dream could be the real reason for my indifferent health." She put a hand to her shoulder, and her husband, who was standing behind her chair, took it in a firm clasp. She looked up at him before returning her gaze to Antonia with a smile that resembled the cat who had found the cream. "Even though it must be many years since your last pregnancy, no doubt your Grace can recall that feeling of utter elation that comes with knowing one is fulfilling the hopes and dreams of an entire family."

"*Grands dieux*, another baby on the way. There must be something in the water," Antonia muttered, then smiled at the happy couple, offering up her congratulations and adding cryptically, "Believe me, Lady Grasby, that feeling of elation of which you speak was only yesterday for me. You have made your family happy, particularly your husband's grandpapa. I pray you have a son, but a healthy child is what is most wished for. But where is Rory?" she continued in a practiced tone of enquiry, head slightly cocked. "You did not wait to share your most exciting announcement until all the family it could be together?"

"That's what I wanted, but—"

"Under the circumstances, Lord Shrewsbury gauged it best not to wait," William Watkins stated, cutting off Lord Grasby, and with a swift glance exchanged with Lord Shrewsbury, which alerted Antonia that both men knew more than the Grasbys as to why Rory was not present.

Antonia's green eyes widened. "Circumstances, M'sieur Watkins? What circumstances are these that preclude a loved family member from such a momentous occasion as knowing a baby it is on the way? I was told Rory she was not unwell…?"

"That's what I said, your Grace," Grasby agreed with a pout at William Watkins. "After all, Rory will be an aunt, and no one would be more excited than she at the prospect! I don't see why we couldn't wait until—"

"She is well, your Grace," Lord Shrewsbury stated, cutting off his grandson not only with words, but with a look. He quickly refocused his attention on his visitor, saying with a forced smile. "But you understand why my grandson's wife could not wait to tell me. Particularly as it is such badly-wanted news. We were about to toast the health of her ladyship and the baby, and would be honored if you would join us."

"Of course," Antonia said, gaze now firmly on the old man. "When Rory she joins us. Please to have her fetched, Edward."

"That is not possible, your Grace."

"I have a great desire to see my goddaughter. That is why me I am here."

"If you returned on the morrow perhaps then—"

"No. That would not suit me at all. It would be most inconvenient. I am here now. I wish to see her, now."

Lord Shrewsbury took a step towards her.

"Your Grace, as I said, I regret that is not possible."

Antonia looked past the old man's velvet sleeve at Lord and Lady Grasby who were exchanging a puzzled glance, while Mr. William Watkins was uncannily composed.

"I am certain her brother he would like Rory to join in the toast. Perhaps, Harvel, you would be so good as to fetch your sister?"

Mention of him by his birth name gave her Lord Grasby's undivided attention and he said without a second thought, "I do want Rory here when we make the toast, your Grace. She should be here with us. I'll go and fetch her and we can—"

"No! I said no," Lord Shrewsbury snarled through gritted teeth. He took a deep breath and was again his urbane self. "I forbid you or anyone to go near her room! Is that understood? Grasby? Is it?"

Grasby looked from his wife to his brother-in-law, to the Duchess, and then to his grandfather.

"Why, Grand? Why can't I see my sister? What's-what's going on?"

"Edward, a word. Alone," Antonia commanded.

She was not required to explain herself. Lord and Lady Grasby bowed to rank and silently shuffled from the room. Antonia gave a jerk of her upswept coiffure to the door, and Michelle curtsied and went off to do her bidding. Mr. William Watkins hesitated in the doorway, as if he were somehow excluded from the imperious command because he was also Lord Shrewsbury's secretary. A haughty lift of Antonia's arched brows and he bowed and was gone, leaving the Spymaster and the Duchess alone in the heated drawing room.

"I am too unwell to expend energy on your stretches of the truth, so me, I will come to the point," Antonia said in her native tongue. "You, Edward, will then do what is best for Rory. *Vous me comprenez?*"

"What I understand, Mme la Duchesse," Shrewsbury replied politely, "is that you are interfering in a family matter that is none of your concern."

"Is it not my concern? You vastly underestimate me if you think Monseigneur and I, we have not had an interest in the happiness of those two children left in your care since the tragic deaths of both their parents."

At that, the Spymaster lost patience and threw up an arm.

"For God's sake, Antonia, why bring up such tragic history on this of all days, when I have just been told I am to be a great-grandfather? Leave my son and his wife to rest in peace, and allow me to enjoy the moment. This is a day for celebration."

Antonia took a turn about the small cluttered room, to distance herself from the smell of stale coffee coming from the tray of used coffee things. She unlatched a mullioned window and pushed it open, hoping for fresh air, before turning to face Shrewsbury.

"I am happy Drusilla she is to give the earldom of Shrewsbury an heir, and me I certainly would like nothing better than to leave your son and his wife to lie peacefully in their graves. But you, Edward, do not deserve your happiness when you have denied Christina's child hers."

"Denied her happiness? I have saved Rory from a lifetime of heartache. I will tell you what I told Fitzstuart: Rory is not equipped to be the center of Society's attention as the wife of a nobleman, and he is not a fit husband for her. I will not give my blessing to such a union, and I will use every recourse available to me to keep them apart. Rory belongs with me. There is nothing you can say or do that will make me change my mind. It is fixed. So, please, Mme la Duchesse, I appreciate you came here with the best of intentions, and no doubt at Fitzstuart's behest, but it is to no purpose. You can tell him from me: If he persists, I will have no hesitation in showing Rory White's betting book as tangible proof his intentions were nothing more than lascivious."

"You do know he loves her with his whole heart and soul?"

Shrewsbury blustered his disbelief. "So he tried to convince me!"

Antonia's green eyes narrowed. "You have never been in love, Edward, so how would you know?"

At that he laughed, as if she had told him something highly amusing. And then his blue eyes went cold and he dared to look her over as a man does a woman he desires but cannot have, gaze finally fixing on her décolletage. "Perhaps not. But I know lust and how to scratch an itch."

"That is a pathetic attempt at intimidation, even for you. Lift your eyes from my breasts to my face, Edward, and attend me! You do not frighten me in the least. This is what you will do: Put to the flame that page of White's betting book with that ridiculous wager scribbled down by a group of silly boys and accepted by an even sillier boy. No doubt in their drunken state they thought it a great lark! You will also give your blessing to Rory marrying the man she loves. If you do not do both these things at once, I will go to my son and tell him what I know about you."

"Go to Roxton? Tell *him* something about-about *me* that *you* know?" Shrewsbury's shoulders shook with silent laughter. "Oh I do love to watch you when you are fervent! God, you must have exhausted my old friend between the sheets!" He lost his smile. "I won't give in to either of those foolish demands. Now, please, Mme la Duchesse, won't you stamp your pretty foot for me, and have done with this melodramatic nonsense."

"I do not think I am being melodramatic when I say you greatly respect my son, because he is a man of the highest morals, and it helps he is also the most powerful duke in England. He Roxton also regards you with great affection. You would not want to lose his respect and worse, have him force you to retire from your post as Spymaster General in disgrace."

Again Shrewsbury laughed, but this time in disbelief.

"Dear God, Antonia, are you threatening *me*? I am more aroused than ever!"

Antonia pulled a face of disgust and put up her little nose. "I do not threaten. It is what will happen if you do not do as I say."

The old man shook his head and put his chin in his hand, done with the playful banter.

"By all means go to Roxton with your tales. I think you will find your son's moral sensibilities will be far more disturbed by Fitzstuart's behavior and his wager to tup a cripple, than anything you can possibly tell him about me."

Antonia took a deep breath and made one last attempt to make Shrewsbury see reason.

"Edward, you would truly break Rory's heart than see her happily married to the man she loves, and who loves her?"

"Yes. It is for her own good."

Antonia's shoulders slumped. But then, resolved, she squared her back and clasped her hands in front of her.

"Then you leave me no choice but to use the promise Monseigneur made to you, against you. We did not become godparents to Rory because you asked it of us, but because her mother, she asked it of me before her baby it was born. Yes. That surprises you. You forget perhaps that your daughter-in-law she and I are the same age, or would have been had she lived. Our sons, too, were near in age. We met in the park and then began having afternoon tea and would watch our babies play together."

It was obvious this was news to the old man.

"What could you possibly have in common with the bastard daughter of a seamstress? She was from Norway; she could barely write her name, least of all speak English."

"I told you. We were of the same age and had baby sons of about the same age. What more than that was needed? We spoke in French. English it was unimportant. *J'ai compris*! You think as a duchess I should have spurned her because of her low origins? She was married to your son and heir, and as such was Lady Grasby. What's more, she had the sweetest temperament and was the kindest person, just like her daughter Rory. They have a great look of each other, although Christina she was prettier. When we strolled up the Mall we would often be mistaken for twins, such was our likeness. We would sometimes wear similar clothes to make it so, and giggle behind our fans as people looked at us and looked a second time..." Antonia made a motion of dismissal with her hand and brought her emotions under control before such bittersweet memories got the better of her. "None of that is important now. What is, is Rory's happiness, and that I know the truth: Christina took her own life because she could no longer live with the shame of what she allowed you to do to her."

There was an imperceptible pause, and Antonia thought she saw Shrewsbury's arrogant façade crack but he quickly regained mastery of himself and gave a bluff response.

"*Me*? She threw herself off a balcony just hours after giving birth to her baby daughter. What mother leaves a newborn to fend for itself? And she made her six-year-old son motherless into the bargain!"

"That is fact, but it is not why she killed herself. Your son, he too, took his own life, out of grief, because he loved his wife, and from shame, because he knew you, his father, was a depraved monster, and he did nothing to stop your abuse of his wife."

"Depraved? Monster?" Shrewsbury blustered. His smile was supercilious. "Fanciful moonshine! I'll grant grief sent my weak-willed son mad. Any amount of unsubstantiated stuff and nonsense comes out of the mouth of the insane. None of my daughter-in-law's pronouncements bear close scrutiny."

"But Monseigneur was not insane, and he never spoke nonsense of any kind, thus what he told me, I believe. He thought you a monster, too. But he wanted to spare Christina's children the torment of knowing what their grandfather had done to their mother, and the truth about their parents' deaths. And he could not let social ruin befall you because it would befall them, if the ugly reality of what you had done ever became public. So M'sieur le Duc he agreed to take your loathsome secret to his grave." Antonia dared to smile slightly. "But before he did, he told me."

"Told you? I don't believe it!"

"M'sieur le Duc he never promised you he would not tell me. Which he did, because he did not trust you, and he knew such knowledge would be useful should England's Spymaster General decide to become an enemy of my family." She frowned. "He did not like telling me. It pained him to have to recount your unconscionable behavior, but he knew I would rather know as not. He also knew it would not change my feelings for my goddaughter. Although, it did forever change how I view *you*. Monseigneur he was clever in telling me because it meant that if some day I needed to protect my family from harm, to protect them from *you*, I had the perfect weapon in your secret. And now that time, it has come, Edward. I intend to protect my family, and you will now do as requested or I will go to my son."

Suddenly the old man looked ill. Yet he made one last attempt to call Antonia's bluff.

"My old school friend would never betray a friend's trust, not for anyone."

Antonia gave a little sigh.

"Again I say, it is obvious, you have never been in love. When you love someone, you will do everything and anything in your power to ensure their happiness and well-being." She came away from the window. "So now, me I will fetch my cousin, and you, you will fetch your family and Rory, and we will all join in a toast to Lady Grasby's breeding, and to the forthcoming marriage between your granddaughter and my cousin."

Before she made it to the door, Shrewsbury caught her by the upper arm and spun her to face him. She was so shocked to be manhandled that she looked up into his face unable to speak or move.

"Perhaps I will snap your pretty neck, here and now," he breathed down at her. "Then all those petty little secrets locked away in that beautiful head will be gone forever, and you can join your precious Monseigneur sooner rather than later."

"To do so would not save you, M'sieur," Antonia replied, his proximity and hot breath making her instantly nauseous.

She pulled her arm free and stepped away, to put distance between them, brushing down the delicate tiered lace flounce of her sleeve, as if cleaning off the stench of him. It also served to give her a moment to compose herself. After all, he had just threatened to kill her. But a wave of nausea brought everything back into clear focus. She knew she must get through this interview for the sake of her cousin and her goddaughter. She also wanted to end this interview as quickly as possible. She forced her morning sickness away, and said in a clear, strong voice,

"I know you too well, and of what you are capable. A sealed letter sits propped on my dressing table. It is directed to my son. I have instructed it be sent to M'sieur le Duc d'Roxton in the event something untoward befalls his maman. My servants—"

"Clever!"

"—they will not fail in their duty. Kill me and you will be ruined. So, too, your grandson and his family, and to the everlasting sorrow of your daughter—"

"You mean granddaughter."

"Do not play me for a fool, M'sieur! I meant what I said. Rory is your granddaughter, but she is also your daughter. N'est-ce pas? You forced your attentions on her mother, your daughter-in-law, and through threats and intimidation you violated her and the sanctity of her marriage. You are a monster and a defiler and were it not for my goddaughter, I would have nothing to do with you, ever!"

Shrewsbury staggered back, as if her words had struck him hard across the face. Shocked to hear it so baldly stated, and with such vitriol, he was momentarily lost for words. Antonia gave him no quarter.

"Christina she pleaded with you time and again to stop your visits to her apartment. But you would not stop. You used the pretext of visiting your grandson. But that was a ruse. You sent your son, her husband, on a pointless diplomatic mission to The Hague so you could spend uninterrupted time in her bed. She endured your abuse for seven long months, and it was only when you had impregnated her did you have your son recalled from the Continent for fear the truth, it would out—"

"No! That is not true! I was never happier when Christina told me she was carrying my child. It was what we both wanted—"

"*Liar.*" Antonia stared at him as if he was mad. "Of course she wanted the child. She thought pregnancy would stop you! And do not speak to me of your-your *happiness*. You broke God's law passed unto Moses by taking your daughter-in-law as your mistress, and you have the gall to tell me to my face that you were *happy* you impregnated her? You—*disgust* me!"

Shrewsbury had heard enough. He held up a hand, as if this would stop Antonia taunting him with the truth. He had thought that episode in his life long buried under two decades of living. He had almost convinced himself it had never happened. He held to the truth Rory was his granddaughter; that she was also his daughter he had carefully suppressed. To have his carnal cravings for his daughter-in-law and their consequences baldly stated to his face made him suddenly ill.

He, the keeper of other people's vile little secrets, who had no conscience in using those secrets to further his ends as Spymaster General, had been bested at his own game, and by the widow of his best friend. In a moment of supreme weakness he had confided in the old Duke of Roxton. He had felt better for having purged his conscience, little realizing that his own vile little secret would be tucked away, but always at the ready should it ever be needed. His shoulders curled in on themselves knowing that day had come. Yet, despite recognizing he had been defeated, enough arrogant self-belief remained that he tried to justify his behavior.

"You must understand. Christina bewitched me. I knew it was wrong. I was ashamed, but there was nothing—*nothing*—I could do to stop myself! Men are but weak creatures against divine beauty. It is a-a sickness—"

"*Ne parlez pas*! I will hear no more! It is no wonder the poor creature she jumped to her death. *Mon Dieu*, I do not know how Monseigneur he did not run you through with his rapier upon hearing your pathetic confession!"

"M'sieur le Duc knew intimately the-the—*agony* of being in the grip of an all-consuming passion for a much younger beautiful woman. He married you when you were half his age, and the most divine—"

Antonia gasped, horrified. And then her face flooded with color and her green eyes glittered with an anger she had rarely experienced.

"How dare you—How *dare* you compare yourself and your wickedness to the great love Monseigneur and I shared! You know *nothing* of love! Never *ever* speak to me of him again. I cannot bring myself to even contemplate your twisted mind. It makes me ill!"

She took a deep breath and forced herself to regain her calm, to remember why she was putting herself through this distasteful ordeal. Yet, she could not help wondering how she had stomached the presence of this abhorrently loathsome man. But Monseigneur had shielded her from the horrific truth about Rory's parentage, and the deaths of Christina and her husband, almost until the end of his own life. The revelation had come just weeks before his passing. But she had been so consumed with grief at losing the love of her life, unable to cope with the reality of her beloved leaving her, that anything and everything else paled into insignificance.

Now, three years on and married to a man she loved and adored, she had returned to the land of the living, strong and determined, and with a desire for all members of her extended family to live happy and fulfilling lives. If she had a grain of sympathy for Shrewsbury, it was because he had been a doting grandparent to both Harvel and Rory.

The supreme irony was that because he had raised Rory to regard her frailty as just another characteristic of her being, and not a hindrance to her existence, he unwittingly gifted her with self-belief and confidence. But he had wrongly assumed no man would want to marry her, and thus she would never leave him. She would be the ideal companion of his old age. It never occurred to him she would fall in love, least of all with the heir to an earldom, and that gentleman none other than the ruggedly handsome Major Lord Fitzstuart.

But this made no difference to Antonia's opinion of Shrewsbury, or her faith that he would spend his eternity in hell for what he had done to Christina. She looked at him now, and saw that her impassioned speech had drained all the fight from him. So she said in a much calmer voice, she the one now in command of the situation,

"I will allow you a few moments to compose yourself, and to find a way to rid White's betting book of the offending page. Then you will give the performance of your life and be happy for the engaged couple. After the toasts, Rory she will stay with me until the wedding day, which is a week from tomorrow. It will be in M'sieur le Duc's private chapel, with family present. If you value her happiness, and her new husband's goodwill, you will attend."

Shrewsbury stared at her with resentment, yet obediently nodded his agreement. When he spoke, his voice was meek and pleading,

"Promise me you will not say a word of this, to anyone. Promise me, for Rory's sake, and the sake of my family, you will burn that letter to your son."

Antonia pretended to contemplate his request. In truth, there was no letter. Not in a hundred years would she commit to ink Rory's true parentage and the sad story behind her parents' deaths. It had been a bluff. One that had thankfully worked, for she had not formulated an alternative plan had Shrewsbury not swallowed her story and her threat.

"For the sake of my goddaughter and my cousin, and your family, yes. I will do as you ask. But only after they have been up before the vicar and are pronounced husband and wife."

Shrewsbury nodded, satisfied. He shuffled across to the fireplace and retrieved an innocuous, leather bound volume that had been propped beside the leg of his wingchair. He opened it out to a dog-eared page. Folding the page into thirds into the margin, he then care-fully tore the offending page from the book. He crumpled it up and tossed the paper ball onto the grate atop the smoldering logs. Antonia's green eyes widened as the fire came to new life and the paper ball was consumed by flame. He did not need to tell her the page was from White's betting book, and that the aberrant wager was now no more.

Her hand was on the doorknob when Shrewsbury called her back. She looked over her bare shoulder, but did not move.

"You are wrong, Mme la Duchesse. I do know how to love. I love my daughter. I love her beyond words."

"*Bon*. Then as a loving father you will be overjoyed she is to marry well and for love. Oh, and Edward, if you dare strip me naked with your eyes again, I will have my husband put out your sight."

THIRTY

THE DUCHESS HAD BEEN INSIDE THE GATEHOUSE LODGE FOR less than fifteen minutes, leaving Dair outside in her carriage, when he decided it was ten minutes too long. He hated being confined, but he hated more being sedentary. He needed to be doing something, anything, than sit idly until fetched. One booted leg was unable to keep still, while the other was stuck out along the length of the silken cushion, toe tapping against the door's silken padding. He took another look at the pearl face of his silver pocket watch for something to do, noted the minute hand had moved all of three minutes, and slid it back in a pocket of his silk waistcoat. He then shoved a hand in a pocket of his light linen frock coat, found his silver cheroot case and small engraved tinder box, which he could not remember placing there, and decided he had had enough of staring at the opulent dark blue watered silk walls of his carriage prison.

He scrambled out into the fresh air, using the carriage door on the far side of the Gatehouse Lodge, and walked a little way off, towards a stand of tall white rose bushes, keeping the carriage between him and the house, so that he would not be seen from the windows. On his haunches he went about using the contents of the tinderbox to light a cheroot. And once lit, he stayed low, and smoked, dark eyes squinting in the bright sunlight at the serene view of a well-ordered landscape familiar to him since boyhood: The gravel path leading to a winding road just beyond the gate that skirted the lake, then spliced through a long luxuriant avenue of majestic elms, crossed a three-span wide stone bridge, and curled on up to the palatial mansion of the Dukes of

Roxton that dominated the second highest point on the estate. Only the family mausoleum commanded a higher vantage point. Yet, on this day the view barely registered. Major Lord Fitzstuart's mind was crammed full with possibilities and scenarios of what must be occurring within the walls of the Gatehouse Lodge.

He was used to taking charge of a situation, thinking through the problem and its logistical challenges, and putting a suitable plan into action. But he had promised his cousin he would wait until called; that he would not do anything rash. She had actually ordered him to "not play the hero", by which he was certain she meant not kicking in doors, climbing a rope or scrambling a drain pipe, and smashing in a window to enter Rory's rooms by force, if not stealth. All these possibilities were given serious consideration until Antonia made him promise otherwise.

So he was reduced to pacing back and forth the length of the blind side of the carriage, from driver's step to footman's rail, cheroot between his fingers. It wasn't long before his mind wandered back to storming Rory's bedchamber. After all, he needed to be prepared in case his cousin's visit did not go as she planned. He decided Rory's room would not be upstairs after all, but on the ground floor. He'd noticed the narrow stairwell the night before, and how the steps turned sharply out of sight. She may have been sitting on the lower step waiting for him, but he was sure she did not use the staircase day-in and day-out.

That got him ruminating about his ancestral home, Fitzstuart Hall, the grand staircase in particular, and the private apartments on the first floor he was going to have remodeled and enlarged for his bride. There were other modifications to the house he intended to have commissioned to make the house as comfortable as possible for her, the first being the installation of a flying chair like the one Shrewsbury had at his Chiswick House. Perhaps he would have two installed, one in each wing so that her ladyship would not need to retrace her steps if she wished to go downstairs, and it would give her even easier access to all rooms of the mansion. And of course there was the Pinery to be built to cultivate pineapples, oranges, lemons and limes, and perhaps exotic flowers, if such things took his wife's fancy.

These considerations kept him occupied as he paced, stopping occasionally to smoke and drop ash and grind this into the crushed stone of the drive with a toe of his jockey boot.

This visit he was dressed for comfort, in knitted breeches and jockey boots, white shirt and a plain linen frock coat of Prussian blue. And though he had let Farrier shave him yesterday, today he would not be shaved. It was partly a superstitious act. The one time he put in an effort to have his suit of clothes as neat as a pin, and his face as smooth as a nymph's lovely behind, Shrewsbury had rejected him out-of-hand as suitable husband material for his granddaughter. But mostly his slap-dash grooming was how he was most comfortable, now he no longer needed to make an impression. This time he expected Shrewsbury to accept him. But he couldn't care less one way or the other. All he cared about was Rory's happiness and marrying her without delay. And that day couldn't come soon enough!

The longer he paced and smoked, the more worried he became that his cousin was having about as much success as he'd had the night before. That is, until a footman fetched him to come indoors.

Dair was so nervous with anticipation his every muscle was as tight as an over-wound watch. He strode past the footman and into the small house, ready to do battle with anyone and everyone. He stepped into the drawing room with a lift of his heavy chin, both hands fisted. His dark eyes quickly scanned the room in search of the only beautiful face that mattered. She was not there. Why was she not there? But before he could ask the question, a crystal champagne glass was thrust between his fingers, and in amongst the chattering and laughing he heard the sound of corks popping.

It was only then he realized he was being greeted with a warm welcome by a room full of smiling faces, while two footmen scurried about pouring champagne into glasses.

"You're just in time!" Grasby announced, stepping forward to greet his best friend. "What luck you happened to arrive just now, as we're about to toast our news. Apologies I didn't write and tell you, but Silla wanted to wait until we'd told Grand. Which is the right way to go about things. Still," he added confidentially, sidling up to the Major to say at his ear, "if I'd known your whereabouts this past fort-night, I'd have told you anyway. What luck you're staying with the Duke."

"What's going on, Grasby?" Dair asked curtly and drank down the champagne without tasting it. He hadn't realized just how parched he was. "Where's your sister?"

"Steady on! We've not had the toast yet! Here, take my glass," Grasby insisted and put out his hand for another from a footman. "You're bleached white as falling snow, as if you've come bang up against a specter. Are you all right, dear fellow?"

"Perfectly. Where did you say your sister was?"

"Grand's just gone to fetch her. She's feeling poorly. Seems she had a bad night of it—"

Dair's brows contracted with worry and then he set his jaw, anger just simmering away under the surface of his congenial façade. If

Shrewsbury had caused Rory any distress, there would be hell to pay. His left hand clenched again.

"—but we can't have a toast to a new Talbot without his aunt present, now can we?" Grasby rattled on. "Oh, drat! There I go and spoil the surprise. You won't tell Silla I told you, will you?"

"What's that you say, Grasby? A new Talbot?" Dair came out of his angry abstraction enough to smile and slap his friend's back. "Not a word, dear fellow! Congratulations. Good for you! About time, too. Rory will be thrilled to pieces to be an aunt."

"Between you and me, I was despairing of ever becoming a father after that whole Romney studio debacle," Grasby confided with a roll of his eyes and a sigh of relief. "At least now Silla's with child she's willing to forget that ghastly night ever happened—

"Surely not ghastly? Well, not ghastly for you…?"

Grasby snorted his embarrassment. "Steady on! Not so loud!" When Dair lifted an eyebrow, he rolled his eyes again and conceded, "Oh, all right, not ghastly for me! They were lovely, weren't they, those girls—"

"Very."

"—but a chap has to remember what's important in life, and being allowed to sleep in the matrimonial bed is important."

Dair threw back his head and laughed, which caused a pause in conversations as heads turned in his direction. "Egad, Grasby! You always put matters into perspective!"

Grasby grinned like an idiot. "Do I? I do! Yes, of course I do! Oh, and you'll be pleased to know the wife has forgiven you, too."

"I hardly deserve such munificence. When did Lord Shrewsbury leave to fetch Rory?" Dair asked, glancing about the room. He saw the Duchess standing by an open window, fanning herself, face turned to the fresh air, and thus he could not catch her eye. He would have crossed to her but Lady Grasby, with William Watkins a step behind, imposed on her solitude and offered her a glass of champagne.

"Don't get too comfortable," Grasby warned. "Silla being Silla, she immediately withdrew her forgiveness upon learning you'd socked her brother in the face and broken his nose!" This time Grasby snorted laughter. "My God, you planted him a beautiful facer! None better, and so I told Cedric and the fellows, who instantly laid down a hefty sum that you'd do it again to him before the year's out."

"No more dares, Harvel," Dair stated and clapped his best friend's shoulder when Grasby's mouth dropped open. "Sorry to disappoint, but that's how it's going to be from now on. No exchange of serious blunt and none of it written up in White's betting book. I'm done being an unthinking ass. I guess that's not a bad thing, for you, too, what with impending fatherhood. Do you think Rory will be much longer?"

"Listen, Dair. That's the third time you've called my sister by her name," Grasby grumbled. "If you've a mind to lead her astray I'll be the one socking you—"

"Not at all, dear fellow. Quite the opposite."

"Eh?" Grasby was baffled, but the smile on Dair's face carried no lewd insinuation. In fact, he looked pleased with himself, and in a nice, happy sort of way that Grasby's fears were alleviated. "Well then. That's all right. I just thought I should mention it because the Weasel has been making some pretty rough insinuations to Silla about your intentions toward Rory. And I can tell you, if he wasn't my plaguey brother-in-law, and you hadn't already broken his nose, I'd be the one socking him in the face!"

"Be my guest. But do me the favor of waiting until he's properly healed before you put a hand to him. And you'll have to forgive me for not being so forthcoming with *you* with *our* news, but it will all become apparent—"

"Forgive you? Forthcoming? Apparent? What will? *Our news?* Whose news? Dair? Dair!"

"Excuse me, Grasby," Dair muttered, distracted with the drawing room door opening wide, and stepped past his friend.

Suddenly he was deaf to his friend's questions, and lost all peripheral vision, so was blind to Lady Grasby and her brother crossing the room to make themselves known to him; Lady Grasby's smug smile shrinking to an undignified pursing of her lips when Dair ignored her. All he saw was the doorway and all he heard was the pumping of his heart hammering in his head. He realized he was still wound as tightly as a pocket watch when he thought he might pass out with the anticipation of seeing Rory, and of what was to come after that.

Lord Shrewsbury walked into view first and then, there she was, his Delight, on her grandfather's arm and leaning on her walking stick. She was tired about the eyes, but in every other respect she was his beautiful darling girl. He unconsciously broke into a grin and stepped forward. And just as he had done when he entered the drawing room, she quickly looked about her, as if she, too, had lost something or someone.

And then she saw him.

JUST BEFORE ENTERING THE DRAWING ROOM, RORY HAD
marveled at the rolling high seas of emotion she had experienced in the
past twenty-four hours, from the heavenly heights of unbridled happiness to then be plunged into the depths of black despair, with seemingly no way to claw herself out, only to be lifted up again into the
heart-fluttering bliss of loving contentment.

From the heightened anticipation of her grandfather's welcome
response when Dair came to call to formally ask for her hand in
marriage, she was left bewildered at finding herself alone in the hall,
Dair gone without a word. And then came the numbing desolation of
being told, in a matter-of-fact way, how much her grandfather admired
Major Lord Fitzstuart's bravery in accepting an assignment to return to
the Colonies on the first available ship, to infiltrate a rebel spy ring on
the outskirts of New York, a loyalist stronghold.

Rory instantly disbelieved her grandfather. She had wanted a
servant sent after the Major, to have him called back. She had to speak
with him. It was a matter of the utmost importance and could not wait.
She would have the news of his departure from the Major's lips and no
other.

Her grandfather had been completely at a loss to understand her
distress. He had patiently sat with her on the stair and asked her to
explain why she was so upset by such news. But as she had fallen all to
pieces to think the Major had not told her grandfather he was engaged
to her, and had accepted a mission to spy on the other side of the
Atlantic—as if there was nothing holding him to England—she could
barely form a coherent word, least of all form a sentence explaining
herself. He had offered her his handkerchief and held her in his arms
while she sobbed until her ribs hurt. He suggested she had exhausted
herself swimming in the sun that day, was even suffering from
sunstroke. He had noticed at dinner there was more color in her face
and to her arms than usual. A good night's sleep would set everything
to rights. They could talk again in the morning.

But Rory knew everything would not be all right in the morning.
She had to see the Major *that night*. Her grandfather had to understand. Tomorrow was too far away. She had to see him now, tonight,
that instant.

Such was her distress that she refused to go to her rooms, and again
demanded her grandfather send a servant out into the night to call the
Major back. He was staying with his cousin the Duchess, just a ten-
minute stroll down the lane. When he again patiently refused, saying
he would not disturb the Duchess's household at such an hour, and
that she was being uncharacteristically unreasonable to make such

demands, she declared her intention of calling on the Major herself, and at once.

It was only then that her grandfather became angry. He called her selfish. She was to desist with her unbecoming behavior at once. Did she not remember who she was, the granddaughter of the Earl of Shrewsbury? Displaying the manners of a fishwife, and before servants, was unacceptable. He would not stand for such behavior from his own blood. He had ended his scolding with the heartfelt hope that she had not lost her head to the likes of the Major.

He had raised her to have a discerning mind, to know her own worth, and to behave accordingly. She was not a hair-brained, penny-pinched nobody prepared to offer herself to any nobleman, body and soul, in the hope of entrapping him into marriage. Did she not have a sense of discrimination? Certainly the Major would one day inherit a noble title. But he, Shrewsbury, knew him better than anyone. The Major was the last man on God's green earth he would allow any female of his acquaintance to marry. He was a known seducer, a reckless risk-taker, with his own life, and anyone else's if it suited his purpose. He had bastard children practically littering the countryside. Did she not understand there was good reason his moniker was Dair Devil?

But what had stopped her sobbing and caught the breath in her throat was his quiet, almost pitiful, prediction that his heart would break and his health never recover if he discovered she had so much as permitted the Major to kiss her hand. As for having her pretty head filled with ridiculous notions that such a man could love her and would offer her marriage, she could banish such thoughts. If the truth be told, he was just the sort of conscienceless libertine to make up to her, all to satisfy some ludicrous wager made between young men of the Major's ilk. But he was confident she had the sense and sensibility to see through such schemes.

Unable to breathe, Rory collapsed.

She awoke in the arms of a footman, who carried her, not to her bedchamber on the ground floor, but upstairs, where she was set down on the bed in the small guest bedchamber over the front entrance. Edith came, and her grandfather, too. She lay there, listless and cold. She honestly wondered if she could be bothered with breathing, such was the pounding in her head and the ache in her heart.

In her fog of despair, she heard her grandfather tell Edith he was locking the door. He did not want his granddaughter doing anything foolish in the night, such as run off to the dower house. He would unlock the door at a reasonable hour in the morning, when he hoped a good night's sleep would see Rory recover her wits.

Rory's gaze must have wandered to the window, for he added that it was impossible, for whatever reason, to open the window. And as there was a considerable drop, and nothing between the window and the gravel drive to break her fall, should she smash the glass and climb out, she would surely break every bone in her body, if not kill herself.

He then kissed her forehead and told her she meant the world to him and that he loved her so very much. With the turn of the key in the lock, she burst into tears and cried herself to exhaustion and fitful sleep. She woke with the dawn and found Edith asleep in a chair at the foot of the bed, most uncomfortable and shivering with cold, the wrap pulled up over her having slipped to the floor. The fire in the grate had gone out, the scullery maid unable to access the room to provide more wood for the night. Rory was so sick in her heart she felt nothing except the ring on her finger…

The ring! The pale lavender sapphire ring Alisdair had slipped on her finger after asking her to marry him. Why had she not thought to feel it on her finger before now?! With dawning wonder she stared at the beautiful stone in the gray morning light until her eyes went dry, fearing that if she blinked it would not be there, that she was dreaming. But it was still on her finger, exquisitely cut, beautiful in its soft lavender hues, and *hers*. The ring became her talisman of hope and belief.

She knew then Alisdair had gone away without a word to her, for any reason other than he had forsaken her. He did love her. He did want to marry her. The proof of his words was in this ring. But perhaps her grandfather had rejected him as a suitable husband—he had said as much the night before—and, dejected, Alisdair had not the heart to face her with such news. But she was confident he had left the house only to come up with a plan, and that he would not leave England for America without her. If she had to elope with him to the war-torn Colonies, then so be it. Nothing and nobody would stop her!

Feeling so much better, and confident the day would bring Alisdair to her with some plan for their future, Rory drew the wrap back up across Edith, and added one of the two coverlets from the bed for good measure, to ensure her maid was kept warm. She then snuggled in and fell asleep almost instantly, she was so achingly tired. Waking to a late breakfast brought up on a tray, she surprised Edith by eating well and then declaring she would bathe, and wear the soft green silk gown à *l'anglaise*, with the embroidered under-petticoats. And to bring her a cold compress for her eyes to take away the puffiness. Then Edith could dress her hair in a coil of braids and curls.

When Lord Shrewsbury enquired of Edith how her mistress was

holding up after the night before, Edith was able to tell him that when she left Rory in her bath, she was singing to herself; it was as if the previous night's melodrama had never occurred. Far from looking pleased, the old man's frown deepened. He wondered what scheme his granddaughter was hatching to see herself reunited with the Major. He ordered the footman to keep his granddaughter locked in the upstairs bedchamber, with only her maid to be given access; a footman to stand guard at the door at all times.

Rory was bathing when Edith brought her the news that Lord and Lady Grasby and Mr. William Watkins had arrived from Chiswick. With this news, she was again locked into the bedchamber, and this time without warning or explanation, which worried her as to her grandfather's motives for keeping her locked up, even from her own family members.

And then Major Lord Fitzstuart did return! She was dressed and ready to go downstairs when a second carriage turned into the drive. Edith was at the window and called her over in time to see the carriage door furthest from the house fling wide and the love of her life appear. Rory could have fainted with happiness at seeing him. She pressed her hands and little nose to the glass to better see him when he went down on his haunches to light a cheroot, and wondered if she shouted he would hear her. But then she reasoned, so would the rest of the house, so best to keep quiet and be ready to flee when he kicked in the door. Perhaps she should think of a plan to help him in his rescue of her. To this end she had Edith help her remove the candles from their brass holders. She played with the weight of them, judging the best way to hold a candlestick to use it with force. Edith swayed with worry at the passion for violence her young mistress displayed when demonstrating the use of a candlestick as a weapon.

But neither candlestick was required to be misused. Nor was the door kicked in. It was unlocked by a footman to admit a short, upright lady who introduced herself in French as lady-in-waiting to Mme la Duchesse d'Kinross. She came with orders for Edith to have Mlle Talbot's belongings packed up and sent out to the Duchesse's waiting carriage. Mlle Talbot would be spending the week at the house of her godmother in preparation for her marriage to Major Lord Fitzstuart. Not understanding French, Edith looked to Rory for translation. But upon hearing the phrase... *in preparation for her marriage to Major Lord Fitzstuart*, Rory again went into shock and forgot to breathe, crumpling to the floor in a heap of billowing petticoats.

Revived, Rory existed in a heightened state of awareness, the mixed emotions of relief and disbelief causing not only her heart but her mind to race. And while Edith went off with the Duchess's lady-in-waiting to supervise the packing of portmanteaux, the footman locked Rory into the bedchamber again with the apology he could not free her until word came from his lordship.

Finally her grandfather did fetch her, and with the news everyone was awaiting her presence in the drawing room. He did not speak of events of the night before, and while there remained so many unanswered questions, Rory could not bring herself to ask him. He looked to have aged overnight. His shoulders stooped and his hands had acquired a slight tremor. Worst of all was the haunted expression in his blue eyes. He could not meet her gaze, and when he spoke he sounded frail; gone was the confident resonance.

How could she stay angry with him? She kissed his cheek, put her arms about him and said she forgave him and would always love him. He broke down, asked her forgiveness for being over-protective, and in an about-face, he said the Major was indeed a good man who was worthy of her. They then both shed a tear. When sufficiently composed, they went downstairs, arm-in–arm, Shrewsbury resigned to being a bystander, Rory to greet the first day of the rest of her life.

In two strides Dair was before her. She smiled up at him. He grinned down at her. They were so happy to see each other they giggled. Rory let go of her grandfather's arm and handed him her walking stick. But when she turned to look at Dair again, when she saw that he was indeed still there before her, she was so overcome with relief she crumpled. A shaking hand to her mouth and tears in her eyes, she sobbed.

Dair instantly scooped her up and held her against him, face nuzzled in her hair, silent, feeling the strong tremors of release coursing through her lithe frame. But then he realized the tremors were not only hers. He did not speak, just held her, and let her cry until she stopped of her own volition. When she moved in his arms, he let her go. He gave her his handkerchief. And when she had dried her eyes, he quickly wiped his own and thrust the handkerchief away.

Neither was certain who moved time on after that. But she was in his arms again, on tiptoe, chin tilted up to kiss him. He stooped and crushed her mouth under his, all social constraint abandoned. They were too relieved, too overjoyed, too in love to be bothered with convention and propriety. All that mattered was they were together, they were to marry, and as soon as possible. Everything and everyone around them disappeared in a fog of unimportant movement and noise.

They would have stayed this way, locked in a passionate embrace, but Rory came to a sense of her surroundings when a glass shattered on the floor.

Lady Grasby had gasped in shock to see the couple embrace and kiss, and dropped her wine glass, champagne splashing the silk ruches of her bodice. Never in her lifetime would she have suspected this outcome. She did not believe her eyes. She glanced swiftly at her brother, who looked just as shocked as she felt, with his jaw hanging loose. But it was at her husband she stared hardest. Lord Grasby's immediate reaction mimicked hers, but then a change came over him, and his mouth lifted into a silly grin. He hugged himself, as if needing to contain his joy, shoulders hunching, shock giving way to enlightenment and then sheer delight at sight of his sister and his best friend so happy in each other's arms. Lady Grasby's eyes filled with tears and her mouth puckered; it had nothing to do with sentimentality. Her moment to shine in the candlelight had come and now it was gone, extinguished by this couple's unbridled happiness.

The breakage caused a general commotion, and footmen ran about picking up the shards, while Mr. William Watkins was heard to comment that he was not surprised her ladyship lost hold of her glass. The shock of witnessing such an indecent spectacle of a couple giving in to such base behavior in such exalted company, and in the broad light of day, was enough to alarm even the most liberal mind amongst the assembled company. He expected the Major to instantly offer up his apologies to Her Grace and to his lordship.

"M'sieur! You have the sensibilities of an old maiden aunt, the manners of a washerwoman, and the face of a rat catcher," Antonia stated bluntly, staring down and then up at the tall reed-thin secretary, from his highly-polished buckled shoes to his fashionable but excessively curled wig *a le faisan*. "I am told your face it is the result of the first two. So me, I have no sympathy. So now, M'sieur," she ordered, pointing her closed fan at Mr. William Watkins, "you will be quiet, as if you are not here at all. Lord Shrewsbury he is to perform the toasts. Then both sides of the family they can be surprised equally by the news of the other. I do not doubt it will provide some of you with conversation for the rest of the week. But my goddaughter and Lord Fitzstuart, they will be excused from such enlivening discussion, because me I am to take them to an appointment with my son and his chaplain, to discuss the wedding ceremony to which you are all invited next week.

And there! I have told you the news, without really meaning to. My lord, the toasts, if you please. M'sieur le Duc cannot abide tardiness."

But as she was handed up into her carriage, the Duchess gave her driver the order, not to take her to M'sieur le Duc d'Roxton, but to drive to the mausoleum. She must share the couple's news, and her own, even more startling announcement, with Monseigneur, before going on to the big house.

SUNLIGHT STREAMED IN THROUGH THE GLASS OCULUS OF THE opulent crypt of the last resting place of the Dukes of Roxton and their relatives, illuminating the Italian marble flooring, and showing the way deeper in to the cavernous space.

A footman and Dair carried in urns filled with white roses. The footman placed the smaller of the two urns at the base of a black marble sarcophagus that had upon its lid the sleeping figures of a man and woman in white marble: The last resting place of the Earl and Countess of Stretham-Ely, known for most of their lives as Lord and Lady Vallentine, Antonia's beloved brother and sister-in-law; parents of Evelyn Gaius Lucian Ffolkes, who, according to Dair, now called himself M'sieur Lucian.

The large urn of white roses, Dair placed at the base of the fifth Duke of Roxton's imposing tomb. The nobleman, sculpted in white marble, was so to the life, he stared down his long nose from his chair, as if he still surveyed all before him with the same arrogant disdain he had shown all but his family when alive. To Dair, the Duke had been a second father, a stern second father, but a loving one for all that. And so after placing the urn, he stepped back and stood for a moment with head bowed, before joining Rory on the marble bench opposite. He put out his hand to her without taking his eyes from the Duke, and when he felt her fingers entwined with his, he smiled and then looked at her. She was staring at him fixedly, and when he put up his black brows in a silent question, she touched his shoulder so he would dip it to allow her to whisper near his ear, and thus not disturb the Duchess.

"When I was six years old, M'sieur le Duc told me that when I was older I could have his beaky nose... He was true to his word... You have his nose."

Dair sat up with a frown, looked at her, then up at the statue of his cousin, for he was related not only to Antonia through their mutual ancestress their grandmother, but to the Duke who had been their grandmother's first cousin. But he had never before thought much about his blood connection to the Duke. And yet, staring at him now, it was glaringly obvious he had indeed inherited his strong nose. That the old Duke had predicted the love of Dair's life would marry a man with the same strong nose as he possessed was mere coincidence, but it still sent a shiver down his back, and formed a lump in his throat. He held Rory's hand just that little bit tighter.

The couple then sat silent and attentive to the Duchess, who remained standing before her first husband's tomb, first to arrange the flowers to her liking, and then to look up at him with a hand to the toe of his buckled shoe. It was as if contact with cold marble was somehow needed for her to feel that little bit closer to him, to bridge the insurmountable gap between the living and the dead. And although she never said a word out loud, Rory was certain her godmother was communicating with her beloved. She knew it was so when the Duchess finally came over and sat on the bench, with her hands lightly in her lap.

"I have told him your news," she said gently. "I know he is overjoyed for you both. But now please leave me and hold hands in the carriage while I have five minutes alone with Monseigneur. Then we will go on to the big house to share your happy news with my son and Deborah and the children."

She watched the couple leave the mausoleum hand in hand then turned to smile up at the marble figure of her first husband, a hand to her flushed throat.

"And now I have something to tell you that will make you shake your head and laugh at me..." She looked over at the tomb with the second urn of roses before it and said, "You, too, Vallentine and Estée. You will scold me severely, but I tell you it could not be helped." She looked back up at her beloved. "You will be happy for me, I know it. Though you will tell me it is an outcome that is nothing less than I deserve for marrying a virile man not much older than our son..."

When she rejoined the carriage, Michelle was waiting for her outside. Antonia understood why, and thanked her lady's maid for giving the couple the privacy of the carriage. She found her cousin and her goddaughter snuggled up together in a corner, asleep. She was not surprised, after the emotionally exhausting events of the past twelve hours—she herself was tired. With a soft gloved knock to the panel above her head, the carriage set off, and she too snuggled into a corner, Michelle beside her, and dozed until the door was opened by an officious liveried footman of her son's household.

Taking the white-gloved hand of the footman, and stepping down into fresh air, she made a most welcome discovery. She was no longer nauseous. Her morning sickness, which had come upon her swiftly and with surprise, had vanished just as it had arrived. Michelle must have been right in her calculations all along. Though she was partial to believing it was no coincidence, she had just been to the mausoleum to receive Monseigneur's blessing for the new life growing within her. Tonight she would write to Jonathon with her news. He would be ecstatic, and no doubt scold her lovingly that he had told her so!

With a confident tread, Antonia, Duchess of Kinross swept into the gigantic foyer of what had once been her home. Her four grandchildren were rushing down the wide curved staircase to greet her, squealing and giggling with delight, nursemaids, servants and tutors in their wake. She floated to the marble floor in a cloud of soft silk, opened wide her arms, and scooped them all up in one loving embrace.

THIRTY-ONE

With the Duchess of Roxton and the Duchess of Kinross putting their heads together to organize every aspect of Rory and Dair's wedding, from the guest list to the dishes to be served at the wedding breakfast, there was little for Rory to do but enjoy each day closer to the ceremony with a heightened sense of anticipation, as if she were living a dream.

She did not even have the drama of indecision regarding what gown would be most suitable. Her sister-in-law tried to convince her an ivory or lemon silk would be best for a bride, but neither suited Rory's pale complexion. And she had promised Dair to wear the pink-lavender open-robed gown of silk and matching shoes he had seen her in on the stair of the Gatehouse Lodge. Edith knew just how to arrange her hair, despite Silla's insistence she was more expert in such matters. And as for jewelry, Rory was perfectly content with her pale lavender sapphire betrothal ring—the color perfectly matched her choice of gown. Again, Silla said this would never do. She would find something suitable for Rory's décolletage and wrists. Secretly, Rory hoped her search was in vain.

The next day Lord and Lady Grasby strolled up to the dower house from the Gatehouse Lodge to have morning tea with Rory on the terrace. Enjoying their second cup of tea, they presented Rory with a flat square jewelry case. Inside, nestled on a bed of velvet, was a four-strand choker of luminous pearls and a matching bracelet. The set had belonged to Rory's mother and worn on her wedding day in Oslo, and now it was Rory's, a wedding gift from her brother and his wife. Rory was brought to tears, surprised Silla could part with such pearls.

Silla ruined the moment with the revelation she had a much more expensive five-strand choker with a long length of pearls fitted off with a gold and diamond clasp, and that it came with two matching bracelets and a pair of earrings. The set was a gift from her parents on her marriage into the Talbot family. Rory made no comment other than she was certain Silla's pearls were beautiful indeed, to which Silla replied Rory would see them for herself when she wore them to the wedding ceremony the day after tomorrow.

Rory exchanged a look with her brother, who merely rolled his eyes, bit down on a retort, and silently drank his tea. Yet not five minutes later, Silla outdid herself with an insensitive reply to Grasby's innocent enquiry as to which of her walking sticks Rory had chosen to use for the big occasion. The Malacca stick with the ivory handle carved in the shape of a pineapple, was Rory's preference. In fact, he had given it to her on her twenty-first birthday, did he not remember? It was also the one she had with her that fateful night at Romney's studio. Grasby laughed at that and said it was the perfect choice, and wondered aloud if his best friend remembered the offending instrument.

Silla found nothing to laugh at. In fact, she was alarmed to think Rory was going to be married with a walking stick. Setting her teacup in its saucer, she said bluntly, oblivious her words were in the least offensive,

"Rory cannot possibly be married with her stick, Grasby. Have you ever seen a bride with a walking stick? No. It simply won't do. You must lean on the Major's arm. That is more fitting and thoroughly acceptable for a new bride. People will then think you are emotionally overcome by the ceremony and will be none the wiser—"

"Silla! How can you say—"

Grasby was cut off.

"As it is a family wedding, Silla, everyone is wise to the fact I use a walking stick," Rory replied without heat. "And I am not such a poor creature that I am likely to faint at my own wedding." She dimpled. "I am more likely to be wearing a silly grin of happiness, which I must temper or I shall appear a fool." She touched her brother's upturned cuff. "You will tell me by some signal or other, if I start grinning like a Bedlam inmate, won't you?"

"But, dearest, you've never been the center of attention before," Silla argued. "And you've never danced. You've always sat in out-of-the-way places at functions. So there are quite possibly those who have no idea who you are! Believe me, having everyone stare at you is more nerve-wracking than you can possibly imagine."

Rory suppressed a smile at her sister-in-law's conceit, and said levelly, but with tongue firmly planted in cheek, "Even more reason to use my stick upon this occasion. After all, one day I will be Countess of Strathsay, so the sooner I become accustomed to being the center of attention the better. Don't you agree, Grasby?"

"Most certainly. In my book, you can't become the center of attention soon enough, sister dear."

Brother and sister laughed, but Silla saw nothing to be amused about. After thoughtful consideration she said, "I suppose that is true, Rory. And with so many titled relatives in attendance, we can't have the bride falling flat on her face."

"No. No, we cannot," Rory agreed and when her brother pulled a funny face at her, out of his wife's line of sight, she giggled into her teacup. When she had regained her composure, she added, "What an inauspicious start to our marriage if I were to trip, twist my good ankle, and land on my face! Poor Alisdair!"

Silla gave a prim little cough into her gloved fist.

"Dearest, it is only ever Alisdair when you are private, and once he is your husband," she enunciated in a patronizing tone. "*Always* Fitzstuart in company, and *my lord* before the servants and other menials."

Stunned by such an unwarranted rebuke, Rory could think of nothing to say, so went about organizing the tea things, undecided if she should be angry or embarrassed.

Grasby stepped in, patience worn thin. His wife might be with child, and he was warned not to upset her delicate nerves at such an early stage in the pregnancy, but he was not going to sit idly by and let his sister be told how to conduct herself, which was none of his wife's business. Irritated to anger, he said what was on the tip of Rory's tongue but which good manners dictated she not voice aloud.

"Where do you get your singular notions to lecture *us*? My sister is a Talbot, and we Talbots know how to conduct ourselves in any company. Besides, she can say what she likes—call her husband Rover or-or Spot if it pleases *him*, for all I jolly well care! By the bye, where is Rover—er—the lucky groom?" he asked, taking his temper down a notch, and shifting in his chair to look left and then right, as if he expected his best friend to leap out from behind a statue to frighten the life out of him. It had happened before. "I thought he'd be here, with you."

"Not until noncheon today," Rory told them. "He has business to discuss with the Duke."

"I thought we'd done all the settlements and such yesterday," Grasby remarked. And when Rory frowned, explained. "Grand and me, Roxton and Dair, worked out the settlements, your dowry and pin money." He smiled as if he was well-pleased with himself. "I don't mind telling you, sister dear, that you are being well looked after, with all eventualities covered."

"Eventualities?" Rory had no idea what he was talking about.

"You know… If anything were to happen to Dair—Not that it's likely to!" he assured her quickly when her frown deepened. "He's given up playing at spy—Now there's something I didn't know about him, and he my best friend! A spy all these years! But, Rory, please. Don't look at me like that! I hadn't the foggiest notion. But he's given all that shadow-and-stab stuff up. And so he should, now he's to be married. He has other responsibilities—you being the most important one, and so I told him! But I haven't any worries, have I, when he's practically stitched himself to your skirts!" He teased his sister. "And if he's not sewn to you, he's looming large like a shadow, just one step away. And the poor fellow can't keep his eyes off you. I'd say he's got it bad—"

"What? What's he got?" Silla asked swiftly, a hand to her bodice. "It's not contagious, is it? The baby—"

Lord Grasby put up a shoulder and stuck out his bottom lip. "That's difficult to say—"

"Oh, stop your teasing, Harvel!" Rory admonished him lovingly, cheeks red with embarrassment. "Your baby is perfectly safe, Silla."

Lady Grasby heaved a huge sigh of relief and fanned herself, as if she truly believed Major Lord Fitzstuart was infected with the plague.

"Thank Goodness! Deb Roxton has put such an effort into your wedding, and she heavy with child, too," Silla said dramatically. "What a disappointment for her and Her Grace of Kinross, if, after all their planning and hard work, the wedding was to be called off because the Major is struck down with the flu!"

"Oh yes! Let's not disappoint the Duchess—*two* duchesses, in fact," Lord Grasby scoffed and put aside his teacup and saucer. "Never mind disappointing his bride!"

When Rory opened wide her eyes at him, he knew he had gone too far with his chastisement of his wife and did his best to temper his annoyance. It was not only Silla who had put him out of charity. If he were honest with himself, he had been out of sorts with the world since learning of his sister's engagement to his best friend. Selfishly, he did not want her leaving the family fold. He did not entirely understand why she was staying with the Duchess of Kinross before her marriage, and not at the Gatehouse Lodge with her immediate family. His grandfather's explanation was that the Lodge was small, and with William Watkins in the house, it was best for Rory to be elsewhere.

But then William Watkins had departed for London under a cloud only the day before. He was not given the full explanation, only that the Weasel was needed in the city on Crown business. Grasby knew that was only part of the story. The other part he had heard loud and clear through the thin walls of the Lodge, because he just happened to be sitting just outside the study, on the first step of the staircase, reading the *Gazette*.

The Weasel accused Dair of being a traitor—nothing new there—he was always trying to discredit the Major, and it had become a long-standing joke between Grasby and his grandfather. But this time, the Weasel said he had proof, a letter in the Major's hand to his brother Charles. It had come into the Weasel's possession by mysterious means he was not prepared to divulge. There was then a lot of back-and-forth arguing between the Weasel and the Spymaster General, and Grasby could only catch the odd word. The upshot was the Weasel screaming for Shrewsbury not to toss the offending letter into the flames.

Mr. William Watkins had then exited the study, took one look at Grasby, and blurted out that the House of Lords was filled with black-guards, and the sooner it was abolished the better for the country! To which Grasby replied mildly that such words were treasonous, and if he really wanted to make a difference somewhere, there was a revolution going on in the American colonies. He was confident the patriots would welcome a man of the Weasel's abilities and philosophical lean-ings with open arms. He then returned to reading the *Gazette* as the Weasel stomped past him up the steps to have his bags packed.

Memory of the exchange brought a smile back to Grasby's face, and he was more in charity with the world, thinking the Weasel might yet decide to throw in his lot with a bunch of revolutionaries and run off to America, and so leave him and his wife in peace.

"There's nothing at all wrong with Dair," Grasby told his wife gently. "To point out fact, all's right with our Major. He's just in love with my sister, and hooray for that." He smiled at Rory. "I couldn't be happier for you both. I should have known it when I saw you at the Banks House wall." He sat back with a wink at Rory. "If Dair's not needed here, Cedric and I will claim him tomorrow morning. We're off hawking with Roxton and a few of the local gentry, all come to cele-brate the poor fellow's last hours of freedom; before he's leg-shackled for life and can never move again without the wife demanding to know his whereabouts."

Silla, not seeing Grasby's wink, sat up very tall. But before she could launch into another lecture, the object of their discussion came into view, crossing from the stables to the house.

Dressed in a riding frock and jockey boots, his shoulder-length hair wind-tussled, Dair had just ridden over from the big house. He was, as always, slightly disheveled, and had not bothered to shave, all the more handsome for the stubble to his face. This was Rory's assessment, and her blue eyes lit up as he came lightly up the stone steps to join them. Her brother was of the same opinion, watching his sister's skin glow pink at the sight of his best friend, and his wife sit forward and gaze up at him with limpid longing—she, too, wishing to be noticed by the Major. But Grasby held no malice, and just shook his head, not only on the effect the Major's untidy masculinity had on the fairer sex, but also that the man himself seemed oblivious to his effect on females.

"I should warn you, two carriages are on their way from the big house," Dair told them as he came to stand by Rory's chair. He placed an ungloved hand gently on her shoulder and her fingers immediately found his and held on. "One full of children, the other full of their attendants. The Duchess has invited them for a picnic lunch. I was able to ride over here, but Cedric had no such luck. Roxton's twins have taken a shine to him, so he was bundled into their carriage before I could save him."

"Ha! I'll wager you made no such effort! Poor chap," Grasby replied without sympathy, as he scraped back his chair. "Serves him to rights for being about as tall as a shrub. Possibly mistaken for a brat himself. Come, wife! Best take you home. You need to rest, and we can't have the baby exposed to mites with coughs and snotty noses, even if they are ducal mites."

Lady Grasby showed no objection. In fact, she could not move fast enough to put distance between herself and the dower house. She was off down the terrace steps ahead of her husband, who stopped to have a last word with the couple.

"Not abandoning you. I'll return as soon as I have Silla settled," he confided. He held Rory's gaze. "Perhaps we'll get to have a proper chat about that matter we touched on yesterday…"

When Rory nodded, Grasby took his leave. But even with her brother out of earshot, and she alone with Dair, she did not elaborate on the cryptic sentence. Dair did not need to be told the subject matter to know something grave was weighing on Rory's mind. Her thoughts should not have been clouded by anything more serious than her wedding gown and last-minute preparations for their impending nuptials.

He did not like to see her so solemn. And although he could not help her if he did not know what was the matter, he knew he could fix the immediate problem. Without warning, he scooped her up and ran with her across the lawn to the pirate ship tree house. Before she could stop gasping and squealing with laughter at the same time, he had hauled her over his shoulder as if she were nothing heavier than his frock coat. He then climbed the ladder up a three-hundred-year-old oak and into the magical world of a two-level tree house fashioned like the quarterdeck of a pirate ship.

Dair lifted Rory onto the boards, and she crawled away from the ladder and the long drop to the ground, to allow him space to hoist himself up to the safety of the wooden floor. Once secure, she sat up on her knees and took a peek over the side of the painted railing at the view.

"Oh! How delightful! You can see everything, from the terrace to the pavilion and across to the jetty. I wish I'd come up here sooner. Though this ship seems to have appeared from nowhere. It wasn't here last summer. Perhaps it was sailed in on a cloud by a band of fairy pirates and got stuck? What do you think?"

"This is only my second time aboard. Kinross had it built for the Roxton brood, just after Easter. But I like your explanation better." He joined her, crossed arms leaning lightly on the railing. "The boys will be here soon enough, and will head straight for the gangway to clamber aboard. This pirate ship is all they can talk about!"

He turned from the view and sat with his back up against the rail, long booted legs sprawled out before him. When she joined him, sitting to face him, he took hold of her fingers and gently pressed his lips to the back of her hand. He smiled wistfully.

"We've not had a moment alone since your grandfather toasted to our future happiness, have we? We're forever surrounded by a hive of activity, and I suspect it won't let up until we can run away together after we're married. I know I've been kept occupied going over settlements, estate documents, and discovering precisely what mess my father left for the old Duke and then Roxton to clean up, after he ran off to Barbados! But what about you? Lady Grasby looks to have recovered from her dead faint at our announcement..."

"Oh, but we must feel for her position," Rory said with a smile that mirrored his own. "She is finally breeding, which is such badly wanted news by the family. And what do we do, but spoil her moment in the sunshine by announcing our engagement. She should still be basking in all the attention. As it is, her baby has become secondary to our wedding. So I do have sympathy for her. Though, I could do without her good advice on being a bride, of which I've had a pailful." Her smile was impish. "The only topic she has *not* broached is the wedding night, and I am certain her restraint is only due to my brother's presence. Poor Harvel would faint from mortification if he ever suspected she would dare try to give me advice about *that*."

"I can't imagine what she could possibly confide in you," he commented with a chuckle.

She misconstrued his meaning and blushed.

"I'm certain I still have much to learn—"

"I meant her advice, Delight."

"Oh! I see..."

He moved closer to lift her chin so she had to look in his eyes.

"What is it? You have not been yourself since yesterday. Have you had second thoughts about—"

"—marrying you? *Never!*"

"—giving yourself to me on the island. Perhaps you would have preferred to wait until our wedding night?"

"Oh no!" She was emphatic. "How could you think that? It is a day I will never forget." Her smile was bashful. "I'm sure every girl dreams her first time will be just as glorious as mine. And you made it so for me."

"Thank you. That means the world to me. *You* mean the world to me."

"As you do to me..."

She shifted to lean in to kiss him gently. First the stubbled underside of his chin, then his throat, on up over his square jaw, across to his cheek, then the bridge of his strong nose, and finally his wide brow. Teasingly, she avoided his mouth. She punctuated these light butterfly kisses with conversation that was just as playful.

"If Silla does try and give me advice, I shall tell her politely that I do not need her wifely wisdom, because I cannot wait to make love, *again*. But this time, with my *husband*. She will fall into another dead faint, but that can't be helped, because I will not lie. In fact, it is most distressing you are staying at the big house and I am here. From my bedroom window I can see Swan Island and it is a constant reminder of our time alone. And then I have the most wicked remembrances of us making love. Of you on your back on the floor of the temple, looking up at me astride you, and I lie amongst the pillows of my bed, alone, unable to sleep for wanting you. If you were staying here, you could row me over there at night, no one in the house the wiser, and we could—"

He caught her face between his hands and kissed her passionately, no longer able to withstand the torture of her barely-there kisses, her banter, and the sweet delicious vanilla scent of her skin. The memories of them making love in the temple, of her straddling him, enjoying him, her straw-blonde waist-length hair falling about her shoulders, and then the imagery she conjured up of her lying in her bed alone, naked and wanting him, was all too much. It sent him beyond reason. He had to make love to her, taste her, fill her, there and then. He no longer cared they were trespassing in a children's tree house and that those children were due to storm the ladder at any moment. He was sure there was time enough.

But as much as Rory returned his kisses and wanted him to make love to her, she was not so lost in the moment that she was unaware of their surroundings and the potential for a scandalous predicament. So she was the one who broke their fervent kissing. The instant she did, he stopped.

He stared at her, short of breath and wondering what he had done, but it only took a few seconds before he came to a sense of his surroundings. He was not only acutely embarrassed for allowing himself to be caught up in the moment in such a place, but it would now require some time for him to return his heated body to its resting equilibrium. To this end he thought it wise to put a little distance between them and he sat back against the wall of the ship. Pulling his windswept hair back off his face, he turned his thoughts to the account books for Fitzstuart Hall, the vast income that had been accruing over the years from his father's sugar plantations, and the unexpectedly welcome news he was now, on the eve of his marriage, exceedingly wealthy. He had to salute his father for having the foresight to withhold his inheritance until marriage, and Rory for giving his life direction and joy.

"That was my fault," Rory apologized, feeling awkward. "I should not have enticed you with my vulgar and silly—"

"It was not vulgar," he interrupted, coming out of his abstraction, physical frustration making him sound harsh. "And never silly. We should always be playful with each other. But you were right to stop me. This is not the place. Now, won't you tell me what it is that has been bothering you? Perhaps that will be enough to pour cold water on my ardor?" He chuckled. "Unless, that is, you do have some cold water to hand!?"

Rory frowned. "Cold water...?" When he looked away, a ready

flush to his face, dawning wonder opened wide her blue eyes. She sighed her understanding. "It is so different for men, is it not? We females can more easily hide our frustrations so no one need know, but for men—Is it painful if you do not find release?"

Acute embarrassment mixed with the studiousness of her enquiry made him burst out laughing.

"Oh, Delight. I do love you so! Yes. In a way it is painful. But more uncomfortable than anything else, and quite embarrassing if not dealt with. He tends to have a mind of his own, and never more than when I see you! So. If you don't mind. I'd like not to keep him center stage. Is there something bothering you that we should discuss before our wedding?" He chucked her under the chin. "We must share our worries as well as our blessings. It's the only way a marriage will work."

She nodded. "Yes. Yes, you are right. I am in a bit of a quandary." She again scrambled to sit before him, layers of her petticoats tucked up under her knees, closing the gap he had put between them. "Grasby was to help me find a solution so that I need not bother you with it. You have been so caught up in business affairs, and I know how much you hate being indoors, that you do not need any more aggravation—"

"Rory, let me stop you there. Firstly, I will never be caught up, be it with business or anything else, that you should ever feel you cannot interrupt me. Secondly, you will never aggravate me. Thirdly, I understand you have been used to going to Grasby for assistance and guidance, he is your brother after all. But I hope now we are engaged and soon will be married, you would be comfortable enough to come to me first." He smiled crookedly. "That sounded as if I am envious of Grasby, didn't it? To own a truth, I am, a little. Mary—my sister—would never think to come to me for advice. I guess because she is older than me, and was married off while I was still at Harrow... Let me guess your quandary... You are worried about your grandfather and how we shall all go on from here, now your allegiance is to me—"

Rory interrupted him.

"How did—"

"Because I know you. And because I don't want you to be troubled, Shrewsbury and I have called a truce. I respect the fact he loves you very much and only wants what is best for you. He has come to the realization that he and I share that common goal. I also know you are concerned about the Royal visit to your grandfather's pinery taking place a week after we are married, when we should be enjoying the start of our honeymoon. I assume you have been wondering how best to tell me?"

Rory's blue eyes grew round.

"How did—"

It was his turn to interrupt, and with a smug smile. But he couldn't keep up the pretense of oracle for long, and shook his head at her look of wonderment.

"Also your grandfather. We were discussing settlements and the like with Roxton and two dreary men of business, and I must have been fidgeting in my chair. Believe me, Delight, three hours stuck in a library surrounded by wall-to-wall books almost undid me! I was ready to throw myself through a closed window, climb the bookcases, anything to get myself into fresh air! Shrewsbury knows me well. So he called me away for a stroll on the terrace, to have a cheroot, while the Duke dealt with an interruption from his surveyor. Your grandfather graciously asked my permission for you to attend the presentation of the Talbot Pineapple to Their Majesties. After all, it was you who cultivated it..."

He let the sentence hang, waiting for her reaction, and to add something to the discussion, but when Rory remained mute, waiting for him to continue, he threw up a hand and then pulled her to him.

"Good God, Rory. What did you think I would say? No? After all your months and months of hard work growing the jolly thing! Other than Portland's gardener Speechly, who else is the foremost cultivator in the kingdom of such a majestic fruit? No one but you. I know how much this pineapple means to you, and to your grandfather, who watched you put your heart and soul into his pinery. The second time I met you, you dropped a gardening treatise at my feet—"

"You remember that?"

"Remember it? It is burned into here," he said, jabbing his temple. "I'd given your grandfather my word I would not let on I remembered anything about our fortuitous meeting at Romney's studio. So here was I wanting to scoop you up in my arms with the joy of having found you again, and forcing myself to pretend I had no idea who you were. I can even remember the name of the book. A first for me. *A General Treatise of Husbandry and Gardening* by Richard Gradey—"

"*Bradley*. Richard Bradley."

"Yes, well, him. So *of course* I know how much it means to you to present the Talbot Pineapple to Their Majesties. You will be there; we both will." He chuckled. "Besides, who better to make the presentation than Lady Fitzstuart, wife of a descendant of Charles the Second, who was the first monarch to be presented with a pineapple—"

"—by John Rose. I've seen the painting by Danckerts."

"Yes. I suggested to your grandfather that he have the auspicious occasion painted, too, and by Romney, and that a second copy of the painting be presented to His Majesty. Shrewsbury thought it a splendid idea. I've requested a copy also, to be hung in the Great Room at Fitzs-tuart Hall. My mother will be impressed."

When she threw her arms about him, he kissed her swiftly, but did not allow himself to be distracted by the feel of her in his arms. Reluctantly, he disentangled himself, as he had more that needed to be said before their big day, and before Roxton's brood arrived with Cedric and came aboard.

"We need to be in accord on an important aspect of our marriage, Rory. When we marry, spiritually and legally the husband and wife become one, and the husband is that one. But that is not how we are going to conduct ourselves as husband and wife. Do you understand me? I have been witness to that sort of marriage—it is degrading and destructive. You are to always be you, and I, well you are going to have to suffer me as I am! And we will make important decisions *together*. You were the one who told me what you consider important in a marriage: Love. Respect. Friendship. Honesty. Trust. And I believe that sincerely. Do you understand?"

Rory snuggled into his embrace and nodded her agreement, adding cheekily in a meek voice, "Of course, my lord. Whatever you say, my lord."

"Desist, wicked creature!" He kissed the top of her hair, adding, "I will tell you here and now, so you can be comfortable and enjoy the ceremony and wedding breakfast without the worry of wondering about our postponed honeymoon. We are spending the first two nights as husband and wife on Swan Island."

Rory gasped. "Truly? How are we to manage rowing over there after the wedding breakfast without our family knowing? Without the Duke knowing? You must have a plan!"

He shook his head, grinning. "No. No. No, dear heart. Nothing so underhanded. Though, I grant the prospect of whisking you off to a forbidden island is a more romantic notion. No, Delight. It is a gift from my cousin, your godmother." Suddenly emotion got the better of him and he swallowed hard and took a moment to collect himself. "She —She has gifted us the leasehold for one week a year for our lifetime. She was delighted when I said we would be honored to continue the tradition begun by her and the fifth Duke. And she has granted my request to hang our story in thread, when we feel the time is right, above the fireplace on the fourth and final wall of the temple."

Rory was too overcome to speak. But there was no need for words. Both were awed by such a gift. And then Dair heard sounds of activity, and the distinct high-pitched crescendo of unbridled excitement that only children can manage. He made movements to leave and helped Rory to stand.

"Time we jumped ship, Delight, before we are boarded and taken captive. Louis and Gus are fierce pirates; so they keep telling me. Louis has even threatened to make me walk the plank should he catch me!"

"You should let him. Nothing would make that little boy happier."

"Yes. Yes, you're right, of course. I will." Dair winked at her. "But I won't make it easy for him." He drew her into his arms. "That which is hard won is all the more precious for the struggle..."

There was the scuff and scramble of many feet competing on the ladder. Whispers and giggles followed. Then a young voice blurted out,

"*Pauh*! Kissing. Gus! *Gus*. Look! It's disgu—disgu—it's *awful*!"

"Louis! Move!" Frederick ordered his younger brother and squeezed past him on the ladder.

The eldest son and heir to the Duke of Roxton then poked his head up into the tree house, took a look around, saw the two people his grandmother was looking for, then squeezed past Louis again to go halfway down the ladder. Meanwhile, Gus passed him and joined his twin, Louis, who had moved up a rung and was determined to enter the tree house regardless of the disgusting sight before his eyes. The twins scrambled up into the quarterdeck and whipped out their painted wooden cutlasses that had been secured in a colored silk sash around their waists. Gus even wore an eye patch. Both pointed their weapons at the two prisoners.

"We've found them, Mema!" Frederick shouted down to Antonia, who was with half a dozen upper servants at the base of the ladder, his sister Juliana in her arms. All were looking skywards into the boughs of the old oak. "They're here, Mema! They're kissing! And Louis is going to throw up!"

THIRTY-TWO

THE WEDDING CEREMONY OF MAJOR LORD FITZSTUART, HEIR TO the Strathsay earldom, to Miss Aurora Talbot, granddaughter of the Earl of Shrewsbury, was due to commence in just under three hours. Every person within the Roxton ducal household, from His Grace down to the scullery maid, and beyond into the estate and village, was in a heightened state of anticipation. Silverware and woodwork were polished to the highest sheen. Floors as well as children were scrubbed. Hot baths were drawn for the family and guests. Valets and lady's maids preened their masters and mistresses, while maids and footmen scurried up and down the backstairs, like ants, to fulfill last-minute requests. Bouquets of flowers and summer fruits filled porcelain urns in drawing rooms, state rooms and the tables set for the wedding breakfast to come. Garlands adorned the Roxton Chapel.

Nothing and no one had been left to chance under the expert guidance and organizational skills of the Duchess of Roxton and the Duchess of Kinross. That is, except for the mother and the sister of the groom. It was almost the eleventh hour and the whereabouts of the Countess of Strathsay, and the Lady Mary Cavendish remained unknown. The last that anyone had heard from them was a missive stating their intention to arrive two days before the wedding. Those two days had come and gone. If the Major was concerned, it was for their well-being. But barring misadventure or death, the wedding would go ahead without them. Nothing and no one was going to stop him marrying Rory on the specified day and at the specified time.

So it was an enormous relief to the entire household when an unidentified carriage spotted on the Treat road was confirmed to contain her ladyship and her daughter. An outside servant rode at full gallop to report the affirmative. The carriage was covered in dust, the horses looked to be hacks harnessed for far too long, and there were only two outriders. Handed down to firm ground by liveried footmen, the Countess, her daughter, and their respective lady's maids, were in such a state of anxiety that their wails of lament could be heard across the broad entrance steps, on up to the Sea Green salon on the first floor. In this salon, those guests who had traveled some distance and been put up for the night at the Bull and Feather at Alston, were being treated to a pre-wedding levee. But the commotion was such that a few guests drifted over to the sash windows to take a peek at what and who had created such a fuss, and on this of all days.

Shown into one of the downstairs withdrawing rooms, and given refreshment while their rooms were made ready, and baths drawn, the Duchess of Roxton greeted them with open arms, pleased to see them safe and well, and just in time! Word was sent up to the Major that his mother and sister had safely arrived. But it took many moments for both ladies to be calm enough to construct an intelligible sentence, and it was left to Mary to speak for both of them, the Countess collapsing onto a sofa with barely enough strength to turn her wrist to fan herself.

From what Deb Roxton could deduce, their journey from Bucking-hamshire into Hampshire was fraught with setbacks before it began. Lady Mary's daughter Theodora was nursing a fever that would not abate. And so Mary had been in two minds whether to leave her daughter in the care of her nurse, but was finally convinced by the Countess's physician there was nothing serious to worry about. And so Lady Mary and the Countess had finally departed for Hampshire. And that was only the beginning of their troubles.

Ten miles into their journey their carriage broke an axle. They were forced to put up at an overcrowded inn for the night while the second-best carriage was sent for. The wheelwright of the village was himself too ill to attend to his duties. It was while their carriage was being unloaded and the portmanteaux secured on the second carriage that they were robbed, and in daylight! The Countess was forced to hand over a diamond brooch and hairpins, the Lady Mary to part with her sapphire earrings. Fortunately, they had managed to hide their jewelry box and guineas in the strongbox secret compartment under a seat. And if this wasn't enough of a trial, another ten miles on, the road was blocked by an overturned bullock wagon. More delays and more drama ensued.

The Duchess listened patiently to so many unnecessary details that it took her more than a few moments to sort the inconsequential from what was important. Still, she managed to make all the appropriate noises of concern and have both ladies calm by the time a footman came to inform her the Countess and Lady Mary's rooms were now ready. Baths were drawn, portmanteaux were being unpacked, and gowns prepared with the help of several of the maids not needed downstairs at this time. With the ceremony only a handful of hours away, the Duchess advised there was not another minute to waste. She herself had to be excused. There was still so much to be done.

It was then that the Countess came to renewed life, and leapt off the sofa as if she had seen a mouse, or a spider had run across her plump wrist. She demanded to see her son *at once*. She had correspondence requiring his urgent attention. There was also a letter for the Duke, and from the same source. There was no time to lose. Indeed, she was of the opinion that once her son read the contents, it was quite possible his marriage would have to be postponed, perhaps indefinitely.

To highlight the urgency of this demand, she searched for the slit in her petticoats that gave access to the pocket tied about her waist. Having found it, she struggled to pull out not one, but two letters, one quite thick. And these she held up high, as if she was displaying aloft a prize pheasant shot from the skies.

That these letters were news to Lady Mary, too, was evident by her astonishment.

"Mamma? I cannot believe you waited until now to divulge this. Why did you not say something in the carriage? Indeed why not tell me when we were still at Fitzstuart Hall?"

The Countess waved her fan at her daughter as if she was an annoying summer gnat.

"What was there to tell you, Mary? The letters have nothing to do with you. They are for Fitzstuart and the Duke." She showed the letters to the Duchess, as if she was offering them to her. "They must be delivered, and at once. They are from the Indies, I am sure of it by the—"

"Thank you, Cousin," Deb Roxton said calmly, despite her heart taking the oddest leap and beating harder. Though she wanted to snatch them away from her, she slowly took the letters before the Countess could protest and take them back. Without looking at them, she slid the two packets between the silken folds of her blue damask petticoats and into her pocket. "I will give them to His Grace at once."

"As Fitzstuart's mother, I should be the one to—"

"Oh, no, Cousin. That would never do," the Duchess said gravely. "It would be too upsetting and not quite the thing for the mother of the groom to disturb her son so close to the ceremony. He is with his male friends, who are keeping vigil with him in his last hours as an unmarried man. I dare not go near that end of the house myself. Only male servants and male relatives are permitted to trespass. I'm sure you understand, Cousin Charlotte. No doubt your son has commenced being dressed. Of course, I will send word of your arrival," she continued, gently taking the Countess by the elbow and guiding her from the room to the double sweeping staircase. "You and Mary have had such a long taxing journey that a few extra moments in your room to settle must surely be welcome." She nodded to a footman, who came forward from his post. "James will show you to your rooms. And word will be sent when it is time to assemble for the walk to the family chapel. It has only recently been refurbished, and I am sure the Duke is keen to know your opinion on the finishes to the family pew and to the pulpit. He read your long letter of advice on the matter, and showed it to the architect."

The Countess was suitably diverted. "Roxton did? He is? Then I will be sure to offer it to him at the wedding breakfast. Though how I am to take in the new interior when my nerves are frayed to bits, what with the trauma of the journey, and my eldest son marrying without me, his mamma, not so much as setting eyes on his bride!" She gripped Deb's arm. "Has everything been done to make certain she did not coerce him with her feminine wiles—that this marriage is what *he* wants? So many unsuitable females have tried to put their talons into Fitzstuart. It takes a vigilant eye to stave them off. Men have no notion of the wickedness that surrounds them, wickedness dressed up to entice and ensnare. I have already lost one son, entrapped into marriage with the daughter of a nabob—"

"Charles was not entrapped, Mama. He eloped with Miss Strang. And her father is not a nabob, he is a Duke in the Scottish peerage, and married to Cousin Duchess."

"Mary! I know well enough who and *what* that man is. I have yet to recover from the shocking fact Antonia remarried, not only beneath her, but a bronzed brute who is so much younger than she. It is simply scandalous!"

Lady Mary's violet eyes widened at her mother's complete lack of awareness that she was casting aspersions on the Duchess's mother-in-law, and in her presence. But Deb was used to the Countess's tactless and often acidic remarks. And while she was angered by them, there was no time for her to be bothered offering a spirited defense, particularly when it would only delay her ladyship from following the footman upstairs. Besides, she had the anticipated satisfaction of the Countess being further scandalized, and couldn't wait to see her reaction, upon learning the Duchess of Kinross was pregnant with her much younger husband's heir.

But Deb did have empathy for Lady Mary, who looked bedraggled and brow-beaten, after spending a week in her mother's company and then three days closed up with her in a carriage. So when the Countess was finally persuaded that what she needed was a hot bath and an equally hot cup of tea in her rooms, and followed the footman up the stairs, Deb detained Mary with a hand on her arm.

"I am sorry Teddy could not be with us. Perhaps, when she is much better, you could both come and stay for a month or so?"

Lady Mary's eyes lit up at the prospect.

"Are you certain? What about the new baby?"

Deb smoothed a hand across her rounded belly. "Oh, he or she, or both—"

Lady Mary gasped. "Another set of twins, Deborah? Are you sure?"

"No. It will be what it will be. And you and Teddy coming to stay won't change that. So please give the offer serious consideration, won't you?"

Lady Mary nodded, sudden tears in her eyes. She kissed her sister-in-law's cheek. "Thank you. You and Roxton have been so kind and generous since Sir Gerald's death. I hardly know where to begin to thank—"

"Mary! Hush! No thanks. Please. You were married to my brother. You are Julian's cousin. You and Teddy are family. Now go and ready yourself for your brother's wedding and we can talk more tomorrow, when all the fuss has died down."

Lady Mary nodded, sniffed back tears and forced a smile. Her husband had died two years ago, in a hunting accident, in what was whispered were mysterious circumstances, but which she refused to countenance. What was not in dispute, having failed to produce a male heir the estate was lost to her and her daughter, leaving them practically destitute. Still, she did not dwell on her circumstances. What was uppermost in her mind was her brother, more particularly his bride. To this end she put her hand on the Duchess's silken sleeve and asked in confidence,

"Deborah, tell me truly: Is she deserving of my brother? She is a Talbot to be sure, and that counts for something, but to me that is as nothing if she is not in love with him."

"She is perfect for him. You will love her, Mary, as we all do. They love each other very much."

"Then I will be happy for them, and welcome her as a sister."

The Duchess and Lady Mary exchanged another kiss on the cheek,

and Lady Mary followed her mother up the stairs, while Deborah
bustled off to find her husband. She had left the Duke talking with his
mother in the library. She prayed the letters in her pocket did not
bring ill tidings. Whatever news was contained within their folded
pages, Deb was determined it would not spoil Dair and Rory's
big day.

DAIR WAS STARING CRITICALLY AT HIS REFLECTION. HIS VALET WAS
to one side of the long looking glass, his two best friends, mute, on the
other. All three were staring at him. Dressing for his wedding had taken
some time and was conducted in solemn silence. Lord Grasby and Mr.
Cedric Pleasant were dressed and ready, and upon being given admit-
tance to their friend's closet, found him as he was, dressing almost
complete and before the long looking glass.

The groom had chosen a silk suit of dark burnished gold, almost
chocolate brown, depending on the light, with matching breeches,
waistcoat, and frock coat. The front of the waistcoat and its pocket
flaps, the lapels and collar of the frock coat, the knee bands of the tight-
fighting breeches, and the fabric buttons to all three garments were
heavily embroidered with delicate arrangements of lavender, rosemary,
dianthus blooms and arum leaves.

It was a stunning ensemble, completed with white clocked stockings over muscular calves, highly-polished black leather shoes with a
low heel, diamond buckles to shoes and breeches, and frothy layers of
lace at firm wrists, with matching lace in the white cravat about the
strong neck.

As well as being uncharacteristically clean-shaven, the groom's hair
was pomaded and scraped back out of his eyes. A wide ribbon of white
silk was chosen by his valet to tie off his hair, but Dair had his own
ideas. He gave Reynolds a much narrower ribbon of lavender silk. This
was obediently tied up in a neat bow, without Reynolds batting an
eyelid; he rightly assuming the ribbon had once belonged to his
master's bride. And while it might not look as elegant as the white silk
ribbon he had chosen, to Reynolds the romantic sentiment brought a
tear to his eye.

It only remained for Dair to be shrugged into his frock coat, slip on
his gold signet ring, which he rarely wore except on the most formal of
occasions, and collect up the various gentleman's accoutrements that
belonged in his pockets: Silver pocket watch, white linen mono-
grammed handkerchief and silver tinderbox.

Yet he lingered before his reflection and tweaked at the lace under his shaved chin as if all was not satisfactory.

"It's all a bit too much, isn't it?"

The valet looked worried. Lord Grasby and Mr. Cedric Pleasant grinned and shook their heads.

"Not a bit of it, dear fellow. You're getting married. You're supposed to look like a prize fighting cock!"

"Fighting cock? Ha! More like a peacock. And I feel as weak as a bloody blancmange!"

"All perfectly natural," Grasby replied, still grinning.

He hadn't stopped grinning since breakfast. He grinned through a quick game of billiards with the Duke, Dair and Cedric, all to calm the groom and make him forget what was to come. He grinned through the impromptu toasts, and even grinned while smoking a cheroot, his first. He just couldn't help himself. If his face didn't ache, his throat did from imbibing too much cognac mixed with tobacco smoke, and all this before midday. He was just so happy that his best friend and his sister were to be husband and wife.

"And while my limbs feel as wobbly as a pudding, my head pounds," Dair grumbled. "It's as if I've just been told I'm destined for the gallows, not the chapel. And I don't want to feel like this at all."

"Yes. Yes. All quite normal," Grasby assured him and gave Mr. Cedric Pleasant a nudge in the ribs so he would add his assurances.

"What? Oh! Er, yes, all perfectly normal," Cedric Pleasant added. "Not that I've ever been in your dire—I mean euphoric—condition, Dair. But I'm told by reliable sources that feeling God-awful is perfectly natural for a groom on his wedding day."

Dair's head snapped round at his two best friends and he glared at them and growled, "You're both enjoying this, aren't you?"

Cedric Pleasant started to shake his head when Grasby laughed out loud.

"Yes! Yes we are! Why not? The tables are quite turned, dear fellow. I've been there and done that. And who better than my best friend, and soon to be brother-in-law, to experience the unmitigated terror as the bell tolls the last hour of a groom's freedom. I was unequivocally petrified, I don't mind telling you!"

"Don't worry, Dair," Cedric assured him. "Grasby and I will be right beside you the entire ceremony, to prop you up, should you falter."

"I won't falter, and I won't need propping up. And I am not terrified! I want to marry Aurora. I love her. You both know that, don't you?"

His two best friends lost their smiles and nodded.

"Yes. Of course."

"Yes. We know that. Wouldn't let you marry my sister otherwise. Come on, let's get you into your frock coat and downstairs," Grasby added, a nod to the valet, who stepped forward with the frock coat opened wide. "The Duke must be wondering where we are by now…"

Dair nodded. He allowed himself to be shrugged into his silk frock coat without argument, and remained docile while Reynolds fussed with the fit at the shoulders and tugged gently on the skirts so that the silk folded nicely. He even allowed the man to take one last look at him from hair ribbon to shoe buckle, before turning away from the looking glass.

"Thank you, John, I'll take it from here," he said quietly to his valet, who nodded and with a bow retired to stand on the other side of the dressing table.

"I have it," Grasby said when Dair started to pat the pockets of his frock coat as if he had misplaced something. He patted the inner pocket of his silver spangled embroidered waistcoat. Contained within it was a small velvet box that had nestled inside it Rory's gold wedding band.

"And I have your cheroot case," Cedric offered. He smiled kindly. "For after the service, at the breakfast. If you need to slip outside…"

A sharp single knock to the outer door had all three gentlemen looking that way. Farrier poked his head into the room.

"Just your vedette, m'lord. Come to tell you that this is definitely the last call-to-arms. Your piquet of His Grace, with Lord Alston, Lord Henri-Antoine and Sir John Cavendish, are all waitin' downstairs to take you on through to the chapel."

The gentlemen silently filed out of Dair's rooms. On the landing, Dair sent Grasby and Cedric on ahead so he could have a quiet word with Farrier. His best friends weren't going anywhere. They continued down the sweeping staircase but only far enough so their friend remained within eyesight, if not within earshot.

"Very smart, Mr. Farrier."

The batman, dressed in a new suit of fine blue linen, courtesy of his master, made him a bow, then held up his silver hook with a smile. "All spit and polished and gleaming, m'lord."

Dair smiled, and in a move that had the batman swallowing the emotion back down his throat, he gave Farrier's upper arm a squeeze as he said, "You've always been there for me, Mr. Farrier. Whether it be running through a hail of enemy fire, helping me escape a painter's studio, or watching me go up before parson. Thank you."

"Always, m'lord."

"I wanted to reassure you. I may be getting married and rusticating on the family farm, but it doesn't mean I won't have need of you. I'll have an estate to run, and I need someone who knows me, whom I can trust implicitly. A home steward of sorts, to run my private household. To see her ladyship and I have everything we need. Someone to oversee that our family—and I include Jamie and the Bankses in my definition of the word—have the privacy we need. Her ladyship and I are in accord on this, and we both want you to take on the job. That's if you're up for it." Dair smiled. "That's if you don't think you'll be bored in such employment."

"It would be an honor and a privilege, m'lord. Always saw m'self retirin' to the country someday."

Dair laughed and nodded, and became serious. Something else was weighing on his mind. "Keep an eye on the boy and his grandparents for me. While they'll be accorded every welcome, there are those who won't be pleased to see them here." He was thinking specifically of his mother and the straight-backed sticklers of her ilk.

Farrier knew his lordship was talking about his natural son Jamie and the boy's grandparents, Mr. and Mrs. Banks.

"Don't you worry about a thing, m'lord. I looked in on 'em yesterday evening. They'd settled in nice and snug at the Bull and Feather. And then this morning, Her Grace sent a carriage to bring 'em here, and I went with it."

"Did she? That was kind of her. And of you. Thank you."

"And Her Grace and me, we put our heads together about the seating arrangements—"

"Her Grace of Roxton and-and you—*put your heads together…?*"

"Beggin' your lordship's pardon—the Duchess of Kinross. Her Grace didn't want to trouble you. Said you had enough on your mind. So it was decided, I would sit with Master Jamie and his grandparents in the chapel, and later, to sit at the wedding breakfast with the Bankses, while Master Jamie is to sit with Her Grace of Kinross at a table with Lord Henri-Antoine, Sir John Cavendish, and Lord Alston."

Dair was surprised but also relieved. "Well then, there's nothing for me to concern myself about…"

"Nothin' whatsoever, m'lord. You just ease up and enjoy the moment with her ladyship. That's all you've got to do." Farrier grinned. "It ain't like you are ever goin' to do this again!"

"Too bloody right, Bill! Never."

Farrier came to attention and saluted his Major. He then stuck out his only hand. "I wish you both all the happiness in the world, m'lord."

Dair returned the salute and then took his batman's hand in a firm grasp. "Thank you, Mr. Farrier."

"Dair! Dair? Oi! Fitzstuart!"

The shouts came from the first landing. It was Grasby and Mr. Cedric Pleasant.

"For God's sake, Alisdair! Get a move on or the bride will be there before us!"

This last exclamation came from the Duke, and it had Dair, with his batman following, down the stairs in an instant, to the applause of his wedding troop.

THIRTY-THREE

Earlier, before the Duke of Roxton joined the groom and his party and headed for the chapel, he was having a quiet respite with his mother in the splendor of his library, his favorite room in the ancestral palace.

There was something about being surrounded by floor-to-ceiling leather tomes and the paraphernalia that went with such a magnificent setting that comforted the Duke: The painted plaster ceiling, the large twin globes, one of terrestrial bodies, the other celestial, the large mahogany desk, the comfortable sofas and deep chairs, and the plush carpets. It reminded him of his happy childhood, of his father behind the big mahogany desk writing, while his mother sat curled in a wingchair, or propped on the chaise, always in a cloud of soft petticoats, with her shoes kicked off, and always reading.

Today was no different. Antonia had her stockinged feet up on the chaise, sipping weak tea; a vision of loveliness in a gown à *l'anglaise* of delicate Indienne cotton. But never in all his days would Roxton have foreseen his mother in these surroundings pregnant with another Duke's child, and at her age. He thought she would always be married to his father... He missed his father's acerbic wit, his omniscient eye, and his company. He wondered what he would make of it all. Particularly on this day, with their cousin Alisdair being married in the family chapel, and to the granddaughter of his best friend from Eton days. He was certain his father would approve of his goddaughter marrying the Major, and no doubt make some quip that she had tripped him up with her stick, that sent their cousin head over heels in love with the little beauty.

He shook such maudlin thoughts away the instant a footman admitted his duchess. His face split into a grin as she strode up the long room with her familiar firm tread, resplendent in blue damask petticoats, her rich auburn hair swept up off her lovely neck and dressed with strands of pearls. She never failed to look majestic, and like her walk, took each pregnancy in her confident stride. He thanked God every day that she had good pregnancies and easy deliveries (if any delivery could be called such) because the thought of losing her in childbirth, or at any other time, would surely make his life meaningless.

"Your face is remarkably transparent to your thoughts, your Grace," Deborah teased her husband, and kissed him. "I didn't go into an early labor dealing with Charlotte and Mary, if that is what is meant by that look in your eye. And I managed to send them up to dress, without Charlotte demanding to see you. So for that I deserve another kiss... Thank you. But I do now need to sit for a bit before we head off to the chapel."

She broke from her husband's embrace and eased herself into the closest wingchair. Roxton quickly placed a footstool in front of her, put up her feet, slipped off her shoes, and sat on the edge of the footstool to rub her stockinged feet.

"Thank you, Maman," she said to Antonia, when handed a cup of tea. She sipped at the tea and shifted against the cushions, a smile at the Duke. "And thank *you*, dearest. You had best have another cup of tea yourself, or perhaps something stronger. I have invited Mary and Teddy to stay—"

"When and for how long?" Roxton interrupted.

"—for a month, as soon as she can arrange it. Teddy is presently still at Fitzstuart Hall nursing a fever. Nothing serious."

"A *month*? I think I will have something stronger! But I am pleased Teddy is not in any danger. A pity she could not join us..."

Daughter- and mother-in-law exchanged a smile at the Duke's expense as they watched him pour out a snifter of brandy.

"That was kind of you, Deborah," Antonia said, and to tease her son, added with practiced naivety, "But is a month long enough...?"

"Yes! Yes it is, Maman. What with the baby due in two months time—Oh! How droll!" he added when both women giggled behind their fans.

"*Mon chou*, I am sure Mary gave up her infatuation for you a long time ago."

Deb glanced at the Duke but addressed her mother-in-law. "I

wouldn't be too sure of that, Maman. Sometimes, when she thinks no one is looking, Mary will gaze at him like this." She opened her eyes wide and fluttered her eyelashes in an exaggerated fashion that had Antonia giggling.

"P-poor Mary!"

"Stop it! Both of you!" Roxton demanded. Blushing, he threw back the brandy and set down the tumbler. "The poor woman has lost her husband and is practically destitute. The least we can do is offer her some comfort in these surroundings."

"What a marvelous idea, my love," Deborah agreed, a knowing smile exchanged with Antonia. "Then I will make the necessary arrangements and let Mary know you have extended her an invitation."

"You could have her stay on and send for Theodora when she is well...?" Antonia suggested. She put aside her teacup on its saucer and looked up at her son. "I will have Mary stay with me for a few days after the wedding, and then, when we know her daughter she is on her way, I will return her to you."

"That is a generous offer, Maman."

"It is nothing of the sort, Julian," Antonia corrected him with a light laugh. "Me I am lonely and bored, and even Mary's company is preferable to that!"

"I had the archery boards set up for the children on the lawn just beyond the terrace," Deb told them conversationally. "They'll be as tightly wound as clocks after the ceremony, so best they run around while we are enjoying the wedding breakfast." She looked at Antonia. "I thought perhaps Harry and Jack might do the honors of keeping an eye on them."

"After all the years I kept an eye on them while they fired off arrows at who-knows-what, and whom! Let them try and get out of it!" the Duke said, only half-jokingly. He glanced at the mantel clock and then checked his gold pocket watch. "We'd best be getting ready to move. I know who's as tightly wound as a clock at this moment, and that's Dair. The poor fellow is quite frozen with nerves. If he faints during the ceremony, I wouldn't be at all surprised."

"And so it is with large vigorous males," Antonia added with a sigh of remembrance. "Your father he was the same—"

"What? Papa was frozen with fear at the prospect of marrying you? I don't believe it!"

Antonia sat up tall. "Julian, you think I would lie about such a thing? Your poor father he was one big block of frozen water I tell you!"

Roxton gave a bark of laughter and shook his head. "*Mon Dieu*, I wish I'd been there to see that!"

Antonia's green eyes twinkled and she smiled a secret smile, saying quietly, "In a small way, you were, *mon cher*."

"Oh! I almost forgot," Deborah said spontaneously into the silence between mother and son, which moved time on and cleared the Duke's furrowed brow. She had remembered the two letters in her pocket, and wished she had not. She gave them to her husband, saying, a worried glance at Antonia as Roxton sat at his desk and put the two sealed packets before him, "Please tell me, Julian, that these letters will make no difference to today's arrangements; to the happiness of the couple about to be married."

Both letters were from the Indies. Both were addressed to the Duke of Roxton. Why both had been sent to Fitzstuart Hall in Buckinghamshire, and not here, to Treat in Hampshire, he could only guess at. But both were vastly different. One letter was sealed with a red wax seal, impressed with the coat of arms of the earls of Strathsay, and in handwriting he recognized as belonging to that of his great uncle, Theophilus, Earl of Strathsay. He had no hesitation in opening this letter. He read the two pages, while his wife and mother waited patiently, if anxiously, for him to tell them its contents.

It was indeed from the Earl, and written some six weeks ago. Roxton skimmed over the words, looking for any sign of what might be to come in the letter with the black seal. But there was no mention of sickness, or symptoms of illness, nothing to suggest the man was in any way not his usual healthy self.

After reading it, Roxton gave it to Antonia to read.

There was news of the sugar plantation, how his two natural children were faring, how proud he was of his son's ability with the cricket bat, and how his daughter was growing into a beautiful accomplished woman. There was even talk of a planned family journey to the Continent, when the twins were a little older, to visit Italy in particular.

Only one paragraph dealt with his legitimate family. And that was all about his second son Charles, his escape to France, and his elopement with a wealthy heiress. There was no mention of Dair. In fact more ink was used up on describing the coming of the hurricane season, and the worrying news from the port that a ship had just docked with talk of a large weather depression headed their way, than there was on his family here in England. And there being no mention of Dair's plans to wed, it was presumed this letter had crossed with Dair's letter to his father informing him.

It was the second letter that bothered the Duke most, and enough for him to turn it over several times before holding it up for his mother to see. This letter was not in his great uncle's fist, and was addressed to both him and Alisdair Fitzstuart, care of Fitzstuart Hall. That it was not sealed with red wax but with an inky black wax, and with an impression the Duke did not immediately recognize, usually meant one thing only: A death in the family.

Seeing the black seal, Antonia was up off the sofa in her stockinged feet, a fist to her mouth, as if to stop herself from crying out. Deborah took one look at her husband, and then one at her mother-in-law, and said aloud what they were both thinking.

"You think it is Lord Strathsay who is-is *dead*, Maman?"

"Julian! Put that letter in a drawer and forget about it this instant!" Antonia demanded. "Do not open it. Do not think about it now. I do not want to know, and he, Dair, does not deserve such appalling news, if it be true, on this of all days! You cannot do this to him!"

Roxton continued to stare at the letter with the black seal, and for so long that Deborah eased herself to her feet and joined Antonia at the Duke's desk.

"Maman-Duchess is in the right, my love. Dair and Rory deserve this to be a day of joy and celebration."

"And what of the day after that, or the day after that one? Surely those days, too, should be joyous?" Roxton asked. "If I don't break the seal today, or tomorrow, when should I? You see my dilemma?"

"If you do not open it, then what does it matter?" Deborah asked in a small voice. "If you put it in a drawer and forgot about it for a-a week, what is a week in Dair's life?"

"A week?" Roxton huffed. "In a week's time the newlyweds will be on their way to Fitzstuart Hall. Should I tell him after he returns from Swan Island, or after his wife presents Their Majesties with the Talbot Pineapple, or perhaps just after that, before they go on to Fitzstuart Hall?"

"Julian! You are being infuriatingly pedantic!" Antonia stated angrily. "Not in a week. In a month. Open it in a month. When Alisdair and Rory their honeymoon it is over. You can grant them that time. And you can think me cold-hearted, but what is a month, if it is true my uncle he is dead? He will still be dead in a month! It is the living we must worry about."

The Duke bit back the retort that less than six months had passed since the dead was all his mother could think about, and now she was telling him to think only of the living? He went to pick up the letter, but she scooped it up first.

Antonia was about to demand that he lock it up, when she realized there was something other than parchment contained within the packet. She held the letter for some moments, weighing it in both hands, and then let her fingers move over the outer parchment, over the string that tied up the letter and held the large bump firm. There was a small heavy object wrapped inside it and from the pattern of indentation, she would hazard a guess the object was a ring.

If it was the ring she assumed it to be, then she knew it well. She had seen it on the finger of her grandfather. Dubbed the Fitzstuart Fire and Ice, the gold ring was set with a large ruby and a diamond of similar size. It had been gifted to her grandfather as a baby in his cradle by his father Charles the Second, to be passed on to the male heir upon succeeding to the title. The ruby represented the blood royal and the diamond was unbreakable; meaning the royal blood bond between father and son, and the male line, could not be broken, regardless of its illegitimate beginnings.

It was only then, feeling the weight of the ring, that the enormity of what was contained within the letter hit her, and so hard she had to sit. She knew then, as surely as if she had read it in ink, that her uncle, her mother's brother, and grandson of Charles the Second, was dead. She did not know how or why, or when, but Theophilus James Fitzstuart, second Earl of Strathsay was no more.

But she would mourn for him another day. Not today. Today was to be a celebration, for the coming together of two people very much in love. For all she knew, her uncle had died over a month ago, such was the time it took for news to travel between the Indies and England. So what was the point of this day becoming one for mourning his death? And then what? The wedding it would have to be called off, postponed at the very least, and Alisdair, what would he have to do then? Journey to Barbados to be assured his father was dead, or wait seven years for him to be declared legally dead? Was that any way to begin a marriage, a new life as husband and wife?

And this is what Antonia told her son and his wife.

She expected her son to argue the morality of withholding such news from their cousin. That he was obligated, as head of the family, and as guardian of the Fitzstuart estate and holdings, to do what was right and proper, regardless of the consequences. And the right thing to do was inform the family as soon as possible. The couple would understand, the guests, too. Dair, indeed the Countess and her daughter, too, all had a right to know the second Earl of Strathsay was dead; that Dair had succeeded to the title and was now third Earl of Strathsay, and third Viscount Fitzstuart.

But the Duke surprised his mother.

"Here, Maman," he said gently, holding out a small brass and enameled key on a short length of gold chain.

Antonia took it unconsciously, so deep was her preoccupation. When she realized she was holding a key she looked up at him with a frown, wondering what she was supposed to do with it. He told her.

"Keep it safe. In a month's time, bring it to me, and I will unlock my desk drawer and break the seal on that letter. And then I will do whatever it is I must do. *Vous acceptez, chère mère?*"

Antonia nodded and slipped on her mules. With her son and his wife, she left the library, the key secured in a pocket under her sheer Indienne cotton petticoats.

The Duke went with the groom and his male attendants to the chapel. The Duchess joined the guests assembled in the Sea Green salon. Antonia took a peek in at the bride, to see how last-minute preparations were progressing. The letter with the black seal was forgotten as the entire congregation watched on misty-eyed and smiling as the beautiful bride joined her handsome groom at the altar of the Roxton chapel.

RORY HAD NEVER LOOKED MORE DELICATELY BEAUTIFUL IN HER pink lavender silk petticoats, her straw-blonde hair upswept and arranged, pinned and beribboned, and with a cascade of curls falling over one bare shoulder. She wore her mother's pearl choker and bracelet, and the pale lavender sapphire betrothal ring. If there was a change in her wardrobe from the night Dair had seen her sitting on the stair of the Gatehouse Lodge, it was her shoes. From her grandfather's home in Chiswick she sent for her pair of specially-made silk shoes with pineapple motifs embroidered across the bridge and heels. They matched her walking stick, and the little pineapple purse, crocheted by Edith for her twenty-first birthday, dangling from her wrist.

When her grandfather brought her to stand beside Dair, she wondered if he was as anxious as she. But she could not bring herself to look at him. The importance of the occasion weighed heavily with her. And being married before their peers, with all eyes upon them, particularly her, made her feel faint. She kept her gaze straight, and could barely feel her fingers about the ivory handle of her walking stick, she was gripping it so tightly. And while she heard the Duke's chaplain speaking, such was the ringing in her ears, she had no idea what he was saying. She doubted then if she would make it through the ceremony without mishap.

And then, within a few seconds, everything changed. She was no longer nervous or worried.

Dair felt for her hand, and gave her fingers a little squeeze.

Rory finally got up the courage to steal a nervous glance up at him. He smiled down at her and winked.

She saw then that he was just as nervous, and yet he had made the effort to put her at ease. And while she continued to appear solemn, as the situation demanded of a bride, she was flooded with such happiness she could not stop smiling on the inside.

A little while later, she dared to glance up at him again. This time she noticed his bronzed silk frock coat with its beautifully embroidered collar, the froth of lace under his clean-shaven chin, and how his hair was dressed formally, and so unlike the Dair she knew. But it was at the ribbon tied in his hair that she stared, and for a good few seconds. Then she quickly glanced away, a hand to her mouth to stop a sob, but she could not stop her tears.

He was wearing the lavender satin ribbon he had taken from her as a spoil of war, the night he had collided with her at Romney's studio. She had quite forgotten about that ribbon, but he had not. It was such a heartfelt gesture she could hardly breathe.

Before she knew what was happening, she had a handkerchief pressed into her hand. But such was her emotional state, she was left bewildered by it, and had no idea what she was supposed to do with it. And then, as if by magic, her chin was lifted and her cheeks gently patted dry. Dair disposed of his handkerchief in a frock coat pocket. He then squared his shoulders and nodded to the chaplain to continue. All of this done with a minimum of fuss, and to the collective sighs of every female in attendance.

The bride and groom survived the rest of the ceremony without mishap. Neither faulted on the declarations. They exchanged vows in a clear voice. And the groom managed to keep hold of the wedding ring when Lord Grasby offered it to him. The slim gold band slipped on to Rory's finger with ease. It was only then that there was a deviation from the service. Dair could not help himself. With the ring secured, he lifted Rory's hand and kissed the gold band, another smile and a wink at her before releasing her fingers and turning back to the vicar. Not only was there another collective sigh from the females in attendance, but one of their number burst into tears and continued to sob throughout the blessing.

With the register signed by both parties, and witnessed, the newly-married couple faced their family and relations with blushing smiles. They acknowledged the Duke and Duchess of Roxton with a bow and a curtsy, and then with the same to the Duchess of Kinross, who blew them a kiss. And then they turned and bowed and curtsied to the

Countess of Strathsay, who was sniffing back tears, her face half-buried in her lace-bordered handkerchief. Dair took a step forward, kissed his mother's cheek and then his sister's, too, before rejoining his wife to accept the smiles of congratulation from one and all as they made their way along the aisle towards the open doors and the crowd waiting patiently to see them. Outside the family chapel, they would receive more congratulations from family, friends, the ducal household, and most of the village, who had walked up to catch a glimpse of the bride and groom in all their splendid glory.

But the couple had not taken many steps along the aisle towards the doors when the new Lady Fitzstuart stopped and smiled up at her husband. Those who were following the bride and groom wondered why. Dair did not wonder. He swiftly kissed his new wife's hand and then stepped forward to embrace his son. Jamie held on so tightly to his father, Dair knew the boy was overwrought and so he gave him a moment. He then kissed the top of his dark red curls, had a word in his ear, and when Jamie nodded, let him go. He then put out his hand to Mr. Banks, and the old gentleman, overcome to be so acknowledged, gripped Dair's hand tightly. All the while, Mrs. Banks cried her happiness into her damp handkerchief, and when Dair leaned over to kiss her cheek, and to say something in her ear no one but she could hear, she wailed all the more, and fell into her husband's arms.

There were those in the congregation who thought this behavior extraordinary, and looked to see what the Duke of Roxton made of it. But the Duke, like everyone involved in this emotional scene, couldn't care less what others thought. They were all so very happy. And happiest of all were the bride and groom.

Dair and Rory left the chapel, and walked arm-in-arm into the sunshine of a bright and loving future, two souls now as one.

AUTHOR NOTE

 WHILE RESEARCHING DISABILITY in
the eighteenth century, in particular
soldiers returned from battle with one
or more limbs incapacitated or amputated, I came across a most remarkable
little treatise entitled *On the Best Form
of Shoe*, by an equally remarkable man
Professor Petrus Camper (1722-1789)
who was Professor of Medicine,
Surgery, and Anatomy, at Amsterdam
and Groningen.

What is self-evident today (but is
still widely ignored by many
consumers) was a revelation to most in the 18th Century. Camper
concluded that shoes were made in ignorance of the anatomy and
growth of the foot, and constructed to the absurdities and dictates of
the fashion of the day. Camper used the term "victims of fashion" to
describe persons wearing a particular shoe form, not for comfort, but
because it was the fashionable thing to do. He voiced the hope that
enlightened parents would avoid inflicting "torture" (his word not
mine), on their children by allowing them to wear shoes that fit their
foot for comfort, and praised enlightened parents who allowed their
children to go barefoot in the house, and thus allowing the growing
foot to form naturally.

Camper's book includes a chapter on club feet and through his
scientific observations and findings concluded (wrongly but enlightened for the time) that such a deformity occurred in the developing
fetus while in the womb, and that it was unlikely to be corrected by the
use of the wooden and steel contraptions of correction available then;
footwear, like those for the normal foot, should be made specific to the
shape of the foot itself.

Camper's findings were so remarkable for the time that *On the Best
Form of Shoe* was translated almost at once into several European
languages and considered worthy of reprinting for the next 100 years.

*Behind the Scenes—explore the places, objects,
and history in* Dair Devil *on Pinterest.*
www.pinterest.com/lucindabrant

*Concept to Cover—costumes, jewelry, models, & photoshoot.
Discover how the* Dair Devil *cover art was made.*
www.youtube.com/lucindabrantauthor
www.lucindabrant.com/blog/dair-devil-cover-reveal

The Roxton Family Saga continues…

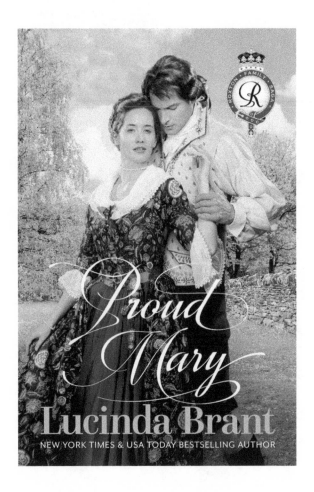

Proud Mary

Lucinda Brant

CPSIA information can be obtained
at www.ICGtesting.com
Printed in the USA
BVHW071119100122
625871BV00005B/26

9 781925 614718